The Tenth

By R.W. Peake
and
L.R. Kelly

Also by R.W Peake

Marching With Caesar® – Birth of the 10th
Marching With Caesar – Conquest of Gaul
Marching With Caesar – Civil War
Marching With Caesar – Antony and Cleopatra, Parts I & II
Marching With Caesar – Rise of Augustus
Marching With Caesar – Last Campaign
Marching With Caesar – Rebellion
Marching With Caesar – A New Era
Marching With Caesar – Pax Romana
Marching With Caesar – Fraternitas
Marching With Caesar – Vengeance
Marching With Caesar – Rise of Germanicus
Marching With Caesar – Revolt of the Legions
Marching With Caesar – Avenging Varus, Part I
Marching With Caesar – Avenging Varus Part II
Caesar Triumphant
Caesar Ascending – Invasion of Parthia
Caesar Ascending – Conquest of Parthia
Caesar Ascending – Pandya
Caesar Ascending – The Ganges
Caesar Ascending – The Han
The Titus Chronicles – Eagle and Wyvern
The Titus Chronicles – Viking

Critical praise for the Marching with Caesar series:

Marching With Caesar-Antony and Cleopatra: Part I-Antony
"Peake has become a master of depicting Roman military life and action, and in this latest novel he proves adept at evoking the subtleties of his characters, often with an understated humour and surprising pathos. Very highly recommended."

Marching With Caesar-Civil War
"Fans of the author will be delighted that Peake's writing has gone from strength to strength in this, the second volume...Peake manages to portray Pullus and all his fellow soldiers with a marvelous feeling of reality quite apart from the star historical name... There's history here, and character, and action enough for three novels, and all of it can be enjoyed even if readers haven't seen the first volume yet. Very highly recommended."
~The Historical Novel Society

"The hinge of history pivoted on the career of Julius Caesar, as Rome's Republic became an Empire, but the muscle to swing that gateway came from soldiers like Titus Pullus. What an amazing story from a student now become the master of historical fiction at its best."
~Professor Frank Holt, University of Houston

The Tenth by R.W. Peake and L.R. Kelly

Copyright © 2021 by R.W. Peake

Foreword

Somewhere in early 2020, my partner on another project and good friend Larry Kelly came to me and said (near as I can remember), "You know, you should tell Titus' story in a new way."

When I asked what he meant, his response was simply, "Like HBO did with *Band of Brothers*." (It was a bit more involved than that, but hopefully y'all get the idea)

And, the more I thought about it, the more I liked the idea. Going further, I watched the excellent series for what is probably the fifth time, and the one episode that stood out was the one where Dick Winters, played by the incomparable Damian Lewis, seems to kill an unarmed German soldier in cold blood. As the episode progresses, however, viewers learn that it wasn't that straightforward, that Captain Winters was acting in the best interests of his own men. Along with *Band of Brothers*, there was another movie, this one made for TV as well, starring the late Luke Perry, titled *Riot*, the subject of which was a fictional event that takes place during the L.A. riot in 1992. I don't remember how it was received, or even much about the movie, but I do recall being fascinated by the premise of viewing an event through the eyes of several different characters and just how different that event can look depending on who it is doing the observing.

It's no secret that we're all shaped by our experiences, which is one reason why, of all the kinds of evidence available to law enforcement, the one that most investigators will name as the least reliable is that provided by one or more eyewitnesses. In fact, the more eyewitnesses, the less reliable it is when it comes time to take it to court. However, that doesn't necessarily mean that what one person sees is more or less valid than another, and sometimes different perspectives actually help provide context to a complex event.

I also liked the idea of fleshing out these characters who played a pivotal role in the story of Titus Pullus, and it may or may not surprise some of you that, of all the characters, I was most interested in Spurius Didius. As anyone who has read the first seven volumes knows, Didius is one of Titus' primary antagonists, the "rock in his *caliga*," but even as I was writing what would become *Birth of the 10th* and *Conquest of Gaul* back in 2008-09, I felt some qualms about making Didius such a simple villain. After all, I spent a fair amount of time developing Titus' and Vibius' characters; given the roles that each of the young men who share the tent belonging to the Tenth Section, First Century, Second Cohort play in Titus' own story, the chance to let readers learn more about each of them was appealing.

With this, Volume I of what I expect to be more than a dozen (much shorter than my normal) books, readers will be introduced to each of the characters who answer the call for the *dilectus* of the 10th Legion in a more in-depth manner, along with their training, albeit from a different perspective than just that of Titus.

I've never made any secret that my own time in the Marine Corps has provided inspiration for *Marching With Caesar*, but with *The Tenth*, I realized how much each of these secondary characters are modeled on Marines I served with, starting in boot camp, both good and bad. I'll let you readers try and figure out which one of these characters might be me; the only hint I'll give you is that it might not be who you think it is!

And throughout this process, which admittedly has taken much longer for me to produce than I anticipated, Larry was an integral part of it, offering his thoughts and suggestions, many of which made it into the pages of *The Tenth – Volume I* and *Volume II*, which is completed and will be released early next year, and since I'm a firm believer in giving credit where it's due, that's why I felt it was important that he be recognized for what he contributed, because without him, this wouldn't have happened.

Semper Fidelis
R.W. Peake
December 2, 2021

Historical Notes

There's not really much to add to these Historical Notes that isn't in *Birth of the 10ᵗʰ*, but there are a couple of points to be made, specifically concerning Corduba and Scallabis. When looking at reference materials, like the *Barrington Atlas Of The Greek And Roman World*, it has to be remembered that Rome's control of Hispania covered several centuries, and as I learned, the amount of documentary evidence about locations is more prevalent for the Imperial period than it is for the Republican period. We do know that Caesar launched his campaign against the rebelling Lusitani tribes from Scallabis, modern-day Santarem, Portugal, when the Praetor for 61 BCE, Gaius Julius Caesar established a military camp outside the city, designating it *Scallabis Praesidium Iulium.*

However, the actual capital of Hispania Ulterior was Corduba, while what would become the Roman province of Lusitania wouldn't be established for another thirty-six years after its final pacification by Augustus, so the question is...where did Caesar govern from during his Praetorship? While it's a vexing question, I ultimately chose to make Scallabis the seat of Caesar's government, at least during this period when he was making preparations to launch a campaign against the rebelling tribes of Lusitania, which is why every young Roman in the story has to make their way to Scallabis.

As far as the *dilectus* itself, given the dispersion of the population of eligible enlistees, it was undoubtedly a fairly drawn-out affair, with parties of *Conquisitores* traveling the province, which I describe in the story. I will ask forgiveness in one area, and that is in how long it's been since I did the research into the Roman system of conscription, so I can't recall exactly where I determined the difference between *Probatio* and *Tirone*, but I use that system to illustrate the length of time it would take someone to go from Gades, for example, all the way to Scallabis.

...And, indeed, if any one does but attend to the other parts of their military discipline, he will be forced to confess that their obtaining so large a dominion hath been the acquisition of their valor, and not the bare gift of fortune...for their military exercises differ not at all from the real use of their arms, but every soldier is every day exercised, and that with great diligence, as if it were in time of war, which is the reason why they bear the fatigue of battles so easily; for neither can any disorder remove them from their usual regularity, nor can fear affright them out of it, nor can labor tire them; which firmness of conduct makes them always to overcome those that have not the same firmness; nor would he be mistaken that should call those their exercises unbloody battles, and their battles bloody exercises.

Flavius Josephus- *The Jewish War*, Book 5, Chapter 3, Paragraph 1

Table of Contents

Chapter One.. 1

Chapter Two 53

Chapter Three.. 106

Chapter Four 162

Chapter Five 226

Chapter One

"*Oy!*" No response. "*OY!*" When this had no effect, Aulus Didius didn't hesitate, reaching down to pick up the small bucket tucked under the bed, and dumped the contents onto the sleeping figure of his son Spurius.

This achieved the desired result, although whether it was from the urine or the stench of the remnants of his son's last meal that he had deposited in the night Aulus didn't know, nor did he care; he was far enough away that it wasn't his problem. Spurius was sitting upright, spluttering in outrage and revulsion, violently coughing, which quickly transformed into gagging as his olfactory nerves informed him what his father had used. He barely snatched up the now-empty bucket to vomit into it, while his father stood there, arms folded, watching with amusement, but when he spoke, his tone wasn't remotely friendly.

"You said that you're going to Scallabis for the *dilectus* they're holding there," he said coldly.

Spurius didn't answer immediately because he was still retching, but once he recovered sufficiently, he managed to croak, "I said I was *thinking* about it. I haven't decided."

"Yes you have," Aulus snarled, "and I've decided for you. I want you out of the house."

In truth, Spurius could be excused for his delayed response, even after he had managed to settle his stomach down, because he was nursing a monstrous hangover. The fact that he had been debauching with his father the night before at their *taverna* Proserpina's Delight only contributed to his bafflement, and he racked his aching mind, trying to recall anything from the night before that might give him a hint as to why, at least in his mind, his father had so abruptly had this change of heart.

Whether it was because Aulus was a seer and knew what he

was thinking, or it was simply the logical next step Spurius would never know, but he still got his answer when his father reminded him, "Remember, I warned you that you weren't pulling your weight and that I'd turn you out if you didn't get back on my good books."

"But that was just last *week*," Spurius gasped. "That's not enough time for me to…"

"It's more than enough time," his father cut him off. "And you clearly didn't take me seriously, or you wouldn't have been with me at the Delight all night."

"*But you invited me!*" Spurius gasped, and as his mind was slowly catching up, he felt the fanning of the ember of resentment he had always held towards his father threatening to burst into flame.

"It was a test," Aulus answered coldly. "And you failed it. Besides," he did smile then, showing the few remaining teeth that he had, "your little brother has more than made up for you not pulling your weight."

"He's not my brother," Spurius snapped. "He's my half-brother, and his mother is that bit…"

"You need to be very careful, boy," Aulus didn't yell, which actually made him more menacing, if only because Spurius had witnessed what his father was capable of immediately after he had used that tone with another man, whose remains had long since been shat out by the pigs Spurius helped his father feed them to. "That's my wife you're talking about."

"For now," Spurius muttered under his breath, but he had determined that his father was deadly serious, and he threw the soiled sheet off of himself and stood erect, which always made him feel better and a bit more powerful. And, he was grimly pleased to see, his father took a step backward, farther away from him, which Spurius took as his recognition that his son was dangerous in his own way. The fact that Spurius was almost a foot taller at six feet tall, and at least forty pounds heavier was something that he had been using to his own advantage all of his life. And, given the family business, it helped to be bigger and stronger than the people you dealt with, considering how likely it was that at some point, they would become enraged and at the very least, want to beat you senseless…and that was if the goddess Fortuna smiled on you.

The pair glared at each other for a moment, then Spurius broke it by asking sarcastically, "Can I at least go to the baths and get this *cac* off of me?"

"As long as you're gone by sundown," Aulus replied. Then, in the same quiet tone, he added, "And I don't have to remind you what will happen if you disobey me, do I, boy?"

This was too much for Spurius, who snarled back, "The day that you could beat me down or kill me is a long time in the past...*Tata*. And you'd be a fool to try it!"

Aulus' reaction was the last one Spurius expected, the son certain that making that kind of challenge would prick his father's *dignitas* sufficiently to make him behave rashly, because in this brief span of time, Spurius Didius had begun to plan his next move, one that would enable him to avoid fulfilling what had, in fact, been a promise to join the *dilectus* called by the new Praetor of Hispania. From Spurius' viewpoint, he had been drunk when he made it, and it had been during the conversation with his father about the run of bad fortune he'd been experiencing, so it didn't really count. Besides, he thought with rising excitement, if Aulus falls for the bait...

Spurius' flight of fancy lasted only for the time it took for Aulus to hold his hands out in what might have been a gesture of surrender as he widened his eyes and replied in mock surprise, "I would *never* kill my own son! But," Aulus dropped his arms, taking the sham of his emotional display with it, "I have men who will. And," Spurius would always wonder if the sadness his father showed was genuine, "I would grieve your loss, my son, but..."

"...Business is business," Spurius finished for him, knowing the words that were coming because they had been pounded into his head since he could walk. After all, he reminded himself, we always thought that he was behind the murder of my uncle because Aulus was the younger son. He said nothing for a long span of heartbeats, while Aulus regarded him unblinkingly, as if it was his turn to know what was coming. Which, this voice was so deep down within him Spurius could almost pretend he didn't hear it, he does, because he knows that I'm afraid of him. I'm afraid of dying, especially at my father's orders.

Aloud, he said quietly, "I'll be gone by dark."

The change in Aulus was immediate, and to his credit, he didn't revel in this show of submission by his son.

Instead, he smiled broadly, as if this tense exchange had never happened, and declared, "Besides, you're going to be following the tradition of serving under the standard just like I followed your grandfather. He," Aulus reminded Spurius for what the son was certain was the hundredth time, "was one of the original Marius' Mules, you know. And I served under Sura when we beat that *cunnus* Mithridates!"

"Yes, I seem to recall that," Spurius answered sullenly, now wanting nothing more than to get to the public bathhouse here in Gades (Cadiz), but his father wasn't through.

What Spurius wasn't expecting was his father, seemingly remembering something, reaching into his coin purse that hung from his belt. Spurius heard his father muttering something as he peered down into the open mouth of the bag and poked about, but when he found what he was looking for, it wasn't the coins that Spurius was expecting, but a scrap of parchment, which Aulus thrust at him.

"Here, you'll need this," Aulus said briskly, but for the life of him, Spurius couldn't think of a possible reason this scrap would have any value, if only because he was illiterate, although his father knew his letters.

"What's that?" Spurius asked suspiciously, refusing to reach for it.

"It's the name of the man you need to see once you get to Scallabis. He'll take care of everything. His name is Marcus Surenas. Show him that when you meet with him."

"Everything?" Spurius frowned. "What does that mean? Why would I need anything to join the Legion?"

His son's question reminded Aulus of just how ignorant Spurius was of so many things, and worst of all in his view, how he had never expressed an interest in finding out. In fact, while he couldn't articulate it in this manner, this was a large part of Aulus' decision that Spurius was not the man to take his place, because the youth had no imagination. He seemed perfectly content to continue making money the only way he knew how, and Aulus had survived in this enterprise long enough to know that one always had to keep an eye out for new ways to make money as their victims began catching on to their old tricks. Now, however, he also realized that he needed to offer Spurius at least a brief explanation.

"Surenas," he pointed to the scrap, "has one of the *conquisitores* in his purse...you *do* know about them, don't you?" Aulus asked with a heavy sarcasm.

"Yes! I'm not stupid!" Spurius shot back angrily, despite knowing that this was a weakness of his that he had long since learned his father would exploit mercilessly. "I know they're responsible for finding men for a *dilectus*!"

Deciding not to prolong his fun, Aulus nodded, and explained, "This man is one I've done...favors for, so he owes me. He has a list of men the right age who will stand in for me in Scallabis since I can't show my face there."

"Ah," Spurius nodded in what for him was a sheepish manner, "that's right, I forgot. You can't go to Scallabis, and I have to have my 'father' there to attest to my status as a citizen and I'm older than seventeen."

He didn't show it, but Aulus was secretly relieved to know that this was just something Spurius had forgotten and not that he had been ignorant of this requirement for enlistment all along. It didn't change anything in a material sense; he was still determined to get Spurius out of Gades, but Aulus Didius had just enough of a paternal instinct to be slightly worried about his son and whatever faced him in the future, and he hoped this was a sign from the gods that Spurius wasn't irretrievably stupid and destined for a bad end because of it.

Aloud, he simply said, "That's right. You'll meet whoever Surenas finds so that you can get your stories straight." He couldn't resist one final jab. "Assuming you remember who you are and where you came from."

This time, Spurius didn't rise to the bait, exacting his own small revenge by answering, "I do. Now," he nodded in the direction of the door, "may I go to the baths...Father?"

Not surprisingly, Aulus quickly stepped out of Spurius' way, and while he knew deep down it was because of the stench,

Spurius consoled himself by saying it was because his father feared what he might do. And, he sighed inwardly as he left the *insula* that the family Didius occupied, it was a nice dream while it lasted. He occupied himself during the walk to the bathhouse savoring what would never be, that he would run the Didius family enterprise, ruling it firmly but more fairly than Aulus. In its simplest terms, what Spurius thought of as a family business was nothing more than a group of men and women, united by blood, albeit in somewhat convoluted fashion; Spurius had long since lost track of how many cousins he had and by what degree they were related, and oaths of loyalty sworn by those few who weren't bound by blood. What their business was based on was almost exclusively criminal in nature, referred to as a *collegia*, although there was a certain level of organization, which Aulus had built on from the original version created by his own father, and ruled with an iron fist. What Spurius and his younger half-brother Septimus were responsible for when it came to bringing in money for the family was from gambling, and the way they brought that money in was by, in simple terms, cheating. Mostly at dice, although they had become competent at the sleight of hand necessary for the game of "Find The Chickpea" and other sundry games of chance where a stealthy hand could defeat even the wariest eye. And, Spurius had to admit to himself, he had become careless and gotten caught with the loaded dice in his hand just before he was switching them out. It was purely by chance; behind him, one of the whores had gotten enraged at what she claimed was a customer who tried to cheat her with some counterfeit coin, and the customer's response had been to punch her in the face, sending her reeling backward right into him with enough force to jar his switch hand. This was the story anyway; once some time had passed, Spurius allowed to himself that it *might* have happened because he had gotten sloppy and hadn't spotted the signs of a setup, which was an inherent danger in their line of work. The only way he had escaped that *taverna*, which was outside the walls of Gades on the Via Costa, was because of his size, strength, and the ferocity he showed whenever he was threatened, managing to get away with only bumps and bruises, while leaving behind a man with a broken jaw and another whose skull he might have crushed with a heavy wine pitcher. That was why his father's giving him only a week confirmed what he had suspected but not really wanted to believe, that Aulus wanted his oldest son gone, and for this, he didn't fault his father but his stepmother Livinia, who he was also certain had poisoned his mother back when they were supposedly best friends. Only occasionally did he allow himself to acknowledge that if this were true, it was likely done with Aulus' tacit acceptance, if not at his urging. Maybe, he thought bitterly, this will be good for me, maybe being under the standard will afford me other opportunities. This was his train of thought as he entered the baths, whereupon he struck the slave attendant for recoiling at the stench and the sight of the *cac* that still clung to his tunic, and this further helped his mood lifting. Using almost the last of his coins, he paid to have his tunic and *subligaculum* cleaned, and by the time he was oiled and scraped, his thoughts had taken flight as he thought of all the gullible farm boys that would undoubtedly flock to the capital of Scallabis, like him, answering the call put out by the new *Praetor*; what was his name again? Just before he dropped into a doze, soothed by the feeling of the warm water that he was sitting in up to his chin, it came to him. Caesar. That was his name, Gaius Julius Caesar.

The one thing that Quintus Artorius knew beyond all doubt was that his father Tiberius hated him. And, when Quintus was honest with himself, he couldn't really blame his father all that much. While his father was of average height, because of his work as a smith, he was quite muscular and robust, whereas Quintus was neither of those things. By now, just a month short of his eighteenth name day, Quintus had heard the story of his birth and infancy more times than he could count, how small he had been and how frail he was, and how often he became sickly. This last part seemed to have passed; the last time Quintus could remember being ill was when he was twelve, but it was because of this that his mother made such a fuss over him and constantly worried about his welfare. It should have been comforting to Quintus, but he knew why his mother was this way towards him; he was the only male Artorius, and his mother, after almost dying delivering a stillborn daughter to go with Quintus' two surviving sisters, was told by the midwife that her childbearing days were over. This put an enormous burden on Quintus' narrow shoulders, and while he did make an effort to learn his father's trade, it was half-hearted at best, which, when coupled with his frailty and size, meant that his father hated him. At least, this was how Quintus saw things, yet in fact, he wasn't far from the mark, and Tiberius Artorius knew he *should* love his son. After all, it wasn't the boy's fault that the gods had chosen to mock Tiberius Artorius, who prided himself on being one of the strongest men in their town of Italica, and he was in fact the undefeated wrestling champion three years running in the town games. Nevertheless, Tiberius just couldn't bring himself to accept that Quintus had neither the build nor the temperament to be a smith, at least of the type that Tiberius was, where most of his business came from shoeing horses and forging large pieces of iron equipment and mechanisms. Now, after Tiberius had toyed with the idea of setting Quintus up as a weapons maker for some time, he finally did so, even going as far as to set up an area of his shop that his son could use to begin learning the process of forging *gladii* and *pugiones,* although he had him start with spear points. And, for the span of the previous three months, it appeared as if Quintus was making an honest effort to apply himself, working hard, or at least what passed for hard work with the boy. Then Quintus began quitting earlier in the day, and going on "errands" for his mother that ate up large parts of the working hour. It was when he disappeared on one of these excursions that, in a fit of anger, Tiberius confronted his wife Fulvia, demanding to know what on Gaia's Earth she thought she was doing using their son as an errand boy. What he got in return was a blank stare from her, whereupon he learned that she had never done any such thing because, as she pointed out, she was as aware as Tiberius that Quintus was the only hope for the Artorius business to continue into the indefinite future.

"But we can't force him, Tiberius," she had told him then. "If his heart's not in it, then what kind of work would he produce anyway?"

This was something Tiberius knew fully well was true, but

it made it no less frustrating, and he expressed this by crying, "What does he want to do then, eh? What is it that *does* interest him?"

"I don't know," she admitted with a sigh. "The gods know I've asked him more times than I can count, but I've never gotten an answer."

Over time, both of his parents became aware that, setting his physical limitations aside for being a smith, the truth was that Quintus Artorius didn't seem to have any ambition at all. And, they both concluded in a rare moment of accord, how could they guide their son if he didn't really want to go anywhere?

"Maybe," Tiberius said jokingly, "he'll join that Legion the new *Praetor* is raising in Scallabis."

The very idea of this made both of them laugh, long and hard.

It wasn't that Quintus Artorius lacked ambition; it was just that, as Quintus grew and matured, he realized something about himself: he had no talent for anything that a man of his class could do to support himself. Only to himself, and never once uttering it aloud, even to his sister Camilla, the one of his two sisters to whom he was the closest, what Quintus Artorius wanted to be was a poet, like Homer. Oh, how he loved to hear the tales of Achilles and Hector that traveling poets offered on festival days! He could lose himself in his imagination as he sat, always as close as he could get to whoever it was declaiming in the small makeshift theater that was nothing more than wooden risers set up in the forum for the performances. He liked the Greek plays of Euripides as well, particularly his play about Hercules, although he was less fond of Sophocles. That he was unlettered and couldn't even write his name were insurmountable obstacles when this realization first hit him, but in a rare show of initiative, he began to seek out someone who would be willing to help him learn and take next to nothing in payment. Unfortunately, this newly found ambition happened to coincide with his father's experiment in trying to teach him how to become a weaponsmith, and Quintus *did* try to apply himself, at least at first. The problem was, now that this idea had been planted inside him, he couldn't seem to shove it aside, and before long, he found himself standing at the forge, wearing the heavy leather apron that provided only a modicum of protection from the heat and the inevitable flaming bits of slag that shot out and away from whatever was being worked on, holding an ingot of iron that, as his father liked to remind him, was more precious than any of Tiberius' children, and have no idea what he had been doing. This was when he began inventing things his mother wanted him to do, and it helped that when Tiberius was working, he was so absorbed in what he was doing that he barely noticed. Italica (Santiponce) was a moderate-sized town for this part of Hispania, numbering about ten thousand inhabitants, and it never occurred to Quintus that he might have difficulty in finding one of the men who hung about the forum offering their services as a tutor, or as an expert in rhetoric. And, truthfully, it *wasn't* difficult to find them, but where Quintus was having problems was in convincing one of them to offer their time for the pitifully small pile of coins, none of them *sesterces* but composed of *as* and *obols*, the small change of the day that was all Quintus had to offer. The reason his errands grew in duration was because he began spending his time pleading his case to a prospective tutor until, more out of exasperated amusement than for any other reason, a bearded man in a filthy tunic cut in the style favored by Greeks who called himself Eusenius of Delphi, finally agreed to help Quintus learn his letters. Quintus' new tutor was certainly literate, but his name was not Eusenius, nor was he from Delphi; he was as Roman as Quintus but had a talent for mimicking accents, which he employed as he had drifted his way from his original home of Latium all the way here, to this provincial town, scratching out a living by any means necessary. Eusenius' agreement with Quintus coincided with the youth finally abandoning the attempt to please his father, and for a brief span, Quintus Artorius was happy, thinking that he was at least doing *something* to achieve his dream of becoming a poet. Eusenius was cynical, and he wasn't above petty thievery, but he wasn't a cruel man by nature, and while he would never say it aloud, he became fond of young Quintus, if only because it was flattering to have someone so eager to learn from him. Sadly, what became clear to the quasi-tutor almost immediately was that, while young Artorius was eager to learn, he lacked the basic intelligence needed to achieve more than the most fundamental level of literacy, able to read inscriptions on monuments or contracts in their simplest form, albeit painfully slowly. And, as the days passed, Eusenius discovered that, while it wasn't particularly well-formed or used that often, he did have a conscience, and he finally resolved to sever this relationship with the youngster the next day.

Quintus could tell that Eusenius was becoming frustrated with him, but he deduced, erroneously, that his tutor's discontent wasn't due to his own limitations. Not without some logic, he determined that, now that he had met with Eusenius more than a half-dozen times, usually for a full Roman watch, the coins he had handed the man to seal their bargain simply was no longer a sufficient amount to justify his time.

"He has to eat, after all," Quintus told himself. "That's only fair."

Consequently, he turned his mind to how to get his hands on a more substantial amount of money, but even after spending considerable time thinking about it, he could only come to one conclusion; he would have to steal it. Not that he thought of it in this manner, instead assuring himself that he was just borrowing a small sum from the hoard of coins that his parents thought he knew nothing about, hidden under a loose stone in the forge in his father's shop. Once he became a poet and had secured a rich patron, having learned from Eusenius that this was the way poets made money, he would not only pay it back, he would repay it with interest! Nevertheless, when he rose from the bed that he shared with his sisters shortly after the midnight watch began on the night he made his decision, he almost didn't go through with it. Stealing was wrong, no matter what the reason, and he was rightly afraid of what his father would do if he found out that some money was missing. It wouldn't be much; he had decided on ten *sesterces*, but even if it had been just one, Tiberius would be furious with him. He already hates you anyway, a small voice inside Quintus' mind pointed out. Almost immediately, the same voice countered, At least you're doing this for a good reason. You're trying to make your future, and he was perfectly fine making another anvil, using that precious supply of iron, along with forging a set of tools, so why wouldn't he understand that you're doing this for that future? This got him moving, and he tiptoed across the room, thankful for the stone floor that aided his silence.

Moving through the darkened house, he paused outside his parents' room, the only one in the house with a door and a latch, listening for a span of several heartbeats. Only when he heard his father snort, which he did every so often in the night, almost always waking Quintus, did he resume his progress, slipping through the door that separated the family home from the business, doing it slowly because he knew the hinges squeaked if he opened it too quickly. Then, he was in the shop, which was completely dark, and he realized how seldom he had been in it when there was no light, so he moved even more slowly, feeling ahead of him with his hands as he strained to remember the placement of things like the large anvil, the bench, and the bins that held different materials. He felt more than he saw the forge, barking his shin against the stone foundation of it, but he managed to avoid crying out in pain, instead dropping to a crouch so that he could feel his way along the foundation, counting the fire-hardened stones with his fingers until he felt the one that was loose. Carefully lifting it up, he placed it to the side then reached down into the hole, and for a brief moment, experienced a surge of panic when his hand didn't touch anything. It *has* to be here! he thought desperately, which prompted him to shove his hand farther into the cavity, which, he discovered, was much larger than he remembered, although he had only peeked down into it once when his father was adding money to the leather sack when Tiberius didn't know Quintus was there.

The clinking sound of the disturbed coins coincided with his fingers brushing the sack, and he quickly extracted it, realizing with a sense of deep surprise that the sack was bulging with more coins than he would have thought possible. Suddenly, Quintus Artorius' greed came rushing forth, surprising him because, to this point in his short life, he had never really experienced it before. No, up to this moment, he had always been content with what he had, the small allowance that his mother passed to him, telling Quintus his father didn't know, which was a fiction that all three of them pretended to believe. What he was holding now was different; it was the most money he had ever held certainly, but he had never even seen this much. Some of this—the same voice that had gotten him moving suddenly returned—belongs to me. I'm the oldest and the only son, so if my father were to die tomorrow, I'd become the *paterfamilias* and this would all be mine. It was not without an internal struggle, but fairly quickly, Quintus discarded the idea of taking it all and just disappearing, yet now he was no longer willing to grab just a small handful of coins. Besides, he realized after he opened the sack and thrust his hand into it, savoring the feeling and clinking noise made when he did so, this isn't just a bag of *sesterces*; he could tell that just by the feel of the coins, some of them having the ridged edge that denoted *sesterces* while others were smooth, which meant that these were *denarii*, each one worth four *sesterces*. I wonder, he thought excitedly, if there are *aurei* in here! Quintus could count on one hand and have a finger left over the number of times he had actually seen an *aureus*, the gold coin that was worth either ten or a hundred *denarii*, when one of the high-ranking plebeians in Italica had paid his father for something. Without thinking it through, he curled his fist and lifted his hand out of the sack, only then deciding that he would be content with whatever the amount he held in that hand was, awkwardly pulling the drawstring tight with his free hand and his teeth, then depositing the sack back into the hole. He was proud of himself that he made sure to shove it back into the cavity to more or less the same place he had found it, then carefully replaced the stone.

By this time, his eyes had adjusted to the darkness a bit better, and he could just make out the shapes of the things that he had had to feel his way around, so he moved more quickly, reaching the door. It was closed, which Quintus thought was odd, because he was certain that he had left it open, not wanting to risk the hinges making noise four times instead of just two. Or, he thought without much alarm, maybe I didn't, and reaching for the latch, he pulled the door open. He would never be able to really remember in what sequence things happened, whether his eyes made out the bulk that was slightly darker than everything around it, giving him an eyeblink of warning before a hand clamped around his throat with such brutal force that he was worried his windpipe would be crushed instantly, but this was only marginally more painful than the bellowing challenge, *"Who are you? What are you doing?"* Quintus would not have thought it possible, but now the voice, which he recognized as his father's, raised to another level as he shouted, *"Thief! There's a thief in the shop of Tiberius Artorius!"*

Quintus wanted desperately to shout back that it was just him, except that he heard nothing but a strangled gasp, and he started using his free hand to strike his father's forearm as he struggled wildly to free his throat. He might as well have been striking iron, and his world began to fade, while another roaring sound began to drown out his father's bellowing that seemed to throb in rhythm with his heart beating. I'm going to die, he thought rather calmly, and maybe that's what the gods want, as he felt his body going limp.

He only dimly heard a new voice, screaming at an unbelievably shrill volume, *"Tiberius! Tiberius! It's Quintus! You're killing Quintus!"*

Then the crushing pressure around his throat stopped, and he collapsed to the ground, hearing the wheezing sound as his lungs were trying to draw in the air that he had been deprived of for what seemed like a full day through a badly damaged throat, but when he tried to get to his feet, he was too weak and he collapsed back onto the floor.

"Why?"

It was the fourth time that Tiberius Artorius had asked the question, but what shook Quintus to his core was that his father wasn't bellowing this as he had been when he thought his son was an intruder. His father angry he could take, and he could understand, but his father sounded more bewildered, and hurt, than anything else. They were seated at the table where they took their meals, the girls, having naturally been roused by the commotion actually being sent to his parents' room with instructions to close the door and not listen in. A lamp had been lit by his mother, but only one of the normal three they used for illumination after dark, but it was enough for Quintus to see that his father's expression matched his tone. Why, indeed? he wondered.

It took Quintus three tries before he could get anything out, and he was rewarded by a look of, if not shame, then regret on his father's face for being the cause of his condition that made his voice so hoarse, it was hard to understand, but he finally managed, "I…I needed it."

"For what?" His mother asked this, and she leaned forward to grab Quintus' forearm. "What would you need that much money for?"

"I don't really know how much I took," he mumbled. "I just closed my hand around a bunch of coins."

This prompted his father to respond, not verbally, but by suddenly dropping the coins that, presumably, had been in Quintus' possession onto the table, the sound almost musical as the coins struck the table and each other. For a long moment, Quintus could only gape down in an astonishment dulled by the throbbing pain in his throat, trying to focus on what he could see were three gold *aurei* of the hundred *sesterces* denomination, perhaps a dozen *denarii,* and several *sesterces.* It was a small fortune to anyone of the Head Count class of Romans, of which the Artorius family was a part; indeed, it was a substantial sum even for someone in the Equestrian Order.

"I didn't know it was that much," Quintus repeated.

"How much were you trying to take?"

When his father put it this way, Quintus realized that he was facing a dilemma; yes, his original goal was to procure about ten *sesterces* or perhaps three *denarii,* but a fistful of coins, even if they had all been *sesterces,* was far more than that.

Rather than answer directly, he offered, "I needed to pay a man who's been helping me."

"Helping you?" Tiberius asked with a frown. "Helping you with what?"

"Helping me learn my letters," Quintus answered.

"Your letters?" Tiberius glanced at his wife, but Fulvia could only offer a shake of her head, although she was frowning, the sign Quintus recognized as the signal his mother was deep in thought. "Why would you need to learn your letters?"

Before Quintus could answer, his mother suddenly interjected,

"I know why! He wanted to learn to help you run the business!"

"The business?" Tiberius was clearly unconvinced. "How would learning his letters help us with the business?"

"Because," she sounded more confident with every word, "you've said it yourself. You can't take any of those big contracts without hiring someone to read them for you, Tiberius. What Quintus is doing will allow you to stop paying them, don't you see?"

While Tiberius didn't look altogether convinced, Quintus knew his father well enough that, if anything, he *wanted* to believe this was the case.

Turning to Quintus, Tiberius asked quietly, "Is this true, boy? Is that why you're doing it?"

If he said yes, Quintus was certain that, at the very least, this crisis would be averted, and it might even improve his father's view of him, so he was opening his mouth to assure his father that this had indeed been his plan, as ill-conceived as it might have been. I can just say that the reason I didn't tell him was because I was certain he would say no, and that I was serious about doing this. This had the advantage of being at least partially true, but in a rare, and in one of his only flashes of insight, Quintus Artorius realized that, while this would enable him to avoid being honest now, this would become apparent over time, and there would be more battles, with every one becoming more bitter and acrimonious.

"No. No, it's not true." He felt sufficiently guilty to turn to his mother. "I'm sorry, Mama. I know you're trying to help. But," he shook his head, "that's not why I did it." If anything, Tiberius looked even more baffled. Taking a deep breath, Quintus said, "I want to learn my letters because I want to become a poet, like Homer and Euripides."

For a long span of time, Tiberius simply stared at his son, while his mother had a hand to her mouth as she looked from father to son back to father, her expression one of surprised horror.

The silence was shattered when Tiberius began roaring with laughter, but it was a mocking, lacerating sound, and he finally managed to gasp, "A *poet*? What kind of nonsense is that?" He turned to his wife, and as quickly as it came, all signs of humor vanished as he snarled, "This is all your fault, you silly woman! You've always coddled this boy, and now here he is wanting to be a pederast Greek *poet*?"

"Homer is famous! Euripides is famous!" Quintus shouted, experiencing his own surge of anger that was so rare for him, he wasn't really sure how to handle it, which was what led to his intemperate words. "Who's ever heard of Tiberius Artorius? You could die tomorrow, and who would notice?"

The blow came, hard and fast, Tiberius' work-hardened hand smacking Quintus on the side of his head with enough force to send him flying sideways off of the bench to land on the floor, his left ear with a ringing sound that would last for the next two days.

"Who do you do you think you are, boy?" Tiberius had leapt to his feet to stand over his son, pointing a finger that was still shaking with rage. "I'm a respected man in this town! I've won the wrestling prize three years in a row. What have *you* done?" he sneered. "You're small, and you're *weak*, boy! You'll never amount to anything if you try to go out on your own!"

Despite how much his head was spinning, Quintus scrambled to his feet, but he had to grab the edge of the table as he shouted, "I'll show you! I'll make you eat those words! I *will*, I swear it on Jupiter's Stone!"

"Oh?" Tiberius laughed again. "And how do you intend to do that, *boy*?"

"There's a *conquisitor* here in Italica." Quintus was surprised at how calm he felt. "He's looking for men to join the *dilectus* the new *Praetor* has called to form a new Legion in Scallabis."

This was something he had actually heard from Eusenius just the day before when he spotted a man in the forum, wearing a tunic with a broad red stripe accompanied by two slaves carrying a stack of wax tablets, and as Quintus watched, he saw that those who approached the man, who had set up a portable desk and stool, were exclusively young men like himself, although they were all accompanied by an older man. He asked Eusenius, who briefly explained the man's purpose, but this was all the thought Quintus had given to the idea...until he was standing there, reeling back and forth and staring up at his father.

Tiberius said nothing for a long period of time, breathing heavily, although he did glance over at his wife, who offered a helpless shrug, and finally, he asked gruffly, "Are you serious about this? You're not going to change your mind or back out?"

"No," Quintus assured him. "I'm joining this new Legion."

While Tiberius considered this, Quintus' mother spoke for the first time.

"Perhaps this is for the best," Fulvia said calmly, which clearly surprised both of them. "Quintus isn't meant to be a smith, Tiberius. You know this. And," she turned to look up at her son, and he saw the glint of tears there, "it's time for you to become your own man. The Legion might be the best way to do that."

"You know that you need me to do this," Tiberius said, and Quintus nodded, but when he was about to mention that he had been told this by Eusenius, he decided it was better not to, not wanting to have to explain who the man was. Tiberius asked, "Where do we need to go?"

"To the forum, in the morning," Quintus answered, then there didn't seem to be anything left to say. "That's where the man spends his time while he's here."

"In the morning, then," Tiberius said, then scooped the coins off the table and headed to the shop to return them. Over his shoulder, he ordered, "Go to bed and get some sleep."

Once he was gone, his mother stood and embraced her son, who, to the surprise of both of them, was still remarkably calm.

"Are you sure you want to do this, my son?" she whispered into his ear as she embraced him.

"I am, Mama," he replied firmly.

In the not too distant future, Quintus Artorius would remember this moment and tell himself, "I did mean it when I said it."

Dawn came earlier than Quintus Artorius expected, but when he tried to break his fast, he found it impossible to swallow any food, so he had to content himself with the cup of *posca*, the warmed wine with heavy spices that mostly hid the inferior quality. His mother worked silently, while Tiberius seemed content to ignore his son, although this wasn't unusual at all. Only Camilla was upset, after Quintus had whispered to her that he would be going away to join the Legion, while the youngest, Atia, was too young to understand anything other than something unusual was happening.

"I'll be outside," Tiberius said gruffly, getting up and leaving Quintus to say his goodbyes.

His mother was obviously upset, but she also seemed to accept that this was the best thing for her son.

"Do your best. Obey your Centurion," she said as she kissed him on both cheeks, then dropped her voice to whisper with a fierce intensity, "and show your father that he's wrong about you."

Even if he hadn't already had a lump in his throat from the bruising, this would have choked Quintus, and he managed to assure her, "I will, Mama. I'll make you proud."

When it was Camilla's turn, she threw herself into his arms, her head already just underneath his chin, sobbing uncontrollably, just managing to get out, "Will I ever see you again?"

Truthfully, Quintus had no idea, but he felt it was for a good reason that he promised that he would come home to visit.

His father was standing outside in the street, arms crossed, staring down it in the early morning as Italica began its day, and he didn't even glance at Quintus when he began striding towards the forum. Quintus was carrying a small bundle, although he had no idea if he would be allowed to keep it, and wrapped in his other tunic was the wax tablet where he had been practicing the words Eusenius had assigned him in his last lesson, but if he'd been asked, he wouldn't have been able to say why it was so important to him now. When they reached the forum, the *conquisitor* was nowhere to be seen, but just when Tiberius was about to slap his son for lying, he appeared, along with the two slaves, and Quintus pointed him out, then the pair watched as the slaves set up the portable desk and stool. Suddenly, it was Tiberius who seemed uncertain what to do, and for a fleeting moment, Quintus thought that perhaps his father was having second thoughts. In the span of a few heartbeats, Quintus Artorius' mind went through the possibilities. He doesn't want me to go! This was the first thought, and he saw himself turning to his father, whereupon Tiberius would blurt out the truth, that he didn't want to see his only son joining the Legions and face an uncertain future. They would reconcile, then and there, and return to the Artorius home to inform his mother and sisters, who would be overjoyed at his return and this last-moment reprieve.

Then what?

It was a voice, cold and distant, that Quintus had never heard in his mind before, one that he would later think of as his adult self, stripped of his boyish fantasies and dreams that, just perhaps, his father would come to love him for who he was. Even if he doesn't want you to go, it doesn't change anything, the voice insisted. He's going to expect you to join him in the smithy, and you're going to fail at it because you're not strong enough, and you're not interested. Yes, perhaps he'll be so happy that you didn't leave that he'll forget all about it...for a time. The fact that it was Quintus who moved first, walking towards the *conquisitor* caught Tiberius by surprise, but he joined his son so quickly that the man wouldn't have noticed.

The man, who appeared to be in his late thirties and was also wearing a chain about his neck with a bronze plate that was inscribed with his title, eyed the pair, then offered them a smile, calling out, "*Salve*, good and noble citizens!" Turning to Quintus, his expression betrayed him for less than an eyeblink at the sight of the scrawny specimen, recovering to boom, "And who is this version of Hercules himself, eh? Are you here to do your duty to Rome?"

Ironically, the bruised vocal cords made Quintus sound manlier than he would have normally as he answered, "Y-yes, Excellency. I am."

Turning to Tiberius, the *conquisitor* said, "I assume that you're this fine young man's father and the *paterfamilias*?"

It comforted Quintus to see that his father was only slightly less discomfited speaking to such an important official, but he did manage to affirm, "That's correct, Excellency."

"Good." The official nodded, then he turned and snapped his fingers, one of the slaves literally jumping across the space to attend to his master.

Things moved extremely quickly from there; the *conquisitor* asked Tiberius Artorius some questions, which Tiberius answered, then made him affirm before the gods that everything he had just said was true and correct. Then, it was Quintus' turn, and again he surprised himself, answering without hesitation. This was followed by the moment where it was made official, both father and son offering their formal oaths, while Quintus got a small moment of revenge when he painstakingly wrote his name on the *vellum* that was his official enlistment document, while his father had to make his X, which was annotated by the *conquisitor* as being the mark of one Tiberius Artorius of the urban tribes known as the Head Count, specifically the Quirina. Then, standing to administer the oath, the *conquisitor* made Quintus and his father swear by all the gods above and below and specifically to Jupiter Optimus Maximus, the supreme deity in the Roman pantheon, that the information they had given was true and correct, and that they were both Roman citizens and had never been slaves. This was the last part of the ceremony in which Tiberius would participate, and he stood watching solemnly as his son then took the oath that made him a *Probatio*, the status that denoted a Roman man who had enlisted in the Legion, but before he actually began training, when he would become a *Tirone*.

"The difference," the *conquisitor* answered when it was, somewhat surprisingly, Tiberius who asked the question, "is that the range of punishment is different for a *Probatio*. We use that designation for the amount of time it takes for a man to reach his new Legion, then for the period of time he's waiting to be assigned his Cohort and Century."

"What's the difference?" Tiberius asked, and Quintus wondered if this was his father's attempt to scare his son, or if he was truly concerned.

"*Probationes* can't be executed," the *conquisitor* replied flatly, already eyeing another pair of men, one younger and one older. "They can only be flogged with the scourge." Before Quintus or Tiberius could respond, he turned to the youth, all hint of warmth gone from his voice. "There's a wagon leaving for Scallabis at the beginning of second daylight watch, which isn't long from now." Turning, he pointed to a spot, instructing, "Go stand under the statue of Mars. That's where the wagon will pull up."

Pointedly turning his attention away, the *conquisitor* called out to the pair that he had spotted, "*Salve,* good and noble citizens! And," he turned his attention to the younger man, "who is this version of Hercules himself, eh? Are you here to do your duty to Rome?"

It was a moment that Quintus Artorius would remember, the moment when he and his father were of the same mind, exchanging a glance of rueful amusement at what they now knew was nothing more than the kind of call any merchant trying to entice customers used when hawking his wares. A fact about which they were unaware was that this particular *conquisitor* had omitted what would have been, given Artorius' size and visible frailty, a step that might have saved Quintus what was to come, the examination by a physician. Completely oblivious to this development, they walked together to the statue, then stood there awkwardly, neither willing to look at the other.

"Would you like me to stay with you?" Tiberius asked his son.

There was a part of Quintus that desperately wanted to say yes, but he was still angry, angry about his father mocking his dreams when he finally had worked up the courage to divulge them to his parents. He was angry with himself for making what he knew was a rash and impulsive decision that, with every heartbeat, was becoming more and more obvious had been made in a fit of resentment.

"No, Father," Quintus said. "I don't need you anymore. I'm going to the Legion, and when I come back, I'll be a man. Maybe," he finished bitterly, "the kind of man you can finally be proud of."

Then, in a deliberate insult, Quintus Artorius turned his back to his father, folding his arms and gazing up the street from where, presumably, the wagon would be coming. His attempt to anger his father one last time failed; if he had glanced over his shoulder, what he would have seen in Tiberius Artorius' expression was the sadness and worry of a parent watching their son heading towards an uncertain and likely dangerous future. Then, without saying anything in return, Tiberius Artorius walked away, crossing the forum.

"Jupiter Optimus Maximus, Fortuna, Mars and Bellona," he murmured under his breath, "please watch over my son."

While Marcus and Quintus Mallius weren't twins, and in fact were born almost exactly a year apart, they were often mistaken as such, which they sometimes used to their advantage. Marcus was the one a year older, and the pair were the youngest of five Mallius brothers and two sisters, although one sister had died at the age of ten. As far as their father, Numerius Mallius was concerned, this was a mixed blessing, because it had enabled him to expand his farm outside the provincial town of Illurco, but with two of his oldest sons already married and with children of their own, there simply weren't many options for the youngest children when it came to the farm. With essentially free labor, Numerius had created a farm that required more than one man to run, and he had informed Marcus and Quintus that, while there was enough land to divide out among the three oldest brothers, both of them would have to learn a trade. That neither of them had shown the slightest inclination towards finding a trade, save for Quintus' half-hearted attempt to apprentice for a tanner in Illurco, was a source of concern for their father. Granted, part of the problem was how small Illurco was, with essentially four businesses who were either looking for help or willing to take his sons on because of his standing in the community. It was more than that, however, and it was why, seemingly on an impulse, Numerius Mallius had invited Marcus and Quintus to accompany him to Scallabis to deliver the olive oil that was the primary product of the Mallius farm to the Legions there. Numerius had quickly recognized the primary reason Quintus hadn't stayed on with the tanner had more to do with the fact that Marcus wasn't there than any real dislike for the trade itself.

"They might as well be twins" was a phrase that Numerius' wife had uttered more times than he could count, but it was a view that Numerius understood and agreed with; they were truly inseparable.

That was why, the night before Numerius and his two oldest sons were going to drive the two wagons and one cart that had already been loaded with the dozens of amphorae of olive oil that they would take to Scallabis, he rolled over to nudge his sleeping wife to say, "I've changed my mind. I'm not taking Gaius and Tiberius with me; I'm taking Marcus and Quintus."

"Why?" she asked with a yawn, not yet fully awake, and frankly, accustomed to her husband making midnight declarations of intent that, more often than not, had been forgotten by the time the cock crowed.

"They've never been," Numerius replied, and while it was seemingly innocuous, this made his wife come fully awake, suddenly aware that there was more to this than she initially thought.

"So? Isn't this contract for five years? They can go next time."

Numerius knew he had to tread carefully here, because despite their shared concern over the fate of the youngest Mallius children, Numerius felt an urgency that his wife simply didn't, at least not yet.

"I think that seeing someplace besides Illurco will be good for them," he said carefully. "They'll be able to see how much bigger the world is than if they stay on the farm."

As he hoped, this clearly struck his wife as she sat up, drawing her knees under her chin as she considered.

"That," she finally said, "is a good idea, husband." Then, as she stretched back out and rolled away from him, she added, "For once."

"Since when have I had a bad idea?" Numerius asked in mock surprise, this being a long-running theme between them, and was one reason why he had no complaints in the choice his parents had arranged for him so many years ago.

"Since last week, when you thought that we needed to start breeding mules," she shot back. "We're farmers; we don't know anything about mules."

"I still think it's a good idea," Numerius grumbled as he settled back down to sleep the rest of the night. "You just have no imagination."

The only reply came in the form of the soft snoring of his wife, who had already fallen back asleep, while Numerius took the time to thank the gods that he hadn't been forced to divulge his real reason for taking Marcus and Quintus with him.

Before noon, Numerius Mallius was beginning to regret his decision, although most of his ire was directed at himself. You were always able to walk away when they started up with each other, he thought with rueful amusement, but now there's nowhere to go. Of his two youngest sons, Marcus was the more outgoing, and he was quite sociable, but the problem was that he talked too much. Quintus, on the other hand, wasn't against socializing; he just wasn't all that interested in doing so. In fact, from Numerius' viewpoint, Quintus' main interest seemed to be in goading his older brother for his own amusement. And, he admitted, at times it could be quite entertaining, but by the gods, enough was enough!

Finally, Numerius twisted around from his seat on the lead wagon to bellow, "By Jupiter, if you two don't shut your mouths, I'm going to dump the both of you right here!"

Holding his glare long enough for both youths to break eye contact and mumble their promise to stop, once he turned back around, he missed the pair offering each other a grin, while Marcus stood on the bench of the other wagon and bent over, lifting his tunic to expose his bare ass to Quintus, who had been consigned to walking alongside the cart, although only after their father promised to allow them to switch at the noon stop. Traffic was light, but what there was of it seemed to mostly be heading west, which made sense when Numerius thought about it. It was always like this in the first couple of months when a new *Praetor* arrived from Rome, as the inhabitants of the province, both Roman citizen and native, hurried to learn more about what they could expect in the coming year. It's almost a ritual, he thought with some amusement, but he had also noticed that, while there was certainly a great deal of horseback traffic, the sign that the rider was a member of the upper classes, at least of the Equestrian Order, or men of his status wealthy enough to either own or rent horses, what Numerius noticed almost immediately was how many wagons there were. Because of the terrain, most of the first two days of the journey headed due west before reaching the main north/south Roman road that led from the coast straight up to Corduba, but Numerius actually got his answer when they stopped at what was essentially a small town, although it had no name, for the noon break. In reality, it was a cluster of buildings, a result of this being the natural stopping point for anyone traveling east or west in this region, situated on a branch of the Illeris (Cubilla) River. There was a ramshackle combination inn and *taverna*, but Numerius' wife had packed enough food to feed the three of them, so there was no need to go inside. However, when Marcus suggested that they have a cup of wine while they allowed the animals to rest, Numerius didn't need much convincing, and the three entered to find the place as full as Numerius had ever seen it, it being a regular stop for his several trips a year for one reason or another. They did find a table, which they had to share with a pair of men who seemed to welcome the company, which wasn't always the case with men of the upper orders, and these two were clearly Equestrians.

"*Salve*, citizen!" the older of the pair addressed Numerius genially. "What has you out on the road?"

"*Salve*." Numerius nodded as he returned the traditional greeting. "I'm Numerius Mallius, and these are my two sons, Marcus and Quintus."

"Gaius Fonteius," the older man indicated himself, "and this is Publius Bibulus Crispus."

The now-named Crispus inclined his head, but in such a way that clearly communicated his reluctance to be seen in the company of a Head Count farmer and his sons, and it was a subtle reminder to Numerius, and to Marcus and Quintus of how rigid and strictly enforced their class system was by those higher up the ladder.

Fortunately, this was nothing new to Numerius, and he chose to address the clearly friendlier Fonteius, explaining, "We're heading to Scallabis to deliver this year's entire crop of olive oil. I recently signed a contract to supply the *Praetorium* for the next five years. Normally, I would have to sell it to a number of buyers instead of like this."

"Congratulations!" Fonteius said amiably enough, though without much interest that Marcus could see, but it was Crispus who spoke up. "It's because of Caesar."

The manner in which he said it gave Numerius the distinct impression that whatever Crispus thought of this man Caesar, it wasn't complimentary, but since he could not recall hearing of the man, he asked, "Who? Who's Caesar?"

This elicited a sharp, barking laugh from Crispus.

"You mean you don't know who you're delivering this olive oil to? You've never heard of Gaius Julius Caesar? By the gods, Hispania is as backwards as I'd heard!"

This was delivered with such mockery that Fonteius felt it necessary to intervene, if only to keep the two pups of this provincial Head Counter from attacking Crispus.

"You'll have to forgive Crispus here," Fonteius interjected with a smile that was partly apologetic. "His family has a...history with Caesar. And," he turned back to Crispus, while he was wearing a smile, he was also sending a warning to his companion, who scowled back but didn't interrupt him, "as you can see, there's no love lost between them."

This was when something registered with Numerius. He had only been partly paying attention when the introductions were made, but suddenly, Crispus' identity took on a new meaning, not because of his *cognomen* of Crispus, but his *nomen* of Bibulus. In turn, this dislodged bits of gossip from his mind that he had heard years before, back when Lucius Lucullus commanded Rome's Legions against the Pontic King Mithridates, who at that time was considered to be a threat to Rome on a level commensurate with Hannibal himself in the first of what would become known as the Mithridatic Wars. It had concerned members of Lucullus' staff, and a supposed feud that had become so bitter that one of the participants had begun a rumor about this man, Caesar, and his supposedly homosexual relationship with a client king, Nicomedes IV of Bithynia. And, Numerius recalled now, that other junior officer had been one Marcus Calpurnius Bibulus. Hard on the heels of this memory came another, that one of Caesar's acts of revenge on his return to Rome was to seduce and bed as many of the leading women of Rome as he could, and if the rumors were to be believed, one of those women was related to Bibulus somehow, although Numerius couldn't recall whether it was a wife, daughter, or perhaps a sister.

Clearly, he thought, this Crispus fellow is related somehow to Bibulus, which prompted him to say carefully, "Honestly, I don't know much about him, although once you mentioned his full name, it's familiar." Hoping to steer the conversation to safer ground, he added, "I will say I'm surprised at how heavy the traffic is that seems to be headed for Scallabis. There are a lot more wagons than I've ever seen before."

"Well, you know why," Fonteius said, as if it were obvious, but when Numerius could only offer a mystified shake of his head, he explained, "Because his first act as *Praetor* was to call a *dilectus* for a new Legion. All those wagons that you're seeing are taking all the materials that are needed to arm and equip a fresh new Legion, as well as supply the three that are already there. And," Fonteius added as an afterthought, "I heard that Caesar intends to go back to the traditional Century size of one hundred instead of eighty with his new Legion."

And just that quickly, the entwined destinies of Marcus and Quintus Mallius changed, although neither they nor their father had any idea yet.

The nearer the Mallius party got to Scallabis, the heavier the traffic, to the point that they experienced delays at the normal stopping points where the animals were watered, so that by the day before they arrived in the capital, they spent an entire Roman watch sitting in a line waiting for their turn to water the animals from a river whose name they didn't know.

"We'd be there by nightfall if it wasn't for this," Numerius grumbled, his sons rolling their eyes behind his back since, they were sure, this had to be the tenth time he had said this.

"I want to get there so I can take a bath." Marcus laughed. "We stink as bad as the animals do!"

"Speak for yourself," Quintus shot back, then lifted his arm to take a deep sniff from his armpit. "I smell fine."

"You smell like my ass," Marcus hooted, thinking that he

had taken the honors, but his brother wasn't done, not yet.

"That's not what Livia Plautus thinks." Quintus said this with a leer, and just as he hoped, it infuriated Marcus, who, as the Fates would have it, was walking with the cart.

Rushing towards the wagon where Quintus was sitting, a broad grin on his face, Marcus shouted, "I told you before, you leave Livia alone! She's in love with me, not you!"

"That's not what she says," Quintus replied with a counterfeit shrug, but this time, Quintus had miscalculated.

Usually, he knew just how far he could push his older brother before it came to blows; he learned that this was not the case when, without warning, Marcus reached up, having to stand on his tiptoes to grab a handful of his brother's tunic, whereupon he yanked Quintus off the wooden bench, pulling him down as Quintus let out a surprised squawk, the pair hitting the ground at roughly the same time, both of them thrashing at each other without any real skill. It was exactly the kind of spectacle to draw the attention of the nearby drovers and wagon drivers who were either ahead or behind in line, so that within a span of a dozen heartbeats, the brothers were surrounded by a ring of laughing onlookers, some of whom immediately began wagering on the outcome. Numerius' response to this, having heard this or a variation of this for the previous days, was to heave a heavy sigh, then without any haste, climb down off the wagon...but he took the goad he used for the animals with him. The struggle had raised a small dust cloud, so that between that and the crowd around them, Numerius couldn't really tell who was winning, and he thought with some amusement, Maybe I should make a wager. If he did, he probably would have put it on Quintus, who seemed to have a bit of a mean streak that Marcus didn't possess. From behind him, Numerius heard someone call out, and when he turned to look, he saw that the line had begun moving again, which helped to partially disperse the crowd, as the men ahead of him in line went trotting away, all of them grinning at him and joking about the two combatants, having deduced they were his sons. Shaking his head in disgust, Numerius strode into what remained of the makeshift circle, and brought the goad down hard several times, using his wrist to snap the braided leather cord, not really caring which one of his sons he hit first. Their growling and cursing was instantly replaced by yelps of pain, and they immediately came apart and scrambled to their feet, both of them holding their arms up around their heads, which meant that Numerius changed his aim, whipping their legs and leaving welts that would be there for the next couple of days.

"That's enough," he growled at them, just loudly and with enough force to reach them and to send the message their father's temper was aroused.

"He started it!"

Despite his irritation, Numerius had to struggle not to smile at the sight of his two sons, who had spoken in unison and were mirror images of each other, pointing at their sibling.

"I don't care who started it," Numerius snapped, then pointed with his goad. "Marcus, it's your turn to drive the wagon, and Quintus, you're with the cart. And if you two idiots say *one more word* for the rest of the day," he brandished the goad, "you're going to get more of this. Do you both understand me?"

With a varying degree of sullenness, the brothers agreed, but not before giving each other a glare that contained the warning that this wasn't finished. Which, Numerius knew fully well, was a lie on both of their parts; his sons had never been able to stay angry at each other long enough, and he doubted they would even remember what it was about by the time they stopped for the day...which was exactly what happened.

When they entered Scallabis early the next day, neither brother could contain their excitement. This was the largest city they'd ever seen, and they were both so absorbed in seeing what, to their provincial eyes, were all manner of exotic people, merchandise, sights and smells in such an overwhelming fashion that they were both slightly dazed. After arriving at the *Praetorium*, Numerius and his sons were immediately directed to a series of warehouses, all of which had been newly constructed along the southern wall. In fact, Numerius was slightly shocked at the level of activity, which was far more than he could ever recall on any of his many visits to the city before, no matter what the season was. While he would never make the connection, the reality was that this would be a hallmark of anyplace where Gaius Julius Caesar was and no matter what role he was fulfilling. Numerius was also pleasantly surprised at how quickly everything went, from the moment he announced his arrival at the *Praetorium* at the Office of the Quaestor, to when the slaves at the warehouse swiftly and efficiently unloaded the amphorae. As impressive as this was, it was the sight of all of the wagons and carts lining the street where the warehouses were located that struck him, and very quickly, Numerius saw an even deeper level of organization than anything he had ever encountered before when dealing with provincial government.

Next to the warehouse where the olive oil was being unloaded was an identical building, but the slaves there were carrying large sacks of grain inside, while further down, a larger gang of slaves were lugging wooden crates that, judging from their behavior, he was certain carried some form of metal, either iron or lead. This piqued his curiosity, and ordering Marcus and Quintus to stay there and keep an eye on things, he walked down the street. About halfway down the block, the wagons being unloaded carried lengths of wood, all of them cylindrical but of varying lengths and circumference, the slenderest of which Numerius correctly identified as shafts for the Roman *pilum*, the javelin developed by Gaius Marius that had proved so devastatingly effective, while the larger circumference pieces would serve as handles for a variety of tools, like axes, spades, and turfcutters. Sheets of tanned and cured leather that would become a number of pieces of equipment, from the Roman *caligae*, the boots worn exclusively by the Legions and auxiliaries of Rome, to the harnesses upon which the Legionaries would affix their weapons of *gladius* and *pugio*, were being unloaded even further down the block. This, he thought with an unexpected upswell of pride, is the might of Rome. *This* is why Rome will never be defeated. What other nation can do this? What other nation is able to organize and equip men like this, in as short a period of time? Numerius Mallius was a farmer who had never served under the standard, as Romans of this day liked to say, nor had he ever been particularly interested in martial matters. Oh, he had trained with the other farmers' sons from the area, armed with spears and shields when he was a youngster, and there was still the odd rebellion here in Baetica with the native tribes, but unlike some of his friends, he hadn't dreamed of or wished for one of those uprisings. Still, it was not just impressive, it was comforting to know that, should it be required, the city that he had never seen but gave him so much as a citizen, could do something like this.

Returning to find both wagons and carts unloaded, Numerius was in an expansive mood, and he surprised his sons by saying, "What do you two want to do? The rest of the day is yours to explore the wonders of Scallabis." Then, with a grin, he shocked them by holding up his coin purse and said, "And I might happen to know of a very nice spot near the forum where the wine is good and the women are better! You two want to go along with your old Tata?" They both opened their mouths, but Numerius held up a hand to add sternly, "As long as you both swear on the black stone that you won't tell your mother."

Numerius was *not* surprised that they both immediately and solemnly assured him that they would never divulge a thing about it. They were telling the truth, as it would turn out, just not for the reason Numerius thought. And, when he returned to his farm, he would still have a great deal of explaining to do to his wife.

Marcus and Quintus Mallius were exactly the type of provincial that, if they had gone to Gades instead of Scallabis, Aulus Didius would point out to his sons Spurius and Septimus as "pigeons ripe for plucking." Numerius watched them, amused and remembering how his three older sons and the one daughter he had brought with him had behaved in much the same manner as he followed them from one temple to another, then stood in front of a statue of a god and argued about who knew more about the deity. He did notice the line of exclusively men standing outside the *Praetorium*, but only gave them a passing glance, so he missed that they seemed to be in pairs, and one was clearly older than the other. Once they finished with the forum, they walked over to the area where the market stalls were located on market days, and even Numerius was slightly surprised to see that, while the stalls weren't completely occupied, they were about two-thirds full, despite it not being a market day that marked the end of the Roman week of eight days.

"It's probably because there are so many people coming to the capital," he guessed aloud, but his sons had already spotted a vendor selling a variety of small pies both savory and sweet.

"Look, Quintus!" Marcus pointed excitedly down to a row of the pies. "They have dormouse pies!"

Both of them turned as if they were a single man, looking at their father, who was already reaching into his coin purse as he said, "You know that I love good dormouse as much as you do." Signaling to the vendor, a woman of about middle age, they watched as she used a flat piece of wood to expertly scoop up three pies, only offering them once Numerius had dropped a coin into her hand. Munching on their pies, the three of them wandered down the aisles, with the two younger Mallius men stopping to banter with the young woman whose father ran one of the stalls. It was as they were doing this that Numerius spotted a man he knew quite well, although he wasn't from Illurco, and he called to his sons.

"I see Spurius Carbo over there. I'm going to talk to him for a bit." He grinned at the pair. "Try not to get into any trouble, eh?"

Marcus waved at their father, and they continued their meandering course, which, as it happened, took them back towards the forum and the two-story *Praetorium* building, but it was Quintus who noticed the line of men.

"I wonder what they're doing?"

Marcus had been ogling a pretty girl who was helping what had to be her parents as they sliced pieces of pork to a customer's requirement, and he only reluctantly turned around at Quintus' call, but his eye was immediately caught by something even more unusual, the largest man he'd ever seen in his life. At least, that was what Marcus assumed, but when he examined the man more closely, he realized with a start that this giant was clearly around his own age. Quintus' attention was elsewhere, forcing Marcus to tug on his tunic, then once Quintus was oriented, he didn't want to take the risk of pointing out this giant in the event he was offended, but he quickly learned there was no need.

"Pluto's thorny *cock*!" Quintus gasped, fortunately not loudly enough to be overheard. "That's the biggest man I've ever seen in my life! Look at the size of his arms!"

"But he's more our age," Marcus commented, beginning to get nervous that the giant might notice the pair of them gawking, totally unaware that the giant had been subjected to this behavior for most of his life.

Now that they had some time to take in the scene, Marcus noticed that the giant was actually a member of a small party of men, another youth their age who was talking to the giant, but was so short that it only emphasized the height difference, although the pair were clearly friends. There were three other men, but one of them was a slave whose only job seemed to be surreptitiously holding the elbow of one of the older men. He must be sick, Marcus thought, and his slave is helping him do whatever he's here for. After only a span of a handful of heartbeats, Marcus had determined that the second older man was probably the father of the short youth, so it made sense that the enfeebled man was somehow related to the giant.

It was left to Quintus to ask what, at the time, came from nothing but idle curiosity, yet would forever alter the course of his and his brother's life, addressing the men in the line nearest to them, "What are you all here for? Is the *Praetor* hearing cases today?"

Since it was so generally directed, instead of answering immediately, the men glanced at each other, waiting for someone to speak up, but when someone did, it was actually from a tall, slender man who, while older than either of the brothers, was still young, "This is the line for the *dilectus*."

"*Dilectus*?" Marcus echoed, but it wasn't because he was confused or unaware what that meant; by this time, they had heard more about the new Legion being formed, and when he glanced at Quintus, once again, he saw their thoughts were running along the same lines.

"Let's go find Tata," Quintus said, and immediately turned around and headed back towards the center of the forum, with Marcus hard on his heels.

"You two are certain about this?"

"Yes," both brothers replied in unison to their father's query.

Numerius rubbed his chin as he thought about it. It was certainly true that he had had *something* in mind when he brought Marcus and Quintus with him to Scallabis, but while only partially formed, his idea of what might take place didn't include his sons joining this new Legion. And, he thought miserably, it will be bad enough that I come back without them, but he knew that his wife would be furious at the reason for it.

More to forestall the moment where he would render his decision, Numerius challenged, "But, why? Why the Legion?" Before they could answer, he made a partial confession. "One of the reasons I brought you two along is I hoped that you'd see someone doing some sort of trade that might interest you."

He saw by their reaction that neither of them was surprised by this, but for once, Quintus seemed to defer to Marcus as the older brother to reply, "We thought that might be part of it. But, as far as why the Legion?" Marcus shrugged. "We've known for years that we won't be getting anything from the farm, and the truth is that we haven't thought much about the future." Seeing his father was growing impatient, Marcus said quietly, "So, why *not* the Legion? We'll be fed, we'll have shelter. And yes," he hurried on, "we both know that it will be hard. But at least we'll get the chance to *do* something with our lives."

"Yes," Numerius muttered, "like get killed."

"You don't seem to have much confidence in us, Tata."

Numerius glared at Quintus, but his son returned it with a level gaze of his own, while Marcus stood there with his arms folded. And, their father noticed with sour humor, they're both wearing the same look on their face, one that he recognized, except there was something different this time in their demeanors, a determination that he never recalled seeing.

"What about Livia Plautus?" Numerius blurted out, hoping to shake them up. "Just yesterday, you two were willing to kill each other over her. And now, you're just willing to never see her again?"

The brothers exchanged a glance, but again, Quintus deferred to Marcus, who said flatly, "There will be other women." Then he grinned as he added, "Maybe I'll be able to buy nothing but women as slaves and they'll take care of me."

This made Numerius chuckle, but the mention of women brought his mind back to what worried him the most about this sudden decision.

"Your mother isn't going to be happy with me if I come back without you because you both found jobs here. But," he almost shuddered at the thought, "when I tell her that it's because you joined the Legions?" It was Quintus who opened his mouth, but Marcus reached out and touched his arm in a warning, shaking his head as his eyes stayed on their father, who was now staring at the ground with his chin cupped in one hand. Neither of them would be able to recall that, around them, life was going on as normal, with people laughing, talking, and doing business, their memory being the same, of how quiet everything was as they both watched their father intently. Finally, after what seemed to be a thousand heartbeats of time, Numerius sighed. "You're both of legal age. I'll deal with your mother. And if your minds are made up, then I only need to know one thing. What do I need to do?"

The three of them joined the end of the line, while Numerius Mallius realized that not only would he be coming back without his sons, but with a lighter purse since he'd have to hire two men to help him get the wagon and cart back. This Caesar fellow, he thought sourly as he watched his sons becoming more excited by the moment, better know what he's doing.

Publius Vellusius was normally of a placid temperament, slow to anger and not really feeling strongly about much of anything, with one exception; he *hated* farming. He hated it with a passion that, frankly, when he first came to terms with it, surprised him because he'd never experienced anything with this much emotional depth in his life. Even when he had managed to feel up their neighbor Lucius Canidius' daughter Cassia, while he had certainly enjoyed the experience, and was looking forward to more like them since she was clearly willing, it didn't come close to how he felt about what he was doing right at that moment, bent over with a hoe, hacking and chopping out the weeds that threatened to overrun and choke off the tiny shoots of wheat that had just begun poking above the furrowed rows on his father Gnaeus' farm. What made it worse, at least in Publius' opinion, was that he was the oldest son of four brothers and two sisters, and his father never seemed to tire of reminding him of how, once Gnaeus was gone, the farm would be his. Despite his antipathy towards the occupation, Publius also had spent every day of his life on this farm, so he had absorbed a great deal of information from his father, even if he didn't want it. For example, he understood that, by the standards of the day, the Vellusius farm was quite a bit larger than average, being almost sixty *iugera*, while the typical farm in this part of Hispania was forty, which had come to his father because he had the good fortune to have an uncle whose sons had died, having come to Hispania as new settlers with Publius' grandfather, and Gnaeus was the nearest surviving male relative. Best of all, at least as far as Gnaeus was concerned, most of the land was river bottom along the Anas River (Guadiana), outside the settlement of Myrtilis, south of Pacensis, which made the Vellusius farm one of the relatively few able to produce wheat, whereas most of the countryside was suitable for only olives and grapes. In turn, this made the Vellusius farm more prosperous because the shipping costs required to bring the grain from Sicily and Africa to feed the hungry people of Hispania were practically nonexistent.

"Which means," his father reminded Publius and his siblings on what seemed to the oldest son to be on a nightly basis, "that one day, we'll be able to buy even more land. We," Gnaeus Vellusius always chose this moment to sit back in his chair, take a deep draught of his wine, then smack his lips before saying, "are going to see a Vellusius in the Equestrian Order one day, may Jupiter and Fortuna make it so!"

Publius loved his father as all sons should, and in most ways, he actually liked him, but if there was one thing that bothered him, it was that Gnaeus was clearly oblivious to the fact that, of all of his children, his oldest son and the one who would inherit the farm, was obviously completely uninterested in the prospect. Not for the first, or fiftieth time, this was what was actually occupying Publius' mind as he brought his hoe down harder than intended on a particularly stubborn weed.

"Oy! Publius! Watch what you're doing!"

Publius' brother Lucius was one row over and had seen his brother's hoe chop down and sever not just the roots of the weeds, but one of the fragile shoots that they were supposed to be protecting.

"Oh, yes," Publius mumbled as he looked down and saw that he had indeed sliced through the stalk of the plant that would have blossomed, ripened, then provided a few dozen kernels of the grain that, in the Roman world, was almost as precious as gold. "Sorry, Lucius. I'll be more careful."

Publius liked bread as much as anyone, he was certain; just the thought of a nice, steaming loaf fresh out of the oven, made by his mother Domitilla made his mouth water. He just didn't care much for all the work that was required to make it. Lucius, on the other hand, loved every moment, and more than once, Publius had wished he hadn't been born first, because in the Roman world, the day Gnaeus Vellusius died, Publius became the *paterfamilias*, so that his own desires became subordinate to the good of the family. He would be responsible for his mother unless she remarried, and depending on when his father died, his younger siblings, effectively trapping him in a place he was desperate to escape. Turning his attention back to his work, Publius gloomily made his way down his assigned row, his back aching as it always did, despite his youth and that this was a chore that, while not done daily, was performed at least once a week, and he had been doing it since he was old enough to hold a hoe. And, he thought miserably, this isn't even the job I hate the most. In fact, most of the time, he didn't mind this so much because he and Lucius got along well, as he did with everyone but his oldest sister Gaia, but nobody got along with Gaia, who was just a naturally disagreeable person; privately, Publius had put this down to the fact that she was quite homely.

The sun was dipping down to the horizon when they were finished and began walking back to what was more than a farmhouse but not quite a villa, mainly because instead of rebuilding the original farmhouse, first Publius' grandfather, then his father had added rooms as the family grew and, while modestly, prospered. It was just before dusk, so there was no light shining through the open windows, which remained open for most of the year here in the southern part of Hispania.

"Mama said that she was thinking of using some of the pork tonight," Lucius commented, knowing that his brother would be indifferent to the idea of meat.

"As long as there's enough lentils and bread, that's all that matters to me," Publius replied, confirming that, if his mother followed through, Lucius could count on Publius' portion.

They both spotted the movement at the same time, although they also both claimed to have been the first to do so, but it was Publius who noticed first. "Isn't that Decimus Norbanus wearing that red cloak?"

Lucius squinted for a moment, then nodded.

"I think so," he said, and Publius heard both the excitement and the concern in his younger brother's voice, even as it cracked slightly, Lucius being at the age where his own body could betray him in any number of ways.

Fortunately, Publius was fond of Lucius, and his own passage to manhood was sufficiently recent that he didn't tease; besides, Lucius' confirmation of his guess suddenly raised all manner of questions.

"Why would Norbanus be coming all the way here from Hispalis (Seville)?" Publius wondered.

"Maybe he's on his way back from Scallabis," Lucius suggested, something that Publius instantly accepted, which he signaled with a nod.

Decimus Norbanus was known by sight to both brothers since, while Norbanus was based in Hispalis, he spent a fair amount of time in Myrtilis, and it was a regular occurrence for the brothers to accompany Gnaeus to the town, just seven miles northwest and the largest town within a day's walk to the Vellusius farm. They did know that Decimus Norbanus was the senior ranking official of Rome for this area, although neither brother really knew exactly what his status was. What mattered was that he was always accompanied by three lictors, the most potent representation of authority in their world, although by this point in time, in the Year of the Consulships of Marcus Pupius Piso Frugi Calpurnianus and Marcus Valerius Messalla Niger (61 BCE), the bundle of rods and the bronze ax that symbolized the official the lictors were accompanying had the authority to mete out punishment ranging from a beating with one of the rods, or beheading by one of the axes hadn't been used in their lifetime, or in the lifetime of their father. But, Publius wondered, why had he stopped at our farm?

He and Lucius got their answer almost immediately, walking into the farmhouse in the middle of Gnaeus telling Domitilla, "Norbanus was returning from Scallabis."

"But why did he stop here? The Via Corduba runs through Myrtilis, so it's not on his way," Domitilla pointed out as, just as Publius had hoped, she set a large pot of lentils down on the table, seasoned with things that Publius had once asked about, but his mother had rapped him on the hand as she declared they were a secret known only to the women of the Vellusius family.

"I actually asked him about that." Gnaeus had already dropped into his chair at one end of the long table, having to raise his voice to be heard as the Vellusius children, from Publius all the way down to little Domitilla, the youngest at four years old, sat down on the wooden benches on either side. "He told me that he'd been instructed to stop at every farm that has men of a certain age."

It wasn't what Gnaeus said but the manner in which he said it that caught Publius' ear, aided by the fact he was actually closest to his father, sitting to his left, and he was certain he heard something evasive in his father's tone. And, he was not alone, because it caused Domitilla to stop on her return to the kitchen to retrieve what Publius' nose told him was the bread he'd been dreaming about. She stared down at her husband, who seemed absorbed in spooning lentils into his bowl, but they had been married more than twenty years, and she was not fooled in the slightest.

"Gnaeus, why is Decimus Norbanus doing that? Why is he stopping at our farm?"

The normal chatter that marked a Vellusius family dinner slowly died down as the seven Vellusius children, just as attuned to the atmosphere between their parents as the parents were to each other, realized something interesting was happening.

Publius' spoon was hovering inches from the pot as he stared at his father, who steadfastly refused to lift his head to meet either his wife's or his oldest son's gazes, and there was a stubbornness in his manner as he shoved a spoonful of the lentils into his mouth.

"Gnaeus, what aren't you telling me?"

Gnaeus chewed his mouthful of food, but he wasn't ready to capitulate, and after he swallowed, he said, "We'll talk about it later."

Just as Domitilla knew when her husband was hiding something, she also knew by his tone that he wasn't going to divulge anything else, and she turned around in disgust to finish her trip to the kitchen, which Publius correctly interpreted as the sign that, whatever this was about, he would have to wait to find out, so he copied his father, shoving his spoonful of waiting lentils into his mouth. Which was when, for what Publius would cross the river believing to be true, his sister Gaia did something nice for her oldest brother, choosing to ignore all of the evidence that this was just another time where his sister instigated a matter to sow discord for her own purposes, whatever they were.

"*I* know what Decimus Norbanus said, Mama," she called out, which as she expected, stopped her mother again.

This time, however, the other Vellusius children rose up in a small rebellion, as Lucius cried out, "She can go get the rest of our dinner before your news, Gaia!"

Reading the mood of her children accurately, Domitilla disappeared, returning with a board with three steaming loaves of bread, and as Lucius had predicted, the remnants of a joint of pork. This time, however, she didn't do the dividing of the loaves, choosing to drop the board on the table, sending the loaves rolling off of the board as she turned and, with arms crossed, stared down at her oldest daughter.

"Well? What is it that your father doesn't want to talk about?"

"Gaia," Gnaeus growled, or at least attempted to, but he had never been the kind of *paterfamilias* to rule over his family with an iron fist, particularly with Gaia, which Publius had put down to sympathy for her ugliness. "You need to be quiet."

Which, as Publius knew she would, Gaia ignored as if Gnaeus hadn't opened his mouth, telling her mother, "The new

Praetor has called a *dilectus* to raise a new Legion, and he ordered Decimus Norbanus to stop at every farm where he knew there were boys who are old enough to enlist because not enough men have been joining from around here."

The instant the words were out, things changed for Publius Vellusius, or at least so he believed, but before he could speak, Gnaeus beat him to it, declaring, "Well, I don't care who this *Praetor* is, Publius is the only one here old enough to enlist, and he has no intention of doing so." To Publius' dismay, his father turned to look him directly in the eye. "Isn't that right, son?"

It had never been in Publius' nature to seek to be the center of attention for any reason, but this was made even worse because every pair of eyes that were now shifted to him were related to him by blood, and if he thought it had been quiet a short while before, now it was total, as if everyone at the table was holding their breath.

"No." Of everyone at the table, nobody was more shocked than Publius at the word that came from his lips, and he felt a stab of deep remorse at the expression in his father's eyes as that short, simple, but explosive word hung in the air, seeing the shock, and worst of all, the hurt reflected there. You've done it now, Publius, so you might as well say what you want to say. "No, Tata," he repeated. "I *do* want to enlist in this new Legion. Tata," he reached out to grasp Gnaeus' left arm, which was resting on the table, and in the recesses of his mind, Publius wondered when was the last time he had had any physical contact with his father; aloud, he pressed, "you *must* know by now that I don't want to be a farmer!" As the words that had been building up inside of him for so long came tumbling out, he couldn't seem to stop himself. "I've told you this, but you never listen to me! I have never wanted to be a farmer, and I don't want to be responsible for this farm once you're gone!" He could see out of the corner of his eye that his siblings were sitting in stunned silence, not just because of what Publius was saying, but because of how rare it was for their placid, calm, oldest brother to be this animated, so much so that he had come to his feet to stare down at his father, trying to send Gnaeus a signal of how deadly serious he was as he continued, "If the gods had wanted me to be a farmer, Tata, then why did they make me like this? Why would they make me *hate* it so much?" Taking a deep breath, Publius tried to sound calm as he finished, "I want to join this new Legion, Father, and I'm going to whether I have your permission or not."

Suddenly feeling somewhat foolish, Publius dropped back onto the bench, but he kept his gaze fastened on his father, who, while a little pale, looked disturbingly calm. Nobody else around the table moved, nor was Publius even aware of them, but when the silence was broken, it wasn't by Gnaeus, it was by Lucius.

"Tata," Lucius said gently, "you know that what Publius is saying is true. He's hated doing all the things we have to do for as long as I can remember. He's not meant to be a farmer..."

"Do you think I was?" Gnaeus cut his second son off in mid-sentence, but he was addressing Publius, in a calm, quiet voice that none of the children could remember hearing. "Do you think that when I was your age, I dreamed of being a farmer, Publius?" He laughed then, but it was one laced with bitterness. "Oh, boy, I had *very* different dreams for myself at one time. And," he added, "I thought about enlisting in the Legions back during all the business between Sulla and Gaius Marius. But," he finished quietly, "my family needed me more than Rome did."

"But your brother..." Publius began, but Gnaeus cut him off with a sharp chopping motion of his hand, and he sounded angry for the first time as he snapped, "You don't need to tell me about my brother, boy. It was because of my brother that I couldn't pursue my own dreams! *He* was the eldest, not me! But Septimus fell in with a bad bunch, and he liked to debauch and gamble more than he liked farming. And," Gnaeus thundered, "it got him *killed*, boy! He had his throat slit because he owed money to the wrong people and he refused to tell our father about it!" Suddenly, Gnaeus' eyes filled with tears, and everyone present heard the pain as he cried out, "And because I was stupid, because I idolized Septimus, when he swore me to silence and keep my mouth shut, I did it! I'm the reason my brother was murdered! If I had told our father, he would have gotten the money somehow, but I didn't!"

Gnaeus Vellusius had never spoken of his brother to his

children before, at least beyond that he had died while Gnaeus was still in his early teens, making him the oldest surviving son, but Publius took one glance at his mother, who was still standing as if frozen to the floor, and seeing the tears streaming down her face, understood that his mother had known the truth all along, but in deference to her husband, had honored his request to remain silent.

Publius was at a complete loss about what to say, other than stammering, "I...I...didn't know that, Tata."

"That's because I never told you," Gnaeus sniffled and wiped his eyes, saying honestly, "because it's too painful for me to talk about. Still," he cleared his throat, pulling himself erect, becoming the Vellusius *paterfamilias* once again, "when I said that you're not joining the Legion, I meant it."

"I said I'd do it without your blessing," Publius warned, but this seemed to amuse Gnaeus more than anything.

"Maybe you're right," he said unexpectedly. "Maybe I had you and your brothers behind the plow too much. Otherwise," the smile he offered was grim, "you'd know our laws, particularly as they pertain to the *paterfamilias* of a family of Roman citizens. If I forbid you to do something, you become an outlaw if you disobey me. Besides," he added with a satisfaction that made Publius' stomach churn, "to enlist, you need for your father to attest that you're not only the right age, but that you're a citizen. We can't have slaves and noncitizens fouling the ranks of our Legions, can we?"

Very deliberately, Gnaeus turned away from his son, and ignoring the stares from the others, reached over to tear a hunk of the nearest loaf, using it to dip into his bowl to soak up the juice left over from the lentil stew. Slowly, the other children resumed their own meal, while Domitilla finally took her seat at the opposite end of the table, yet despite glaring at her husband, Gnaeus studiously ignored his wife, choosing to focus on his meal. Publius' appetite was completely gone, so he shoved his bowl over to Lucius, muttering to him to finish it.

When he stood, Gnaeus didn't look up from his meal, but said, "I don't recall giving you permission to leave the table, boy."

In all of his eighteen years, Publius Vellusius had never

defied his father, at least openly, but something shifted inside him, and he snapped, "What are you going to do? Have one of Norbanus' lictors come and beat me with his rod?"

He didn't wait for an answer, nor did his father offer one, choosing instead to ignore Publius' exit from the farmhouse, leaving his family to finish their meal in morose silence.

Publius didn't return to the farmhouse until he was certain that everyone had gone to bed; days always started early on a farm, and even with all this drama and excitement, none of them wanted to begin their day of what was strenuous work for all of them already tired. Just to be sure, Publius didn't enter through the door, instead climbing through the window of the room he shared with Lucius and his two other brothers. Fortunately, only Lucius was awake, and they talked in whispers.

"Are they asleep?" Publius asked.

"They went to bed, but I heard them talking for a long time," Lucius told him. "They just stopped a little while ago." He watched as Publius climbed into the bed they shared, then asked hesitantly, "What are you going to do, Publius?"

"I don't know," his brother answered with a sigh. "I know he's right about the law, and that he needs to sign for me to enlist. I just thought that he'd do it."

"Maybe he'll change his mind," Lucius offered, though not with much enthusiasm, but this caused Publius to chuckle softly.

"When is the last time Tata has changed his mind about anything?"

This, Lucius knew, was simply the truth, so he didn't try and argue, and within a few moments, both of them were breathing regularly; it was a singular talent that Publius Vellusius would be calling on for most of the rest of his life, the ability to not worry about things that were beyond his control, which meant that he fell asleep almost immediately.

While Lucius had heard his parents talking and had briefly thought of trying to sneak to the door of their bedroom, he quickly discarded it since none of the children had ever managed to pull this off without being caught. Consequently, he was ignorant of the events transpiring a few feet away that would have a profound impact not just on his older brother, but on himself.

"We need to talk," was how Domitilla had started the conversation, just after she closed the door to their bedroom, which actually had a lock on it. Which, she would sometimes think with amusement, is why we've had ten children, although only seven of them survived and she rarely allowed herself to think of those who were taken from her and Gnaeus.

Nor was she surprised at all when Gnaeus cut her off, "No, we don't. My mind is made up, Domitilla."

Normally, this would have been enough for Domitilla to demur; she was the model of a good Roman wife, but tonight was different, because tonight, she had decided that it was time she take control of this business between her husband and oldest son. Perhaps a dozen times over the course of the years, Domitilla, seeing how unhappy Publius was whenever it involved the farm, had broached the subject with Gnaeus, and he had always dismissed her concerns. And, before tonight, she had relented, yet now, while she couldn't say how she knew, Domitilla was aware that this was important for the future not just of her oldest son, but the entire Vellusius family. How she knew this, she could never have articulated, but in her mind, she saw what would happen when Publius, feeling obligated but without any pleasure, followed in his father's footsteps, becoming angrier, and more bitter every day he was chained to this piece of land. Which, she knew very well, men all around them would have rejoiced to own. One of those, though he wasn't a man yet, was Lucius. Whereas Publius viewed everything involved with running a prosperous farm as an onerous chore, Lucius actually enjoyed the work, although much of this was due to his naturally cheerful disposition, a reminder how, while every one of her children came from the same parents, each of them were different and unique. Even in the moment, her thoughts of this led her to Gaia, who, next to Publius, she was worried about the most, although for completely different reasons; if she was being honest, while she loved her children, she didn't *like* Gaia at all, and from what she had seen, neither did her siblings. Gaia could wait, however;

this was a battle for another day.

Which was why she actually replied to Gnaeus, "Then you need to change your mind, husband. Because Publius is going to join the Legion."

Even if it had been in his nature, Gnaeus Vellusius had never struck his wife, but when he leapt to his feet from where he'd been sitting on the edge of their bed and moved towards her and she didn't flinch, just regarded him steadily instead of showing any fear, he realized that he'd been defeated.

Closing his eyes, he staggered back and dropped back on the bed, saying only, "Tell me why this is so important to you."

And, for the next length of time, and for one of the relatively few times in their marriage of more than twenty years, Domitilla Vellusius talked, and Gnaeus Vellusius listened.

The gods had deemed that Publius Vellusius would go on to live a long, and very eventful, life, but for the rest of his days, what occurred at dawn the next morning would be one of the most memorable, and on the few occasions that he thought about it, not being naturally introspective, he would always feel a deep gratitude, not just for his father, but for his mother Domitilla, and most surprising to him, his sister Gaia. Not that this was his first thought when someone gave the bottom of his foot, which had been sticking out from under the covers, a resounding slap to bring him from his slumber, bringing him bolt upright with a shout of pain and surprise that caused his three brothers to wake as well. Blinking several times, he found it difficult to focus his eyes because of the glare of what he only gradually realized came from the oil lamp held in his father's hand. Gnaeus was holding it above his head, which actually gave his features a sinister cast that caused Publius' heart to go from the steady trot it had been doing to a gallop, his thought being, my father's going to kill me for disobedience.

"Get dressed, Publius. And hurry up." Gnaeus turned away, then called over his shoulder, "And pack your things."

Lucius was now awake, rubbing his eyes as he sat up, as were the two younger brothers, the youngest, also named Gnaeus and seven years old, starting to cry, frightened by the atmosphere in the room.

Ignoring the turmoil he'd created, Gnaeus disappeared from their room, while Publius, moving like one of the automatons in a Greek play, did as he had been instructed, with jerky motions as his mind tried to catch up to the possible meanings of this, and none of the alternatives offered any solace.

"Gnaeus?" Lucius tried to sound brave, but his brother heard the fear there. "What do you think Tata's going to do?"

"I don't know," Publius answered honestly, then despite the gloom, or perhaps because of it, he realized that his younger brothers were looking for some form of reassurance from him; he was the oldest, after all. "But you don't need to worry. Everything will be all right."

Then, he was done gathering up all of his possessions, which, if he was being honest, wasn't very much to show for his eighteen years. Before he left the room, he went to his brothers, starting with young Gnaeus, who was now crying pitifully, then Aulus, who was ten and wedged in age between Gaia and Fulvia, finishing with Lucius, who he embraced as he had his other brothers, but he whispered, "You deserve this farm, Lucius, and I know you'll make it even better."

Then, he walked out of their room but came to an immediate stop, seeing that his mother and sisters were standing there, while Domitilla was holding a bundle. Walking to Publius, she thrust the bundle out to her oldest child.

"Here," she said briskly, although her cheeks were wet with tears, "you'll be hungry and it's a long way to Scallabis."

"Scallabis?" Publius echoed, completely confused now, but when he looked for Gnaeus, he was nowhere to be seen.

His mother, seeing and correctly interpreting his confusion, assured him, "He's outside on the cart, waiting for you."

"Waiting for me?" Publius had been certain he couldn't be more confused, but this was proving to be a foolish thought. "Why?"

"Because the *Conquisitor* that was in Myrtilis has already moved on, so he's going with you to Scallabis so that you can enlist in the Legion, of course," Domitilla answered as if this was a foolish question.

For a horrible instant, Publius thought he would collapse, but he managed to whisper, "Are you serious, Mama? He's going to let me enlist?"

"Yes, my son," Domitilla assured him, then swept him into an embrace so that he would not see the tears streaming down her face. "Your father loves you, Publius. And," she kissed him tenderly, "so does your mother, who only wants the best for her children."

Publius, understanding the import of her words, gasped, "You changed his mind? How, Mama?"

"That," she smiled through the tears, "is between me and your father. Now," she gave him a gentle but firm shove, "kiss your sisters goodbye."

As he had with his brothers, Publius started with the youngest, picking up young Domitilla Minor and, despite their tears, swung her about as he had done so many times before so that there was as much laughter as there was crying. Setting her down, Publius hugged Fulvia, who was eight, but it was when he stood in front of Gaia that there was a surprise waiting for him. Before he could say, or do, anything, Gaia threw herself into his arms, wrapping her arms around his neck with a grip that almost strangled him.

"I love you, brother," she whispered in his ear. "And I want you to be happy. May the gods be with you and give you all that you deserve. I," he heard the sudden sob, "couldn't have asked for a better big brother. That's why I spoke up."

From that moment on, Publius Vellusius never viewed Gaia in the same light, and while neither of them knew it, their bond would remain strong for the rest of their respective lives. Then, with the farewells over, Publius walked out of his farmhouse, and while he had no idea this would be the case, it would be the last time he ever set eyes on it, or most of his family. As Domitilla had said, he saw Gnaeus sitting on the seat of the two-wheeled cart, not the larger wagon in which they hauled the grain to market. Feeling awkward, Publius hopped up onto the seat next to his father.

"I'll be back in a few days," Gnaeus called out, and Publius noticed that his father had referred only to himself, which marked the first moment where he thought this might actually be really happening.

With a crack of his whip, the mule threw itself against the

traces and the cart rolled out of the farmyard created by the Vellusius house, barn, and a low wall on the other two sides, while Publius waved once to his family, all of whom had gathered to see the oldest son of the family off. The quiet sobs of his younger siblings tore at his heart, but conflicting emotions began surging through him as he began to accept that this wasn't a trick by his father to lull him into a state of complacency before he unleashed some sort of punishment, although Publius didn't entertain this for more than a handful of heartbeats, knowing that it just wasn't in his father's nature to be cruel in any way. Nevertheless, Publius was still nervous, neither of them speaking as the mule plodded on the track that would take them to Myrtilis, where they would take the better road north to Pacensis, where they would hit the paved Roman road that was part of the Via Corduba, which was more than a hundred miles to the east.

Finally, Publius couldn't take the silence any longer, and he blurted out, "Why did you change your mind?"

Gnaeus didn't reply for several moments, and Publius was beginning to resign himself to never hearing the answer when his father said simply, "Your mother is right." If a strong wind had blown right then, Publius Vellusius was certain that it would have toppled him out of the cart, but while he was staring at Gnaeus, his father kept his eyes on the bobbing head of the mule. At last, he continued, "You weren't born for this, Publius. And," he took a deep breath before he went on, "I've known that for years. I was just too…"

When he didn't continue, Publius supplied, "…stubborn?"

To his intense relief, his father, rather than reacting angrily, laughed and agreed, "Exactly. But Domitilla, your mother," he added this as if Publius needed the clarification between his mother and youngest sister, but he wasn't about to say anything to break this moment by pointing that out, "she forced me to not just see what was in front of my eyes, but to accept it." Another span of silence, then Gnaeus did look at his son, saying softly, "It was wrong of me to saddle you with my expectations the same way that my father did to me, Publius, and I ask your pardon for it."

Naturally, Publius assured him that none was needed, if

only with a nod because he couldn't have found the words, nor could he have gotten them out.

This time, when silence fell, it wasn't uncomfortable, and father and son, having passed through Myrtilis, rode among the early morning traffic of fellow Romans, and while Publius noticed that it was heavier going in the direction towards Scallabis, he didn't think much of it.

"You know," he spoke up, "I noticed that the wall at the northeast corner has started to sag again."

"You're right," Gnaeus said, his tone betraying none of his thoughts. "I noticed that as well. It's because the ground's too soft. I should have dug a drainage ditch to let the ground dry out, but I never got around to it. It needs to be done."

"Put Lucius to it," Publius answered immediately. "He told me some of his ideas about how to strengthen the wall, not just there, but all along the eastern side."

Gnaeus glanced over at his son, yet while he opened his mouth, what came out surprised both of them.

"Why do you want to join the Legions, Publius? Why do you want to be a Legionary?"

Within a heartbeat of the words coming out of Gnaeus' mouth, Publius suddenly realized something, which prompted him to admit, "I don't know, really, Tata." He thought for a moment, and as his comrades and superiors would learn but his father already knew, while Publius Vellusius' mind might not have been the quickest, he nevertheless was methodical and thoughtful, so that when he finally did speak, he did so with enough confidence to say, "What I do know is that being in the Legions will give me the chance to at least see what the gods mean for me."

"But it's twelve years," Gnaeus countered, neither of them knowing that this was incorrect. "It will be twelve years before you can do the thing that you want to do. What if you find it in your first year?"

"Then," Publius shrugged, "I'll wait twelve years." With a laugh, he added, "Who knows? Maybe I'll love the Legions so much that's what I'll do for the rest of my life." He could see that his father wasn't satisfied, but he was grateful that Gnaeus didn't press the issue. Then, after another silence, something occurred to Publius, who asked his father curiously, "Who is the new *Praetor* anyway?'

"His name is Caesar," Gnaeus replied absently, still wrestling with the doubts he was feeling about taking his son to an uncertain fate. "Gaius Julius Caesar."

Chapter Two

"You're as bad as your father."

The words weren't delivered with any particular force or venom, just a simple statement of fact that was aimed at the supine figure lying facedown, with his head hanging off the side of the wooden bed just a few inches above the slimy, sour-smelling puddle of vomit. When the figure didn't stir, the woman, with iron-gray hair drawn so tightly back that it seemed to stretch her already taut features to the point where one might be forgiven for expecting her sharp cheekbones to burst through the flesh, walked to the bed, and with an ease that told of long practice, used the sheet to dump the body off the bed and directly into the pool of vomit, which landed with a wet, smacking sound that was instantly followed by a low groan. Standing with her hands on her hips, Fabia Atilius looked at her son impassively, waiting for his wine-soaked brain to communicate that he was lying face down in a puddle of his own vomit. How many times has it been this month? she wondered. Five? Or was this the sixth? Her thoughts were interrupted by her son suddenly jerking to life, roaring in disgust as he tried to push himself up out of the puddle, only for one hand to slip in the slimy liquid to send him right back down to the floor.

Fabia wasn't normally a woman who saw the humor in things, but this made her smile, while her son Marcus complained, "Pluto's *cock*, Mama! Why did you do that?"

"You know perfectly well why," she snapped, the moment of levity gone. "You're supposed to be at your job now, Marcus! You *know* how I had to beg Asinius Afranius to give you that job!"

"It's shoveling *cac* from his stables!" Marcus protested. "That's not fit work for a Roman citizen!"

"It's the only work you're fit for," she shot back. "You can't stay sober long enough to be trusted with anything else!"

This was, Marcus Atilius knew, nothing more than the truth, but the fact that it was coming from his mother made it more painful.

"You're as bad as your father," she repeated, then stopped suddenly, frowning. "I thought you two were together last night."

"We were," Marcus mumbled as he got unsteadily to his feet, then used the already soiled sheet to wipe what had been the contents of his stomach from his face and arms. He was deliberately stalling, because he knew that if he told his mother the truth, it would be worse for both his father and for himself. "But I don't remember much, Mama."

"Where did you two go?" Fabia demanded, evincing a groan from her son that he hoped she thought was because of his aching head and not because the answer would enrage her. However, before he could reply, she said accusingly, "You went to Pan's Delight, didn't you?"

Atilius closed his eyes before he answered, which was something he'd been doing since he was a child and was what Fabia knew was the sign that what he was about to say would either make his father's temper explode or incite the ire of his mother, so she was at least somewhat prepared for it when he said, "We didn't start there. We met at Temple of Bacchus first. But," he sighed, "yes, we went to Pan's Delight. But it was his idea!"

"Oh, I have no doubt of that!" Fabia snapped, but she was already moving towards the door, alarming Marcus, who was certain he knew what was coming.

He hurried after her, the sudden movement sending what he was certain was a bolt from Jupiter through his head, but he forced this aside as he pleaded, "Mama, don't do it! Not again!"

"Don't do what?" Fabia spun about, her already sharp features even tauter, worn down by the years of disappointment in her husband, and in herself for being foolish enough to fall in love with Gaius Atilius, but it was her eyes that communicated not just anger but the pain that comes from constant betrayal. "Don't go retrieve my husband from the arms of that *whore*?" This last word was more of a shriek and almost unintelligible, but this wasn't the first, or even the fifth time a conversation of this type had taken place in the Atilius *insula*, and honestly, Marcus did have sympathy for his mother's plight.

"You know what will happen, Mama." Marcus tried to be patient. "You and Dafne will get in another fight, and Pacuvius will throw the both of you out into the street so that you don't wreck his place, and then everyone in the district will be laughing about it for the next week."

For just a moment, perhaps a half-dozen heartbeats, he thought that he might have finally gotten through to his mother as she stood there, regarding him thoughtfully, or at least this was how it seemed.

"I should have expected this," she finally spoke, and even without the words, Marcus recognized the tone and braced himself for what was coming. "You're always on his side! You're both against me, and you always have been, ever since you could talk!"

"That's not true!" He protested, but it was to her back as she snatched up the threadbare shawl that should have been discarded years earlier, and as was her habit, she slammed the door with enough force to shake the floor under his feet.

Marcus stood for a moment, his physical misery compounded by what was a depressingly frequent occurrence, that the Atilius *paterfamilias* and his wife would be making a spectacle of themselves again. And, he admitted to himself, his mother wasn't wrong; Gaius Atilius was a scoundrel and petty thief who had long since surrendered his soul to Bacchus and to debauchery and, while it would have surprised his mother, Marcus shared her contempt for the woman that was his father's current passion, the whore named Dafne. She was almost as old as Atilius' mother, which she disguised with a disgusting amount of makeup that only worked as long as she remained in the dim lighting of the combination *taverna* and brothel named Pan's Delight that was in the poor section of Nova Carthago, where the Atilius family lived. Dafne wasn't just ugly to look at; to Marcus, there was a sharp ugliness to her personality, and she made no attempt to hide the fact that part of the reason she had attached herself to his father was because of the pain and embarrassment it caused Fabia. The problem was that Gaius Atilius was a handsome man, even now in his early forties, although the years of dissipation and debauchery had created bags under his eyes, and he had recently lost another tooth. And, Marcus had heard from the few relations on either side of his family who still had anything to do with Gaius, he had always known he was attractive to women, as well as to men of a certain persuasion, and had never been shy about using that to his advantage. The other attribute possessed by Gaius Atilius was a glib tongue that made him sound cleverer than he actually was, so that, on three separate occasions in Marcus' life, he had been roused from his sleep by his father, who took his family with him when he fled after one of his schemes was discovered.

At one point in time, Marcus, who was the youngest, had two sisters and a brother who at least helped him adjust to what had become a habit for the older siblings, learning their way about another new town or city around Hispania. He was nineteen now, and their three years in Nova Carthago had been the longest stretch they had stayed in one spot for his entire life. Now, he was the only Atilius child left; both of his sisters had taken the first opportunity presented to them, one of them marrying a baker who had already lost two wives and was twenty years older, the other marrying a drover who was passing through when they lived in Corduba. His brother Lucius he didn't think about, or at least he tried not to, because anytime he did, it only made him want to drink more wine. Lucius had been nine years older than Marcus, and like many younger brothers, Marcus had idolized his older brother, who was also the firstborn. And, as Fabia had said more times than he could count, the gods had favored Lucius by making him as handsome as his father, but with the brains of Fabia, who was, even her husband acknowledged, the clever one in the family. What had happened to Lucius wasn't his fault, unless doing as your father and the *paterfamilias* directed was a crime. It had seemed so simple, really; at least, this was what Gaius had impressed on Lucius, back when Marcus was ten years old. Like his older siblings, Gaius had made it clear that every Atilius had to pull their weight in the family; of course, as far as Gaius was concerned, he was the exception. Marcus had long believed that, if he'd been left to his own devices, Gaius Atilius would have pimped out his sisters, either managing them himself or leasing them to one of the brothel owners, but this was one area where Fabia was ferocious in her refusal to allow it, so they had both ended up taking more mundane, and lower paying, work.

Fabia Minor, who was Marcus' favorite and the older sister, had worked with her mother taking in laundry from the higher-ranking families wherever they were. Lucretia, the one closest to Marcus in age, had been hired as a cleaning girl for a patrician family, and when Marcus looked back on it, he would have described this as the happiest period of his life, where for an all too brief time, the Atilius family seemed to be just like every other family of their class. Yes, they were poor, but there was enough money to feed the children and to keep a roof over their head, despite how much money Gaius Atilius siphoned off for things that he would describe as "business deals" that always involved copious amounts of wine. Marcus had been put to work as well, assigned to spend his time in the forum, watching for rural Romans from out in the province who had come to what passed for the big city, who his father called "the pigeons." It didn't take long for Marcus to learn how to spot the signs; the gawking at the statues and temples was a dead giveaway, and he would follow them to wherever they were staying, usually at one of the inns, although sometimes they stayed with friends and relatives. He'd relay this information to Gaius, then Gaius and Lucius would disappear from the *insula*, sometimes staying out overnight. More than once, Gaius and his brother had returned to the apartment with torn clothing, bruised knuckles, and on two occasions, cuts that, when Marcus asked his mother where they came from, were described as "accidents," but what he fairly quickly deduced were knife wounds. Usually, but not always, when they returned, it would be with things like coin purses whose strings had been cut, rings, necklaces, and other items of value.

Corduba, being the provincial capital, was the largest city in the province of Baetica, and was where the *Praetorium*, which served as not only the residence of the man sent from Rome to govern in the name of the Senate and People of Rome, but where most of the government offices were housed. The family Atilius had fled there from Scallabis, far to the west, once more leaving in the night after Gaius' attempt to cheat one of the local officials was exposed, although Marcus never learned how, marking his father's most ambitious criminal attempt yet. The two-hundred-fifty-mile journey to Corduba had been a nightmare, and more than once, young Marcus thought about sneaking away in the night; the only reason he didn't was because he knew he wouldn't survive without his family. So he stayed with them, and while it was difficult in Corduba in the beginning, it was no less so than any of the other cities that the Atilius family had settled in. Time passed, and things fell into a pattern that, for Marcus Atilius, was comforting in its routine, even if it was essentially criminal activity, but it was all he knew. His father had never made a secret that he was with other women, but in this, he was no different than most other Roman men, and he never flaunted his latest conquest in his wife's face. Then, everything changed, because of one random act, and because the Atilius *paterfamilias* overestimated his abilities once again.

It didn't surprise Marcus all that much that, when he arrived at the livery stable much later than he was supposed to, the owner Asinius Afranius, who was only hospitable to the animals in his care, was standing there, arms crossed. Since his stable catered to the members of the higher orders, it had been difficult for Fabia to convince Afranius to take her youngest son on, but Marcus had managed to keep this job for six months.

"You're late," Afranius said, biting off each word. "I've already warned you once."

There was no point in arguing, so Marcus didn't even try, saying only, "I know."

"I don't give third chances," Afranius said, but when he paused, Marcus was confused.

Was Afranius giving him the opportunity to beg for his job? *This* job of mucking out stables? There's no way that I'm begging him to allow me to keep shoveling *cac*, he thought. Marcus Atilius may not be much, but he's better than being a stable boy! In something of a rarity, Marcus had read Afranius correctly, that he was waiting for Marcus to offer him a reason, no matter how flimsy, to keep him employed. What neither Marcus nor Fabia would ever learn was that Asinius Afranius, despite his gruff demeanor and prickly behavior with his fellow citizens, was at heart a kind man, and he lived in the *insula* directly across the street from the one occupied by the Atilius family, and they had been here in Nova Carthago a few years, more than long enough for Asinius to take the measure of Gaius Atilius and what he was, and what he wasn't.

Finally, once it became obvious that Marcus had no intention of offering any kind of justification or excuse, he gave a curt nod, saying only, "No need to come back, boy. You're of no use to me."

Spinning about, Afranius stalked off, leaving Marcus standing there knowing that he needed this job, but when he opened his mouth, nothing came out, and he was quickly left alone, standing in the yard of the stables with only the horses, most of them paying him no attention as they munched their hay and swatted flies with their tails. Knowing better than to return home to the apartment, Marcus debated for a moment what to do with his time, while his feet behaved as if they had a mind of their own, taking him back to the quarter of Nova Carthago where he lived, and where the majority of the *tavernae* catering to his class were located. The only problem standing in the way for him to debauch himself was not having any money, but he knew where to get some, so he made a slight detour, heading for the forum. His father had been right about one thing; there were always pigeons to pluck.

Just as Marcus had predicted, the scene between Gaius and Fabia Atilius would be the talk of the neighborhood for the next several days, and while their clashes were too numerous to mention, what made this one different was that, finally, Fabia managed to get her hands on Dafne. In fact, if the story was correct, and Marcus felt certain that it was, Fabia had made it deeper into Pan's Delight than ever before, actually catching her husband and Dafne in the same bed, where both of them were sleeping off the effects of their revels the night before. This time, however, instead of attacking Gaius, Domitilla grabbed a handful of Dafne's hair and, despite the fact that this involved his parents, Marcus chuckled when he heard that the prostitute's "hair" came off her head because it was a wig, but his mother recovered more quickly than Dafne, getting a purchase of her real hair, which she used to drag the woman, screaming and kicking, down the stairs and out into the street.

Marcus wasn't terribly surprised that the version of this battle that he heard immediately after it happened, and what he heard just a matter of a watch later were vastly different, with the latter sounding more like one of the gladiatorial contests that were held on festival days. Whatever the truth was, the end result was that his mother had managed to strip Dafne bare, then proceeded to kick her down the street as the whore tried to scramble away, to the delight of an audience, which like the version of the fight itself grew in size so that by the time the people of Nova Carthago lost interest, Marcus was certain that the crowd of supposed witnesses would have filled the city arena to the brim. As far as his father was concerned, according to witnesses, he was every bit as entertained as the other onlookers, which Marcus would always wonder about, whether this was the final humiliation that was one too many for his mother to bear. Where this irreparable, and deadly, rift had begun between his parents Marcus held no doubt, and he knew that both of his sisters, while they were still under the same roof, felt the same way. It had begun with Lucius; specifically, his execution by order of the *Praetor* in Corduba, when he had been caught in the private quarters of the *Praetor*'s wife and charged with attempted rape. The truth was quite different; Gaius Atilius, who always had a sharp eye out for an opportunity, had heard about this particular wife and her tendency to…roam from her marital bed. Normally, tales of these kinds of actions by the upper classes were relayed from one Head Counter to another with great enthusiasm and amusement, if only because they viewed it as proof that, once the *toga* and *stola* came off, upper class Roman men and women were not much different than the people they sneered at and avoided at all costs. Gaius Atilius, however, had seen something more substantial than the chance for a laugh; he saw an opportunity. As both of his parents said more times than Marcus could easily count, Lucius

Atilius was the mirror image of his father at that age, and hadn't Gaius been able to conquer any woman he desired? Whenever his parents talked like this, usually when Gaius shared his wine with his wife, which had occurred frequently in Marcus' early years, it made Marcus uncomfortable to hear them speaking of such things, and the frank way his mother admitted that she had been one of his conquests. Burned into his memory was the night that his parents and Lucius sat at the table, discussing Gaius' latest plan, after he and his sisters had been banished from the room, which was a practical guarantee that Marcus would find a way to listen in. It had turned out to be deceptively simple, and he always wondered if one of his parents actually wanted him or one of his sisters to listen in; if that was the case, he was certain that it was his father, who always liked to boast about his cleverness to his children about one scheme or another.

"Figulus is almost thirty years older than his wife Aurelia," was the first of the conversation Marcus heard from where he was crouched behind a cupboard that, for some reason, had been moved from its normal spot against the wall to a spot just a few inches away from it but large enough for him to squeeze into, and he instantly recognized his father's voice. "And I heard from Plancus that she's...bored having an older husband. In fact," Gaius' voice took on a laughing quality, "the rumor is that she already rutted with one of the slaves that carries her litter!"

"You know how people love to talk," Fabia interjected. "Just because someone is saying it doesn't mean it happened."

"What better way to find out?" Gaius countered.

Initially, Marcus assumed that it was his father who would attempt to seduce the wife of this Figulus, who had recently arrived from Rome after he had served as Consul, which was the normal arrangement for the ruling class. A year as Consul, followed by a year as a *Praetor* of a nice, fat province, where it was such a longstanding tradition by this point that it might have been one of the laws engraved on bronze tablets that was the basis of the Roman system of government, that the main goal of the *Praetor* was to essentially squeeze and extort every last *sestertius* from the inhabitants of that province. The rationale, what there was of one, was simple: running for

Consul by this point in Roman history was an extraordinarily expensive proposition, and more than one high-ranking patrician family had ruined themselves by trying to attain this office that was the supreme authority of what was by this point a world power. This systematic raping of the province by the *Praetor* was supposed to be confined to the native population and not to Roman citizens, but there was a huge difference between the theory and the practice. All of which was meaningless to young Marcus Atilius, squeezed behind the cupboard; besides, he was concentrating on what his parents were talking about.

He wasn't surprised when his mother objected, "I can think of several better ways to find out that aren't nearly as dangerous."

It was who spoke next that rocked Marcus to his core, when Lucius, for the first time, interjected, "Mama, I can do this, I swear it! I've already seen her twice at the market, and I caught her looking at me several times! I pretended not to notice, which is what will make her even more interested."

Fabia didn't reply, at least not immediately, but she clearly still wasn't convinced, asking finally, "Let's say you go through with this, and it works. Then what? Where's the money?"

"Where's the money?" This came from Gaius, his voice expressing a disbelief that quickly turned to mockery when he repeated, apparently to Lucius since he mimicked his mother's voice, "'Where's the money,' she asks! Why, you silly woman, we'll be *rolling* in the money once we let her husband know that he's been humiliated by his wife! It will be bad enough that *he* knows, but he'd pay *anything* to make sure that none of the other patricians know about it!"

"That," Fabia said quietly, "is a very dangerous thing to do. Men like Figulus are *very* powerful."

"I've thought of that," Gaius countered. "And I have a plan to make sure that he never finds out who's behind it."

"Mama," Lucius spoke again, and Marcus recognized the tone as the same one when he was charming their mother into giving him and his siblings an extra candied fruit. "I can do this, I swear it. And," he paused, and Marcus assumed it was because he was looking at his father, "I trust Tata. He knows what he's doing."

In later years, Marcus Atilius made it a point not to allow his mind to wander back to this point in time, but in the immediate aftermath of what began the disintegration of his family, he found himself wondering what might have happened if his mother had forced his father to explain what that plan was, because they would all come to learn that, like most of the things out of Gaius Atilius' mouth, this was a lie.

At first, things seemed to be going as Gaius and Lucius had predicted, as just more than a week later, Lucius rushed back to their apartment to inform his parents that Aurelia's body slave, who, like the majority of slaves Roman ladies trusted the most, had been with her since infancy, had sidled up to Lucius as they both pretended to be examining some merchandise on offer at one of the market stalls to whisper an invitation to come to the *Praetor*'s residence at the midnight watch that night. Marcus had already heard that Figulus was on a tour of the province and wasn't expected back for several days, which made this the perfect opportunity, and for once, even Fabia seemed, if not willing, then at least resigned to her son accepting the invitation. The first few times were the tensest, to the point that Marcus would rouse himself earlier than normal to wait for Lucius to return from the *Praetorium*, but as days turned into weeks, and he always returned and there was no pounding on the door, the Atilius family began to relax.

"I'm certain that she's in love with me," Lucius offered at the evening meal about two months after the affair began.

"That's not surprising. You're an Atilius!" Gaius laughed, but it was Fabia who asked what turned out to be the crucial question.

"And what about you?" she asked Lucius bluntly. "Are you in love with her?"

Lucius didn't reply, but Marcus saw the answer by the manner in which his brother's face flushed a deep shade of red.

Fabia gave her version of a laugh, which sounded more like a snort. "That's what I thought."

"I warned you about that!" Gaius said angrily. "I told you not to fall in love with the bitch! You," he leaned forward to jab his finger at Lucius, "can't trust these patrician bastards, not a one of them! To them, we're nothing but the dirt under their feet!"

"Your father's right," Fabia added her voice, but she at least was calm, and for her, was gentle with her oldest child. "You can't allow your emotions to get involved in this, my son."

"Aurelia is different!" Lucius insisted. "She'd never betray me!"

This clearly didn't make an impression on Fabia, and she turned to address Gaius to suggest, "Maybe he should break it off with her."

Marcus wasn't the least bit surprised when Gaius snapped, "He'll do no such thing! Not when we're this close!"

"She's already given him a gold necklace and a ring!" Fabia objected, but Gaius only sneered, "That's *nothing* compared to what we're going to get!"

"And when is this going to happen?" Fabia demanded. "Every time he sees her, the danger goes up!"

"Soon," Gaius said, but Marcus had heard his father say this before, and he saw by his mother's reaction that she wasn't fooled either.

Lucius, meanwhile, was staring down at his bowl, saying nothing, and Marcus wondered what was going through his mind, but what mattered was that Lucius continued to see the wife of the *Praetor*.

When things fell apart, it began with a pounding on the door that every member of the Atilius family feared would happen long before their arrival in Corduba, when men of the town watch or some other official came to take one or all of them into custody. It wasn't that, but it was in some ways even worse.

"Who is it?" Gaius demanded through the door, but none of them were prepared to hear a woman's voice.

"You don't know me, but I serve Mistress Aurelia! Your son is in serious trouble!"

This got Gaius moving to the door, but when he flung it open, there was nobody there, the only sign the sound of footsteps echoing as the person fled down the stairs. For once, Gaius Atilius didn't bluster, nor did he try to downplay the seriousness; Marcus couldn't recall a time when his father ever looked this shaken.

"Wait here," he said tersely to Fabia and his children. "I'll be back as soon as I know what's happening."

They sat waiting for most of the day, and with every passing watch, Marcus saw his mother age in front of him. His sisters mostly huddled together, leaving Marcus to his own devices, and he retired to the room where the Atilius children slept, crawling under the bed, craving darkness and solitude. Somehow, he fell asleep, but when he was awakened, it was by a shriek of such pain and loss that he instantly knew the truth, that Lucius was dead. They left Corduba two days later, ending up here in Nova Carthago, though not before Marcus and his sisters heard the gruesome details of their brother's fate from neighbors, some of whom seemed almost happy to paint a vivid picture of Lucius' demise.

"The *Praetor* was supposed to be gone for another day, but he supposedly became ill in Gades, and he hurried back here," a woman who lived two doors down from them told the children who were unfortunate enough to have been sent down to the neighborhood fountain for water.

Another woman took up the tale. "When he went into his wife's quarters, he caught your brother there. And," Marcus was certain this bitch was trying not to laugh as she went on maliciously, "they were humping like rabbits! I heard that Figulus had gotten suspicious that she was up to something, so when he returned to the *Praetorium,* he made sure to stay quiet."

The first woman, seemingly irritated at having her chance interrupted, broke back in, "But Aurelia Figulus said that your brother was raping her."

"That's not true!" Fabia Minor said angrily. "They were in love! Lucius told me so, and he wouldn't lie!"

For the first time, both adults seemed to feel a sense of shame about their cruelty, and it was the second woman who said gently, "I'm sure that's what she told your brother, young Fabia. But," she sighed, "it just proves that patricians can't be trusted."

This knowledge was bad enough, but then another neighbor,

this one a man with a grudge against Gaius, wasn't as circumspect, taking obvious delight in describing the mutilation of their brother when his body was dumped outside the *Praetor*'s residence as if it were a piece of refuse that needed to be dragged away. In fact, this was exactly what Figulus intended, so that when Gaius Atilius came to claim his son's body, he was warned that if he touched the corpse, he would be joining Lucius. The final humiliation, and the ostensible reason the family left Corduba was because Lucius' body, along with the severed parts, were left on display for an entire day as a silent warning to the citizens of the city that Gaius Marcius Figulus was not a man to cross, for any reason.

Now, here in Nova Carthago, Marcus resolved to steal enough money that he could not only stay out all night, but he wouldn't have to spend it alone, but he was only partially successful. He had managed to cut one provincial's purse without arousing the man's attention, yet to his disappointment, when he opened up and examined the contents, he saw that he had enough to get drunk or enough for a whore, but not enough for both. In what would become a pattern of his life for the rest of his days, Marcus Atilius chose the former, and by the time he staggered to the family apartment, it was shortly before dawn. He did pause outside the door, listening for any sign that the drama between his parents had dragged into the dark watches, but after several moments, he decided they had exhausted themselves. Opening the door, he let himself in, then performed a drunken version of tiptoeing to his parents' room, where the door was closed, then listened some more, but when he didn't hear his father's customary regular snort, he didn't think much of it, and made his way to his room. His last conscious memory was to make sure he collapsed on his stomach, with his head turned so that if he did vomit, which seemed likely, it would be onto the floor again, thinking, at least Mama had cleaned up the last time and washed the sheets.

Surprisingly, when he awoke, it wasn't to a puddle of vomit because somehow, he had managed to keep everything down this time, although it didn't really help with the headache or the sour taste in his mouth. Sitting up, he tried to remember the events of the day before, and it came to him fairly quickly. Maybe, he thought, that's why I didn't hear Tata snoring last night, maybe he didn't come home again either. However, this wasn't part of the pattern for these battles between his parents; in the past, Gaius always spent the night in their apartment after he had been caught, usually for several days, although the interval had been steadily shrinking since they had been here in Nova Carthago, after Lucius' death. There was only one way to find out, and Marcus stood up slowly, then shuffled out of his room, where he found his mother, sitting at the table alone, sipping from a cup that, from the smell, he could tell wasn't *posca*. Which, he thought blearily, is unusual.

Fabia didn't bother looking up at him, although she said, "There's bread and some butter that's still good. If," he heard the acid in her tone, "you can keep it down, that is. I don't want you throwing up and wasting food. And," at this, Fabia did look up and give her son a direct gaze, "I'm not cleaning up after you anymore. From now on, you make a mess, of any kind, you clean it up."

She had certainly uttered these kinds of warnings before, but he sensed there was something different this time, although he was too hungover to put a finger on what it was. Deciding that he could keep the bread down, he pulled off the pieces of mold, then slathered butter on it as he sat across the table from her.

"Have you eaten, Mama?" Marcus asked curiously.

"I'm not hungry," Fabia replied, still keeping her eyes on the cup.

Then, she reached over and poured another cupful, and Marcus saw with surprise and some alarm, that it wasn't water as he had deduced, but wine. And, now that he was closer, he could smell that it wasn't cut with water, which was the custom, at least for those people who didn't want to get drunk. Now, he thought uneasily, why would Mama want to get drunk so early in the morning?

This thought prompted him to ask, "Where's Tata?"

"He's still in bed," Fabia responded, which was perfectly reasonable; Gaius was never an early riser, but somehow, to Marcus' ears, there was something different now, but when he got up to go check on him, his mother said sharply, "Leave him be, Marcus. He's…tired."

Perhaps if she hadn't said that, Marcus would have sat back down, but it had been years since Fabia had shown any kind of concern for his father. When he began to move, she behaved as if she intended to try and stop him, half rising to her feet, but then dropped back into her chair, instead giving him only a listless, indifferent wave. Opening the door, he smelled the vomit immediately; if that had been all he smelled, he would have turned around and closed the door to let his father wake up in his own time, but there was another smell, a mingling of odors that still *might* have been normal, if his mother hadn't yet emptied their night soil bucket, except there was something…else there. In his not so distant future, Marcus Atilius would become all too familiar with that smell, the stench of decay that, as he would learn, begins to emanate from a body almost the instant they expire. It was dark in the room, but he forced himself to approach the bed cautiously, and he saw what had happened; or, the thought struck him like a lightning bolt, what Mama wants me to think had happened. Although Marcus had always made certain to lie on his stomach, this time, his father was on his back, his mouth wide open, as were his eyes, but it was the glistening substance pooled in his father's mouth, the vomit that had choked him to death that told him what had happened…or had it?

Staggering out of the room, Marcus whirled about to face his mother, asking in shock, "Wha…what happened, Mama? You *always* turn Tata over on his stomach when he comes home like this!"

Fabia sat there, saying nothing for a stretch of heartbeats, but when she finally lifted her gaze from her cup, what Marcus saw in her eyes chilled him, a look of cunning, malicious triumph.

"I must have forgotten."

Unbidden, the words his mother had uttered to him just the day before came back to him: "You're as bad as your father," she had said, and even in his state and despite the fact that she had said this before, he remembered thinking that there was something different in her tone this time. Suddenly, Marcus

Atilius was afraid of his mother, certain that he saw the light of madness in the steady gaze she was directing at him, the look of a woman who had been finally pushed too far.

Aloud, he tried to sound as normal as possible given the circumstances as he said, "I need to go talk to one of the priests at the Temple of Dis and let him know that we're sending Tata across the river, Mama, so they can make the necessary arrangements. Will you be all right?"

This seemed to surprise Fabia, although she didn't seem suspicious.

"Of course I'll be all right. And," she nodded absently, "you're right. You need to do that."

Marcus didn't hesitate, turning and walking quickly to the door, although he did think to call over his shoulder, "I'll be back to help you with Tata as soon as I'm finished, Mama."

She didn't say anything, or if she did, it was after he closed the door and hurried down the hall. When he reached the street, he didn't hesitate, except that instead of heading towards the forum where the temples to all the gods were located, Marcus Atilius headed for the western part of Nova Carthago, specifically the western gate. There had been talk about the city for a couple weeks about the new Legion that was being raised by the newly arrived *Praetor*, and there had in fact been *conquisitores* in the forum as recently as a week ago, but it hadn't even occurred to him to enlist. That had all changed in the span of a morning, because Marcus Atilius was as certain as he could be that his mother had succumbed to the bitterness and hatred she felt towards her husband, and by extension to Marcus, and he held little doubt that one day she would "forget" to turn him over after a night of drinking. The fact that it also didn't occur to Marcus that the best way to forestall this was to stop drinking, at least to excess, would set the pattern for the rest of his days. Now, he was walking to Scallabis, more than four hundred miles away, although in the back of his mind, he hoped to stumble across a recruiting party along the way, but no matter how it happened, he was leaving all of this behind and making a new life for himself, like his sisters had when they had the chance. What, he wondered as he walked at a steady pace on the edge of the nicely paved Roman road to stay out of the way of the wagons, carts, and horses, was the name of that *Praetor*? However, even after thinking about it for a few miles, the name didn't come to him. Honestly, that didn't really matter; he'd find out soon enough.

It took Spurius Didius the better part of two weeks to reach Scallabis from Gades, finding shelter where he could for the night after using some of his small hoard of coins to hitch a ride on a cart or wagon. Twice he had approached a farmhouse he could see from the road to beg a meal and a place to stay for the night, but on both occasions, he was unsuccessful, neither man hesitating to say no to him, not that he was all that surprised.

"I have two daughters, and I don't need the trouble," was how one of the men expressed it.

The fact that he was holding a pitchfork, while another man who might have been his son and was around Didius' age had sidled over to the stack of firewood, sending a clear signal that the farmer would not be swayed, but Didius felt compelled to try.

"I'm on the way to join the Legion called by the new *Praetor*," Didius ventured, hoping that perhaps an appeal to patriotism might work.

It didn't, and after the farmer made a stabbing gesture, he backed away, seething with impotent fury, and for the span of the next mile, he debated with himself about going back after dark and teaching that *cunnus* farmer and his whelp a lesson they'd never forget, that Spurius Didius wasn't a man to insult. By virtue of being bigger and stronger than his peers, Didius had earned a reputation for being good with his fists; what he never acknowledged, even to himself, was that he deliberately picked on those he was certain that he could beat, and there were actually two versions of that reputation of which he was so proud, although the one that was most popular, although it was never voiced within his hearing, was that he was a common bully with a streak of cruelty that was notable even in these crueler times. Fortunately, Didius' stomach intervened, and he forgot about the insult done to his pride, managing to find a ramshackle roadside inn that was still open. He couldn't afford a room, but he did buy a loaf of bread that didn't have much mold on it, and a bowl of lentils and chickpeas that he was certain was the worst thing he had ever tasted, making him wonder if either of those staples could go rotten.

Once he was back outside, he saw that he wasn't alone; there were what he counted to be a half-dozen forms lying on the ground in a rough row, hard up against a low stone wall that provided a bit of shelter from the prevailing winds that came down from the north at that time of year that could get chilly at night. There was a low hum as at least two of the prone figures held a conversation, although he couldn't hear what was said, and he briefly considered staying out of sight and waiting for them to fall asleep, then see what they might have on them that would be worth his time. Fairly quickly, he decided against it, if only for the reason that it was entirely possible these men were heading in the same direction that he was, and he might run into them again. Instead, he dropped down a short distance away, wrapping his threadbare *paenula* around him, and within a matter of moments, was doing the same as his fellow travelers, snoring softly.

A footsore Spurius Didius entered the capital of Scallabis at midday on his tenth day of travel, having managed to hitch a ride on the back of a cart full of stinking hides that the driver of the cart had collected from the surrounding area to bring to one of the tanners in the city.

"If you can stand the stench," he had said cheerfully enough, "you can ride in the back."

Within a few hundred paces distance, Didius was seriously considering hopping off, his stomach revolting at the smell of raw animal hides, some of them still dripping blood, although it was the swarm of flies that was almost as bad. That he didn't was for the simple reason that he was too footsore to contemplate walking the last ten miles to the capital, so he managed to choke the bile down and settled down in his misery. When they arrived, there was a short line of vehicles waiting to enter through the southern gateway, where a pair of men, not in uniform but wearing some sort of insignia around their necks, were questioning each driver, so Didius hopped out of the cart, and without a word of thanks, strode to the gateway, not hearing the muttered curse from the driver at his rudeness. While there was a similar line for those entering on foot, it moved much more quickly, and Didius was surprised when all he had to say was that he was there to answer the *dilectus*. The lone member of the town watch handling the foot traffic simply pointed in the general direction of the city forum where the *Praetorium* was located, already asking the man behind Didius his business, which as it turned out, was the same as Didius', and despite not being normally friendly towards anyone, particularly strangers, he lingered for a moment until the second man entered.

"You're here to enlist too?" Didius asked abruptly, which surprised the second man, who was slightly taller than Didius but with a slender build, although he answered readily enough.

"Yes, I am," he replied, then offered his arm. "*Salve*, my name is Sextus Scribonius."

Didius was more startled than anything; this wasn't how men of his class greeted each other unless they were engaged in some formal business, and he could instantly tell by the other man's accent that he was from Latium, perhaps Rome itself, but he reacted quickly enough that Scribonius didn't seem to notice as he mumbled, "*Salve*. Spurius Didius."

They stood there in awkward silence as the business of Scallabis went on around them, then Scribonius broke it by clearing his throat. "Yes, well, I'm not going straight to the *Praetorium*. There's something I have to do first."

"That's fine," Didius answered abruptly. "I'm going there straightaway myself. Perhaps I'll see you later."

"I'm certain we will." Scribonius said this with a smile, and it was so genuine that, despite his normal antipathy towards strangers, Didius thought, Maybe he's not a bad fellow.

It wasn't until they parted and Didius had traveled half a block in the direction of the *Praetorium* that the scrap of parchment riding in his coin purse pushed itself into his mind.

"Pluto's cock," he groaned aloud, coming to a stop. "I forgot."

Opening his purse, he extracted the parchment, and while it had no meaning to him since he was illiterate, he recalled his father telling him that it was essential for him to hand this to Marcus Surenas. More importantly, he couldn't just go to the

Praetorium on his own, because he needed a "father" to attest to his identity and eligibility, both by age and citizenship. He had to stop and think, experiencing a stab of what might be called panic as his mind drew a blank when he thought about the directions that his father had given him to find this Surenas.

It finally came to him, and without thinking, he reached out and grabbed the sleeve of a passerby, a stout man wearing a tunic that was spattered with blood, the sign that he was a butcher, and demanded, "Where's the Temple of Apollo here?"

The man jerked his arm from Didius' grasp, seemingly about to take issue with the rude treatment, but clearly thought better of it once he had a chance to take Didius in, something that pleased Didius a great deal, always enjoying being viewed as a dangerous man.

"It's, er," he turned and pointed to the intersection Didius had just passed, "down that street, towards the western gate. You'll have to go a block past the statue of Marcus Marcellus to the next street, then turn right. It's in the middle of the block...Citizen."

"Thank you, Citizen," Didius mumbled, but the man was already hurrying off.

Retracing his steps, Didius turned down the street, where he could actually see what he assumed was the statue of Marcus Marcellus, who he was vaguely aware had something to do with Scallabis being here, and that he had done something noteworthy in one of the wars with Carthage, but Didius had never been curious about Roman history, and in fact, never gave much thought about the advantages and privileges he had when compared to those inhabitants of Gades who were from one of the native tribes of Hispania, or from across Our Sea somewhere. As the butcher had said, he saw the Temple of Apollo, and he passed it to the next intersecting street then turned left, and by doing so, he entered the poorer quarter of Scallabis, which made him feel slightly more comfortable, ignoring the whores lounging outside a nondescript, dilapidated, two-story structure with a sign above it that was so faded, he couldn't make out what it said, but was clearly the brothel that served this quarter of the city. Counting two doors past the brothel, Didius stopped, and out of habit, glanced in both directions before rapping on it three times. He heard the scraping of a footstep, followed by the rattle as the latch was engaged, but when the door opened, he was surprised to see a young female, Didius guessing she was no more than twelve, but with a small bronze placard around her neck that announced her status, and while Didius was illiterate, he did recognize that the symbols that spelled out Surenas on his parchment were the same ones engraved on her placard.

"I'm looking for Marcus Surenas," Didius told her, feeling unusually nervous, unsettled by the unexpected presence at the door, but she simply stepped aside, dropping her eyes as he entered.

He was in for yet another surprise, although it was closer to a shock, which was why it took him a moment to recall the name of the man he had met not long before and was the only other person in the room.

"Scribonius? What are you doing here?"

Scribonius looked distinctly uncomfortable, but before he could say anything, a door at the far side of the room opened, and a man dressed in a toga that, even in the dim lighting, Didius could see was filthy, entered the room.

The man gave barely a glance at Didius, yet he immediately said, "You're one of Aulus Didius' sons. Which one?"

"Spurius," Didius answered, but his unasked question of how this Surenas knew that was answered when Surenas said, "You're the image of him when he was your age. Do you have something for me?"

Didius produced the scrap of parchment and handed it to Surenas, who read it with a frown, then gave a grunt that could have meant anything, but instead of addressing Didius, he turned to Scribonius, asking, "You have the money?"

Scribonius' reaction was a small gasp, followed by a glance at Didius, but Surenas assured him, "He's here for the same thing."

Now it was Didius' turn to gasp, but when he looked over at Scribonius, he refused to meet Didius' gaze. Whether this was what prompted what Surenas said next, neither would ever know.

"You two don't need to worry. I do this all the time."

"How can you do it all the time when this is the first *dilectus* in years?" Scribonius asked quietly, but in a manner that reaffirmed Didius' initial impression that this tall, slender Roman who appeared to be a few years older was educated and probably from the upper classes.

And, for some reason, Surenas didn't seem to take offense at what might have been a challenging question, if only because of the tone Scribonius used.

"I've been doing this for more than ten years," Surenas replied. "And I also have other... arrangements at the *Praetorium* aside from the one I have with the *conquisitores*. Although," he added this as an aside that seemed aimed at neither of them, "this new *Praetor* seems to be a bit of a prig, and I've heard he's got a longer beak than most when it comes to dipping it into our purses."

None of this was really relevant to Didius, but he saw Scribonius stiffen slightly, then he asked, "What is the *Praetor*'s name?"

"Caesar," Surenas answered. "Gaius Julius Caesar."

This clearly troubled Scribonius, but by the time Didius had a chance to ask his new acquaintance why this was the case, hoping to get some information about this Caesar that might be useful, he had forgotten about it.

Surenas told Didius to wait as he took Scribonius away, but when Didius called out, "We'll talk later, *neh*?" Surenas wheeled on him, snapping, "No, you won't. Until you take the oath, neither of you know the other, do you understand? You've never seen each other; you have no idea who the other is. Is that clear?"

Under normal conditions, Didius would have not responded well to being spoken to in this manner, but he was sufficiently nervous that he gave a sullen nod, although Scribonius didn't seem offended in the slightest.

"We won't say a word to each other," he assured Surenas, which satisfied the older man, then they disappeared, leaving Didius to sit alone, the young female slave nowhere to be found, even after he called out.

It was a shame, really; while he had learned to hide his interest, Spurius Didius was attracted to young girls, and he wondered whether he had the time to indulge himself before Surenas returned, although he dismissed it as unwise, not knowing how Surenas viewed the young slave, other than as a piece of property, knowing that often masters viewed slaves as more than just an investment; the idea that she might have been unwilling wasn't a consideration for Didius, and it would be something his future comrades in the Legion would learn about him. Subsequently, he occupied his time trying to recall whether his father had ever mentioned this Marcus Surenas before, and he was still engaged with this thought when Surenas returned, but without Scribonius, and while Didius wasn't nearly as clever as he thought he was, he did deduce that it probably wasn't Surenas who was going to the *Praetorium* to masquerade as a father; even with whatever arrangement he had, Didius had heard the concern in Surenas' voice about this new *Praetor*.

"You're next," Surenas said abruptly as he passed by Didius, adding only, "Wait here, I'll be back in a moment."

Again, Surenas disappeared, but thankfully for Didius' growing frustration, he returned quickly, with a wax tablet.

"You're going to use your real name, *gens* and Urban tribe," Surenas said. "I have a man who will play Aulus. And with that," although Surenas didn't need to explain this to Didius, the younger man understood, for some reason seemed to feel compelled to add, "your father and I are on evens again."

Before Didius could respond, Surenas strode to the door, causing Didius to scramble to his feet to catch up, so that they were out on the street before he could ask, "How do you know my father? And how do you know my father will accept that whatever you owe him is forgiven?"

"That doesn't matter," Surenas snapped, then relented slightly, "at least about how I know Aulus. As far as the other?" He shrugged, though he didn't slow down. "I just know."

They didn't go far, only a matter of two blocks, followed by a turn down another street that took them deeper into the quarter that Didius now could see was exclusively for the members of the Head Count and the poorest freedmen and non-Romans. It was essentially identical to his own quarter in Gades, just a bit smaller, and after another block, Surenas headed towards a *taverna* on the corner. Like other such establishments, it was cramped and filthy, with the wine on offer of the poorest variety that was more vinegar than wine; and, Didius thought with some amusement, If whoever runs this *cac*hole is like my father, that's by design because it means that the customers who are drunkards have to drink more to get the same effect. Sitting at a table was an unshaven man in a tunic that was almost more patch than original material, and Didius learned he had guessed correctly when Surenas stopped at the table. He's the right age, at least, Didius thought, but he wasn't encouraged by the man's bleary expression, and his reddened eyes indicated that he had been imbibing for some time despite the relatively early time of day.

"This," Surenas' voice was flat, "is Aulus Didius, who will be attesting to the *conquisitores* and with an oath to Jupiter Optimus Maximus that his son, Spurius Terentinus Didius, of the *gens* Didia and a member of the rural Terentina tribe, is a Roman citizen and is eligible by age to enlist in the Legion being raised by the new *Praetor*, and he does this on pain of torture if he's lying. All you need to tell him is your name day and the year you were born." He handed Didius' counterfeit father a small stack of coins, but Didius didn't have a chance to get an idea of how much money was changing hands, mainly because he was consumed with curiosity about something else.

"Do you memorize the names and *gens* for everyone you...help?" Didius asked.

"No," Surenas answered immediately, then addressing the other man, said, "You may as well go now. I've seen there's a line, and we need to get this done today."

Didius' concern about the imposter wasn't helped when the man lurched to his feet and had to grab the edge of the table to steady himself, but he was more interested in something that he thought was very odd. Later, when he had time to think about it, he convinced himself that he had already divined the truth when he asked the question; the reality was that he was completely unprepared for the answer to his question. "If you didn't memorize that, then how could you know? I've never seen you before in my life, and my father never mentioned your name before he gave it to me before I came here."

"There's no reason he would have mentioned my name," Surenas answered, but said nothing more for a long stretch of time, while Didius stood there, forgetting his counterfeit father still weaving on his feet next to him. He was about to say something, but then Surenas seemed to come to a decision, although Didius was unprepared for him to ask, "Did your father ever talk about his brother Gaius?"

"Yes," Didius nodded slowly, "but not often. They had some sort of…disagreement, he said, and that Gaius was murdered. But that's all."

This seemed to amuse Surenas, and for the first time in their short association, he smiled, but there was a bitterness to it.

"That," he agreed with a sardonic humor, "is certainly one way to put it." Surenas paused again, yet this time, Didius held his tongue, while the third man, grumbling to himself, dropped back down into his chair. Finally, Surenas said, "I was born Gaius Terentius Didius, but it's a name I stopped using before you were born, and I had to leave Gades suddenly and disappear. Now," he lifted his arms to indicate himself, "I'm Marcus Surenas of Scallabis. And," his voice turned harsh, "I intend to stay that way. Your father promised that you'd keep your mouth shut and never mention my name, and that goes for my *real* name. Do you understand, boy?"

Didius normally would have bristled at someone using that tone with him, but his mind was spinning with this new knowledge, for which he had a hundred questions.

However, at the same time, he also heard the echo of his own father's tone, the one he used when he was deadly serious about something, which was why he only mumbled, "I understand."

"Good." Surenas nodded, then reached down, and this time, he jerked the imposter back to his feet. "Now get to the *Praetorium* and enlist."

He turned and headed for the exit to the *taverna*, but before he opened the door, Didius called out, "If I have the chance, can I come see you later?"

"No," Surenas said without turning his head, although he paused at the door. "And if you do, you'll regret it. Go join the Legion, Spurius." Then, he was gone, the door closing, so

Didius didn't hear his uncle's final words. "Get as far away from Aulus as you can if you want to live to see your thirtieth birthday."

By the time Didius and the counterfeit Aulus arrived at the *Praetorium*, while he spotted Scribonius in the line with his own "father," he was just a couple of pairs away from the entrance. Resigning himself to the ordeal, Didius split his time between eyeing the other men around his age in the crowd, sizing all of them up as possible marks for one of his games, or as an adversary, and repeatedly asking his "father" about the information he was supposed to provide after supplying the man with his name day, the year from the founding of Rome, and the Consuls for the year as every Roman citizen was taught. He was pleasantly surprised that, despite the man's inebriation, he didn't slur his words, and he was able to answer Didius with the correct responses every time, so that by the time they had shuffled halfway up the line, he was cautiously optimistic that this might work. He saw Scribonius emerging, clutching the clay token that each new enlistee was given by their *Conquisitor*, although Didius had no idea what came after that. He'd be learning soon enough anyway, and besides, Scribonius had turned and headed in the opposite direction from the line so that their eyes never met, something that created a thought that Didius couldn't seem to shake that it was a deliberate act on the other man's part. Probably scared of me, he thought to himself, but then his attention was diverted by another party of arrivals, coming from the direction that Scribonius had gone, and for some reason, his heart started pounding rapidly at the sight of a Roman who was even larger and more muscular than himself. He counted that there were actually five in his party instead of just two, and as they drew closer, Didius could see that the giant Roman was young, as was another member of the party who Didius was certain couldn't be taller than the five feet, two inches that was the minimum height for the Legions, although he was tightly muscled, with bandy legs that seemed perfectly shaped to straddle a horse. They made a contrasting pair, but he could see by the way they were talking to each other that not only did they know each other, they were undoubtedly close friends, talking excitedly as they passed by, so absorbed in their conversation that they didn't even glance in his direction to see him staring at them with an intensity that they might have cause to remember. The odd number was slightly unusual as well, since it was universally fathers, real or otherwise, and sons, but Didius spotted the bronze placard of the man who was standing just behind and to the side of one of the older men. Didius didn't need more than a glance to tell him that the other older man was the father of the shorter youth, which meant that this seemingly frail Roman who looked like a farmer was the giant's father, prompting the thought, how could someone as puny as that have a son that size? This was followed immediately by what he was certain was the solution, and while they weren't paying attention, Didius gave them a sly grin as they moved past him, certain that the giant was doing essentially the same thing as he was with a counterfeit father. And, now that the party had gone by, he had gotten enough of a whiff to recognize that the older farmer wasn't frail; he was in essentially the same condition as his own imposter.

This prompted him to turn back to the man and say, "Are all of you..." Suddenly, he realized the danger of saying aloud what role the man was playing, so he amended, "...who are helping us lovers of Bacchus?"

This didn't seem to offend the man, just puzzled him, but after a heartbeat or two, his face cleared. "Ah, you mean that farmer who just passed by? Is he like me?"

Normally, Didius wouldn't have cared whether he offended someone, but he still needed this man, so he managed to answer awkwardly, "Yes, something like that."

"I wouldn't know." The man shrugged. "I've never seen him before in my life, so I know he's not from Scallabis."

The five men had reached the end of the line by then, and while he didn't want to get caught doing so, Didius couldn't stop himself from stepping out of the line just enough so that he had a relatively unobstructed view of the young giant, thinking, I could take him. I'd wager that he doesn't know anything about fighting anyway, not like I do. While he did his best to ignore it, he heard his father's mocking laugh from somewhere in the recesses of his mind, feeling a completely irrational but unmistakable surge of hatred towards that giant, who was still completely oblivious to Didius' scrutiny, or existence for that matter. You'll learn about me soon enough, you big oaf, he thought. I'll show you. By this time, there were only two pairs ahead of them, but when he turned to his companion, without even looking at him, the man quietly repeated the information he would be giving in the very near future, further irritating Didius, who was suddenly in a foul mood. Fortunately, he was distracted by another unusual sight, this time by what he was certain were a pair of twins, accompanied by an older man, crossing the forum from the direction of the market area. They passed by too far away to hear what they were saying, but in their demeanor, he saw much the same excitement that he had witnessed with the giant and his diminutive friend, and he wondered idly how the Centurions would tell them apart, but then, he was struck by a sudden stab of anxiety. Shouldn't I be excited about this like they are? he wondered. Seeing the others like him, they all seemed to be eager to become Legionaries, whereas he felt more resigned than any real excitement, and what little anticipation he held was in the prospect of new prospective victims for one of his games. Any further thought along these lines was interrupted when he felt a tug on his elbow.

"We're next," the imposter said, then stepped inside the open door, forcing Didius to hurry to catch up.

Once inside, he saw that it was a large room that served as a sheltered spot where fairly large groups of men could gather, and along the opposite wall, there were three tables, each with a *Conquisitor* standing behind it, their badge of office affixed to their tunic, while they each had a slave clerk sitting at the desk with them. A slave was standing inside the entrance, and he pointed to the center table, where a thin, sallow-faced man was standing, looking both bored and impatient, while the seated clerk wore a neutral expression that could have meant anything, but what Didius had long before learned was the expression worn by slaves.

"Hurry along," he snapped, beckoning to Didius and his companion. "We're very busy here, and if you're joining the Legion, you're going to be moving a lot faster than that!"

Didius bit his lip as he grabbed the other man by the tunic, moving the pair of them until they were both standing in front of the *Conquisitor.*

"You're here to join the Legion, yes?" the *Conquisitor* asked, and Didius nodded, which wasn't enough, "Speak up, Citizen! You must affirm that's your purpose here for the official record!"

"Y-yes, Excellency," Didius got out, but the official was already turning his attention to the other man, demanding, "And you're his father?"

"Yes, Excellency," the man replied without hesitation. "My name is Aulus Terentius Didius, of the *gens* Didia and a member of the rural Terentina tribe, and this is my son Spurius, who was born in the year of 428, as reckoned from the founding of the Republic, and under the Consulship of Marcus Tullius Decula and Gnaeus Cornelius Dolabella, in the month of January, three days before the Ides."

To Didius' surprise, the clerk, who was writing in a wax tablet, instead of handing it to the official, extended it to Didius, while the *Conquisitor* pointed to a door that Didius hadn't noticed, "Take that in there to be examined by the physician."

Didius did as he was told, finding two men, one of them wearing the robes that identified him as a physician, with his own scribe and to whom he handed his tablet, while the physician ordered him to disrobe, and he did so, while the physician walked around him, visually inspecting him. After a revolution, he was satisfied, ordering Didius to put his clothes back on as he dictated to the scribe that the subject appeared to be physically sound and fit for duty. Only then did Didius realize that he had been expecting some sort of comment on his size and musculature, if only because it was often a topic of conversation. The scribe finished, snapped the tablet shut, and handed it to Didius, while the physician instructed him to go back to the *Conquisitor*, and if Didius had to guess, he wouldn't have wagered that he was with the physician past the count of one hundred. Returning outside, he handed the tablet back to the slave, whereupon the clerk, who now had a fresh sheet of vellum, carefully but quickly transcribed the information contained on the tablet onto the vellum. Once he was done and had sanded it, he handed it to the *Conquisitor*, who scanned it quickly, then gave a grunt that could have meant anything, then leaned over, placing it on the desk but facing Didius and his imposter, to whom the official beckoned, pointing to a spot at the bottom of the document.

"You need to write your name, or make your mark here," the *Conquisitor* instructed, but the man was already leaning down and reaching for the quill, igniting a stab of fear in Didius' heart.

He knew what to do, like he's done it before! He's going to give it away! This was racing through Didius' mind, although if anything, it was his demeanor that would have given away the game simply from the look of fear that flashed across his face, and for a horrifying instant, he thought that it was all over, because the *Conquisitor* clearly noticed Didius' agitation, his eyes going from the other man bent over carefully inscribing an "X" to Didius' face. But then, the official actually gave Didius a faint but unmistakable smile before returning his attention back to the older man, and Didius felt himself relax. Of course, you fool, he thought; he knows what's going on because he's getting a cut of whatever money men like Surenas got from those like Didius.

When the man laid down his quill and straightened up, the *Conquisitor* returned his attention back to Didius, all trace of the smile gone as he said in a manner that betrayed it was something he said dozens of times a day, "Spurius Didius, your father's part is done, and I'll now administer the oath that will make you a *Probatio* of the Legion raised by the *Praetor* Gaius Julius Caesar. It's not the full oath that you'll take once you complete your training, but you're now under the authority of Rome through its Legions, and as such, you will be punished for any violation of those regulations as apply to *Probationes*. Do you understand?" Actually, Didius didn't, because he had no idea what any of that meant, not really, although he still felt his head nodding up and down, but before the official could reprimand him, he remembered to say aloud, "Yes, Excellency, I understand."

The oath, such as it went, was made before the gods Jupiter Optimus Maximus, Mars, Bellona and to Roma, the sacred spirit of the city, attesting that Spurius Didius was indeed a Roman citizen of eligible age, and that he recognized he was now under the authority of the Legions of Rome. He repeated the words without error, but there was a queer, fluttering sensation in the pit of his stomach as he did so, and he wondered if the gods were sending him a signal of some sort since he was never prone to nerves like this. Once he was done, the last thing was the slave handing him a clay token with a series of numbers incised into it that meant nothing to him, and the *Conquisitor's* explanation made even less sense.

"You're part of a different group that doesn't need to report immediately, so you'll present that to whoever meets you at dawn tomorrow at the main gate of the camp outside Scallabis," the *Conquisitor* instructed. "And," he warned, "do *not* be late. Remember, you're no longer a civilian, although you're not a Legionary yet. And that," for the first time, the official smiled, but it wasn't warm as much as grim, "will be up to you, and if the Centurions and the gods decide you're worthy."

This angered Didius; didn't this oaf have eyes? Couldn't he see just how big and strong he was? Fortunately for him, the warning about being a *Probatio* was sufficiently fresh that the only thing Didius did as an act of revenge was a sullen nod.

The *Conquisitor* was already looking past them to the next pair when it occurred to Didius to ask, "What do I do until then? Is there somewhere we're supposed to stay?"

This amused the official, but he wasn't unkind as he shook his head. "What you do and where you stay isn't the business of Rome until dawn tomorrow, *Probatio* Didius. Just," he reminded, "be outside the camp gates at dawn."

Didius' counterfeit father was already halfway to the door, but Didius thought of one more thing, and asked, "Does this Legion have a name yet? Or a number?"

"Yes," now the *Conquisitor* was clearly irritated, but he answered, "it does. It's the 10th Legion, and you're going to the First Century of the Second Cohort."

With that, Didius hurried outside, but while he wasn't sure what to say to his benefactor, he was relieved of that choice because the man was nowhere in sight, leaving Didius standing alone, although he actually spotted the giant, who was standing next to a cart at the far edge of the forum, and he saw the man who Didius had deduced was the giant's father being helped into the back of the cart by the slave. For the briefest moment, he thought about going over and introducing himself, but there was something that wouldn't let him do that, as if he recognized that this huge youth would be some sort of rival, or maybe an outright enemy. Over the course of his life, Spurius Didius would think about that moment and wonder how things might have been different for him if he had made that one effort to be sociable to the man who would have such a huge impact on his life. Instead, he turned away, and thought for a moment, reflexively hefting his purse before cursing his fortune, hearing the faint clinking sound that signified only three or four coins.

"I've got enough to get a whore, and I've got enough to get drunk," he said aloud, disgustedly, "but not enough to do both."

In this case, the needs of the flesh won out, and despite the warning he had been given by Surenas, Didius headed back in the direction of the brothel that was two doors down from his uncle's place. If I run into him, he thought, it will be by accident.

Quintus Artorius was miserable, and he had been so for several days, but it was only partly because of the wretchedness of sitting in a wagon that wasn't traveling on just the good, Roman roads that had slowly spread over Hispania that, along with the aqueducts, were the most potent symbol of Rome's power, and the improvements it brought to the natives, and it wasn't just because of the surly driver and his "assistants" that, while he was not overly bright, Quintus immediately understood were guards whose task was to make sure that none of the new *Probationes* that was their cargo had a change of heart in the night. Escape during the day was impossible, because one of the men, a burly, scarred man who wore the type of leather bracers favored by men who competed in the *pankration*, the brutal boxing game where there were no rules, was mounted. His name was Prixus; at least, that was the name the wagon driver and man in charge had given him, while the driver was attached to the Legion in some way, because he wore what Quintus had learned was the soldier's tunic, and his *baltea* was more elaborate than the kind certain tradesmen wore, with long, metal-studded strips hanging down to protect his groin. He had identified himself as Aulus Vulso, and he was the only man armed with a *gladius* and *pugio*, although Prixus carried a cudgel that was attached to his own *baltea* with a leather thong, as did the third man who rode on the wagon next to Vulso. Of the three, Quintus felt most warmly towards this man, who was only referred to as Publius, if only because he wasn't interested in taunting the new *Probationes* with lurid and horrifying tales of what awaited them.

When Artorius got into the wagon in Italica, there were three others waiting for him, but over the course of the next few days, Vulso would drive the wagon to the forum of the scattering of towns and settlements on the way to Scallabis, so that by the end of the first week, there were ten young men crammed into the back of the wagon, which had two boards on either side that served as benches, and while they were sitting thigh to thigh, there was enough room to sit. While he didn't feel that way, Quintus knew, grudgingly, that he was better off in some ways than his new companions, most of whom, after brief introductions, mostly ignored him. He learned this was the case on the first night when there were just four of them, when the wagon pulled up to a roadside inn, whereupon Vulso hopped down and ordered them off.

"Go inside and they'll feed you," he said curtly.

One of the others, whose name Quintus had already forgotten, raised a tentative hand and asked, "Are you paying...*Dominus*?"

The laugh Vulso gave sounded more like a bark of a small dog.

"First, I'm not your *Dominus* because you're not a slave..." Suddenly, his eyes narrowed, suddenly suspicious. "Or are you, boy? Eh? Are you a slave who managed to fool the *Conquisitor* but now you just slipped up?" The words were menacing enough, but it was the drawing of his *gladius* that caused the youth to give a yelp of fear.

"No, *Dom*...I mean, Legionary! I swear I'm not! I just don't know how to address you!"

"Likely story," Vulso snarled, and he dropped into a crouch

while drawing his right hand back so that it was just behind his body while holding the blade at waist level and parallel to the ground. "I think you're a fucking slave!"

The youth thrust his arms out, hands open in an obvious plea as he began moving backward away from Vulso, and Quintus Artorius' stomach turned over at the thought he was about to see a man killed for the first time, and when his new companion tripped over his own feet to land in a small cloud of dust onto his ass, his face contorted with terror, Quintus turned away, unwilling to watch. Because of this, he was completely unprepared for the sudden roar of laughter from the three men, but he turned in time to see Vulso sheathing his *gladius*, then wipe a tear from his eye.

"Get up, boy," he instructed Quintus' companion, who now seemed to be equally bewildered and fearful. "I was just having some fun."

Quintus didn't blame the youth for being suspicious as he clambered to his feet, but without taking his eye off of Vulso.

"What's your name?" Vulso asked, then guessed, "Are you Artorius?"

"No," Quintus surprised himself by speaking up. "I'm Quintus Artorius."

"I...I'm Publius Crus," the youth managed.

"Well, Crus, first thing, you address me as either Legionary or Gregarius. Understand?"

"Y-yes Gregarius," Crus managed.

"So," Vulso continued, "you were asking about how you'll eat if you have no money?"

"Yes, Gregarius," Crus replied, and Vulso turned to the other three, demanding, "What about you?"

To his surprise, only Quintus was able to reply that he had some money, his father having allowed him to keep a handful of *sesterces* and a few *as* for smaller purchases that he had snatched from the family hoard.

"Right." Vulso didn't seem surprised, although he was clearly disgusted. "So you three are already on the books."

This had no meaning for any of them, until Vulso went to the wagon, and reaching into the large leather satchel that contained the records of the *Probationes*, he extracted a wax tablet and a stylus.

"Follow me," was all he said, then headed directly to the inn, with the four behind him, while Prixus and Publius unhitched the wagon.

Naturally, Quintus followed, but while he was allowed to purchase his own meal, a quarter loaf of bread and a bowl of porridge that was nothing like his mother's, with the other three, Vulso carefully recorded the cost of their meal in the wax tablet.

Once they all had full bowls and bread, Vulso pointed to a corner table, instructing, "Sit there, and eat quickly. No fucking about. Once you're done, go outside."

"Gregarius," this time, it was not Crus who spoke, but a sandy-haired youth that hinted at some Gallic blood, of an average size and build, "why are you recording everything we eat?"

Quintus braced himself for a display of temper, but Vulso didn't seem put out in the least, shrugging as he answered, "So that your meals will be deducted from your pay." Then, for the first and only time, Vulso gave them a grin that was not overtly cruel, and his tone was almost friendly. "You boys are going to learn that now that you're in the army, you're going to be fucked every single day." He paused, then added cheerfully, "Just not in a way any of us like!"

Not that surprisingly, he was the only one who thought it was amusing.

That had been a week earlier, and the days had begun to blur into a dull monotony punctuated by small acts of what Quintus supposed might be called cruelty, at least compared to what he was accustomed to, yet somehow he sensed that this was probably just what his future would be like. He wasn't naturally talkative, so for the most part, he was ignored as the party grew in size, and those *Probationes* with stronger personalities began to assert themselves. One of those who joined on the third day had brought dice with him in his coin purse, the only belonging the *Probationes* had been allowed to keep. His name was Lucius Papiria, and while Quintus was quiet by nature, Papiria was the exact opposite, a boisterous and boastful nineteen-year-old, making him one of the older men to that point. Fairly quickly, he became the *de facto* leader of the *Probationes*, although there was another youth who didn't see it that way, and was constantly carping and making biting comments until, without any warning, Vulso himself handed the reins to Publius while giving him the order to stop as he snatched up the goad used on the animals, and twisting at the waist, began slashing down indiscriminately at the occupants, all of whom yelped in pain or shouted some kind of protest.

"If you *cunni* don't shut your fucking mouths and stop arguing like a bunch of women, the instant we get to Scallabis, I'm going to the Legate and put you all up on charges that will get you scourged, each and every one of you!"

For once, Quintus was happy for his diminutive size and the fact that he had been consigned to one of the spots at the front of the wagon, directly behind Vulso, but the Legionary's fury, and the fate he promised would befall all of them, terrified him.

Fortunately, he saw that he wasn't alone, and it was left to Papiria to beg Vulso, "I'm sorry, Gregarius, truly! We won't behave this way again, I swear it!" He turned to the others, demanding, "Isn't that right, boys?"

Quintus was every bit as vocal as the rest of them in their assurances that they had learned their lesson, that behaving in such a rowdy fashion was unacceptable. For a long moment, Vulso, breathing heavily, glared down at them before, finally, he turned back and exchanged the goad for the reins from Publius with a disgusted grunt. The wagon resumed moving, and not a word was said for several miles, which Quintus took advantage of, choosing to doze as his body rocked gently back and forth as the wagon moved over the uneven surface. By the next day, however, spirits had been restored to the point that the *Probationes* went back to their chatting, swapping stories about their exploits with village girls that made Quintus both envious that he hadn't experienced anything close to some of the things he heard from his companions, and doubtful that they were telling the truth. However, the one thing they were careful about was avoiding arousing Vulso's temper, which for reasons they didn't understand, seemed to be getting worse with every passing day. On the sixth night, there was a storm severe enough that sleeping under the wagon wasn't an option, while any hope of sleeping in an inn was out of the question because Vulso directed Publius to a farmhouse a few miles short of their intended stop. Instead, they were offered the barn, but at a price that sent Vulso into a fouler mood, which he took out on his cargo of new recruits, using the goad from the wagon to strike at the first *Probatio* he could reach, which happened to be Crus this time. Driving the group ahead of him towards the barn, they were met by the farmer, who had opened the door, the smell of animal manure so overwhelming that several of them gagged. They were wet, they were miserable, and while they were at least relatively sheltered, despite several leaks, they were also penned up with Vulso, Prixus, and Publius, who for the first time, seemed as angry as his two comrades at their fate.

Quintus desperately wanted to ask, but he didn't have the courage, so he was intensely relieved when one of the newer members of the group, Gnaeus Lentulus, asked Vulso, "Are we going to be eating tonight, Gregarius?"

"Of course," Vulso answered, seemingly surprised, and it was then that Quintus noticed that Publius was holding a sack that appeared to be quite full of something. Then, Vulso asked, "Oh, did you mean are *you* going to be eating tonight? Lentulus, is it?"

Lentulus nodded, which pleased Vulso, and as he reached and took the sack from Publius, he said with mock regret, "I apologize. I thought you were asking if I, Prixus, and Publius are eating tonight? Of course we are, boy. We're veterans! We plan ahead. Didn't I tell you beforehand that you needed to squirrel away some food every time we stopped for a meal?"

By virtue of the time spent with Vulso, seven pairs of eyes turned to the original four, but again it was Crus who answered, with a flat resignation, "No, Gregarius. You didn't tell us that."

"I didn't?" Vulso's eyes went wide, but it was apparent to all of them this was one of his "jokes." "By the gods, it must have slipped my mind! Now," he snarled, "find a place where you're not lying in *cac* and get some sleep. And," he added menacingly, "tonight, I don't want to hear any fucking mice talking or rustling about, do you understand? I'm not in the mood for it."

He seemed content with the response, which was nothing

but a sullen mumbling, while the more enterprising of the group immediately headed for a spot with more hay or was at least not below one of the leaks. Quintus wasn't particularly surprised that, spying a spot in the far corner next to a stable containing a mule who had been watching the proceedings while placidly munching a mouthful of something, when he headed for it, he was intercepted by the youth who had caused trouble with Papiria.

"I saw that spot first," he said, then gave Quintus a hard shove that, thanks to his slightness, sent him reeling across that part of the barn.

Quintus Artorius was slow to anger, but now he was angry, and for the span of a couple heartbeats, he stood there with clenched fists, his chest heaving, working up the courage to go charging at the larger youth. He actually had an opportunity because the youth had his back turned as he kicked some loose hay to cover the dirt floor, but just as he was about to launch himself, the youth turned around, saw Quintus standing there and instantly understood what he was contemplating. The others, warned somehow in that way that a group of people who have been together for a length of time can tell when there's a change in the atmosphere, turned their attention to this small drama, though nothing above a whisper was said. Quintus felt the eyes on him, and he knew that he needed to do something; then, Vulso's warning about what would happen to them if any of them created a disturbance came rushing back. The Legionary was already in a foul mood; being roused from whatever he and the other two were eating on the other side of the barn would undoubtedly enrage him. This was why Quintus Artorius pointedly broke his gaze, and began to look for another spot, ignoring the broad grin of triumph from the victor; at least, this was what he told himself. Choosing a spot by virtue of the fact that it was the best of the bad choices remaining, Quintus dropped to the ground, curled up, and turned his back to the others, ignoring the snickering and whispered comments. Consequently, it was because of his spot in the barn that placed him just a few feet closer to the corner where Vulso, Prixus, and Publius had selected that he learned the cause of Vulso's distemper.

Quintus didn't know how long he'd been asleep, just that he came to consciousness by the sound of low voices, while he somehow managed to avoid moving or indicating in any way that he was awake.

"These *cunni* are eating all of our profits." He recognized the voice as Vulso's, but he was shocked that it was Publius who answered; he was certain that he hadn't heard the man say more than a dozen words.

"That was a neat trick tonight," he said. "You know we could have made it another mile to the inn."

"You know that, I know that, and Prixus here knows that," Vulso sounded amused, "but thank the gods these thickheaded bastards don't know that."

This amused all three of them, but it was Prixus who had the most distinctive laugh, if only because he sounded much like a pig snorting, which Quintus supposed was a result of a nose that was barely recognizable as such.

"But," Publius continued after their mirth subsided, "how many more times can we do that?"

"How many more days to Scallabis?" Vulso asked, which pricked Quintus' ears, but the Legionary showed that the question was rhetorical since he knew the answer. "Three. So," he paused as he thought, "I think we can only do it one more time."

"That's not going to be enough," Publius answered grimly, and for the first time, Quintus got a sense that, just perhaps, Vulso wasn't the true leader of this trio. "We'll have less than a hundred left at that rate." There was a silence, then he said, "But I have an idea."

Naturally, Quintus was intensely interested, thinking that for the first time, he would have something to offer the group that they'd find valuable with this bit of information. To his frustration, which almost caused him to groan aloud, Publius had dropped his voice to a whisper, and he couldn't hear anything that was said, although by the grunts of the other two men, it sounded like they approved of whatever it was. This was when he made the decision that he had been toying with for the last few days, and he settled down to wait.

It was almost two weeks later that Quintus Artorius limped into Scallabis, alone and near the end of his strength and endurance, days behind Vulso and his wagonload of *Probationes*. The fact that he was doing so, despite his certainty that he would be facing some form of punishment was based on one thing, his recognition that he was out of options. After successfully sneaking out of the barn, he was certain that the gods had favored his decision to return home and make peace with his father; after all, hadn't it been just the night before that, for the first time, Vulso hadn't required a nightly guard by Prixus and Publius? And, hadn't he managed to avoid detection because the noise of the rain covered what small noise he made as he squeezed himself through a crack in the barn where a board had either rotted or been damaged and not replaced? True, he was soaked to the skin within a matter of heartbeats, but, just as he had with his idea of learning his letters, Quintus Artorius showed that he had the ability to remain committed to a course of action once he made his mind up. Consequently, he had forged ahead, or back, as it were, walking in the darkness and rain until, exhausted, he simply couldn't keep going, and he found a shelter of sorts in a copse of trees a few hundred paces from the road. Collapsing under one of them, he huddled, shivering and miserable, but whenever Quintus Artorius looked back on that span of time, it was with rueful amusement, because he had been certain that this was as bad as it would get for him.

He didn't sleep, but fell into a doze, and was awakened by the dappled sunlight on his face, his heart going immediately to the gallop as he sat bolt upright to peer through the low brush that had grown up underneath the trees and provided him cover. He half-expected to see Prixus on the road searching for him, but the stretch that he could see was deserted. Despite this positive sign, he didn't move immediately, as the first tendrils of doubt wrapped themselves around his mind, making what had seemed to be such an obvious decision just a matter of watches before no longer seem as such. However, once he determined that the road was clear of traffic, he resumed walking, with every intention of returning home. He didn't go down to the road, however, still worried that Prixus would be hunting for him, although he took care to move under cover as much as possible, while stopping whenever he was hidden by a wall or trees to scan the road in both directions. Traffic had begun to appear, mostly carts and wagons, with most of them heading in the opposite direction, towards Scallabis. By midday, his hunger pangs were threatening to double him over, and by his estimate, he had only covered about three miles because of his cautious pace. When daylight had come, he had recognized the landmarks, estimating that he had gone three miles in the night, meaning that he was only six miles closer to home, and this was when the enormity of what he was trying to do hit him, so that his already cautious pace slowed even more until he stopped within sight of a farmhouse barely two miles farther along. There was a drainage ditch, and Quintus dropped into it, staring at the farmhouse where, from inside, someone had just lit a lamp that shone through the open window.

"They'll have food." He said this aloud without thinking, and the sound of his own voice startled him, but he decided he liked hearing something other than the sound of his own panting. "I could pay them." As soon as the words were out of his mouth, he countered himself, "But I'm hundreds of miles from home, and I'll need all of what I have left. So," he sighed, "I'll have to sneak in there after dark and steal something."

It would turn out to be the only time he was successful, if by that one meant that he managed to snatch a fist-sized chunk of bread and one hard ball of cheese that was mostly mold, before being forced to run in terror because the farmer had burst from his room with a piece of firewood and chased him out into the night. He didn't stop running for at least a mile, although he tripped once and landed heavily, scraping his chin, but worst of all, he lost his grip on the bread. Only after several moments of feeling along the ground did he retrieve it, then found another spot where he was concealed before, still shaking, he devoured the bread, then downed the cheese, ignoring the taste of the mold. By his third day alone, Quintus Artorius was convinced that there would be no pursuit; by the fourth, he realized that trying to make it all the way home was out of the question. They had been just three days away from Scallabis when he escaped, and while it was now four days later, he knew he hadn't covered nearly as much ground as they had when he was in the wagon with the others. That night, he returned to an inn they had stopped at the night before the farm, using all but one of his remaining coins to buy a meal and some extra food. He thought about sleeping inside but decided against it since it would have exhausted his money, but he actually slept better than he had in the previous days, because in his mind was the reminder from the *Conquisitor* that, while he presumably would be punished for his attempted escape, he would be allowed to live. There wasn't much that he remembered of his retracing of his steps, although he managed to convince a wagon driver to let him ride in the wagon until the driver turned south towards the coast, away from Scallabis, which he informed Quintus was now a full day's walk away. The fact that he had been wrong, that it was more than another half-day was something that might have angered Quintus, but he was at a point where he was simply too exhausted to have much emotion about anything. At least, so he believed until, after being allowed into the capital after the noon watch the next day, he was given directions to the *Praetorium*.

"They're just about through," one of the town watch had informed him. "I heard yesterday that they're going to be finished by the end of today."

"Why?" Quintus asked, his heart suddenly thudding against his ribs.

"Because," the older man shrugged, "they've enlisted enough men for the new Legion, I suppose."

If he could have, Quintus would have run to the *Praetorium*, but he was simply too tired, so he just walked as quickly as he could manage. He didn't know whether to be relieved or terrified that there were still people outside the building, but he went to the back of the line, both hoping for and dreading that an official step outside to announce that the *dilectus* was now over. As usual, he was completely ignored by the men in front of him, which was fine with him since he was completely occupied with what he would say when the time came to stand in front of whoever was inside. How would he explain his tardiness? He might not have been particularly clever, but he also knew that his record, which had been created when he became a *Probatio* back home and was in the leather bag Vulso had with him on their journey, was likely somewhere, either in this building or nearby. So absorbed was he that he barely noticed the huge Roman who was just entering the building, nor did he notice the two twins who were chattering away just a couple people ahead of him, but by the time it was his turn to enter, he was no closer to coming up with an explanation for his tardiness than when he joined the line. The slave standing at the entrance pointed to the table farthest from the door, where the *Conquisitor* was drinking something as he waited, a body slave standing just behind him holding a small pitcher. Because he was draining the cup, his view of Quintus was obscured for a moment, but when he was finished and handed the cup to the slave, he saw the youth approaching, frowning at the sight.

"Where is your father?" the *Conquisitor* snapped. "If he's gone to piss, you'll have to go back outside. We're trying to finish this today!" Quintus' mouth opened, except nothing came out, yet neither did he turn around, prompting the official to demand, "Are you simple, boy? Is that it?"

"N-no, Excellency," Quintus finally managed. Swallowing, he said, "My name is Quintus Artorius, and I was sworn in as a *Probatio* in Italica. I was part of a group that was under the command of Gregarius Vulso, who brought us by wagon."

The *Conquisitor* listened with barely concealed boredom, although he was sufficiently engaged to ask, "Then why didn't you come in with his party?"

"I got sick," Quintus said, astonishing himself by how quickly, and smoothly, the lie came out. "I had a fever, I believe, and I was too sick to travel."

For a heartbeat, the *Conquisitor* said nothing, then commented offhandedly, "Yes, that happens quite often. So," he snapped his fingers and the scribe handed him a wax tablet, "what did you say your name was? And," he looked up at Artorius, "who were the Consuls when you were born, what *gens* and what tribe are you from? That information better match what's on your record," he finished severely, "or there will be consequences."

He couldn't stop himself from shaking, despite the fact that he knew the information and he was certain that it would match, but Quintus was never very self-confident, and he was worried that he would fulfill his father's judgment that he was just too stupid to be of much use. The *Conquisitor* recorded the information in the tablet, then handed it to the scribe, who without a word, walked past Quintus to the far side of the room, where there was a closed door.

"Go wait over there." The *Conquisitor* pointed to the opposite wall. "This may take some time." Without waiting for an answer, he called out for the next pair to come forward.

Quintus leaned against the wall, barely paying attention as the next two men stood in front of the *Conquisitor*, although he saw by their dress they were farmers of some sort, and he thought he heard the name Vellusius, but he wasn't sure, nor did it matter as far as Quintus' own fate. He did watch as the younger Roman, whose black hair seemed to stick straight up from the top of his head, raised his hand and swore the oath that Quintus had what seemed like a month before. Although it reminded him that he had done the same thing, what he remembered most of all was the warning that had come with it. They can't execute me, he told himself, only flog me; not surprisingly, this idea didn't offer much comfort. Just as the pair stepped away from the desk, with the younger man clutching a clay token, Quintus saw the scribe returning, except that along with the tablet, he was carrying a scroll, and, Quintus noticed, there seemed to be a scrap of vellum attached to the scroll. Unsure what to do, he decided to stay put, which turned out to be the right thing, so he could only watch as the scribe handed the *Conquisitor* the scroll, who unrolled it then opened the tablet next to it. He was obviously checking for discrepancies in the information between what Quintus had supplied in Italica and just a bit earlier, and when he saw the official give a slight nod as he shut the tablet, he began to hope. Then, the man pulled the scrap of parchment from the larger scroll, unfolded it and read it, but whatever was contained there made the man utter a curse, and for the first time, he looked at Quintus.

"Come here, boy!" On shaky legs, Quintus did as directed, stepping in front of the small desk. "According to this," the *Conquisitor* said angrily, "you're dead."

Of all the things Quintus had been expecting, this was the

last thing, and he had no idea how to respond, other than to say, "But I'm not dead!"

"I can see that," the official snapped. Then, without any warning whatsoever, Quintus Artorius was saved, although he didn't realize it immediately, when the *Conquisitor* demanded, "Who did you say the name of your escort was?"

"Gregarius Vulso, Excellency," Quintus answered.

"So," the official said with a grim smile, "that scoundrel wrote you off so that he could keep some of the money that he was provided to feed you *Probationes*." He shook his head, his tone reflecting his disgust. "It's a common enough problem, and it happens every *dilectus*. But," he shrugged, "it's been going on long before I took the post, and I'm certain it will be that way after I'm turned to ash."

Then, he reached down to a small stack of clay tokens, which Quintus could see was inscribed with three numbers, which the *Conquisitor* recorded on the outside of the scroll.

Handing the token to Artorius, he said brusquely, "Report to the camp at dawn tomorrow, at the *Porta Praetoria*." Seeing Artorius' blank stare, he explained impatiently, "That's the main gate. There's a road leading directly to it from the northern gate of the city. You can't miss it."

And with that, Quintus Artorius was dismissed, and he walked out of the *Praetorium* in a daze. He was halfway across the forum when he realized that he had no idea what he was supposed to do until dawn, or where he was supposed to stay, but while he did turn back towards the building, he instantly dismissed it as unwise. Somehow, he had gotten away with his desertion without a flogging, and while he wasn't overly religious, he still wasn't willing to risk angering the gods by going back and asking. Instead, he pulled out his purse and looked into it, sighing at the sight of the two *as* and one *obol*. It would be enough to get a bowl of porridge, he supposed, but that was all. Besides, he thought, after tomorrow, I won't have to worry about it; the army will be feeding me.

The fact that Marcus Atilius had actually managed to make his way across the entirety of southern Hispania was based on one, and only one factor; he had nowhere else to go, and nothing much better to do. And, while he would barely admit it to himself, he was terrified of his mother and that she'd somehow track him down if he had stayed in Nova Carthago. He also experienced a run of good fortune that, for a brief period of time, almost convinced Marcus that perhaps this decision was ordained by the gods because they had something better in store for him. It began when he hired on as a drover for a native Spaniard, a member of the Turditani tribe, who once owned the land around Corduba and Italica. The man, Isauricus, had a sour disposition, and his Latin was atrocious, and he was offering such low wages, he had been unable to attract any help to go such a far distance, while he only had his son, also named Isauricus, who was twelve, to help. Making it worse, at least to Marcus, was that he wasn't driving cattle but sheep, but Isauricus Minor not only spoke much better Latin than his father, he was more than willing to share information.

"These sheep are from Campania," he had explained proudly to Marcus, who knew nothing about sheep. Seeing his blank expression, the Turditani boy continued, "Their wool is much softer, and they're bigger than the Latxa sheep we raise. My father plans on crossbreeding them."

By the end of the first day, Marcus was mostly accustomed to the smell, and while he didn't appreciate it at the time, he learned how to get by on short sleep since Isauricus Major made it clear that one of his duties was to stand guard against the wolves that came down from the hills. The Turditani had four dogs, of a kind that Marcus had never seen before, but he quickly learned that these animals did the majority of the work, both during the day, nipping and harrying the animals to stay on the road, then standing guard much more alertly than Marcus ever did. They had a cart, and at night, the boy was responsible for erecting a crude shelter that used the side of the cart, but Marcus was never allowed to sleep under it, and he was only grudgingly given a blanket that stank of sheep and, judging from the amount he was itching after the first night, was infested with vermin. As might be expected, their progress was slow, and Marcus chafed at what he viewed as the leisurely pace, but he desperately needed the two *sesterces* that Isauricus had promised. Somewhat surprisingly, the food, while not plentiful, was not bad, as Marcus was exposed to a different style of cooking and preparation.

Over the course of his ten days with the Turditani, he grew close to Isauricus Minor, although the boy talked a great deal, yet he was so likable that it made Marcus ache for the days when he had a brother that he could talk to like the boy was talking to him. The biggest disappointment was that the Turditani only drank water, and by the fourth day, Marcus realized this was the longest period he had been completely sober since he could remember. They parted outside Italica, when, as promised, the older man handed him two coins with a grunt that could have been his form of thanks, or might have been a curse, while Isauricus Minor wrapped his arms around Marcus' waist, wailing at the thought of their separation. It was awkward, and he was embarrassed, but Marcus Atilius also would remember that moment for some time. He watched them taking the road south towards the coast; Isauricus' farm was five miles away, and while it was never explained to him, Marcus supposed that they were confident between the dogs and the pair of them, they could manage five miles, and for whatever reason, the older man didn't want Atilius to see where they lived.

Once they were out of sight, he headed into Italica, slipping through the gates as part of a small knot of men returning from the fields outside the walls. He spent barely more than a full day in the town when he learned of a pair of wagons that were hauling grain to Scallabis, and he was able to bribe one of the drivers to allow him to ride along for a *sestertius* and a promise to help hitch and unhitch the teams, along with feeding and watering. As with the sheep, he knew nothing about livestock and wagons, but he had perfected the art of appearing to be sincere when he lied, and he was taken on. Normally, the price required of the driver, a squat man with one crossed eye who went by the name Censorinus, although Marcus was certain he was lying about that, would have been too high, but he had managed to make a circuit of the town after sunset that day and found a *taverna* where there was a large crowd. Slipping inside, he waited until a man who looked drunk enough got up and staggered towards the exit, where Marcus had chosen to stand against the wall next to the door, holding a cup that he had snatched from a table before the slave who cleaned up could pick it up. He was further aided by the party of men and a couple of whores at the table nearest the door listening as one of them told some sort of joke that made them roar in laughter, which Marcus immediately joined in, although he had no idea what it was about. As he had learned long before, blending in like this meant that his target gave him no more than a bleary glance, while Marcus' cause was further aided by virtue of a pair of men who were entering at the same time as his prey was leaving, just as Marcus stepped behind the drunken man. It was something that happened all the time, when people squeeze past each other, and Marcus Atilius' father had taught him well, and he cut the leather strings of the man's pouch with the small knife he kept razor sharp as they all jostled together. And, as he had been taught, Marcus didn't turn in the opposite direction as his victim, but the exact same way, knowing that if the man instantly sensed his purse had been stolen, the initial instinct would be to turn around, and seeing someone hurrying the opposite direction would be a telltale. Nor did he walk much more quickly than his newly fleeced victim, for the same reason, so the man was still in the edge of his vision when he came to a sudden stop, looking down at his waist with a frown. This was the crucial moment; back when he was first learning the game, he tended to panic and speed up, and while most of the time he got away, sometimes he didn't, once taking a particularly bad beating from one of his targets before suffering the indignity of having the money he'd already managed to steal taken from him, meaning that he was beaten again by his father. Consequently, he maintained the same sauntering pace, making it to the corner and turning left; only then did he lengthen his stride, although he wasn't particularly worried. Ducking into the first alley, he opened the stolen purse and examined the contents, happy to see a mixture of coins that came out to about five *denarii*, which was why when he agreed to pay Censorinus five *sesterces,* it didn't bother him that much, and the driver turned out to be a decent enough sort, but it was when Marcus told him why he wanted to go to Scallabis that the man's entire demeanor changed.

"I marched with Lucullus," he said proudly. "Against Mithridates."

Marcus was impressed, and he said as much, but Censorinus laughed and said, "Truth be told, I did more digging than marching."

This seemed odd to Marcus; over the course of that journey, Marcus Atilius received an education on what life in the Legions was really like, to the point that, when they reached Scallabis, he was beginning to wonder if he had made the right decision after all, but in another sign the gods had favored his endeavor, once they were within sight of the city walls about five miles distant, Censorinus turned to him.

"How do you plan to enlist without anyone to vouch for you?"

"What do you mean?"

This was when Marcus Atilius learned that it wasn't just a matter of telling some official that you wanted to enlist.

Censorinus said with a laugh, "Boy, you can't just walk up and say you want to join the Legion! If that was allowed, Rome would have Legions full of slaves and freedmen, not citizens!"

Suddenly, Marcus' feeling that the gods had finally started smiling down on him evaporated, and he would have sworn on Jupiter's black stone that he actually felt the abrupt coldness of his body that seemed to envelop him as the moment when they turned their face away.

So obviously despondent was he that Censorinus actually reached out and gave him an awkward pat on the shoulder, and he was sincere when he said, "I'm sorry, boy. I thought you knew that and had already made the arrangements."

This served to rouse Marcus out of his stunned stupor to lift his head, although it wasn't with much enthusiasm that he asked, "Arrangements? What does that mean?"

Now it was Censorinus' turn to look back to the team pulling the wagon, an expression on his face that indicated he had broached an awkward subject, although he did answer, "It means that there are...ways for men who are citizens to enlist in the Legions, even if they don't have a father or uncle to attest to their status."

It was more how Censorinus said it that meant Marcus

immediately understood, and he asked bluntly, "How much does it cost to find someone?"

"I don't know what it might cost now," Censorinus answered honestly, "but I had a comrade in my *contubernium* from Etruria who said he paid twenty *sesterces*. Now?" He shrugged. "It's probably more."

And as quickly as his flickering hope was revived, it was snuffed out for Marcus Atilius; there was no prospect of being able to steal that much money in time to enlist in this new Legion. In an odd way, however, Marcus also felt more comfortable with this downturn, if only because that seemed to be the fate of anyone with the Atilius name. The gods, he thought gloomily, are doing what they normally do to my family. The pair lapsed into a silence that stretched out for about two miles, then Censorinus cleared his throat.

"Marcus," he asked simply, "how badly do you want to enlist in the Legions?"

"It's the only thing left for me," Atilius admitted. "I don't have any other prospects."

Censorinus didn't respond to this right away, seemingly content to let that sit with him for a bit.

Then, he turned to regard Marcus, and when the younger man sensed eyes on him, he turned to face Censorinus, who said, "I have an idea."

Afterward, Marcus Atilius was *almost* a believer that, at last, the goddess Fortuna was smiling down on him. Because they were still more than a mile away from Scallabis, it was more than enough time for Marcus to give Censorinus the information he would need to perpetrate the fiction that he was Atilius' uncle, not his father, the only other legal entity that Roman law recognized as being acceptable for vouching for an enlistee into the Legions.

They had discussed the idea of Censorinus posing as Marcus' father, but it was a short discussion, and it was Marcus who pointed out, "We don't look anything alike. You're fairer than I am, and our hair is a different color, and you're taller than I am."

Censorinus saw the sense in this, and they settled on the

story that Censorinus was his maternal uncle, not paternal, exploiting the one loophole in the law, which didn't decree that an uncle had to be patrilineal. And, as Atilius learned and took as another omen that Fortuna was on his side, they arrived in Scallabis on the last day of the *dilectus*, but the final sign that convinced Marcus Atilius the gods approved of his decision was in how smoothly the whole process went. In fact, from Marcus' perspective, the *Conquisitor* who took his information and administered the oath barely glanced at the pair of them, and he supposed that it was because this was the end of a long process, while the physician who examined him showed similar disinterest, barely glancing at Atilius before incising something in the wax tablet before handing it to him. But, after he took the oath, then was handed the token and told to report at the main gate at dawn, he found himself slightly dazed and standing out in the forum with Censorinus. Marcus Atilius had been trained, almost from birth, to never offer someone else money if there was the slightest chance he could get away with not paying for something, but without thinking, he reached down into his coin purse, and extracted the rest of his coins, offering them to Censorinus.

"I want to thank you, Censorinus," Marcus said past the lump in his throat, "and I want to pay you for what you did for me."

Censorinus' response was a shake of his head, and he reached out and gently closed Marcus' hand.

"I didn't do it to be paid, Marcus," he said simply. "I did it because I remember what it's like to be out of opportunities and chances, and this is my way to repay the gods for the kindness they showed me in allowing me to join Lucullus and fight against Mithridates, and to survive it all."

Nothing in Marcus Atilius' relatively short life prepared him for this sort of kindness, so he didn't know what to say, other than an awkward, "Thank you, Censorinus." Then, he had an idea. "How about I at least buy you a cup of wine? You've been here before. Surely you know of a place?"

"That I do," Censorinus said with a laugh. "There's a place called Dionysius' Cave that's a few blocks from here." His smile faded. "But I'm afraid I have to decline. Trebonius was angry enough that I took the time to do this, and if we hurry, we'll have time for another load before the Legion is equipped." He indicated in the general direction of the southern gate, through which they had entered. "He's already waiting for me at the gate with both wagons."

Trebonius was Censorinus' partner, and he had never accepted Marcus as a member of their party, however temporary it was; Marcus despised him, and being honest with himself, he would have had no qualms in lifting Trebonius' purse even after the man delivered him to Scallabis.

"I suppose this is goodbye, then," Marcus said awkwardly, then thrust out his arm, which Censorinus took.

"May Fortuna watch over you, Marcus Atilius," Censorinus said soberly. Then, true to his nature, he joked, "And I'm wagering that you'll be cursing my name in about a week."

This made Marcus laugh, then without another word, Censorinus turned and strode across the forum, heading for the southern gate, leaving Marcus Atilius alone, and with a fair amount of money for one last night. What did he call it? He tried to remember, then nodded to himself. Dionysus' Cave, that was it.

As it happened, a tradesman of some sort was walking past, and Marcus called to him, asking for directions to the *taverna*, which the man gave without breaking stride. Although he had enjoyed some wine once he attached himself to Censorinus, Marcus' thirst was barely touched. Besides, he said to himself, it will be the last time for only the gods know how long, and feeling better and more optimistic than he could ever remember before, Marcus Atilius headed off for one last night of debauching.

Chapter Three

Lucius Calienus wasn't particularly happy that his section had been selected by his Pilus Prior Gaius Crastinus to fill empty spots in the other Centuries, but he understood it. He just hoped that the new meat that was showing up the next morning turned out to be a solid bunch and not mostly the liars, lame, and lazy, one of the terms used for those men who created most of the problems in a Century. His concern was based in the fact that Crastinus had informed him that, if some of these new *Tirones* didn't work out, this time, they wouldn't be replaced.

"The *Praetor* is already chomping at the bit to get started on this campaign," he had informed Calienus. "So, if some of these new boys don't work out and are dismissed, you're going to have a short section."

This wasn't a prospect that Calienus relished, but he also wasn't as concerned as if he had still been marching in the 1st Legion, or as it was more commonly known, Pompeius' 1st Legion. For some reason that Calienus would never learn, this new *Praetor* Caesar had ordered that this new Legion, the 10th, consist of the pre-Marian tradition of one hundred-man Centuries, and not the currently common eighty-man Centuries. It created a unique set of challenges, but to Calienus, who tended to be something of an optimist, it also meant that even if one or two of these new men didn't work out, at least they wouldn't really be shorthanded, since all he had ever known was an eight-man section. Like Crastinus, the Optio, and the nine other section Sergeants, Calienus was a veteran, and while he hadn't been at the end of the twelve-year term set by the great Pompeius Magnus when he had reconstituted the 1st Legion, he had already served ten years and was twenty-eight, but accepted the new *Praetor*'s sixteen-year term in exchange for a promotion to Sergeant (Ducanus) of a tent section, called a *contubernium.* He was looking at one of the challenges, in the form of the eight wooden cots in the now-empty tent, waiting for the nine new replacements instead of ten, as the men who had been occupying this tent earlier were now spread out among the rest of the Second Cohort. Being a brand-new Legion brought a number of challenges; that the *Praetor* required ten-men sections was one of them, but he also had…unusual ideas about training, with special emphasis on getting the raw *Tirones* ready for battle more quickly than normal, and less time on the kinds of things that his former Legate Pompeius Magnus had insisted on, like drilling and making sure the men knew how to care for their equipment and uniforms. Pompeius had always liked a tidy, well-presented Legion, whereas Caesar's primary concern was getting the men trained to a degree that, when they marched, they would be likely to survive. Calienus, like most of the men from the Pompeian Legions, admired and respected Pompeius, but while he would never say such a thing aloud in front of his Pompeian comrades, Lucius Calienus suspected that Caesar's approach would prove to be the better one. His reasoning was straightforward: the job of the Legions of Rome was to fight anyone who the Senate decreed was an enemy, and most importantly, defeat them. How they looked and how disciplined they were certainly had their place, but it was common knowledge that, as soon as the new 10th Legion was deemed ready, Caesar would lead them north, where a number of the tribes in Hispania were in open rebellion and attacking Roman towns and settlements. Satisfied at what he saw, Calienus went out to the training ground to report to the Optio of the First Century, Aulus Vinicius.

"Tenth Section tent is empty, clean, and ready for the new meat, Optio," Calienus said as he was saluting.

Aulus Vinicius returned the salute, but his attention never wavered from the men who were now arrayed opposite large wooden poles planted in the ground. Each man held a *rudis*, the wooden *gladius*, the edges of which were lined with lead, along with lead in the hollowed-out handle of the weapon, making it heavier than a real *gladius*, which was the entire point; if men got accustomed to performing the thrusts and slashes with the *rudis*, when it came time to do it for real with a *gladius*, their movements would be even quicker.

"First position!" Vinicius called out. "Ten thrusts!"

Instantly, the air filled with the sharp cracking sound of wooden blades striking the poles as each of the twenty men obeyed their Optio's orders. Not only was Vinicius Optio, he was also the weapons instructor for the First Century, and supervised the instructors in the other five Centuries. Not for the first, nor the last time would Calienus reflect on how if he knew nothing about Aulus Vinicius and had been asked to pick out the most proficient man with a *gladius* in the entire Cohort of veterans, Calienus would have put Vinicius near or at the bottom of the list. Part of the problem was his demeanor, which was placid, almost bovine in nature, as if nothing roused his interest to a point that he became animated, but it was also his physical appearance. Of average height, he had a stocky build, although there seemed to be a layer of fat that hid his muscular development, and because of his habit of seemingly staring vacantly into the distance with his mouth hanging slightly open, more than one man had thought him slow-witted. Fortunately for Calienus, he had learned differently back when they had served in the 1st Legion together, albeit in different Cohorts back when Vinicius had transferred in from the 3rd Legion in exchange for a promotion to Sergeant, and he had also witnessed firsthand that anyone who chose to spar with Vinicius was headed for defeat. In fact, Aulus Vinicius was the only veteran Calienus knew who bore no scars on his body, the most eloquent testament to his prowess.

In a seeming proof that his stare was anything but vacant, Vinicius suddenly called out, "Your feet are too close together again, Papiria. I won't warn you again." Keeping his eyes on the men, Vinicius told Calienus, "Your new section will be here at first light. Once the Primus Pilus welcomes them to the Legion, they'll be turned over to the Pilus Prior."

Calienus had also come to appreciate Vinicius' dry wit, which was why he chuckled at Vinicius' description of what the new *Tirones* would be facing at the hands of Primus Pilus Favonius.

"How many do you think he beats? And," he grinned, "does he use his fists first or the *vitus*? Care to make a wager?"

Vinicius gave Calienus his version of a smile, but he asked, "How will we know?"

"I'll ask the new meat when the Pilus Prior brings them to my tent after they draw their equipment."

Vinicius nodded, then signaled his acceptance by saying, "I say fists first, and he'll beat at least three of them."

"I say *vitus* first, and that he hits four of them," Calienus countered.

"How much?"

"Five *sesterces*?"

"Done," Vinicius answered, and extended his hand, which Calienus took, sealing the wager.

With his part done, Calienus had nothing much to do as the Optio worked with the new men, so he decided to stay and watch, thinking of the five *sesterces* he was going to win the next day.

Neither Marcus nor Quintus Mallius got any sleep the night after they took the oath as *Probationes*, so when the slave charged with keeping the time at the inn they were staying at called out that it was the last third of a watch before dawn, they were immediately on their feet, ignoring the complaints of some of the occupants who didn't have somewhere to be when the sun came up. Fortunately, they were not the only ones who had somewhere to be, and in the darkness, they saw at least one other figure rising and quickly donning his tunic. They left the room, going to relieve themselves in one of the night buckets, then entered into the large common room where the meals were served, where a bleary-eyed slave was sitting on a stool, tasked with the job of providing the food that was a part of the cost for staying there.

"We need to eat while we're walking," Marcus decided for them; somewhat unusually, Quintus didn't argue, and the pair exited the inn, devouring their small meal as they headed for the northern gate.

Unusually, neither of them felt like talking, and since the streets were almost completely deserted, the loudest sound was their footsteps on the paving stones.

It also meant they were completely unprepared for someone

to call out, "Are you two heading for the camp?"

As Marcus reminded him later, it was Quintus who gave a completely undignified yelp of surprise, but they both turned to see a lone figure behind them by a matter of perhaps a dozen paces.

"Yes," Marcus answered, then he made the connection. "Were you the other one in our room?"

"I was," the man said, and now that he was just a couple paces from reaching them, they saw that he was very tall, but with a slim build. "I'm reporting to the 10th Legion today."

"So are we," Quintus confirmed, then the three of them resumed walking, though none of them said anything more as they reached the northern gate.

Normally, it would still be closed, but the *Praetor*, or so they supposed, had given orders that they be opened early, while the man of the town watch who had the duty stood there and watched them exit through the one gate that was open. None of them were aware that this had been the daily practice for the last three weeks, since the training of the new Legion began, and the watchman had long before tired of making the same old jokes about the fate that awaited the three young men and how they would regret their decision. They would be finding out for themselves soon enough.

Like the Mallius brothers, Quintus Artorius had been unable to sleep, although he was staying in a different inn, using the last of his coins for the chance to sleep on a straw-filled pallet, which he immediately regretted given his sleeplessness. He rose even earlier than the Mallius brothers, slipping quietly out of the room without rousing anyone, but after he relieved himself then went for some food, he felt as if he was nailed to the bench, sitting there after picking at the food, a small bowl of cold porridge and piece of bread smaller than his fist. He knew he should eat, but he had no appetite, and he was still forcing himself to consume his meal when he heard a noise that he identified as someone walking across the floor above him. Immediately after that, he heard footsteps descending the stairs, but there was only one small lamp allowed in the common room, so while it was lighter than in the room he had been sleeping, it wasn't by much. The figure entered the common room, and Artorius was certain that he hadn't been seen, but then he heard the figure mutter something to the serving slave. Although he couldn't make out the words, the tone of the voice was familiar, and he spent several heartbeats trying to place where he had heard this man before. It came to him a few heartbeats later; it had been when he was waiting for the scribe to return with his records, when the man with hair that stuck straight up from the top of his head and the man who was his father went through the process of enlisting. What was his name? He tried to remember, but all he could recall was that it started with a "V." It was when the man turned around, with the identical-sized bowl and piece of bread, that he saw Artorius, and he crossed the room.

"Are you going to the camp?" he asked uncertainly, standing there as if waiting to be invited by Artorius.

"Yes," Artorius replied, then, embarrassed he hadn't thought of it immediately, indicated the seat across the table. "Please, join me, Citizen." Suddenly, a thought occurred to him, "Or are we not Citizens anymore? I mean," he added hurriedly, "I know we *are*...but what are we supposed to be called now?"

The other man sat down, and it pleased Artorius that he didn't laugh, and instead seemed to consider the question seriously.

"I suppose," he finally said, "we'll be finding out soon enough. But," he reached an arm across the table, "for now, I'm Publius Vellusius."

That was it! Artorius thought, but aloud, he said as he responded with his own arm, "Quintus Artorius."

"I see you've already finished." Vellusius pointed to the bowl. "If you want to go on to the camp, don't worry about me."

"I was up earlier than I needed to be," Artorius answered honestly. "So, I'll wait."

He saw this pleased Vellusius, which in turn made Artorius happy, not relishing the idea of walking to the camp alone. Vellusius ate quickly, then stood up before Artorius, although he quickly drained his cup of water then stood as well.

"Let's go find out what we've gotten ourselves into," Vellusius said with a cheerfulness that Artorius was certain was false, but he appreciated the effort of his new friend.

They left the inn, their journey to the northern gate shorter because it was closer to their inn than had been for the Mallius brothers and their companion, and who, unknown to the pair, were barely five minutes ahead of them. As he had with every group, the town watchman simply observed them silently, although his eyes lingered on Artorius, immediately selecting him as the most likely of this bunch on this morning to not make it through training. Not surprisingly, if he had been asked, the watchman would have immediately picked one man of the first pair to leave the city to be the most likely to not just survive the harsh training regimen of a Roman Legion, but to excel, if only because he was probably the largest Roman the watchman had ever seen. They had been the first through the gates that morning, but while the other youth was much smaller, they both seemed equally eager. Not, he thought with some amusement, like this one; he looks as if he's going to his execution. This was not to say the other one with the black hair that stood straight up looked joyful or eager by any means, but he didn't have the air of resignation of his slightly smaller companion. He was still watching them walking away from the city, realizing that he could now see farther than he had just moments before, when the echoing sound of footsteps from inside the walls drew his attention. This man was alone, and once he materialized out of the gloom, the watchman noticed that this man was almost as tall, and almost as muscular as the giant.

"What the fuck are you looking at, watchman?" this one snarled at him as he walked by, and the watchman saw he was clutching a token in one hand.

It was the glare that the watchman, who didn't answer, would remember, thinking that this one would welcome an opportunity for a confrontation. He's certainly spoiling for a fight, he thought, and from what I hear, this new *Praetor* is as well, but there was something else in the large man's eyes that, even in the light from the single torch he had lit, the watchman was certain he had seen. A moment's consideration led him to silently conclude that what he had also seen was fear, although for that the watchman couldn't blame him. When he assumed the duty, he had been warned to expect nine new men to need early exit from the town, and that had been eight. He remained there until the sun came up above the horizon, which was his signal to fully open both gates for the day's business to begin, yet the ninth man had never shown up. It happened, he knew; sometimes, a man's nerve failed him at the last moment and kept them from fulfilling their sacred oath. And, while there wouldn't be a manhunt for this man, if he was stupid enough to remain in Scallabis then ran afoul of the authorities for some reason, no matter how minor the offense, he faced a flogging with the scourge, and not many men survived that. The watchman quickly forgot about the missing man, preparing for the real start of his day, one that would be like all those that had gone before. Regardless, he also knew there were much worse ways to earn your daily bread.

"What do you think it will be like?" Artorius asked of nobody in particular of the group of men standing a short distance from the main gate, waiting for them to open.

It was not fully dark, but it was still gloomy enough that it was difficult to make out facial features if the other person was standing a pace or more away, but Artorius had seen that there were five others besides him, although they seemed content to remain with whoever they had arrived with, so that there was a pair in Atilius and Vellusius and one group of three, two of whom were sitting on the ground while the third man chose to remain standing, with another man standing by himself.

"It will be the hardest thing we've ever done."

To his surprise, it was his new companion Vellusius who said this, essentially the only words he had spoken since they left the inn.

"I'm not worried about it." The man standing off by himself said this slightly louder since he was a bit farther away, although Artorius thought it could be for other reasons. "By the gods, I can't wait to kill some barbarian scum! I wager anyone that I'll have the most kills of anyone in this Legion!"

"*Gerrae*," one of the seated men responded, his tone mild enough. "That's awfully big talk."

"You'll probably be the first one to piss yourself the instant one of those barbarians look cross-eyed at you." This came from the other of the pair sitting on the ground, and although it was delivered with a laugh, it clearly offended the lone man, who actually took a step closer to the pair on the ground.

"Watch your tone! I've beaten better men than you, I swear by Hercules I have!"

Neither of the pair seated got to their feet, but the first one said, "That's easy to say."

"Easy, boys," the tall man standing next to the pair on the ground spoke up for the first time and Artorius saw that, while he was tall, he had a slender build, but what Artorius instantly deduced was that this man was older than the others, and the manner in which he had said it at least hinted that he might know what he was talking about. "There will be plenty of time for everyone to get as much fighting in as any man could want."

His words also seemed to ease the tensions somewhat, but then, seemingly out of nowhere, two men suddenly materialized in the darkness, and the surprised alarm that was shared unanimously by the six of them, in the form of gasps and squawks at the sight of these apparitions probably did more to dispel the tension than anything else.

"*Salve*, Citizens," one of them greeted the others as the pair approached, but while Artorius tried to offer a reply, nothing came out of his mouth, although the others had more success in returning the greeting that had come from the largest man Artorius had ever seen.

That he wasn't the only one who noticed was confirmed when one of the pair who had been seated but had scrambled to their feet at the sudden appearance of the pair blurted out, "Gods, you *are* a big one! Remind me to stand next to you, Ajax!"

This brought some laughter from the others, but it was now light enough for Artorius to see that not everyone was amused, and the man who had been standing by himself, who was large and muscular himself, simply glowered at the giant. Only then did Artorius turn his attention to the giant's companion, and he was slightly heartened to see that, as large as the giant was, this man was close to his size; certainly he was no taller than Artorius, although he did have a more muscular build. Before anyone else could speak, however, they heard a rattling sound, followed by the creaking as one of the gates to the camp was opened by a man wearing mail armor and helmet.

"Well," the giant said this over his shoulder since he was already moving towards the camp, "I guess that means they're ready for us."

Lucius Favonius, Primus Pilus of the 10th Legion, stood in the gateway, clutching his *vitus* in both hands just below his waist, watching as the group of new *Tirones* made their way towards him. Not surprisingly, his eye was immediately drawn to the one in the lead, not so much because he was the first one, but because of his size. That, Favonius thought, is one big fucking lump of meat, and he gave a small smile, knowing that this lump of meat was completely unaware that the welcome Favonius had prepared, the one that Calienus and Vinicius had laughed about, would be used on him first. All Favonius needed was the slightest excuse, and he knew from experience that, with new *Tirones*, or as they were most commonly called, *Tiros*, each of them would be offering an opportunity very quickly.

Once they were within earshot, Favonius pointed to a spot on the ground in front him with his *vitus*. "All of you fall in, in a single line starting right here, with the tallest first to my left."

As he expected, the giant Roman, who Favonius could see was very young to be so large, moved immediately to that spot, which told Favonius something. He's always been the biggest and the strongest, so he's gotten accustomed to being singled out. Well, he thought with grim amusement, he's about to learn that that comes with a price when you're under the standard. Outwardly, he watched impassively as the small group gauged each other to determine where they would go, although one of them did essentially as the giant, walking immediately to the opposite end, and in one glance, Favonius marked this *Tiro* as the weakling of this bunch. The man who stood immediately next to the giant was older than the others, though not by much, and an inch shorter than the giant, while the man who stood on the opposite side from the large one might have been as muscular as the giant but a bit shorter than the second man. To Favonius' embarrassment, this was the first time he noticed that there were only eight men and not the nine that had been expected, and he muttered a soft curse, though he didn't say anything aloud, thinking, Pluto's cock, we already have a deserter out of this bunch? It just happened that this was also the moment that the giant chose to turn his head to look down the line of men that had just settled into place, and Favonius moved immediately, and quickly, so rapidly that the giant was still looking to his left when Favonius, using the end of his *vitus* and with perfect aim, rammed it, hard, into the *Tiro's* stomach, knowing exactly where to strike right under the breastbone so that it took a man's breath away. To his satisfaction, the giant dropped immediately to his knees, his breath exploding from his lungs with so much force that he couldn't even cry out, whereupon he bent over, clutching his stomach.

"Nobody told you to look around, did they, you *cunnus*?"

As Favonius knew, the youth hadn't regained his breath enough to answer, and he was prepared when the *Tiro* could only respond with a shake of his head.

This time, Favonius aimed his *vitus* at a spot just above the giant's left ear as he roared, "I asked you a question, boy!"

By this time, the *Tiro* had regained enough of his breath to stammer out, "No, sir…I mean, Your Excellency!"

Again, Favonius had known what to expect, except this time, he brought the *vitus* down on top of the *Tiro's* head with a sharp crack.

"I work for a living, you *cunnus*!" For this, Favonius had leaned over so that he could bellow directly in the *Tiro's* ear, causing the youth to wince from the auditory assault. "I'm no Excellency! I work for a living!"

Then, as if it had never happened, Favonius stood erect, and said in a normal, almost conversational tone, "On your feet, boy. And look straight ahead. Understood?" The youth pulled himself to his feet, although he was weaving a bit, but when he opened his mouth, Favonius cut him off, using the same tone. "Of course, none of you know what my proper title or my name is because you haven't been taught such things. So we'll begin with that. My name is Lucius Favonius, and I'm the Primus Pilus of the 10th Legion. I know that means nothing to you now, but you'll learn what it means in time. Right now, all you need to know is this." He pointed to his transverse crest, which was white. "I and anyone who wears a crest like this, no matter what the color, are to be considered on the same level as your household gods, because like the gods, we exercise the power of life and death over each of you."

As far as Lucius Favonius was concerned, this was one of his favorite moments of this little drama that he had been conducting since the first day of the *dilectus*. He had insisted on being the first Centurion to meet every bunch of new *Tirones*, which meant that in the hectic early days, he had stood on this spot for most of the day as the *Conquisitores* at the *Praetorium* sent men as rapidly as they could finalize their paperwork, and this was the last time he would ever do it, since he had no intention of being under the standard sixteen years from this moment, when this Legion would hold a new *dilectus*. The reason he enjoyed this moment would have surprised every one of those he greeted, that it wasn't about the chance to be cruel, but it was his chance to administer the first dose of what life under the standard was really like, that it wasn't the glorious pursuit of arms that so many of these youngsters who answered the call had in their heads. And, he was satisfied to see, this bunch looked as if they were a group of men who had been suddenly awakened from a pleasant dream, which was precisely the effect that Lucius Favonius had intended. The rest, he knew, would come later.

"I'll escort you to the *Praetorium*," he said, breaking the brief silence and pointing to the largest tent in the camp, then turned and began walking.

As he expected, the group hurried behind him, and because his back was turned to them, they didn't see his broad grin as he recalled what one of his Centurions had said about this sight.

"They look like a bunch of baby ducks following their mama when you take them to the *Praetorium*."

It was an apt observation, and it amused Favonius every time he did it. There was no sign of humor when he reached the entrance, which had both flaps pulled open and where two Legionaries, also wearing their full uniform were standing, and he pointed with his *vitus* at the ground.

"You'll go inside and hand in your tokens, and then you'll return to this spot outside the *Praetorium*, where you'll get into the exact same line, facing the tent, then you'll wait for me. Is that clear?"

Favonius got a surprise of his own then, when the giant said instantly, "Yes, Primus Pilus."

"Maybe you're not as stupid as you look, boy," he said with a chuckle, then stepped aside to watch the group file into the tent.

For Spurius Didius, the sudden appearance of the Roman youth he had seen the day before outside the *Praetorium* had unsettled him deeply; while he didn't know with any certainty, his sense was that he and the giant were going to be in the same group for the foreseeable future, and the idea angered him. Adding to this emotion, his embarrassment about how he had yelped like a girl when the giant and his friend had seemed to come from out of the ground meant that he was already developing a deep hatred for this giant. Although, he thought as he followed behind Scribonius, the only man whose name he knew at that point, as this Favonius character led them to the big tent in the middle of the camp, it wasn't all bad. Seeing how the giant had dropped like a sack of grain thrown from a wagon had given him an instant of happiness. Most importantly, while it had been hard, he had managed to keep looking straight ahead, forced to use the far edge of his vision as Favonius struck the giant twice more. Unfortunately, by the time they reached the *Praetorium*, much of Didius' anger had returned as his mind took flight at all the injustices that he was likely to endure, simply because that *cunnus* just happened to be bigger and, from the looks of it, at least as strong as Didius himself. Inside the tent, his attention was occupied by the scene before him, as several men hurried about, a couple of them wearing the uniform of the Legions but most of them wearing only tunics of the type that designated that they were either a freedman non-citizen or a slave, all of whom were wearing a bronze placard. Every one of them were moving quickly, and like his new comrades, Didius would learn this was a feature of life for any man under Julius Caesar's command.

A clerk sitting at a desk next to the tent wall to their right, seeing them enter, called to them, and naturally, the large *Tiro* led the way, handing over his token first, which the clerk then used to identify the correct record from a stack of scrolls that were sitting on a small table next to the desk. Didius didn't really pay attention, understanding that he would be finding out in a moment what was happening anyway, so he instead watched the activity around him. Scribonius stepped forward, breaking Didius' attention from the other clerks, and when he took his step into Scribonius' former spot, he saw that the giant had moved to a desk that was placed just a couple of paces away to the left. Then it was his turn, the clerk taking his token, then turning to the small table, selected one and unrolled it. Didius was illiterate, but he also recognized it as the one that he and his counterfeit father had signed the day before from the markings.

"As of now," the clerk intoned, not even bothering to look up at Didius, "you're no longer a *Probatio*; you're now a *Tirone* in the 10th Legion."

"What does *that* mean?" Didius blurted out, which did earn him the attention of the clerk, who looked up at him, his mouth a thin line.

"If you had waited," the clerk said icily, "you would already know." Didius was enraged at this freedman clerk for speaking to him in this manner, but the clerk had been doing this a long time, and he had long since learned that, even as lowly a status as a freedman clerk may occupy in a Roman Legion, it was higher than a *Tirone*, so he ignored Didius' glare to continue, "As *Probatio*, the list of punishments are limited, but now that you are a *Tirone*, you are under the full authority of the rules and regulations that govern the Legions of Rome, which include the penalty of death if the violation is deemed serious enough by the Legate in command. Do you understand this, *Tirone* Didius?"

As he was certain it would, the mention of the possibility of execution shook Didius sufficiently that he had to swallow once before he answered hoarsely, "I understand."

The clerk turned the document around and pointed to a drawn line that Didius hadn't noticed the day before, at the very bottom of the scroll.

"Since I can see that you're illiterate, make your mark again on that line," the clerk said, and Didius bent over, took the quill lying next to the scroll, dipped it in the inkpot, then drew the same symbol that he had used the day before.

If the truth were known, Didius was actually secretly proud that he chose not to use the customary "X" that also meant the number ten, but from what he was certain was one of his initials, the letter "D," and he repeated that.

The clerk, however, was unimpressed, because Didius was far from the first man who couldn't read or write but had learned the first letters of their names and used one of them as their mark.

"Go to the next table," the clerk ordered as he sprinkled a handful of sand on Didius' mark, then called out, "Next man."

Didius did as he was told, although he had to pause for a brief moment as he watched Scribonius quickly sign his full name on yet another document presented to him by the clerk at the second table, igniting a stab of envy in Didius, along with the thought, Maybe I'll ask him to teach me to read and write. As if he read Didius' thoughts, when Scribonius put the quill down, he glanced over at Didius and gave him a smile before he stepped away.

"This concerns your pay," the second clerk told Didius as he stepped in front of the desk.

Although they did not physically resemble each other, the demeanor and attitude of the pair of clerks might have made them twins like the two men of his group, although he still didn't know their names either.

The mention of his pay caused Didius to demand, "So when do we get our pay?"

The clerk's reaction baffled him and made him angry in almost equal measure, because the man burst out laughing.

"Why don't you ask your Primus Pilus about that?"

Scribonius, following the large *Tiro's* lead, had chosen to stand near the entrance as they waited for their new comrades to go through the process, and they both heard the clerk's response, exchanging a glance, and as they talked about it later, they had both arrived at the same conclusion at roughly the same moment, that this would be a monumentally bad idea for a new *Tiro*.

Didius, however, was too angry to notice, so he shot back as he bent down to repeat making his mark, "I'll do just that!"

Throwing the quill down, he gave the clerk a glare before he stalked off, seeing Scribonius and the giant standing near the entrance. The fact that they exchanged a quiet word, then both turned and exited the tent before Didius reached them he didn't notice or attach any significance to, unaware that they had originally intended to wait. Once outside, he saw they were standing at the spot Favonius had indicated, but both of them were looking straight ahead and not speaking, which Didius realized was probably a good idea, and he joined them. One by one, the others emerged and resumed their spot in the line, facing the tent, until finally, Artorius emerged, joining the others in complete silence, waiting for what came next.

As he intended, Favonius didn't return to the *Praetorium* until the new *Tiros* were back in line, facing the tent, whereupon he approached them from behind, except this time, he wasn't alone. Accompanying him was another Centurion, several years younger, although taller and a bit slenderer, and with a long scar that began midway next to his right ear down to about the middle of his jaw. The other differences were the color of the transverse crests they each wore, Crastinus' being red, and there were a few more *phalarae* on Favonius' harness, along with a couple of arm rings and a torq, but otherwise, they were identical in their demeanor and even in the manner in which they moved. Now, they approached the new *Tiros* from behind, slowly and quietly, stopping just a matter of a couple paces behind them, whereupon they were content to stand there, while the Legionaries guarding the tent and facing their direction who knew what was in store for these *Tiros*, having seen it happen over the previous weeks, were expressionless as the *Tiros* stood, silently, knowing they were waiting for something but having no idea what lay ahead of them next.

"Pluto's cock, what are they waiting for?"

If Favonius and his companion would have been disposed to do so, they would have told the *Tiro* who spoke from his spot in the exact middle of the line that his outburst was it, but Favonius was already in motion, crossing the distance in two quick strides as his *vitus* came swinging down, except this time, it was not aimed for the head or torso, but right across the back of the *Tiro's* knees, although it had the exact same result as with the large *Tiro*, dropping the man to his knees, whereupon he fell forward, catching himself so that he was on all fours.

"Did anyone tell you to speak, *cunnus*?"

"N-no, Primus Pilus," the man half-gasped and half-sobbed as he shook his head.

"Then get on your feet, you miserable piece of *cac*," Favonius sneered. "I didn't hit you nearly as hard as I hit that big oaf on the end, so get up and quit sniveling like a woman."

As the *Tiro* climbed unsteadily to his feet, Favonius walked around the end of the line, followed by the second Centurion, and turned to face the group, while the other Centurion stood next to and just behind him.

"This is Secundus Pilus Prior Gaius Crastinus." Favonius used his *vitus* to point over his shoulder. "He's the commander of the Second Cohort of the 10th Legion, and you will be in his Century, the First Century of the Second Cohort. You'll accompany him to the *Quaestorium,* where you'll be issued your equipment. And," his voice hardened even more, "you'll obey him in the same manner you obey me, or you'll wish you had never been born. Is that understood?"

For the first time, the *Tiros* managed to all reply in the correct manner, and although it was more ragged than would be allowed in the future, Favonius didn't press the issue.

Turning his back to them, he grinned at Crastinus and said quietly, "They're all yours, Gaius. You know what to do."

Crastinus nodded, and Favonius stepped aside, then walked into the *Praetorium*, leaving Crastinus and his new charges alone.

Artorius' case of nerves had almost immediately escalated to the point where he was in a state of terror that was close to outright panic, beginning when Primus Pilus Favonius brought the huge Roman to his knees with an ease that was truly frightening, and as he quickly learned, it was making it extremely difficult for him to concentrate. He managed to avoid drawing attention when they were met by Favonius and followed the instructions inside the *Praetorium*. It was when Pilus Prior Crastinus took over where his difficulties started, when the Pilus Prior began with the basics of instructing them in the position of *intente*, the position from which all other movement commands began. To Artorius, he thought he was following the instructions Crastinus gave, with his arms held down by his sides, feet together, chin pulled in and staring straight ahead, but when the Pilus Prior reached him, Crastinus uttered a curse, and then struck him on the upper arms with his *vitus*.

"Your arms need to be straight, you miserable piece of *cac*," the Centurion snarled, but even when Artorius tried to comply, it wasn't good enough, earning him two more swipes that, as he would learn later that night, left bruises.

And it only got worse from that point forward, because Crastinus was simply moving too quickly for Artorius, going from one command to the next more rapidly than the youth could absorb. What followed learning *intente* was how to turn so that the line of men went from side by side to back to front, which happened to be the moment when, because of his panic, Quintus Artorius temporarily forgot his left from his right. Part of the problem was with the timing of the commands, because Crastinus would say something, then pause an instant before bellowing the word that was supposed to initiate the movement, and the first time, Artorius wasn't the only one who moved early, nor was he the second, or the third time. And, fortunately for Artorius, it was other men who drew Crastinus' wrath on the third, which was exacerbated when the man who was two men down from the giant who had been so belligerent earlier that morning tried to correct himself without Crastinus noticing.

He was unsuccessful, as Crastinus bellowed, "Do not move!" Running to stand in front of the man, he stuck his face a matter of three or four inches from the *Tiro* as he snarled, "You miserable bag of *cac*! I said to wait for the *final* word of the command!"

Artorius thought about taking advantage of Crastinus' attention being elsewhere to correct himself so that he was facing in the same direction, but the man next to him who had also made the error didn't move, so Artorius followed suit, and he could only hear the *Tiro* protest, "But, Pilus Prior…"

He got no further, and Artorius knew why just from the sound of Crastinus' *vitus* smashing into the man's body, followed by the thud of his body hitting the ground, while the man made a choking sound.

"But what?" Crastinus was leaning over the man as he shouted, "There is no *but*, you *cunnus*, you piece of filth! You'll wait for the command!"

Without warning, Crastinus spun and stalked down the line to smack one of the brothers, though he wasn't knocked down, then to Artorius' comrade next to him, striking the youth who had been with the giant at the end three or four times on the arms. Artorius braced himself, trying not to flinch, certain that he was next, but Crastinus was satisfied that he had made his point and strode back to his position facing the rank, while Artorius thanked the gods he had escaped; it would prove to be short-lived.

"We're going to do it again," he announced, then paused before he barked out the first two words. "*Ad Gladium…*" Then, after a bare heartbeat's pause. "*CLINA!*"

And, as one, for the first time, all eight men pivoted their facing. Unfortunately for Artorius, seven of them turned to their right, as indicated by the word "*Gladium*" since they carried their blade in their right hand, while Quintus Artorius turned in the opposite direction.

"By the gods, what has been sent to me?"

Crastinus was moving as he bellowed this, suddenly appearing in front of Artorius, who was still facing in the wrong direction, and once again, he thrust his face just inches from the terrified *Tiro*.

This time, he did not yell, which frightened Artorius even more than if he had been bellowing, asking, "Are you daring to tell me that you don't know your left from your right?"

Of *course* he knew his left from his right!

"N-n-no, Pilus Prior," he answered, thinking that he was providing the right answer, that no he was *not* telling the Centurion he didn't know his left from his right, because he did, despite the evidence to the contrary.

"What's your name, boy?" Crastinus asked quietly, and in

a deceptively mild tone, although Artorius was still terrified.

"Q-Q-Quintus Artorius, Pilus Prior."

Crastinus nodded, and still with the same tone, said, "Well, Quintus Artorius, since your whore of a mother and your slave of a father never bothered to teach you left from right, let me show you."

The blow was delivered with an open hand that Artorius never saw coming, igniting what seemed to be a thousand stars behind his eyelids, but it was the sound that he, and his comrades, would remember.

"That," Crastinus said calmly, "is the left side of your face."

He was too stunned to understand what was coming, and if this one wasn't quite as powerful, it was by a matter of a small degree, as Crastinus slapped him with his left hand.

"That's the right side of your face," the Centurion said, still speaking in the same, almost conversational manner, but he was not through. "Which hand do you eat with?"

Artorius somehow managed to retain enough of his wits to raise his right hand as he answered shakily, "This one, Pilus Prior."

This time, Crastinus used his *vitus*, smacking it across Artorius' palm, which wrenched another yelp of pain from the hapless *Tiro*.

"That's your right hand, Artorius," Crastinus said. "That's the hand you hold your *gladius* in, do you understand?" Artorius nodded, then flinched, thinking that he would be hit for doing so, but Crastinus continued, "So, when I give you the command, *Ad Gladium, Clina*, which direction do you suppose you'll turn towards?" Artorius opened his mouth, eager to correct his mistake, but Crastinus stopped him. "No, don't tell me, point." Artorius did as he was told, seeing his hand shaking as he pointed to his right, which Crastinus ignored. "Very good, Artorius." He nodded. "Now, turn around and face the way everyone else is facing. And remember, if you obey an order and you find yourself as you just were with everyone else doing something different, you were the one who was wrong. Got it?"

"Y-yes, Pilus Prior."

Satisfied, Crastinus resumed his post to begin instruction in how to perform the next movement, which was the order to march, while Artorius swore to himself that he would pay attention from this point forward. And, to his credit, he did try and was successful enough that he wasn't singled out for the rest of the time they were drilled before Crastinus deemed they could go to the *Quaestorium*.

While it was another new experience for the *Tiros*, most of the group had begun to grasp that at the very least, the wisest course of action was to keep their mouths shut and do as they were instructed. Most, however, was not all, although in the case of one of the *Tiros,* his complaints were more practical in nature, for the simple reason that nothing fit him. It was the giant young Roman who, by virtue of being first in the rank, was also the first to be told to disrobe, but when he was handed two of the new soldier's tunics, which were a freshly dyed red, he had to struggle to put one on because it was much tighter than his own shabby civilian's tunic. Scribonius, the second in line, watched with some amusement as, similarly as they did in the *Praetorium*, the giant sidestepped to the next station while he was still grumbling about the tight fit. The Legionary behind the counter thrust the two tunics at Scribonius, and while almost as tall as his new comrade, there was no problem with the fit, and he had just shrugged one on when the giant was thrown a pair of what the man called *caligae*, the soldier's boot that was as identifiable as the red tunic. Even given the circumstances, Scribonius had to struggle to keep from laughing as the giant stared down at his feet, where his largest toes were poking through the open front almost an inch. The Legionary behind the counter felt no such compunction, and he burst out laughing, and even called out to the man doling out tunics and his companion on the opposite side who was holding a chain mail vest, the three veterans roaring at the hapless youth.

"Don't you have any larger pairs?" he asked plaintively, and Scribonius winced, certain this would earn the giant some sort of rebuke, even glancing over his shoulder, but Crastinus was nowhere in sight, and to his surprise, the man simply shrugged and said, "I'll look."

This engendered a delay for a few moments for the rest of the others, although they were all given their tunic and spares and changed into them, leaving their old clothes in a heap that they were told would be burned for vermin. Scribonius watched as the giant tried on a half-dozen pair, and the best-fitting ones still left his toes exposed, though not by as much.

"How can I get *caligae* that fit?" the giant asked, earning him another indifferent shrug.

"You'll have to have one of the cobblers out in town make you a couple of pairs."

"How much will that cost?"

It was easy to hear the dismay in his voice, but the man behind the counter had exhausted his knowledge, and his interest in this minor diversion from a boring day.

"No more than a few *sesterces*, I expect. I wouldn't know."

Only then did their progress resume, the giant obviously recognizing further attempts to learn more would be fruitless, and to Scribonius' relief, the pair he was handed, while they did not fit perfectly, at least covered his toes and his heel didn't slip much. His new companion ahead of him had just been handed a chainmail vest the man called the *lorica hamata*, while Didius was just putting on his *caligae*, standing next to Scribonius.

"That big oaf might be strong, but he's thick, *neh*?" he whispered to Scribonius. "He's slowing us all up!"

Instead of answering, Scribonius stepped into the spot vacated by the giant, who was being handed a leather *baltea*, including the metal-studded strips that hung down to provide a modicum of protection for that part which every man, even if they weren't in the Legions, held most dear. Didius, irritated that his jibe had neither been appreciated nor remarked on, glared at Scribonius' back as the slender *Tiro* donned the *hamata*, and while Didius noticed the ease with which Scribonius did so, as if this wasn't his first time, it didn't register with him as anything but an idle thought. Then it was his turn, and while he was still irritated, it was at himself because he hadn't really paid attention to Scribonius, so he fumbled with the two flaps of chain mail that hung over the shoulders and were secured in place by two hooks. When Scribonius glanced over his shoulder and noticed, he returned to Didius, and without saying anything, demonstrated the proper way, while Didius felt a pang of embarrassment for his unkind thoughts just a matter of heartbeats earlier, prompting him to mutter a thanks.

"That's because when those barbarians try to kill you, they're going to aim for your head," the man behind the counter commented, though he made no attempt to do anything to help Didius, "but their aim is terrible, so you need that extra reinforcement."

He clearly thought this was witty because he burst out in laughter, although from what Didius could see, his comrades behind the counter had either heard this before or didn't find it particularly amusing. This time, Didius did pay attention to Scribonius, while the giant was now being handed a helmet along with a felt cap, and Scribonius showed Didius how, once the *baltea* and the harness was properly fitted, bunching the mail up a bit above the *baltea* actually lightened the perceived weight that Didius was feeling on his shoulders, and this time, Didius made sure to thank him, although he only received a small smile in return. Once he was handed the helmet, he saw that it had two hinged flaps to protect his ears and jaw, while there was a flange about half the width of his hand in back to protect his neck. It also had a protuberant knob on the crown, but Didius saw that there was a hole drilled in the knob, correctly assuming that this was how the horsetail plume he had seen the men guarding the *Praetorium* wearing would be attached. Then they were handed a shield, the largest piece of kit, which was both an oval and slightly curved, with a large iron boss in the center to provide room for the knuckles of the hand that would grip the leather wrapped wooden handle. The shield itself was made of wicker, but Didius had noticed that the shields carried by the soldiers around the gate had all been made of wood and painted red, and with what looked like a bull painted on them, and he wondered when they would get those instead. From one station to the next, in a systematic and very Roman fashion, the new men received the bits and pieces of their gear, which they were told to place in a pile in a row that mimicked their line in formation.

Like the others, Didius had resolved to keep his mouth shut, and he actually managed to do so when, for the third time in a row, the man behind the counter made the same joke when he handed him a spade. "You're going to get to know *that* piece of equipment very well."

However, it was when Didius reached the final man behind the counter that he could not contain himself.

Staring down at what to him was clearly a toy *gladius* made of wood, although the edges were lined with a dull gray metal, he burst out, "What's this? Are we children that we don't get a real *gladius*?"

Didius learned he wasn't alone in his indignation because, almost immediately, one of the pair of brothers echoed, "Exactly! Aren't we good enough to have a real weapon?"

This was also the moment Didius learned that Pilus Prior Crastinus had returned when, hearing rapid footsteps from behind him, he turned just in time to receive the end of Crastinus' stick in almost the exact same spot as the first time, with the identical result of knocking the wind out of him and sending him to the ground to land next to the pile of equipment.

He also happened to be oriented so that he could see that the twin who had spoken after him received the same treatment, which elicited a sense of grim satisfaction as the *Tiro* ended up on the dirt floor in an almost identical posture, but when his brother leaned down to help him out, the second brother joined his sibling, also clutching his stomach, as Crastinus bellowed, "Nobody told you to touch him!"

"I'm sorry, Pilus Prior, he's my bro..."

He got no further, Crastinus bringing that infernal stick down with a resounding smack, striking the *Tiro* on his upper thigh as he snarled, "And nobody asked you for an explanation, you *cunnus*!" Crastinus took a step away from the trio and ordered, "On your feet, the lot of you."

Didius was determined not only to be the first back on his feet, but to assume the position they had just learned, drawing himself to *intente*, but he was disappointed to see that the brothers clearly had the same thought.

When Crastinus spoke, it was with a tone that, while pleasant, didn't deceive any of the *Tiros*, asking, "Now, is there anyone else who wants to complain about not getting a real *gladius*?" Eight heads moved in a universal back and forth motion, and Crastinus continued, "You *cunni* can barely walk in a straight line, so you don't really expect us to hand you a real weapon, do you? You have a *long* way to go to reach that point." Crastinus glanced over at one of the men behind the long counter, who gave him a nod, which prompted him to say, "You've gotten your basic allotment of equipment. Now, pay attention and I'm going to show you how you're going to be carrying it all."

The new *Tiros* watched as, with an expertise that spoke of hundreds if not thousands of repetitions, Crastinus put some of the items into the large leather pack, then placed some of the tools in the wicker basket they had been given, which not just Didius was curious about, unable to come up with a possible use for it. As if by some sort of magic, the pile of items that had been at the feet of one of the brothers vanished, leaving only the basket and pack...and a long pole that had a shorter crosspiece lashed securely just a few inches below one end.

"This is your *furca*," Crastinus explained as he then slung the pack from one arm of the crosspiece, then the wicker basket from the other. Then, he hefted the *furca*, placing it on his left shoulder so that the load of equipment dangled behind and, because of the angle, slightly above his head. "This is how we march in the Legions, and it's why we can carry more of a load than any barbarian. Now," he set the *furca* down, "pack your equipment like I showed you."

It didn't surprise Crastinus that the *Tiros* he had just thrashed had clearly paid the closest attention, although his expression never changed from the permanent frown as he stood watching. Nor did he give a flicker of surprise when he saw that the tall, lean *Tiro* behaved as if he had done this before, as did the giant and the second smallest man in this section, those three just beating out their freshly thrashed comrades. And, as he expected, it was Artorius who seemed to have the most trouble remembering what went where, but Crastinus didn't intervene when he saw the *Tiro* try to stick the turfcutter into the pack instead of the basket, although he did instantly see that the handle protruded. Unknown to these youngsters, Crastinus had already been through this process with those new men who were now advanced in their training, which was what saved them from another thrashing because, as a group, these

Tiros actually were ready more quickly than the others had been a couple weeks earlier.

"Fall in outside the tent, in formation," he instructed, then paused for a moment to allow them the time to rush out of the *Quaestorium* before following them outside to see that they had gotten themselves in the proper order.

From the *Quaestorium*, he marched them down a neatly ordered street lined with tents, only stopping them outside a tent near the front wall whose flaps were tied open, showing an empty space, save for several wooden frames.

"This," Crastinus indicated the tent, "is where you'll be living. As you see, there are eight of you here, but your Sergeant has already been selected." He paused, then in a slightly different tone, continued, "This is your *contubernium*, your tent section. Look around at the other men," he indicated the rank with his *vitus*, watching as the *Tiros* did as instructed, turning their heads to look at their new comrades, "because they'll be the ones you're living with from here on until your time in the Legion is up. Or," he gave a grim laugh, "until you die, whichever happens first." He wasn't surprised to see that the new men didn't find this particularly funny, but Gaius Crastinus was far more experienced in these matters, and he knew that sooner rather than later, they would be making jokes about one of them dying on their own.

Aloud, he issued another, very important instruction. "Before you go in, each of you needs to select one other man from this section. This man will be your companion, your closest comrade and friend for the time both of you are in the Legion. He'll be the holder of your will, he'll be the man who watches your back wherever you go. Whenever possible, you'll go together, even when you go out into town, so choose wisely. I'll give you a few moments to do that, then you're to go into the tent, and with your choice in mind, pick a spot where you'll be sleeping. The cot that your Sergeant occupies is the one closest to the entrance; you can tell because his gear is under the cot. Now, I'll return in," he glanced up at the sun, "a sixth part of the watch. Or maybe sooner," he warned, "just to make sure you're doing what you're supposed to be doing and not already fucking off."

With that, he turned and strode away, leaving the *Tiros* in something of a bewildered silence, but it was Scribonius who broke it by turning to his right to address the only man taller than him in the section, "I'm Sextus Scribonius." With a grin, he said, "You seem to have your wits about you like I do. What do you say we pair up?"

The giant immediately accepted Scribonius' outstretched hand, saying with a deep voice that matched his size, "*Salve*, I'm Titus Pullus." He had returned Scribonius' grin, but it faded and he sounded a bit uncomfortable as he said, "While I appreciate the offer, I actually joined with Vibius Domitius," he indicated the short youth who even then was striding towards them with a broad grin on his face, "and we've been friends since childhood. So..." He offered a slightly embarrassed shrug but did not finish.

There was no need, and Scribonius, while disappointed, assured him he understood, turning in the opposite direction to see what his choices were. Behind him, the newly identified Pullus and Domitius had a brief whispered exchange, then immediately the pair entered the tent with their gear, which didn't surprise Scribonius. Nor did it surprise him when the pair he assumed were twins, seeing Pullus and Domitius, made a mad dash for the tent, leaving Scribonius with rapidly diminishing options.

Didius, having seen Scribonius turn to the giant, immediately spun about, but the problem was that the brothers were next to him, and while he had been insulted that Scribonius had not deigned to ask him instead of the big oaf, he immediately understood the inevitability of their pairing up. Next, he eyed the bandy-legged short *Tiro*, mainly because he was heading in his direction, but he saw that the *Tiro* was looking past him to where Scribonius was just turning away from the giant, who he had overheard was named Pullus. With a sense of growing frustration, he spun back about as, like Scribonius, he saw his options rapidly evaporating. Unlike Didius, however, Scribonius didn't hesitate, but when he walked past Didius and didn't even look in his direction to approach the weakling Artorius, it sent a bolt of fury through

Didius. He'd rather be with that...that *idiot* and weakling instead of me? He didn't even know his left from his right! Didius could hardly believe it, but while he wouldn't admit it even to himself, he was as hurt as he was insulted. The consequence was that the only one left was the youth whose hair stuck up straight on his head, and while Didius saw the expression of resignation for what it was, he chose to at least partially ignore it, not bothering to offer his arm.

"I'm Spurius Didius," he said abruptly. "What's your name?"

"P-Publius Vellusius," the other man stammered, thrusting out his hand, which Didius accepted, albeit grudgingly.

"It looks like it's just you and me, *neh?*" He gave Vellusius his version of a smile, which as he would learn, others viewed as nothing more than a baring of the teeth. "So I suppose you'll do."

Vellusius certainly understood this, yet he still hesitated, both of them missing the approach of another man from behind them, although he stopped at the tent opening to lean against the pole.

"I...I suppose so," was all Vellusius said. Then, he grabbed his *furca*, saying, "We better go see what's left."

Didius glared at Vellusius' retreating back, then bent down and picked up his own gear and followed suit, but he had not made it inside the tent when the newly arrived man spoke up.

"So apparently, someone can count." It was spoken in a dry, somewhat humorous tone, and he continued, "In case you haven't guessed, I'm the Sergeant of this tent section, and my name is Lucius Calienus. I was a member of Pompeius' 1st Legion, and I was promoted to Sergeant to help fill this Legion with some men who know their asses from their elbows. And," he added a sigh for effect, "judging from what I'm seeing in this lot, I might as well kiss my ass goodbye because I'm as good as dead the moment we go into battle." This was just another insult to Didius' already battered pride, but because of where he was standing just outside, he saw that the giant Pullus, who was now seated on the first cot next to the entrance on the left wasn't any happier about this Calienus character's jibe. The Sergeant chose that moment to step into the tent, and it was actually to Pullus and his short companion who was seated on the cot next to him that Calienus turned as he continued, "So I see that you, or at least some of you were catching on that there seems to be a problem with the numbers in this tent." None of them, Pullus included, seemed to know the proper manner in which to address Calienus, so they all simply nodded, but the Sergeant didn't make a comment about that, saying instead, "Well, you'll be happy to know that you're correct in your assumption, so there may be some hope for some of you yet."

Then, to Didius' mortal embarrassment, Calienus turned to face Didius, standing just inside the tent now because Vellusius had ducked into the tent first, giving Didius his first glance at the man's face. He wasn't as tall as Didius, nor as muscled, although he was well-built, and he had somewhat unusual-looking eyes that, he would learn later, were almost grey in color.

"It looks like you're the odd man out, *neh*?" Copying the behavior of the others, instead of replying verbally, Didius nodded, which elicited a laugh from Calienus, yet another stab to his pride. Smiling, Calienus said, "Maybe you're just slow to make friends. Or," the smile vanished as if it had never been there, pinning Didius with a stare that, for reasons he couldn't understand, triggered a fluttering of fear in him, "it means you're someone I have to keep an eye on. Either way, you're out of luck, *neh*?" Without waiting for an answer, Calienus turned away from Didius to address the others. "The reason for the lack of cots is because there's no room for them, because this tent," he pointed at one wall, "was made before the *dilectus*, and our new *Praetor* and Legate Julius Caesar ordered that the 10th be returned to the standard one-hundred-man Centuries that were used before Gaius Marius reformed the Legions and made it possible for bastards like us from the Head Count to die for Rome." This caused a few chuckles, but Calienus ignored the nervous quality. "What that means is that two men will be forced to store their gear in the corner, and sleep on their *sagum*, that cloak that you were given that you stuffed into your packs." Didius was opening his mouth to argue how unjust this was to him, since Vellusius had gotten the last cot, when Calienus said, "And you'll all take a turn sleeping on the ground, so nobody can complain about how unfair it is."

With that, Calienus directed those who had a cot to stow their equipment underneath, while Didius was forced to drop his in the back of the tent in one corner. Suddenly, without any warning, a shrill blast from outside the tent made the occupants jump, but while it was a sound that neither Didius, nor most of the others, had ever heard judging from their reaction, the giant Pullus and his comrade Domitius instantly reached under their cot to grab their helmets, snatch up their shields where they were placed between the cot and wall of the tent, along with the wooden swords, and dashed outside. This prompted a frenzied reaction as the others followed the pair's lead, while Calienus sat on his cot, observing with what, to Didius, looked like amusement. Scribonius was the third man, and despite being at the far end of the tent, Didius was determined not to be the last man out, and once he had everything, he didn't hesitate, shoving the weakling Artorius out of the way, sending him sprawling back onto his cot, following the two brothers out to stand next to Scribonius. Not surprisingly, Artorius was last, but for some reason, Crastinus, who still had what Didius now saw was a bone whistle clenched in his teeth, didn't seem to notice.

Instead, he dropped the whistle from his teeth, but he was looking at Pullus when he asked, "Who told you to come out with helmets, shields, and *rudis*?"

All eyes turned to the big Roman, who Didius was pleased to see didn't look happy to be called on, although he answered immediately, "My brother-in-law was in the Legions, Pilus Prior, and I asked him a lot of questions about what to do."

Crastinus pursed his lips, and while he didn't say as much, he was impressed by this giant youngster's initiative. Instead of saying so, he walked over and grabbed the *rudis* from Pullus' hand then stepped back so that he could be seen by the others.

"Since we don't have sheaths for your *rudis*, when you carry them, you need to carry them like this." He demonstrated by holding it vertically, along the right arm with the point up. Then, he had Pullus hand him the shield. "When we march with our shields in our hands, but we're not expecting contact, we hold it out like this." He pivoted his arm at the elbow so that the shield was not in danger of striking the left leg as they marched.

Handing them back, he said, "But you won't need those now. We're going back to the forum to work on your marching."

"Stupid bastard," Didius muttered this under his breath, but loudly enough for Scribonius to hear. "He thought he was clever, and he made us look foolish!"

"I wouldn't say that," was all Scribonius said.

Once they were back outside, Crastinus barked out the order to step off, and they marched back to the forum to continue what Didius was realizing would be a very long, very trying day.

If a *Tiro* like Didius was being tested, Artorius was certain that this was the worst day of his life, even counting his travails in getting to Scallabis. When they returned to the forum, the Pilus Prior had them watch other groups of men for a bit, all of them larger in number than just their section, including a couple of full Centuries, but most of them were being commanded not by a Centurion, but by men with a white stripe sewn on their shoulder to signify that they were the Optios, the second in command of the Roman Legion Century. It was easy to see that these men were farther ahead in training, bearing little resemblance to the sight of Artorius and his new comrades on their first day.

Finally, Crastinus said, "You can see that you'll be spending a great deal of your time just learning how to march in the proper manner, and obey the commands given you while you march. And, know this, you *cunni*, my Century and Cohort will be the tightest, best drilled Cohort in the Legion. Or you'll all die trying." He laughed at his joke, though not surprisingly, neither Artorius nor his comrades saw much humor, mainly because by this point, they had no idea if he was jesting. Finally, he said, "All right, that's enough watching. Now we go to work."

Thus began what would turn out to be two full watches of marching, back and forth along the large open area of the forum, with Crastinus resuming his teaching them how to execute a right turn, then a left turn, and how to stop instantly on command. In the process, almost all of them earned blows from Crastinus with what Artorius and the others now knew was the *vitus*, which was carried by both Centurions and Optios, although only Centurions carried it with them everywhere they went, even out of camp, as a symbol of their authority when out of full uniform. One small blessing was that, with his first lesson still making his ears ring, Artorius actually escaped punishment, the only member of the section to do so, each of them, even the huge *Tiro* Pullus, who terrified Artorius, feeling the sting of Crastinus' wrath in the form of a slashing blow from his *vitus*, all of them aimed at the thighs or upper back, whereupon the stricken *Tiro* would limp along for a few paces before recovering. Despite the fact that Artorius escaped punishment, executing every order Crastinus gave well enough to escape his censure, just the act of marching back and forth took a toll on him, particularly now that he was wearing the *hamata*, and his only consolation was the sight of his new comrades, their faces dripping sweat and panting from what was, in essence, nothing more than walking back and forth. Although Crastinus was far from satisfied, he finally marched the section back to the tent, where Calienus was waiting, leaving the exhausted *Tiros* in his care without so much as a backward glance.

"It's almost time for the evening meal," Calienus informed them, "so I might as well show you a trick that veterans use." Sitting down on his cot, he explained, "You need to stow your gear under your cot in the same spot." He began to demonstrate as he continued, "Let's say it's the middle of the night, and you're sound asleep, thinking of the women you're missing back home." The *Tiros* reacted in the manner of all young men, chuckling as they elbowed each other and muttered something, usually a name, which always amused Calienus, who was certain that at least half of this section hadn't done anything more than squeeze a tit. "Then, out of nowhere, the horns are blasting and men are shouting because an attack on the walls has started. It's pitch black and you have to fall to your defensive positions, which I'll show you where ours are on the wall on the way to draw our meal." He had pulled out his *hamata* as he was talking, pausing to lift it up and over his head then dropped it down on his shoulders. "Anyway, everyone's screaming and shouting, there's a horrible racket from the barbarian horde outside the wall, and it's utter chaos and confusion." He was strapping on his *baltea* and harness as he said this, then reached under the cot for his helmet. "So you've got just a moment to get your gear and stand to on the wall, or there will be Hades to pay, or worse." Tying the leather thongs that secured the helmet, as he leaned over and grabbed his shield, a wooden one already painted, from its spot against the wall of the tent, he finished, "What if the breach to the wall happens in your area because you couldn't get armed and ready in the proper amount of time?"

By the time he was finished, Calienus had transformed from a man wearing nothing but a tunic to a fully armed and ready Legionary of Rome, and Artorius was deeply impressed; a surreptitious glance at the others told him that almost all of the others were of a like mind, with the exception of the largest *Tiro* and his companion who stood next to Artorius in the rank. They were looking at each other, both of them with what he thought was a knowing smile, and he wondered why. He wouldn't dream of asking himself, but he saw the one named Didius glaring at the pair, and he assumed that Didius might demand to know why they looked like cats who had gotten into the cream, perhaps during the meal. Calienus doffed his armor and helmet, instructing the others to take off their armor and harness, then rearrange their gear under their cots to match his, which Artorius did; at least he thought he did, but he felt a hand on his shoulder. Turning, he was surprised to see Scribonius standing there with a smile on his face.

Talking just loudly enough to be heard over the other muttered conversations as their comrades were busying themselves, Scribonius asked, "Quintus, do you mind if I make a suggestion? Remember," he added, "we're close comrades now and we have to watch out for each other, eh?"

In fact, Artorius had completely forgotten this, despite it having occurred a bit more than two watches earlier, but he didn't say anything, just nodding for Scribonius to continue.

Scribonius crouched down in the narrow space between the cots, pointing to Artorius' as he asked, "See how your helmet, *baltea* and *hamata* is on the same side as mine?" Artorius nodded again, although he didn't understand why it mattered. In a mark of the patience for which Scribonius would become known for among his new comrades, he explained, "That means that you and I would be rolling out of our cot on the same side, and there's barely enough room for one of us."

To Artorius' credit, the instant the words were out of Scribonius' mouth, he saw the problem, and he felt his face grow hot.

"I apologize, Scribonius," he mumbled. "I should have thought of that."

"Why?" Scribonius laughed. "It's not like you've done this before."

It was not the words as much as the manner in which Scribonius said it that Artorius would remember, because it sounded to his ears as if Scribonius actually *had* done this before, which made him intensely curious, but he was far too shy to ask about it.

Calienus gave a final inspection, then informed them they were returning to the *Quaestorium* to draw their evening meal, having them retrieve their bowls, small flask, and cups from under their cots before marching them there for more practice. As they did so, he explained to them, "When we're on campaign, each section is responsible for its own meals, and we're going to be issued a grindstone. Which," he was walking alongside the large Roman, and it was to him he said with a grin, "you're going to be carrying for us." Since Artorius was at the end of the marching line, he didn't hear if the giant said anything, but if he did, Calienus ignored it. "We also are issued with the wheat, lentils, chickpeas and salted pork, usually for at least three days, although sometimes it's for longer, but the mule that carries our tent will be carrying that."

By then, they were at the *Quaestorium* again, except this time, Calienus led them to the opposite side of the huge tent, where there was already a line of men, all of them holding their bowls, and Artorius followed his comrades as, once again, they sidestepped along a long table, where they were served by what Artorius would learn were the slaves that were as integral a part of a Roman Legion as the men themselves. The first slave held a ladle that he had dipped in the largest pot Artorius had ever seen, dumping the contents into his bowl, and despite his exhaustion and nervousness, Artorius' mouth filled with saliva at the aroma of stewed chickpeas and lentils. He was then handed a round, flat loaf of bread, one of the largest he had ever seen, and copying the others, he placed it on top of his bowl. Moving down the line, he again copied what he saw the others do, holding out the smaller of the two flasks that they had been issued, which a slave filled with olive oil, which he placed atop the loaf then automatically held out his cup to another slave holding a large amphora, then exited the tent where Calienus and the others were waiting. Once they marched back, Artorius was surprised to see that there was now a fire, on the same blackened spot that he had noticed that was several feet in front of each tent, and he wondered how that happened. Later, he would learn that every section, all ten of them, had a slave whose duties included attending to the section mule, setting up the tent as the men worked on building the camp ditch and walls, and lighting the fire that would be used to cook the meals, whether it was from wood or charcoal, a supply of which the Legion carried in one of the wagons of the baggage train. Many of these slaves would also work as stretcher bearers, and some of them were also trained as *medici*, bandaging and stitching up wounds that were minor enough that the skills of one of the camp physicians weren't needed.

Calienus dropped to the ground, and without being told, the others arranged themselves, not as they were in formation, but with their close comrade next to them. At least, that was what the giant and his comrade did, dropping onto the ground on the opposite side of the fire from Calienus, which the brothers immediately copied, and Artorius felt a tug on his tunic, turning to find that Scribonius was settling down, and he sat down next to him.

"We get bacon every other day," Calienus said once the others were settled, "but today's not the day. And you're lucky we're in camp and only training, or it would be straight water, no wine. And," Calienus cautioned, "if I were you boys, I'd save a bit of the bread and oil for the morning because we only get one meal a day." This caused a reaction, most notably the largest Roman, who let out a gasp of dismay, but Calienus assured him, "Once we begin marching, our rations will increase, but while all we're doing right now is drill and weapons training, the Legate doesn't want us getting fat and lazy." Artorius' first thought was perilously close to panic as he thought, We're going to be working harder than *this*? The thought almost made him cry, but then Calienus said, "All right, this is where I'm supposed to ask each of you your names, where you're from, and all that sort of thing." Nobody was surprised when Calienus looked directly at the giant, and Artorius was somewhat happy to see that the *Tiro* had his mouth full, which he hurriedly gulped down then began coughing, which caused the others to laugh.

Clearly embarrassed, he still spoke with a deep voice that seemed to be a perfect match to his size and musculature to Artorius, "My name is Titus Pomponius Pullus. I'm from Astigi." He shrugged as if that were all to be said.

Calienus asked him, "And what does your father do, Pullus?"

"He's a farmer," Pullus answered, but while his father's occupation wasn't surprising, there was something in the way Pullus said it that some of the others, including Calienus, noticed, but rather than press him more about his father, Calienus asked, "How old are you?"

"Seventeen," Pullus answered immediately; it was something he had been rehearsing ever since he had essentially forced his father, who loathed Titus with a passion, blaming his son and his large size for killing his mother in childbirth and which enmity Titus returned in full measure, to lie about his age to the *Conquisitor* in Scallabis, adding a year to his sixteen years so that he could join with his best friend.

Calienus gave no indication that he suspected Pullus was lying, although he did remark, "By the gods, does that mean you're going to get bigger?"

The others laughed, but Pullus didn't seem offended, and in fact replied ruefully, "If I do, I hope it's not my feet. I'm already going to have to have a pair made as it is." He pointed down to his feet, and for the first time, Artorius saw the ludicrous sight of Pullus' toes sticking out, which made Calienus roar with laughter, and he was immediately joined by the others, although Pullus was last, initially scowling at his new comrades before succumbing to the humor of the sight.

Wiping his eyes, Calienus turned to the short *Tiro* sitting next to Pullus, who announced, "My name is Vibius Domitius, and I'm from Astigi too, but my father's a tanner in town. I'm seventeen as well, and," he gave Pullus a sharp jab of his elbow, "I've been friends with this oaf since we were ten."

Now that they all knew what was expected, the others murmured a greeting to their new comrade, while without being prompted, Scribonius, who was sitting next to Domitius, said, "My name is Sextus Scribonius. I'm from Corduba, and I'm twenty-two."

He stopped, and was turning to Artorius, who was to his right and next, but Calienus said, "And what does your father do, Scribonius?"

Scribonius didn't hesitate, yet there was something awkward in the way he said, "He's a merchant. Although," he added quickly, "I honestly have never really known exactly what type of business he's involved in."

"Ah, he's a rich boy."

This was muttered just loudly enough to be heard, but when Artorius looked at the others, everyone seemed occupied with their meal, but Artorius was almost certain it had been that Didius fellow who said this. If Calienus heard, he ignored it, as did Scribonius, and he seemed to accept the *Tiro*'s vague explanation, turning to look at Artorius.

"I-I'm Quintus Artorius," he stammered, suddenly uncomfortable with everyone's eyes on him. "I'm eighteen, and I'm from Italica. My father is a blacksmith there." It was all he intended to say, but before he could catch himself, he blurted out, "He wanted me to be a smith like him, but I wanted something else, but he said I couldn't do that, I had to be a smith! So," he finished bitterly, "I told him I was going to join the Legion, but he didn't think I would."

By the time he was through, Artorius was staring down at his partially empty bowl in his lap, so he didn't see the looks exchanged by his comrades, and he would never know that behind his back, the wagering was about to start on how long he would last of the four months of training.

Calienus regarded Artorius thoughtfully for a span of a couple heartbeats, then turned to the next *Tiro*, and his tone was jovial as he said, "Does just one of you want to talk for the both of you since you're twins?"

"Oh, we're not twins," the youth next to Artorius said, then with a laugh, he added, "but everyone thinks we are. I'm Marcus Mallius, and this is my brother Quintus. I'm nineteen and he's eighteen, and my father has a farm outside Illurco. In fact," there was no mistaking the pride in his voice as he pointed to the small flask that Calienus had set on the ground next to him, from which he and the others drizzled the olive oil onto their bread, "that olive oil is probably from our farm."

"How could you know that?" Didius scoffed, but while Marcus didn't seem offended, his brother Quintus, who had remained silent, gave Didius a glare that sent a clear message, and he was the one who answered, "Because Marcus and I helped our father deliver it yesterday, and we decided to stay here and join the Legion."

Artorius was quietly amused that this seemed to put Didius in his place, and he was far from alone in that view.

It was the turn of the *Tiro* to Didius' left to speak up, and he nervously cleared his throat before saying, "My name is Publius Vellusius. I'm eighteen, and my father is a farmer too. His farm is outside Myrtilis." He paused, then added with a shrug, "I'm the oldest, but I don't want to be a farmer."

"Neither did we," Quintus Mallius agreed fervently, which caused the others to chuckle.

Then it was Didius' turn, and the others would have been surprised to know that he was almost as nervous as Artorius had been, but it was because he knew himself just well enough to know that he might not be able to keep himself from boasting, although he started out well enough. "My name is Spurius Didius, I'm from Gades, and I'm twenty years old. My father," he said with pride, "runs half of Gades. He was in the Legions too!" Before he could stop himself, he was saying, "He served under Sura during the campaign against Mithridates, and he was awarded the Civic Crown, along with a set of *phalarae*!" His father had never mentioned such a thing, but Didius was certain that these fools wouldn't have any idea he was lying. He could have stopped then, but he added, "My grandfather was one of Marius' Mules, and he was even more decorated than my father! The Didius name is well known in the Legions!"

He stopped talking then, offering each of his new comrades a stare that was a clear challenge, but when it was his turn, Artorius immediately dropped his eyes to his bowl. Out of the corner of his eye, however, he surreptitiously watched Pullus, noticing that while he was munching his bread in a seemingly placid manner, he was returning Didius' stare without flinching.

Maybe this was why Calienus decided to speak up, saying blandly, "I've never heard of either of them."

The others immediately erupted in laughter, and while this enraged Didius, he also knew it would be the height of foolishness to try and challenge this Calienus. Besides, he consoled himself, there will be a lot of time to make him sorry that he ever mocked Spurius Didius! If he had known that Calienus knew exactly what was running through Didius' mind, having seen more men like Didius than he could count in his years under the standard, it might have given Didius pause.

Aloud, the Sergeant said, "You already know my name and that I come from Pompey's 1st Legion, but what I didn't tell you is that I also served in this last campaign against Mithridates, along with our campaign against the pirates. I've been in thirty engagements, and I've been wounded four times. And," he grinned, "I'm an *Immune* for the armorers. Does anyone know what that means?"

Both Pullus and Domitius raised their hands, but Calienus pointed to Domitius, who answered immediately, "It means you get paid extra for having a skill."

Calienus waited for a heartbeat, but when it was clear Domitius was through, he said, "You left out the most important part." His face split into a grin as he informed them, "It means that I'm excused from all the *cac* details, like unloading wagons or repairing roads. Or," he finished with a laugh, "actually dealing with *cac* on latrine detail, which means that while you bastards are sweating your balls off, I'll be sitting on my ass working on someone's armor."

As Calienus intended, this raised a chorus of groans and muttered curses, and it was the new men's introduction to the rough and cruelty-tinged humor of the Legions. It had gotten dark by the time they were through, and after visiting the latrines, the new *Tirones* of the Tenth Section, First Century, Second Cohort of the 10th Legion returned to their tent, and unanimously collapsed, all but one of them onto their cot, while Didius was forced to wedge himself on the ground between his and Vellusius' gear, who Calienus confirmed would get the spare cot for this night. Didius correctly assumed this was something of a punishment, but he was far too exhausted to care, and he was immediately snoring like his new comrades, a group of young men of which he would be a part for the next sixteen years.

Contrary to what the town watchman and Primus Pilus Favonius thought, Marcus Atilius, who was the missing ninth man, didn't desert. What he *did* do was drink so heavily that, for yet another time, he woke up in a puddle of his own vomit, except this time, it was not in his apartment in Nova Carthago, or even one of the inns of Scallabis. In fact, it took him a moment to determine that he was in a shed of some sort, although it was the smell and not the low-pitched grunting that informed him that his fellow occupants were pigs. Not surprisingly, the stench triggered another round of retching, but now there was nothing coming up, and if he had been in a better frame of mind, he might have thought it amusing how he was on all fours and sounding a great deal like the other inhabitants as he went through the dry heaves.

Finally, the spasms subsided enough for him to half-gasp, "Pluto's cock, how did I end up here?"

It took him two tries before he came to his feet, and he had to grab for one of the support beams to steady himself. The fact that it was dark inside the shed he took as a good sign, because while he couldn't remember exactly what it was, he did recall there was something important he was supposed to attend to at dawn. It happened gradually, as his wine-soaked brain struggled to shake off the last tendrils of the fog that, for as long as he could remember, Atilius loved, but finally he realized that, while it was dim, it wasn't completely dark, and the reason it wasn't was because of the rays of light that came streaming through the cracks in the boards of the shed.

He heard someone gasp, but it was his voice in his ears as

he realized, "I was supposed to be at the camp! At dawn!"

For the span of a couple dozen heartbeats, Atilius stood there, trying to think of what to do. There was a voice in the back of his mind that told him that he should run, and run now. Yes, he had had every intention of enlisting in the Legion, but like an Atilius, he had fucked that up, and while he couldn't recall exactly what the punishment for men like him was, he did remember the part about the scourge. Atilius had actually seen a man flogged with the scourge, back when they had lived in Corduba, and the memory of it made him shudder. You could see the man's spine and ribs gleaming a dull white through the torn meat of his back, and while men said that it was better than being executed, he wasn't so certain about that. Regardless, even as this voice was telling him to run, he still stood there, mainly to try and clear his head so that he could think things through. More than anything, it was the stench of the pigs that got him moving outside the shed, but he opened the door a crack to peer out, thinking that, even drunk, he wouldn't have sought refuge in a pig sty unless he had to get out of sight immediately, but he couldn't think of anything from the night before that would warrant it, although the fact that the reason he couldn't think of anything was due to his inability to recall a single moment wasn't unusual either. It was when he turned his head to locate the way out that he learned something else, when a sharp, stabbing pain in the back of his head made him gasp, and he automatically reached up, giving a cry of pain as his fingers touched a large, sticky lump on the back of his head. Obviously, he had been hit, but again, he had no idea how, when, or why it had happened, and he paused a moment to let the pain subside before he began moving. Stepping outside, the relatively fresh air helped clear his head, but when he glanced up at the sky, his heart sank; it was well past dawn, not yet midday, but about halfway in between. He glanced down at himself, and immediately knew that, before he did anything else, he had to get cleaned up because, no matter what, smelling and looking as he did was an invitation for more trouble even before he got to the camp. Automatically, his hand dropped to his waist, feeling for his coin purse, yet despite being almost certain that it would be empty, he experienced a rush of happiness at the feeling of two coins, along with the token he'd been given the day before. I'll get a bath, he thought, and as I do, I'll figure out what to do.

"*Oy!* You! Yes, you! I see you, you bastard!"

It was through long practice that Marcus Atilius didn't waste precious time looking over his shoulder to see who was yelling, or if he was even the target; he just broke into a run, heading for the nearest corner, ignoring the other pedestrians who, hearing the shouting, turned to see what was happening. Getting to the first corner was crucial, because once you turned it, you had options, and Atilius needed them, although he still had no idea why he was being chased. As he darted around the corner, he saw that this street was crowded with people; normally, this would have been a perfect way to escape since he was experienced in weaving his way through a crowd, but he also was now sober enough to realize that just the stench was going to attract attention, giving his pursuer a way to track his progress by the shouts and curses that would inevitably come. Hearing the slapping sound of leather soles against the paving stones, the signal that his slender advantage was rapidly diminishing, he began moving, resigning himself to a longer chase. This was when, just ahead to his left, a door opened then a woman stepped out into the street, and Atilius didn't hesitate, reaching the woman before she pulled the door closed, throwing himself in between the woman, who screamed in surprise and terror at her malodorous attacker, but Atilius only came in contact with her arm, which she had extended to pull the door shut. He fell through the doorway, landing heavily on the floor, but he had the presence of mind to roll over, seeing the woman framed by the doorway, her mouth open in shock before he kicked the door shut, hearing the latch engage. It wasn't much, but he was already scrambling to his feet as he searched wildly for something, either another escape or a place to hide, and this was the moment that Atilius would later come to believe was one of the few times the gods smiled on him, because what he saw was that this door was an entrance into an open courtyard known as the atrium, and all Roman villas were essentially of the same design, the only difference being the number of rooms and stories.

This building was two stories, and as was the custom, the atrium was open to the sky, but it was the knowledge that, on the other side of the atrium, through perhaps just one room, there would be another exit that mattered. He didn't hesitate, dashing across the atrium, in between the small trees and hurdling the shrubbery, while outside the building and muffled by the closed door, he could hear a male and female voice, sounding like they were arguing, which hopefully would buy him a few more heartbeats of time. Reaching the other side, he had to slide to a stop, looking both ways for a doorway, seeing that it was farther down the hallway that bound this side of the atrium, and he dashed to it, but once more he saw it open just before he reached it. This time, it was a man, one wearing a bronze placard, who had clearly been drawn by the sounds of an intruder, but when Atilius pushed him out of the way, he didn't try to resist, nor did he raise any kind of alarm. In the back of his mind, Atilius remembered that some wealthy Romans liked their slaves, particularly the important ones, to be mute, yet it was just a fleeting thought because, once he entered this room, which was clearly the room for the woman of the house with a distaff lying in a chair, he saw his salvation, the open window on the other side of the room. He was through it and out of the house within a heartbeat, even managing to land on his feet in what was a narrow alley, which ended with a wall to his left, while to the right, it opened out onto another street.

This time, he approached more cautiously, pausing at the corner to take a peek around each corner, immediately seeing that this was a different street than the one he had turned onto. Nevertheless, he took his time, doing as much listening as watching, but when he didn't hear any shouting from the direction from which he had come, he turned onto the street, matching the pace of the other pedestrians, stopping only long enough at a butcher shop to ask directions to the nearest bath, ignoring the jibe from the butcher about whether he was a man or whether he should be hanging from a hook in his shop. Using his last two coins, he paid the slave to wash his tunic while he went into the *tepidarium*, thankful that because of the time of day, there were no other bathers, knowing that they would have strongly resisted sharing the large tub of warm water with someone covered in pig *cac*.

As he soaked, he tried to think of what had taken place the night before, but while he thought he could remember bits and pieces, there was no memory of a quarrel or any other kind of conflict that would have been the impetus for him to hide himself in a pig sty, nor for this bloody lump on the back of his head which, after probing it tenderly as he sat in the tub, he was relieved to feel that while there was a gash and a bump, it had already scabbed over and he couldn't feel any obvious fracture. Honestly, the headache he was suffering could just as easily have come from his hangover. This *might* explain why someone would spend whatever remained of the night and part of the next day searching for him, but for the moment, it remained a mystery. He did remember dicing, and although he had played it honestly, he also remembered he had won a few *sesterces*, then left that *taverna* near the southern gate with the vague idea of finding a place to sleep. It wasn't until he had emerged from the *tepidarium* to spend a few moments in the *caldarium*, the steam rising from the water that was heated to a much higher temperature to create a steam-filled room that he recalled being drawn by the sounds of revelry at another *taverna* that delayed his search for a place to sleep. Had there been a girl? He thought there had been, remembering an oval face framed by straight black hair, and with a nice set of tits. She had been friendly, he remembered, and had even sat in his lap as he gulped down more wine, and when his free hand had gone up to squeeze one of her breasts, she hadn't complained; not much at least, he remembered. It was his plunge into the *frigidarium*, the tub of water that was kept as cold as possible, that did more to sober him up than anything to that point, and with it came the rest of the story, or as much as he would ever remember.

Climbing out of the tub, shivering slightly and his skin pimpled from the cold, he moved into the final room, where a slave was waiting with a flask of olive oil that, as Atilius stood naked, his arms extended, the slave rubbed into his skin. She had gotten up, he remembered as he stood there, arms out from his side, and he was certain that when she walked towards the back of the *taverna*, to a place beyond the bar where the storeroom holding the amphorae of wine and other supplies was located in such establishments, she had looked over her shoulder with an expression that he interpreted as an invitation, so naturally, he had gotten up and followed her. He was very drunk by that point, so he didn't notice the glare of the man standing behind the counter as he staggered past. The girl had pushed through a curtained doorway, and when Atilius shoved the material aside, he remembered pausing because this room was even more dimly lit than the main room, but after a moment, he made her out, at the far side of the room, the walls of which were lined with stacks of amphorae and boxes. Her back was to him, and he saw that she was busy doing something, her hands moving, yet in that moment, he was convinced that this was just a pretense, an excuse to make it seem that she was working when, in fact, she was waiting for him.

"I'm finished, *Dominus*."

Atilius actually started a bit, surprised by the slave's pronouncement, but a glance down at his clean skin that was slightly glistening from the residue of the oil informed him that he was indeed now finished.

"What about my tunic?" he asked the slave, who left the room, assuring Atilius he would find out.

Now that he was clean, Atilius considered what to do, although he didn't see he had any option other than to go to the camp. Better to be late than to never show up, he thought to himself. Otherwise, I'll spend the rest of my life looking over my shoulder, wondering when Fortuna will decide to piss on me, and given how often the goddess squatted over anyone named Atilius, it wasn't a matter of if but when it happened.

The slave returned, holding Atilius' tunic, but he apologized, "It's not dry yet, Master. If you wish to wait…"

"No," Atilius said shortly. "I'll wear it now."

It would dry out soon enough; besides, it was time to face his fate, and he donned the threadbare garment that, honestly, was more patch than original fabric at this point, but it least it no longer stank of pig *cac*. Now, completely destitute, Atilius left the bath, but he had the presence of mind to pause to check the area, although he realized that he hadn't actually gotten a good look at his pursuer. It was this thought that dislodged another fragment, because as soon as this thought crossed his mind, an image of a man's face leapt into his mind, but it was less the face than how it was contorted in rage. And, he recalled, it belonged to a man older than he was, with a beard…and the girl was there, standing just behind this man. It was as he reached the northern gate that it occurred to him; had that been the girl's father? Was that why he had been so enraged? Although Atilius was now certain this was the case, and it would at least explain the blow to his head, he couldn't understand why the man had been so upset; he hadn't actually *done* anything with, or to, the girl…had he? This was a troubling thought, mainly because it wasn't the first or second time that Marcus Atilius had at least been accused of attempting to force himself on a woman, but those had also been because of misunderstandings. Well, he thought as he approached the camp, if that was her father, and he's still looking for me, he won't be coming here. The gates of the camp were open, but he saw that the two wooden towers on either side of the gate were occupied by two men apiece, and he could tell they were watching him approach. He was too hungover to be nervous, and when he reached the gateway, another Roman stepped into view, this man also in uniform but with a white stripe sewn onto one shoulder.

"State your business, Citizen!" the soldier said. "Civilians aren't allowed into the camp unless they have a reason."

This reminded Atilius, and he reached into his coin purse, and withdrew the token, holding it out for the other man to examine. For some reason, the soldier frowned at him as if he'd done something wrong, but he quickly learned why, and in the process received an even deeper shock.

"You were supposed to be here yesterday, *Probatio*!" the soldier snapped, although he was already moving, his hand held out. "You're officially a deserter!"

At first, Atilius could only stand there, dumbfounded, then he finally repeated, "Yesterday? What do you mean yesterday?"

"The last *Tiros* arrived yesterday!" The soldier snapped, "You should have been here at dawn!"

He had been lying in that pig sty for more than a full day? His mind whirled with the implications, but he couldn't fully comprehend the idea that he was now more than just a watch or two late.

"I-I-I had too much wine," Atilius stammered, thinking that, since he had heard men in the Legions drank and debauched heavily that this might strike a chord with the Legionary; he learned differently

"That's no excuse!" the soldier snapped, but he turned and beckoned Atilius. "But it will be up to your Primus Pilus to decide your fate."

For an instant, Atilius thought about turning and dashing away, but when he had glanced up at the men in the tower, he saw they had javelins, which meant there was a chance that he would be cut down. His momentary hesitation meant that he had to break into a trot to catch up, his mind reeling with the implications; he had been passed out for an entire *day*?

The soldier glanced over at him, and his tone, while still hard, was a fraction softer as he allowed, "But you did show up, and that might count for something."

Atilius noticed several groups of men, wearing tunics that were a bright red and not faded like the one worn by his escort, and there was a smaller group as another soldier, his helmet sporting a feather crest that ran ear to ear and not the horsetail plume of his escort, walking alongside the group, bellowing at them and, in the span of time Atilius watched, used the long stick he was carrying to bash two of the men for some reason. Being completely ignorant of life in the Legions, Marcus Atilius had no idea that he was looking at the men with whom he would be sharing a tent.

"Wait here," the soldier ordered once they reached the largest tent in the center of the camp, and he disappeared inside.

Unlike his future comrades, Atilius didn't have to wait long before the man emerged from the tent, followed closely by another, and while he was wearing the same kind of crest as the Roman who was still bellowing at the small group of men, this man's crest was white.

"Here he is, Primus Pilus," his escort said, nodding with his head at Atilius as if he was not even worth the effort to point at, and there was certainly nothing comforting about either his words or his tone as he told this Primus Pilus, whatever that was, "He said he had too much to drink and was passed out all day yesterday."

The other man didn't respond immediately, instead just regarded Atilius, who eyed him warily, not sure what he was supposed to do, but finally the Primus Pilus spoke, his voice reminding Atilius of a bucket of gravel being shaken. "Leave him with me, Optio."

Atilius' escort stiffened into what, to Atilius, was a bit of a silly posture, then the Optio brought his right fist to his chest before thrusting his arm out as he barked out crisply, "I understand and will obey, Primus Pilus."

There was something in the way in which the man pivoted about to face in the opposite direction that hinted to Atilius that he might have to learn how to do that himself, and he regretted that he hadn't paid attention, so he turned his head to watch the Optio stride away, which meant he was completely unprepared for the end of the stick the Primus Pilus was holding to be rammed into the pit of his stomach, nor was he aware that the day before, a much larger and stronger *Tirone* had been in an almost identical position, curled up and gasping for breath, along with several of his future comrades. However, the Primus Pilus wasn't satisfied, and he struck Atilius three more times; that he took care to strike the prone man on the meaty part of his thighs was something that Atilius would only learn to appreciate later.

"All right, get on your feet, you piece of *cac*," he growled, but when Atilius made no move other than to peek through his arms wrapped around his head, he raised the stick again. This served its purpose, and Atilius scrambled to his feet, although he was still gasping for breath and clutching his stomach, which earned him a rap on the knuckles, as the Primus Pilus snarled, "Get your hands down by your sides! From now on, you will be in this position unless you're specifically given permission to move, do you understand?"

Atilius guessed that a nod would only enrage this already angry man further, so he took a risk that he was guessing correctly when he hurriedly said, "Yes, Primus Pilus!"

This did surprise the other man, who was prepared for the most common mistake new meat made, and he was slightly disappointed that he had been robbed of another chance to impress upon this *cunnus* the harsh new realities of his life.

Instead, he said only, "Now, follow me inside."

He did so, then immediately went through the same process of those who had gone before him, completely unaware at the moment that he was the very last man enlisted into the 10th Legion. What he did know was when he was asked to confirm his identity that he did so, and when he was told to make his mark on what he guessed was the same document he had made his mark on before, he did so again. Then some clerk said a bunch of nonsense that he was only dimly aware had to do with his pay, whereupon he made another mark, then turned to see that the Primus Pilus was standing there watching, but the manner in which he was tapping that stick into his other hand made Atilius distinctly nervous.

"Come with me," the Primus Pilus snapped, then strode out of the tent, Atilius trotting to catch up, where he found the Centurion standing there, glaring at him as Atilius stopped in front of him, remembering to keep his arms down by his sides, his hands flat against his legs. The Centurion regarded him for a span of heartbeats, giving Atilius the sense he was trying to decide something, which seemed to be confirmed when the Primus Pilus said, "By regulations, I should have you flogged before your training starts. Why shouldn't I do that, boy?"

At moments like this, the skills he had learned from his parents often proved useful, because without hesitation, he said, "Primus Pilus, while it's true that I got drunk, that's not the reason I wasn't here yesterday."

"Oh?" One gray eyebrow raised, the Primus Pilus' expression softening fractionally. "Explain."

Once again, Atilius proved that he wasn't completely witless, because before he moved, he said, "I'd have to turn around to show you, Primus Pilus."

"Very well, turn around and show me."

He did so, then lied, "I was attacked and robbed, Primus Pilus, night before last. They struck me on the head," he pulled his hair out of the way with one hand, "and took everything but that token. I suppose," he thought this was a nice touch, "they thought it was worthless."

As he expected, the Primus Pilus had taken a step closer to

examine the bump and the gash, and while it was painful, normally, Atilius wouldn't have gasped, but if by doing so it helped his story, he was happy to do it.

"It's a nasty bump," the Primus Pilus said gruffly, "but you won't need stitches. All right, turn back around." Atilius did so, whereupon the Centurion extended his hand, demanding, "Give me your purse." Atilius did so; now that he had turned in the token, as he had said, the purse was empty. Tossing it back, the Primus Pilus said, "While I think there's something rotten about your story, it *could* be true. Besides, you'd just miss more training while you recover, and you're the last man to join the Legion." Atilius couldn't help heaving a sigh of relief, but if the Centurion noticed, he gave no sign, saying instead, "My name is Lucius Favonius. I'm the Primus Pilus of the 10th Legion. You're going to be assigned to the Tenth Section of the First Century of the Second Cohort. Your Centurion is Secundus Pilus Prior Crastinus. Who," he turned and pointed to the Centurion who was marching next to the small group Atilius had noticed, "is right over there with the rest of your section. But before you join them," at this, Favonius turned and began walking, "you're coming with me to the *Quaestorium* to get your issue of gear."

When the thin, high-pitched wailing sound jerked the new *Tiros* of the Tenth Section to wakefulness on their second day, for one of the first times, they were all of a like mind; it was still dark, and they were certain they were too sore to do anything remotely resembling what they had done the day before. Only Calienus was unaffected, and in fact seemed almost obscenely cheerful as he stood and used his foot on one of the brothers who was slow to react, dumping him unceremoniously out of his cot.

"*Salve*, ladies! It's time to start the day!" he said, sitting down on his cot to pull on his *caligae*. "You've got a few moments to eat whatever you held over from last night, go to the latrines to piss and *cac*, then the Pilus Prior will be around to collect you for another day of festival games!"

This produced a raggedly unified chorus of groans from the other eight occupants, but rather than bellow or bluster as

Artorius was certain Crastinus would have responded, this made Calienus laugh.

"Having second thoughts, eh?"

He chuckled, then began consuming the bread he had left over, which prompted the others to follow his lead, although the big *Tiro* Pullus and his comrade Domitius took their food outside.

For Artorius, just the prospect of eating was unappealing because of the nausea he was feeling that stemmed from the realization that he had, in fact, *not* been dreaming, that he was really sitting here in a tent located in a Legion camp. Nevertheless, he forced the food down, knowing that he would need the strength it would provide. More or less in a group, the *Tiros* went to the latrines, although there was a line, and Artorius noticed two things: every man around them was staring at Pullus, who was easily the largest among them, whispering to each other, while Pullus ignored them, or at least seemed to, and it occurred to Artorius, He's probably used to this by now.

He also noticed that, when he was through, the others were waiting for him, since, as would become a habit, the *Tiros* tended to do things together, and by virtue of being the smallest, he was usually the last to be finished. Nothing was ever said, but fairly quickly, Artorius became certain that it was at Pullus' behest that they did so. When they returned to the tent, Calienus informed them that they wouldn't need to don their *hamata*, and Artorius heaved a sigh of relief, although he wasn't the only one. With the instruction to wait in their rank outside the tent, Calienus disappeared, presumably to do his work as an armor *Immunes*, but it was actually one of the Mallius brothers who voiced the suspicion that he was off somewhere loafing.

Crastinus appeared, his mouth pulled down into the same frown he had worn the entire day before, and he growled, "Well, you *cunni*, I was expecting half of you to be gone like the sorry specimens you replaced."

This caused a ripple of murmured surprise, and Artorius was one of them; it had never occurred to him that they were actually replacing men who had joined earlier, nor that it was in the realm of possibility to get up in the night and run away, and this would turn out to be a recurring daydream by Quintus

Artorius for the rest of his time in training. This was all Crastinus said about it, barking the order to *intente*, then marched them back to what Artorius now knew was the camp forum, which was large enough for four Legions to assemble in formation, although it would be cramped. Once more, Crastinus began to drill them, but this time, Artorius didn't escape the *vitus* because, to his horror, it seemed as if he had forgotten half of what he had learned the day before. Perhaps the only saving grace was that it wasn't the difference between his left and his right; otherwise, he had forgotten on which word barked out by the Pilus Prior was the one to move on. Thankfully, he wasn't alone; even Pullus earned a swipe or two, but Domitius didn't, and Artorius began to draw encouragement from Domitius, who stood next to him and was able to whisper hints about what to do next. Even so, it was still a matter of marching up and down, back and forth until, without giving any reason, Crastinus marched them directly to the *Praetorium*, where Calienus was standing with someone they'd never seen before.

"This is Marcus Atilius," Crastinus announced. "He's the tenth member of the section." Pointing at Atilius, who, at least to Artorius, appeared to be almost as old as Calienus, he said, "Come here so I can see where you'll fit in your section rank."

Atilius approached, but his eyes were on Crastinus' *vitus* as he did, something that amused Crastinus, though he gave no sign. Grabbing him by the arm, he moved Atilius down the line, while now Atilius' eyes were on the huge Roman at the end of the line who improbably seemed to be another *Tiro* like him, given the bright red tunic. Finally, Crastinus pointed to a tall, slender *Tiro* who was almost as tall as the giant, and then to the man to his left who, a bit shorter, had a build more like the giant's, with a broad chest and arms that were almost as large as the largest *Tiro*'s.

For some reason, he was glaring at Atilius, but Crastinus said, "Right, once you join the section, this is where you're going to be, got it? Between these two. But," for the first time, Crastinus' face split into a grin, "you're going to be my special project for a bit." Addressing the others, he ordered, "Right, I want you to run around the camp using the *Via Sagularis*." He pointed to the beaten path that ran along the base of the wall that enclosed the camp.

To Atilius' and Crastinus' surprise, none of the *Tiros* moved, but then the tall, lean *Tiro* asked Crastinus, "How many times, Pilus Prior?"

With a surprising speed, Crastinus crossed the two paces separating them, and brought his *vitus* down in a slashing blow that struck the *Tiro* on his upper arm as he snarled, "Until I tell you to stop, you idiot."

This got them moving, with the large Roman leading the way at a trot that, to Atilius, looked very fast, but he soon had other things on his mind.

"All right, you *cunnus*," Crastinus smiled, but it wasn't friendly in the slightest, "the Primus Pilus decided not to stripe you bloody, but he told me that I might need to give you some...*extra* attention. So, let's begin with the position of *intente*."

They hadn't gone more than two hundred paces before Artorius knew he was in serious trouble. Pullus was setting an infernal pace, and the pain in his side was increasing in intensity with every heartbeat, while his mouth was open as wide as he could make it, yet he couldn't get enough air into his lungs. Before they were halfway around the first time, Artorius was weaving, since running in a straight line was impossible because he was seeing double, but he had other aches and pains courtesy of Crastinus' *vitus* that, for the first time in his life, caused him to experience a sense of grim determination that he would endure this, somehow. Domitius unwittingly came to his aid when he gave a quick glance over his shoulder, and Artorius saw that his face was bright red, while his tongue was hanging out of his mouth, which made him feel a bit better knowing that he wasn't the only one in distress. Someone, he didn't know who, managed a gasped shout, although it was nothing more than an inarticulate noise, but Pullus kept running. The next shout, again nothing more than a cry, came from one of the Mallius brothers, but it was followed immediately by Vellusius.

Suddenly, Scribonius managed to get enough air in his lungs to shout, "Pullus! Pullus!" When this had no effect, somehow even more loudly, he bellowed, "*Eho,* Pullus! By the *gods,* man, are you trying to kill us all?"

Because of his height, Artorius could see Pullus turn to look over his shoulder in surprise, instantly slowing down before coming to a stop, whereupon he leaned over to put his hands on his knees. He looks as bad as the rest of us, Artorius thought, so how could he keep running that quickly? Pullus was quickly joined by the others in this posture, although Artorius, one of the Mallius brothers, Vellusius, and Scribonius all immediately began retching.

Finally, Scribonius gasped, "Didn't you hear us shouting for you to slow down? I swear that all of us were begging you to slow your pace, but you just ran along like Mercury himself!"

From what Artorius could see, Pullus was breathing just as hard as the rest of them, but his surprise seemed genuine as he asked, "Really? No, Scribonius, I'm truly sorry. I didn't hear a thing. I just thought I was running at a pace that wouldn't get us in trouble with Pilus Prior Crastinus." Scribonius didn't say anything, but the others weren't as circumspect, each of them offering some choice words at their large comrade, and Artorius was interested to see that Domitius was no less angry, actually poking Pullus in the chest as he chastised him.

Surprisingly to Artorius, instead of arguing or expressing his own anger at the manner in which Domitius was treating him, Pullus held up his hands and protested, "I already told Scribonius I was sorry! I didn't realize I was running so fast."

"Well, clean out your ears, damn you!"

Whether it was the words, or who said them, the atmosphere immediately became charged, Pullus turning to face Didius squarely by moving Domitius aside, and Artorius didn't need to know him well to see that Pullus was angry now.

"If you can't keep up, that's not my problem!"

This got Didius moving, and he took a step towards Pullus, but then Domitius interposed himself between the two, although he had his back to Didius as he looked up at his friend.

"None of us could keep up, Titus, because you forget that you have these great long legs!"

This clearly got through to Pullus, whose shoulders slumped, and he mumbled another apology that at least sounded heartfelt.

Suddenly, from across the forum, they heard Crastinus roaring, "I don't believe I told you *cunni* to stop! The next time I look around, you'd better be running, ladies!"

Scribonius spoke up, saying quickly, "I have an idea. We're going to reverse our order and put Artorius in front."

This was immediately accepted by everyone, except that none of them bothered to ask Artorius his feelings about the subject, and while he did as he was told, he just didn't seem able to set a fast enough pace, which was confirmed when Crastinus bellowed once again that they were loafing and they'd be sorry. They paused once again, but this time, they put Domitius in the front, while Artorius found himself once again at the rear, just behind Pullus. It took every bit of energy he had, but when Crastinus blew his whistle after two more circuits of the camp, he was still with the others, and he felt good about that at least. Atilius now joined the section, then Crastinus resumed drilling them, it quickly becoming apparent that the new addition had taken his lessons to heart, and they managed to finish the rest of the day without any major mistakes. When they returned to their tent, they were informed by Calienus that they would be standing watch for the first of what would be many times, and they would be doing it in pairs of close comrades. Now that their tent was full, it also meant that two of them would have to spend the night on the ground and rotate sharing a cot, but before that happened, Calienus made another announcement once they had returned with their evening meal.

"As soon as we finish eating, I'm taking you boys to the bathhouse, because you stink," he made a show of wrinkling his nose, and Atilius was secretly amused, thinking, If you smelled me this morning, you wouldn't be complaining about them. Naturally, he kept this to himself as Calienus continued, "I'm not going to share a tent with a bunch of animals."

Following their Sergeant, they immediately learned that Calienus' use of the word bathhouse had been a euphemism for a tent where men stripped down, then stood with their arms out as one of the section slaves vigorously rubbed them down with olive oil, in effect performing a massage before using their strigil to scrape the oil away, taking the accumulated grime and sweat with it. As they stood waiting their turn, some of the men who were either in the process or putting their tunics back on, seeing the newly arrived *Tiros,* began calling out a variety of taunts.

"Look, boys! They haven't even worn out the creases in their tunics!"

"Those can't be men of the 10th! They're children!"

While this angered the subjects of the taunts, including Artorius, it was Pullus who began to walk towards the Legionary who had thrown out the taunt about being children, but Calienus reached out and grabbed Pullus' arm.

"Hold there, Pullus. You can't go getting upset when someone runs his mouth at you. Besides," he grinned, "you *are* fresh meat and the boys are just having some fun."

Pullus obeyed readily enough, but it was easy to see that he didn't like it, and it made Artorius wonder what might happen if Pullus truly became enraged. Finally, it was their turn, and to Artorius' deep surprise, once the slave had finished his work, the stiffness and soreness was noticeably reduced. Maybe, he thought, the army knows there's more than just getting clean from this kind of thing. As they returned to their tent, his comrades voiced the same thoughts, but it was Scribonius, his new close comrade, whose comment he remembered.

"It's one of the reasons Rome is impossible to defeat. The barbarians don't have anything like this. They don't have our organization, they don't have our training, and they don't have things like these baths to keep us strong."

Artorius was not alone in making note of Scribonius' words; over his ensuing time under the standard, Titus Pullus would have cause to not only remember their comrade's words, but understand the profound truth behind them.

Chapter Four

Aulus Vinicius was aware of what men who didn't know him thought about him, that he didn't physically resemble what most believed a Legionary would and should look like, but it didn't bother him. It had been like this his entire life, people underestimating his strength, and given his chosen profession, his catlike reflexes and speed of movement. His father, who knew better, had used this to his advantage once Vinicius became a teenager, traveling about Campania, where he was originally from, going to neighboring towns on festival days when there were always a variety of athletic contests, along with wrestling, where he would offer up his son to what the ignorant townspeople thought would be certain defeat. Vinicius didn't mind all that much; his one complaint was that his father didn't share any of the proceeds from what his son had garnered for him. Otherwise, he quite liked seeing the look of surprise on his opponent's face when he was defeated by a pudgy youth with a vacant expression that suggested that he was simple. His decision to enlist in the Legion, originally in the 3rd, had been a pragmatic one formed by his recognition that his father showed no inclination to stop using his son as a source of money, nor any intention of sharing the winnings. Despite appearances, along with Vinicius' physical talents, he also possessed a sharp mind, and he made the case to his father that, since they had to go farther afield as Vinicius' reputation began to grow, their profits would be eaten up by the expenses accrued traveling. He was surprised when his father almost immediately relented, but he quickly learned that his father would only help him enlist on a condition, that Vinicius send half of his pay home to the Vinicius *paterfamilias*. The reason he agreed was also for practical reasons; he had already planned on doing that to help his mother care for his five brothers and sisters, all of them younger than he was, something he didn't mention to his father, knowing that his father needed to feel as if he had won against his son.

Now, twelve years later, Aulus Vinicius was in a new Legion, and like all the other veterans, had agreed to a sixteen-year term, which was four more years than the traditional twelve that had been the term when he enlisted into the 3rd, and when he had transferred to the 1st. However, as he and all the other veterans had quickly learned, Caesar didn't give a rotten fig whether something was a tradition or not, which was just one more thing that made him extremely unusual among his fellow patricians. The members of the upper class would have characterized their attitude as reverence for the memory of their ancestors, those men who brought down Carthage, conquered Greece, Hispania, and a large expanse of the East. From Vinicius' viewpoint, this was just a bunch of superstitious nonsense uttered by old men who were terrified by change of any kind, and it was one reason he was growing to appreciate Caesar's leadership even more. He hadn't been an Optio very long, but such was his reputation that none other than Gaius Crastinus, who was already something of a legend in the Legions despite being a bit under thirty, had approached him personally to persuade him to accept the offer of a promotion to come serve as his Optio in this new Legion. Granted, it was another sixteen years out of his life, but not only did Aulus Vinicius not have anywhere else he would rather have been, somewhere deep inside him, he knew he wasn't going to make old bones. All in all, he was about as content as a man in his position could be, and while his demeanor would never betray it, he was particularly happy today, because Crastinus was bringing the new replacements for their first day of training at the stakes.

Much to the frustration of some members of the Tenth Section, they had learned that the Legions didn't care about their eagerness, which meant they had spent their first weeks learning how to march and obey commands before getting to what they considered the most important part of their training. In that, Vinicius absolutely agreed with them; marching and learning to obey commands immediately had their place, but this was secondary to what he was about to teach them. Now, he stood there watching as Crastinus led the group to where the training stakes were located outside the camp walls. Because of Caesar's order for hundred-man Centuries, instead of twenty large wooden poles buried in the ground, he had ordered that there be fifty, which all of the officers of the 10th immediately appreciated because it rapidly accelerated the training by having two men per stake instead of the more customary four men, and Vinicius had reserved a set of ten on the outer edge, ignoring all the other men from other Cohorts who were practicing their forms. Because the 10th was a new Legion, they were also given priority over the other three Legions, the 7th, 8th, and 9th, with whom they were sharing the camp, although Caesar had them involved in a variety of projects like road repair that kept them afield. Bringing the section to where Vinicius was standing in front of one of the ten stakes, Crastinus introduced his Optio and what his role was, both as second in command and as the weapons instructor, not just for the First Century, but the entire Cohort. While Crastinus talked, Vinicius surveyed the new *Tiros*, who would have been shocked at how much he already knew about each of them because of his friendship with Calienus. Who, as far as Vinicius was concerned, should have at least been a *Tesserarius*, but the Sergeant didn't seem to have much ambition.

"May Fortuna go with you, Vinicius," Crastinus said to his Optio as he handed the *Tiros* over. "You're going to need it with this lot." Addressing the section, he warned, "You'll spend the day with the Optio, but I'll be by to check on you, so don't think I won't know if any of you are slacking off! All this marching and drill is fine, but this is what our real purpose is, to fight and kill for Rome. And die, if that's the will of the gods."

It was the same speech Crastinus had given to all the new *Tiros*, and with a nod to Vinicius, he walked back towards the camp, leaving Vinicius to beckon to the section, pointing to one of the stakes. "All right, the first thing I want you to do is gather round this stake right there."

His choice in taking the *rudis* from the largest *Tiro* wasn't an accident, although nothing in his face betrayed that he was anything other than a new man to the Optio. Neither was his instruction about gathering around one stake random, because with such a large training field, and with several dozen men training already, he knew they would be easily distracted.

"Before I demonstrate the positions, I'm going to show you how we hold our *gladius* in the Second Cohort, because it's different than the traditional method," he began. Holding the *rudis* out in front of him, he turned his wrist so that his fingers were facing the *Tiros*. "As you can see, I prefer tucking my thumb *under* my fingers instead of wrapping my fingers around the handle and leaving the thumb exposed." He scanned the faces as he spoke, and he wasn't surprised to see that *Tirone* Pullus and his close comrade Domitius were actually looking past him with obvious disinterest, but unlike Crastinus, who would have immediately erupted, Vinicius was actually amused, because he knew what was going to be happening before the day was out. Once he did so, he turned to face the stake, dropping into a crouch with his left foot forward, and the *rudis* held at waist level with his arm pulled back as far as it would go, with the wooden blade parallel to the ground. "This is called the first position," he explained. "It's the most basic position used by the Legions of Rome, and it has two advantages." Now he saw that all of them were paying close attention, just as he had anticipated. "The first is that, because we use the *Gladius Hispanensis*, it's short enough that you can hide it behind your shield, and your enemy can't guess where your blade will be coming from. The second," for the first, and one of the only times that these *Tiros* would see, Vinicius smiled, but it was a wolfish one as he continued, "is that when you come up from under your shield in a first position thrust, your point will be aiming right for his cock." The reason Vinicius smiled was because he knew what was coming, as, almost as one man, every *Tiro* involuntarily moved one hand to their groin with expressions of horror, which happened every single time he made this point the first time. The smile disappeared as he said, "Now, watch me perform a first position thrust."

As he expected, all eyes were on him, but despite warning them, as he had learned, the first time Vinicius performed a thrust of any kind, they would react with shock at the speed and raw power, signaled by a sharp crack that was of a different quality than those created by the men around them as they made their own thrusts. It was the gasp of shock that followed that Vinicius always relished, the one sop to his vanity that he allowed himself, though nothing in his demeanor indicated this.

Aloud, he said, "Did you see how I didn't use just my arm, but my lower body?"

"No, Optio," the tall, lean *Tiro* that Calienus had identified as Scribonius, mainly because he stood next to Pullus, spoke for the others in a tone that was close to awe, "I've never seen anyone move that fast before." Addressing the others, he asked, "Have you boys?" As one, they shook their heads, and Scribonius asked, somewhat timidly, "Can you do it again, a little more slowly?"

Vinicius didn't say that he had already planned to do so, simply nodding as he dropped back into the crouch. "Ready?" he asked, and when they nodded, he repeated the motion at what he estimated was about three-quarters speed and with about half the power. As he did so, while he appeared to be focused on the stake, he watched Pullus' expression, and he recognized it. *He's certain that he can do at least as well as I can, and if Calienus is right about him, he might be able to.*

Didius was as absorbed in watching Optio Vinicius as the others, but occasionally, he glanced over at Pullus, who he immediately knew would be his closest rival when it came to sheer power. Like the others, he also instantly detected the stark difference between the sound created by Vinicius' first thrust to the clattering racket created by the other men training around them, and he looked at the Optio with a new respect. *He doesn't look like much, but he's clearly immensely strong, and I've never seen anyone move that fast before.* Once Vinicius had demonstrated the first position thrust several more times, including doing it very slowly, almost as if it were a step-by-step motion instead of one smooth action, Didius was confident that the very first time he struck the stake, Vinicius would take notice...and so would that *cunnus* Pullus. If he'd been asked, Didius couldn't have articulated why he had instantly hated the oaf, but neither did he question that he did, with a deep and abiding passion. Finally, Vinicius had them move in front of their own stake, arraying them in their rank order, which meant that the new man Atilius was to his right instead of Scribonius, putting him farther away from Pullus. For a brief moment, he debated asking the Optio if he could switch places with Scribonius, wanting to be next to Pullus so that he could demonstrate that he was Pullus' match, but he quickly dismissed it.

"Get into your first position," Vinicius ordered, and Didius obeyed along with the others, and the Optio warned, "Do *not* execute your thrust until I give the command." Starting with the weakling Artorius, he examined each *Tiro*'s posture and position, pulling Artorius' arm farther back then kicking one of Artorius' feet backward before he was satisfied. Didius' view was partially blocked, although he saw that Vinicius paused next to Pullus' friend Domitius, but Vinicius only gave a grunt before moving to Vellusius and finding some fault with him. When he got to Didius, Vinicius examined him, starting with his right arm, which he was satisfied with, but when he dropped his gaze to Didius' waist, he frowned.

"You don't have your right hip twisted back enough," he told Didius. As if noticing for the first time, Vinicius commented, "You're almost as muscular as the big one." This made Didius flush with pride, but it evaporated when Vinicius continued, "I bet that you've always been stronger than other men. You've always been able to use that without having to bother knowing what you're doing. That makes you lazy," he said bluntly. "And it can get you dead." He grabbed Didius' *baltea*, using it to twist Didius' hip to the point that he couldn't stop the grunt of discomfort, which earned him a nod from Vinicius. "Like I said, lazy. It should hurt the first few times until you get used to it and your muscles stretch out. If it doesn't, then you're doing it wrong."

Leaving Didius enraged and embarrassed, which was exacerbated by his knowledge it would be foolish for him to show it, he watched as Vinicius stopped at Scribonius, and as he had with Domitius, he simply nodded before going to Pullus. By Dis, Didius thought, he *better* find something wrong with that bastard! What happened next was even better, although it didn't start that way because Vinicius seemed to be satisfied with Pullus, and was turning to walk away when something caught his eye, causing Didius to lean over slightly so he could look past Scribonius to see that Vinicius was looking down at Pullus' *gladius* hand.

He was also close enough to hear Vinicius say, "You're not holding your weapon the way I demonstrated."

"No, Optio," Pullus answered readily enough, but from where Didius stood, it didn't look as if he changed his grip.

"And, why aren't you holding it the way I showed you?"

Now Didius could see that Pullus was a bit flustered, answering, "I...I've had training Optio, from a man who was in the Legions. This is the way he taught me to hold it."

Didius was certain this would earn Pullus a bash of the Optio's *vitus*, so he was shocked when Vinicius actually nodded his head.

"You're right, that's the way the majority of the Legions are taught to hold the *gladius*, but that's not the way *I* teach it." This time, Pullus didn't seem to have an answer, but to Didius' utter delight, he saw that the *Tiro* made no attempt to alter his grip as he straightened up, still holding it, though point down, in the same manner. *Now* Vinicius will thrash him, Didius was certain, but to his consternation, he didn't seem angry, instead just saying with a sigh, "All right, I see you need some convincing." Vinicius took a couple steps away from the stake so that the rest of the section had a good view, then told Pullus, "Come here and face me, and assume the first position." Pullus' mouth opened, then he shut it and, with obvious reluctance, obeyed the Optio, dropping down into the crouch that, as far as Didius knew, Pullus had just learned this day like he and the others had, not believing for an instant that Pullus was telling the truth about having training. "Now," Vinicius said, "strike me. As hard as you can. Give me a killing blow." Pullus stood there, mouth open and looking as if he hoped the ground would swallow him up, and Didius thought that he couldn't be any happier than he was in that moment. He was quickly proven wrong when, seeing that Pullus wasn't moving, Vinicius repeated, "I said, strike me. Give me all that you've got." Then, in a clearly taunting tone, he added, "And don't worry, if you land the blow, I'll absolve you with my dying breath."

While he was ecstatic about the outcome, Didius was also frustrated because what occurred happened so quickly that it was impossible for his eyes to follow. What he did see was the sudden change of expression on Pullus' face in the fraction of the eyeblink before the large *Tiro* launched a thrust that clearly had all of his power behind it. The blow never landed because, somehow, Optio Vinicius used his bare left hand in a sweeping blow across his body that sent Pullus' *rudis* flying across Pullus' body, to his left, while at what seemed to Didius' eye the same time, Vinicius stepped forward to punch the *Tiro* in the stomach with his *vitus*. More than anything, it was the manner in which Pullus collapsed that told the others he was essentially out cold before he hit the ground, despite the fact that he was wearing his *hamata*. Didius heard a bellow of delight, unaware that it was him until from behind, he was shoved violently, sending him staggering, but when he whirled about, Domitius was already past and leaning over his comrade. The sight of Pullus lying prone, then flat on his back after Domitius rolled him over, was so satisfying that it washed away his rage at Domitius, and he joined the others as they ringed Pullus, staring down in a combination of awe and worry, with one notable exception. Didius quickly realized that when Pullus opened his eyes, he wasn't in the right spot for him to see Didius' face, so he shoved Artorius aside just in time for Pullus' eyes to flutter open.

"I thought you were dead!" Domitius cried, having dropped to his knees next to his friend.

It took a couple tries, but Pullus managed to gasp, "So did I."

This was when his eyes began moving around, looking up at the circle of faces, and Didius saw the change of expression on Pullus' face when his gaze rested on Didius, who was offering him what was one of his very rare truly genuine smiles. I can't remember the last time I've been this happy, Didius thought, but he was disappointed when, with some help from Domitius, Pullus climbed to his feet, one hand clutching his stomach. For his part, Vinicius had been standing there watching expressionlessly as Pullus stood up; to Didius, he almost seemed bored.

Once Pullus was more or less steady, Vinicius asked, "Do you know why I was able to do that?"

Pullus didn't reply immediately, and after the silence stretched out a bit, Didius began to hope that somehow his brains had been scrambled, despite being hit in the stomach.

To Didius' disappointment, it was because Pullus was seriously considering the question, and Didius could see by the dawning recognition that Pullus at least thought he had the answer, saying, "Because my thumb was exposed." Vinicius didn't say anything, just offering a nod, giving Didius the sense that he was waiting for something more from the big *Tiro*, and Vinicius was rewarded when Pullus frowned and said, "But..."

Now Vinicius interjected, and despite the short acquaintance, Didius heard the approval there as Vinicius said, "But the problem with that grip is that it restricts your blade from moving laterally, so that you don't have the same freedom of movement. Is that what you were about to say?"

Pullus nodded.

"Yes, Optio."

"Well," Vinicius agreed, "you're correct, *Tiro*...?" Neither Pullus, Didius, nor any of the others for that matter were aware that Vinicius already knew Pullus' name, and Pullus supplied it. "You're correct, *Tiro* Pullus, that at first, your movement is more restricted. But, you'll regain that with practice. By the time I'm finished with you, nobody will be able to tell how you grip your weapon." For the first time, he turned to address the others. "Except that you'll be alive, and your enemy dead."

"You were right," Vinicius told Calienus that night when the Sergeant came to the Optio's tent for a report on his section. "Pullus and Domitius have been trained. And," he admitted, "aside from the grip, whoever trained them did a good job."

Calienus grinned, holding out a hand as he demanded, "You owe me a *sestertius*."

"I should have known better," Vinicius grumbled, showing a side of his personality that very few men got to see. "You're a sharp operator."

"I'm still a *sestertius* behind from the bet about Favonius!" Calienus protested good-naturedly.

As Vinicius made a show of reluctance at dropping the coin into Calienus' palm, he said, "But he's not the only one in your section, I'm certain of it."

"Who else?" Calienus asked curiously.

"The one who stands next to Pullus. What's his name? Scribonius?"

"*Gerrae!*" Calienus exclaimed in surprise. "Are you sure?"

"As much as I can be without asking him," Vinicius answered seriously. "What's his story?"

"He said he came from Corduba, but his accent is pure Rome," Calienus replied. "He's educated too. I'm sure of that."

"Maybe he's from the upper orders and trained on the Campus Martius," Vinicius mused, then shrugged. "Either way, it's none of our business."

Calienus nodded in agreement. Romans who had never served under the standard would have been surprised to learn that, among the assortment of rules and regulations, there was one unwritten one that was almost as sacrosanct as any written down, and that was that men didn't ask their comrades about their past. If they volunteered the information, that was one thing, but once Gaius Marius opened the Legions to the men of the Head Count, there were some questions better left unasked, and this was one at the top of the list.

The pair sat in companionable silence, sipping wine from their cups, then Calienus asked, "So Pullus not only has training. Is he as strong as he looks?"

"Honestly," Vinicius replied soberly, "I think he might be stronger than he knows. And there's an...anger there."

"How's Domitius? I'm guessing that whoever trained Pullus trained him as well."

"From a skills perspective, he's very, very good," Vinicius replied. "And he's fast, Lucius. He might even be as fast as me."

Calienus knew that if Vinicius was saying this, it wasn't said lightly, and he was deeply impressed.

"I suppose he'd have to be if he and Pullus sparred together," Calienus mused. "The best way to defeat power is speed."

Vinicius nodded, then he said, "Actually, while Pullus is slower than Domitius, it's not by much. I can tell you this, I've never seen someone his size move that well."

"How many men his size have you seen?" Calienus laughed. "Only Tubero in the Fifth Cohort, and that bastard Bassus in the Ninth are near his size. I've seen a couple men in the 9th who might compare as well. And," Calienus reminded his friend, "he's only *seventeen*, Aulus. Still," he shrugged, "until they actually get stuck in, you don't know if he'll be worth an amphora of goat piss. He could freeze up the instant some Lusitani looks at him cross-eyed."

"That's true," Vinicius granted, "but somehow I don't think that will be a problem. If anything, it might be the other way around," he finished cryptically.

In the moment, it was just a passing remark, but it wouldn't be that long before Calienus would have cause to remember Vinicius' words.

Still, his mind had moved on from Pullus, and he asked, "What about the others?"

"The usual," Vinicius shrugged. "Right now, I'd put Scribonius third, then that one with the hair that stands straight up."

"Vellusius?" This surprised Calienus. "What about Didius?"

"He's strong, certainly," Vinicius allowed. "But I think he's an empty jug, Lucius. I think he's a bully who's been able to get by because he *is* strong, maybe as strong as Pullus is right now. But as you said yourself, Pullus is only seventeen, and I think Didius is as strong as he's going to get. We won't know about Didius until he faces someone who's his match physically. And," now he gave Calienus a smile, but it was a grim one that might have been tinged with cruelty, "I've got an idea of who that will be, and judging from what I've seen, Didius already hates Pullus for some reason."

"Well, whatever you have in mind, make sure I'm there to see it," Calienus said with a laugh. His smile faded a bit. "And Artorius?"

Vinicius didn't hesitate, nor was Calienus surprised when the Optio said flatly, "I'd wager fifty *sesterces* that he's not going to be marching out of the gates with us once the campaign gets started."

Calienus didn't take the bet.

Not just for Artorius, but for the entire section, the days blurred together into a seemingly endless cycle of repetition: wake up before dawn, eat and eliminate, then spend the day working relentlessly on whatever skill was the focus of the training. The only punctuation was how after a week, a new skill was introduced, and the week after being introduced to the *rudis,* the training focused on using the shield, as the Tenth Section tried to catch up to their comrades further ahead in training. Pilus Prior Crastinus still deemed it necessary to keep the new *Tiros* separated from the rest of the Century, but for Artorius, it was even worse because the day Calienus told them to take their shields to the training field to meet Optio Vinicius, he called Artorius by name.

"Not you, Artorius," Calienus informed him. "Optio Vinicius told me that you still need work with the *rudis*, so you just need to bring that and not your shield."

It was embarrassing, certainly, but Artorius wasn't surprised, nor were his comrades, although only Scribonius and Domitius offered him any encouragement, his close comrade patting him on the shoulder.

Domitius, however, whispered, "Once we're done for the day, I'm going to help you."

Consequently, while his comrades were taught how to handle a shield in the Roman style, which made it both an offensive and defensive weapon, Artorius stood at a stake as Calienus watched, the Sergeant stopping to correct him as Artorius worked through what were known as the forms, the three basic thrusts used by the Roman Legions. First position, come up from under the shield; second position was the exact opposite, aiming for the face and neck, while third position, which they had been assured they wouldn't use as often as the other two, was delivered with a sideways thrust that, when holding a shield, was for the purpose of taking advantage of a foe who had extended his shield too far out in front of him and aimed for the spot just under the ribcage. The reason they were given for it not being used very often was because, unlike the other two, the third position thrust relied more on arm strength.

It wasn't that Artorius wasn't trying; it was simply a matter of strength and coordination, since each position required a different motion and used different muscles. He'd resigned himself to being sore for the foreseeable future, but while he was encouraged that he was clearly stronger and fitter than he had been, it just wasn't up to the standard demanded by the Pilus Prior and Optio Vinicius. Calienus didn't have a *vitus*, but he had other ways to make sure Artorius' mind didn't wander, which it had a tendency to do, that were almost as effective.

"You know that I'm in charge of deciding who from our section deserves being put on *cac* detail, don't you, Artorius?"

"No, Sergeant, I didn't," he managed to pant after performing fifteen repetitions of the second position thrust.

"Well, I am, which means that you need to stop looking over at the boys and think of that stake as your enemy," Calienus said firmly.

In their short association, none of the section had heard Calienus raise his voice, yet somehow, he was able to impress on his new comrades that he was, in fact, in command.

"I will, Sergeant," Artorius promised...and he *did* try, but while nobody in this new world he was now a part of had bothered to ask, he had always had difficulty concentrating for long periods of time, although he also knew none of his comrades and officers cared.

Calienus did offer encouraging words whenever he executed a particularly well-done thrust, but even to Artorius' ears, while the jolting impact that traveled up his arm told him he had hit where he had aimed, the thrust didn't make the same sharp cracking sound that Domitius was capable of producing, and it was nowhere near Pullus or Vinicius. Finally, Calienus patted him on his shoulder, and he was shocked to see that the sun was well on its downward arc, while the section was gathering to march back into camp.

"That's enough for today, Artorius," Calienus informed him. "Fall in with the others. We'll do it again tomorrow."

This alarmed Artorius; he had assumed that this was only going to last a day, and without thinking, he blurted out, "How long am I going to be held back, Sergeant Calienus?"

"As long as it takes until the Pilus Prior is satisfied that you'll last more than one rotation in battle," Calienus replied, again not unkindly, but firmly, telling Artorius that any argument would be pointless.

They had reached a part in their training where once they were back at their tent, they had perhaps two-thirds of a watch of free time, although most of it was spent in attending to their equipment, which showed a surprising amount of wear in a short period of time. Usually, this meant that the close comrades spent time together, although anyone with eyes could see that of the pairs, Publius Vellusius was the unhappiest of them all, and now that Atilius had joined the section, he was spending more time with the late arrival than his nominal close comrade Didius. Not that it mattered, because Didius had taken to disappearing from the circle around the fire, which now had short sections of tree trunks or unused crates that they had scrounged up that served as makeshift seats, which was where men preferred to spend their time. Most of the others had actually ventured over to the other section tents, but on their return, they had reported that they were greeted in the same manner as when they had gone to the bathhouse, with teasing and taunts that, for the most part, the *Tiros* had resigned themselves to as a fact of their lives for the moment. Artorius hadn't done so, choosing instead to try and recover from the day's exertions, but on this day, immediately after Calienus dismissed them, Domitius turned to Artorius.

"Are you ready to do some more work?"

The truth was that he wasn't, yet Artorius also knew that he needed the help, so he tried to show his appreciation as he went with Domitius back to the training ground.

Didius put the dice into his issued cup, then shook it, making a rattling sound that anyone who'd set foot in a *taverna* recognized, while he tried to make his smile genuine.

"Any of you boys want to test Fortuna? How about a game?"

Atilius was the first to respond, although it was to ask, "Where did you find some dice?"

"I traded half my bread yesterday with a lad from the First Section," Didius answered casually, although it was a lie.

The truth was more straightforward, but Spurius Didius knew better than to admit that, during his prowling of the Legion area—every man had been warned about entering the area assigned to another Legion without permission, the punishment being a flogging—he had noticed an empty tent on the Fifth Cohort's street. Sitting on one of the cots had been a set of dice, and with a quick glance around, he had stepped inside the tent just long enough to scoop up the dice.

"We don't have any money," one of the Mallius brothers pointed out, although by this moment in time, they had been given the nicknames Romulus and Remus by Calienus.

Didius thought that it was Marcus, or Romulus, who had spoken, but he was still having trouble telling them apart, but he already had an answer prepared.

"We don't have to gamble for money," Didius answered quickly. "We can gamble other things, like," he pretended to think about it, "our guard duty, or rations. Or," he shrugged, "just doing favors for each other."

The brothers glanced at each other, and the other one, Remus, lifted one shoulder, which Romulus interpreted, and he nodded to Didius.

"I just wish we could gamble for our wine ration," Atilius, who Didius had seen was the most eager to play, spoke up as he settled down on one of the cots. "I haven't been this thirsty in my life."

"You mean you haven't been sober this long in your life," Scribonius, who was sitting with Pullus just outside the tent spoke up, which evoked laughter, especially from Atilius, who countered, "Is there any difference?"

Ultimately, of the section members, there were three who never participated in any of Didius' dice games, which quickly became a regular occurrence every evening; Pullus, Domitius, and Scribonius all offered up an excuse. This angered Didius a great deal, because he had been eagerly looking forward to fleecing that big bastard, certain that Pullus was too slow-witted to even know he was being cheated, because of all the skills Spurius Didius possessed, he was extremely skilled at cheating. Even after suspicions began to mount and his comrades demanded to inspect the dice, they never found how he had altered them, nor did they ever learn that, after another week, he had managed to steal another set of dice which, using his skill at sleight of hand that his father Aulus had pounded into him, literally, switched them out once the pot was to his liking. In this manner, Didius managed to avoid having his sleep interrupted, nor did he have to waste time on such dreary tasks like mending or polishing gear. As satisfying as it was overall, the fact that Pullus never owed Didius rankled him, deepening his enmity towards his fellow *Tiro*. Somewhere in the back of his mind, he knew a reckoning was coming before the training was over, and he swore to Dis that he'd be ready.

Midway through their second week, Crastinus deemed that the Tenth Section was sufficiently trained not to embarrass themselves and him by joining the rest of the Century for drill purposes, so that from this point forward, they weren't trained as a section but as a Century. By the fourth week, the Second Cohort, along with the other nine, began training as such, composed of six Centuries, and as the pace and complexity of the training increased, Quintus Artorius struggled even more. If it hadn't been for Domitius and his unwavering support and encouragement, Artorius knew that he would have been dismissed from the Legion by this point. In Artorius' eyes, Vibius Domitius was the best friend someone like him could have, because he was infinitely patient, and always cheerful, even when he was castigating Artorius for some mistake. And, Artorius noticed, Domitius was almost universally liked, not just by the members of his section, but now that they were working as a Century, with the other men of the First. Only Scribonius had shown Artorius the same kindness and compassion, but he hadn't fought very hard to be the one to help Artorius with his forms and the other skills they had been taught. He was helpful in other ways, however, while the attitudes of the others ranged from being slightly sympathetic, like Vellusius, to indifference like the Mallius brothers. Didius made no attempt to hide his contempt, but it was Pullus who Artorius was as concerned about as he was Domitius, because it had become obvious to all of them that, along with the size and strength, Pullus was already more skilled than the others, save for Domitius.

However, when Artorius insisted that his friend was every bit as skilled as Pullus, Domitius had unhesitatingly said, "I appreciate that, Artorius, but that's not true. Titus is the best of us, and it's not really that close. I even think that he could give Vinicius a hard time sparring," he added confidently.

Artorius wasn't sure about that, but if Domitius said this was the case, he accepted it as likely. As the days passed, so too did the anxiety begin to increase, not just with the Tenth Section, but with all the *Tiros* of the new 10th Legion, because they had been informed that the entire Legion would be performing their first march out of camp and into the countryside, where they would construct a marching camp, then return the next day. They had begun marching with their *furca*, in formation, but only within sight of the walls, essentially marching around the camp several times, and nobody, not even Artorius, had been surprised to see that this was an ordeal for him. Adding to the pressure was the knowledge that the man responsible for the creation of this Legion would be leading the march, and for most of the men, it would be the first time they ever laid eyes on Gaius Julius Caesar. To help him, Domitius stopped tutoring Artorius' weapon skills, and instituted a strengthening regimen consisting of pushing himself up off the ground using just his arms and lifting buckets loaded with sand, yet despite the exercises and his feeling stronger, as the day neared, Artorius experienced a leaden ball of dread that only got heavier with every passing day. The night before the march, he didn't get any sleep, but he wasn't alone; every *Tiro* in the Legion spent an anxious night, even Pullus, which had the effect of increasing not only Artorius' apprehension, but everyone else in the tent except Calienus, who snored peacefully. Not only was there the prospect of their first full march as a Legion, Crastinus had informed them that they would be marching in full dress uniform, with the horsehair plumes, all black, while their leather *balteae* had to have varnish applied, and the metal pieces that were attached, called *bullae*, to the strips of leather that hung down to protect the groin polished, along with their helmets.

Crastinus had spent the rest of the daylight watch circulating his entire Cohort, but not surprisingly, he spent the most time on the part of the street belonging to the First Century. What was something of a surprise was that Artorius escaped the lash of either Crastinus' or Vinicius' *vitus*, both of them offering acceptance of his job with a grunt in the Centurion's case, and a curt nod by the Optio, before turning their attention on the others. It did make him feel guilty that Domitius earned a smack by Crastinus, who spotted a smudge on the buckle of Domitius' *baltea*, knowing that it was because Domitius had paid more attention to Artorius than to himself, but Domitius didn't say anything. With the sound of the horn that they had learned was called the *bucina*, which was used in the camp to record the watches, the time to rise, the time to retire, and other messages involving the camp and the march, like the others, Artorius rose, eating quickly then heading to the latrines. Returning to the tent, like the others, he shed his normal tunic to put on the spare that they had never worn, which would become their inspection tunic. Nobody talked above a murmur, moving quickly, then dragging their packs outside the tent before retrieving their shields, which they strapped to their backs. They now had two shields apiece, the wicker one made for training, which was now kept outside the tents and leaned against the walls, and the shield they would carry in battle, although they had been expressly forbidden from taking the leather covers off. Consequently, they were ready for Crastinus blowing on his bone whistle, whereupon they stepped into the street and fell into their spots, ready to march to the forum. It was now dawn, the sky already going from the pink of predawn to the golden yellow, and for the first time, Quintus Artorius and his comrades were treated to the sight of a fully equipped Legion of Rome, arrayed in their Cohort formations, with the first three Centuries aligned in the front row, then a dozen paces behind and perfectly aligned with the front ranks, the other three Centuries.

"By the gods," Domitius' whisper still managed to convey the awe he felt, "isn't this a glorious sight?"

Despite his trepidation about the coming ordeal, Quintus Artorius wholeheartedly agreed, and he felt his heart quicken, not from fear this time, but from the excitement and pride of thinking that he was part of this. Following hard on the heels of that was the thought, *I wonder what Tata would think now? Would he be proud of me, finally?* Unfortunately for Artorius, and all but a couple men of the Tenth Section, being in the rear rank of ten, even in the First Century, meant that his view was seriously limited, so when, after being called to *intente*, a man that he knew was the *Praetor* began speaking, he still had no idea what Caesar looked like. He could only see his Cohort standard, and off to his right, the silver gilt Legion eagle; everything else was a sea of black plumes and the gray of the armor they were all wearing, with the sun glinting off the polished helmets, and best of all, the silver wings of the eagle, which Artorius was certain was a good omen from Jupiter himself. He could hear Caesar well enough, and as he listened, his heart stirred again as he thought, *I've never heard anyone who speaks like that before.* His accent was strange to Artorius' ears, although he was dimly aware that Caesar must be speaking with the accent used in Rome, but to this moment, his contact with anyone who was actually from Rome had been nonexistent, or so he believed, but he did have a fleeting thought that his close comrade Scribonius had a similar accent. Although Caesar spoke with a diction that Artorius supposed came from being educated to the level expected of a Roman patrician, somehow Caesar managed to speak plainly enough that he didn't have trouble following the words, which was essentially a greeting by the man responsible for them standing there today, in uniform and armored, ready to march. Caesar spoke of how, despite the Legion just being formed, they were all carrying on a long tradition of men who had served Rome, making mention of how he was certain that there were new *Tirones* in the ranks whose fathers, grandfathers, and even great-grandfathers had all marched for Rome. *Didius will love hearing that*, he thought with some amusement, but while he was tempted to turn his head to see if he could see the expression on his face, Artorius maintained his position of *intente*. The end of the speech was signaled by a shouted command from Primus Pilus Favonius, prompting the men of the 10th Legion to offer a roar of approbation, startling Artorius, though he quickly added his voice. As soon as they stopped, the horn sounded again, sending the signal for the First Cohort to follow their general, who strode to the front of the column towards the *Porta Praetoria* to lead the way. Since they were marching in single column, it meant that the Second Century waited until the First Century began, then their Centurion sounded the order to follow, and like a strange, multi-segmented beast, one Century followed another, in their Cohort order.

"Get ready." Calienus, who, now that he was integrated into the section, was actually next to Didius on his left, making him fifth in the rank. "We're about to fall in behind their Sixth Century."

Hoisting his *furca*, Artorius experienced a moment of instability at the sudden weight on his shoulder from the pole pressing down, but he was prepared for this, as his left hand wrapped around both javelins, although they were still training javelins, making them heavier, which he had learned to use as a walking staff.

"First Century," Crastinus bellowed, paused a heartbeat, "*Ad Clinum!*" A pause, then, "*Move!*"

Stepping off at the same instant as the rest of his Century, Artorius offered up a brief prayer, although he wasn't certain which god or goddess he should be addressing, then he was marching, a man of the 10th Legion.

To the dismay of most of the *Tirones* of the 10th Legion, within a third part of a watch, they discovered that their experienced comrades' dire warnings about the ordeal had, for the most part, been warranted. For Titus Pullus, it was especially dismaying, and he took absolutely no solace in seeing how Scribonius marching next to him was puffing from the exertion required for what, as they would learn, was the normal pace that would be set by Julius Caesar. As his comrades had learned, Pullus expected more of himself than his comrades, even Domitius, but once the horn sounded after two-thirds of a watch, he longed to collapse just as much as the others.

Fortunately, they were saved from a lashing by either Crastinus or Vinicius when one of the men in the front rank, after dumping his pack, dropped to the ground, and Crastinus pounced, his *vitus* slashing down as he roared, "Nobody told you to sit down, Flavius! Get to your feet, or by the gods, I'll flay you!"

"He's doing you a favor, boys," Calienus spoke up. "If you sit down, some of you won't be able to get up."

As soon as their Sergeant said it, Pullus understood this was the truth, immediately thinking of Artorius, who was becoming a point of contention between himself and his best friend, but what Pullus would never admit was that he was growing jealous of Artorius for robbing him of time with his best friend. Glancing over at their Sergeant, Pullus copied him, leaning over to relieve the ache in his back, putting both hands on his knees, Scribonius following suit.

Scribonius, who was rapidly becoming his closest friend save for Domitius, turned and asked him, "What did you think?" Seeing Pullus' blank stare, he said, "About Caesar, I mean."

Pullus considered for a heartbeat, then shrugged.

"He gives a good speech. Why, what did you think?"

Scribonius frowned, trying to frame the words, but the best he could do was, "I don't know, really. All I do know is that I've seen him somewhere before, but I can't remember where."

This made Pullus curious, but then the horn sounded the warning call that the march was about to resume, evoking an almost universal round of groans and curses as the men bent down, grabbed their *furca*, and picked them back up, some with a sense of resignation, others with a fair amount of fear, and at least one who was grimly determined to prove to his comrades, his Centurion, and even to the commanding general that he was equal to the task.

The 10th had one more rest stop, then after another two parts of a watch of marching, they arrived at the spot where the *exploratores*, the group of scouts, led by a man skilled in surveying, had selected for the day's camp. For the *Tiros*, it looked like a bewildering array of stakes, with the exposed ends painted a variety of colors, but if you had told them that before long most of them would be able to read them and know exactly how the camp would be oriented and what part they would be occupying, none of them would have believed it. To Pullus, and the other *Tiros*, it looked as if it was nothing but chaos as Centurions ran to where Caesar was standing, next to a large red standard that designated his status as Legate in command of the Legion, then after a brief conference came trotting back, whereupon Centuries began moving in a seemingly haphazard fashion.

Crastinus returned to the Century to announce, "Right, we've been assigned the ditch." This elicited groans from the experienced men, which of course meant the *Tiros* joined in, but Crastinus snapped, "Shut your mouths, you lazy bastards! Now, I expect you Sergeants to take your tent section and give these fresh young things a quick lesson on what they're about to do. I'll give you some time to explain, and then," he turned and used his *vitus* to a spot outlined by a series of stakes, "get to work. That's our section. I'll be around to make sure that you don't make a mess of things."

With that, he turned and strode off towards the Second Century, a reminder that Crastinus was responsible for more than just the First Century, and the section gathered around Calienus, the other nine sections doing the same with their Sergeants.

"You're going to need your turfcutter and spades," Calienus told them, his face expressionless, which they were beginning to learn meant that he was simply resigned to his fate. When they had retrieved the tools from their wicker baskets, Calienus said, "Follow me." He walked over to the spot that Crastinus had indicated, and once they were closer, told them, "All right, what we're going to do is dig our section of the ditch. You'll need your turfcutters first." Once they were equipped, he had them stand in their rank order, and since he was in the middle, the section turned inward to watch as he thrust the turfcutter into the grassy ground. "First, we need to cut squares of sod like this." He worked as he talked, quickly and expertly thrusting the turfcutter down a total of eight times, twice per side to create a square that was more than a foot long on each side. "Then," he used the turfcutter to pry up the square from the dirt below, "you need to pick it up." He did so, then turned and walked several feet away, dropping the square on the ground, although none of the *Tiros* noticed that Calienus was counting the paces he took. Turning back around, he pointed to the set of stakes that, unknown to them, was a precise fifteen feet away as he explained, "We cut out squares all the way to those stakes, and we stack the sod behind us on top of the first square, so you should have fifteen squares of sod."

"Why do we do that?" Didius demanded, then pointed to the opposite side. "By the time we're through, we'll be closer to that side, so why can't we just drop them on both sides? Wouldn't that save us walking back and forth?"

Instead of angering Calienus, the Sergeant just shrugged and said, "If you think that's the best way to do it, go ahead."

To everyone else, this would have been sufficient warning, knowing Calienus well enough by this point to know there was a reason he was seemingly indifferent, but Didius just grinned, certain that he was about to show the others that he could be every bit as clever as anyone in the Legion. Now that he had demonstrated, the rest of the section went to work, using Calienus' first square as an example, but once they were more than halfway across, they all carried their square back to the original side, except for Didius. Meanwhile, they were surrounded on one side by men from their Second Century, and on the other men from the Third Cohort, all doing the same thing, and it was Pullus who noticed something, nudging Scribonius as they were cutting the last square on the far side.

Keeping his voice low so that Didius, who was adding to the pile of seven squares on this side couldn't hear, he asked Scribonius, "Notice anything?"

Matching his tone, and grinning, Scribonius replied, "You mean that Didius is the only idiot who's stacking squares on the far side?"

Pullus chuckled in appreciation that Scribonius had noticed, and he wondered, "Do you think he'll figure that out?"

They were walking back to the original side of the ditch, that was now bare dirt but no more than a few inches deep, and Scribonius glanced over his shoulder.

"It doesn't look like it."

They were joined by Didius, who had at least trotted across

the ditch to catch up, but he was still smirking.

"Now what?" Romulus asked Calienus, who pointed to their spades that were lying on the ground.

"Now, we dig."

It wasn't until the ditch was almost waist deep that Spurius Didius realized not only that he had made a mistake, much to the enjoyment of not just his own section, but also by the men on the other side of the Second Century and the Third Cohort to their right who had been alerted by Calienus that Didius had thought he was clever. Climbing out of the ditch to the guffaws of laughter, he snatched up the squares of sod, dropped back down and crossed the ditch, but then he was forced to scramble up and over the pile of spoil that hadn't been packed down yet, meaning that he slid back down into the ditch, bringing a fair amount of loose dirt with him. His misfortune was compounded by the appearance of Pilus Prior Crastinus, drawn by the sound of laughter from his men, but it was made even worse when Crastinus saw that some men from the Third Cohort were enjoying the sight. He was standing on the top of the low mound of spoil, waiting for Didius, he did wait until the Tiro's second attempt, when Didius finally managed to scramble to the top, then allowed him to walk to the stacked sod and drop his armful before he struck.

"*Who told you to waste fucking time doing things your way, you ignorant* mentula?" Crastinus bellowed while swinging his *vitus* down in a rhythm that matched his words, driving Didius to his knees, while he covered his head with both hands.

Because his comrades were down in the ditch, the only man who could see what was happening was Pullus, and that was just the upper part of Crastinus' body, but with every blow, Didius yelped in pain.

"S-S-Sergeant Calienus!" Didius shouted. "I asked him, and he said it was all right!"

"What a load of *cac*," Crastinus snarled. "Even *if* he said that, all you had to do was look around and see you were the only one doing it, you oaf!" This was punctuated with one last smacking sound, then Crastinus said in disgust, "Get on your feet and get down in that fucking ditch, Didius." Didius scrambled to his feet, practically sprinting up and over the spoil as Crastinus called after him, "And the next time you have an urge to be clever...ignore it!"

It was exhausting work, to be sure, but even so, Pullus was grinning for the rest of the time.

Once the ditch was dug, their part was over, climbing up the ladders that were carried in one of the Legion wagons as part of the baggage, but on the opposite side of the newly constructed wall, entering the camp through the nearest of the four gates, where they were greeted by erected tents and fires outside each one, seeing firsthand for the first time the tasks for which the section slaves were responsible. The learning process wasn't over, however, because this was also their first time to feed themselves, using the section grinder that Pullus had been forced to carry from the time they had begun marching outside the camp, as Calienus showed them how to add water drawn from the barrels that had been hauled from the nearby river into the large section pot, also carried by the mule. Once the dough was created, Calienus expertly divided it into equal portions, dropping the dough onto the round flat clay pan each man carried that served as both plate and a means to bake the *castra paneris* that Calienus had just made, showing them how to use their *pugio* to slice the dough in four places, then placed their lids, called the *clibanus,* on top of each pan. While the pans of bread were baking by placing them directly on the coals of the fire, the pot was now refilled with the nightly ration of chickpeas, lentils, and ten chunks of salted pork, whereupon it was attached to the iron tripod so that the pot dangled a matter of inches over the baking bread pans. All around them, identical scenes were taking place, albeit with minor variations that were unique to a Century or Cohort, some trick that had been adopted as the best way to prepare the meal. As filthy and exhausted as they were, the smells of baking bread and simmering porridge tortured the men, but perhaps none more than Pullus, who was in a state of perpetual hunger and always willing to consume whatever was left uneaten. This night, he was thankful for the pork, because he had already learned that the Mallius brothers and Artorius didn't normally consume it, but he was disappointed to see that this night, only Artorius was willing to hand over his hunk. It was as they were eating that the Pilus Prior appeared again, and Pullus was amused to see that Didius looked very much like he was considering leaping up and fleeing in the opposite direction. That amusement wasn't destined to last long, however.

"The Second Cohort has the guard tonight," Crastinus announced.

Before he could stop himself, Pullus let out a groan, although he only earned one swipe of the *vitus* because he wasn't alone, both Romulus and Remus joining him so that Crastinus barely paused, smacking them both before striding over the next tent. The section could track his progress through the Cohort by the shouts of pain, which made Pullus feel a bit better.

The only reason Artorius made it through his turn on guard duty was because he was with Scribonius, who, while admitting that he was exhausted as well, managed to stay awake and keep them upright for the full watch. Now that they were more advanced in their training, the expectations, and the punishment for failing to meet those expectations, increased, and all the *Tiros* of the 10th had been warned that the days of suspending punishments like flogging were over, and falling asleep on guard duty was near the top of serious breaches. Relieved of their duty, Artorius staggered alongside Scribonius to the tent, collapsing on his cot without bothering to shed his *hamata* or his *caligae*. When the *bucina* sounded the morning call to wake, Artorius was certain that he had literally lay down, closed his eyes, and the horn signal came immediately afterward. Trying to roll out of his cot caused him to gasp from the pain caused by the strained muscles and tortured ligaments, but Fortuna smiled on him because, despite his involuntary cry of pain, he was joined by the other *Tiros*, including Pullus, all of his comrades save Calienus groaning. For the first time, the large youth seemed to be as hobbled and bent over as his comrades, yet as they had begun to learn, the Legions didn't stop just because of the aches and pains of new men, and they broke their fast, went to the latrine, then learned what was expected of them.

Crastinus addressed the Century, "Before we march back, we're going to fill in the ditch, replace the sod, and burn the towers that the Fifth Cohort built. Sergeants, take command of your sections; you know what to do."

Immediately, Calienus was surrounded by his younger comrades, who bore expressions ranging from bewilderment to anger, and it was Pullus who spoke for the others, demanding, "Did you know we were going to do this?"

"Of course," Calienus replied with a grin. "That's how we do things. We don't want to leave a well-fortified camp empty for some barbarians to use, do we?"

"But we're in the province! Nothing's happening here!" Remus exclaimed, which was met with agreement from his comrades.

"Why didn't you tell us?"

This came from Scribonius, and this evoked a chuckle from the Sergeant, who admitted, "We Sergeants talked and decided it would be a nice surprise. Now," he pointed down to their wicker basket, "you know what you'll need. We're just going to do the same thing in reverse."

Artorius joined his comrades without saying anything, but he was convinced that he wouldn't be able to help, yet somehow when he shoved his spade into the dirt, he was able to participate, and it was at least easier to fill the ditch in than it had been to dig it in the first place. The towers were set ablaze, then the Second Cohort learned their order in the marching column for their return to camp, which added further insult to their aggrieved feelings, taking their place at the very end of the column, behind the section mules and the wagons of the baggage train. And, as they quickly learned, it wasn't just the dust churned up by thousands of hobnailed soles and hooves that they had to suffer with, but the leavings of the mules and oxen, which Artorius learned when he stepped directly into a fresh steaming pile of dung because he hadn't been warned by the men of his file. Frankly, he was too miserable to care, nor did he care that their Legate Caesar had chosen to march back as well instead of riding, and he set the same pace of the day before. Before they had gone three miles, Artorius knew one thing with certainty; he couldn't keep this up much longer.

"Are you all right, Artorius?" Domitius gasped, faced with the same added challenge of shorter legs like Artorius. "I know it's hard, but you can do it! You just have to dig deep inside yourself!"

Even if he had been able to spare the breath, Artorius probably wouldn't have informed Domitius that he was certain that he had already tapped into his reserves to complete the march and building the camp the day before. It wasn't his intention, yet somehow, the next time he looked up from watching his feet moving, Domitius and the section were a few paces ahead of him.

"Get out of the way, you bastard! If you can't keep up, move aside!"

Because of his burden, Artorius couldn't turn his head to look over his shoulder, although he did as he was told, moving to the side just as the front rank of the Second Century strode by, its men viewing him with a mixture of sympathy and disgust at this clear sign of weakness. Seemingly from nowhere, Pilus Prior Crastinus appeared, invading Artorius' world by thrusting his snarling face in front of the *Tiro* as he marched backward, matching Artorius' pace.

"You're not going to drop out, Artorius," he growled. "I swear by Hercules, you're going to get back up to the First where you belong, or I'm going to thrash you into raw meat!"

"I...I'm trying, Pilus Prior," Artorius protested, barely understandable because of his panting.

"Don't try! Do it! *Now!*"

To his astonishment, somehow Artorius found the energy to increase his pace to a stumbling trot that was just a bit faster than the marching pace, rejoining his Century.

Trotting past him back to his spot, Crastinus snapped, "Don't let it happen again, Artorius!"

"See? I knew you could do it!" Domitius managed to gasp out. "One foot in front of the other, that's all it takes, eh?"

How simple it sounds, Artorius thought miserably, even as he was certain that his legs would collapse under the burden, or his heart would explode from the exertion. Before another half-mile had been covered, Artorius stepped to the side again, resigned to a beating from the Pilus Prior. He was behind the column to the point that, just as he reached their resting spot, where his comrades were once more bending over at the waist, the horn sounded the signal to resume, giving Artorius time for nothing more than a sip of water from his large flask. Choking from the dust, Artorius watched the Legion, *his* Legion, leaving him behind, and it was a feeling of such helplessness that he came very close to dumping his *furca*, shedding his armor, and just sitting down to wait for whatever came next. He was proud of himself, because he didn't do that, and it was with Domitius' admonition in his ears that Artorius put one foot in front of the other, even if it was at a slower pace. After all, he knew where they were headed, so he would get there eventually.

The second month of training saw the new Legion learning how to operate in battle by being introduced to the various formations used by the Roman Legions. From battle lines like the *acies triplex*, a formation where four Cohorts were in the front line, either in a line of double Centuries so that each Cohort had three Centuries in the formation with a Century behind them, or in a long line of Centuries that extended the area the Legion could cover, while the second and third lines were composed of three Cohorts apiece, and the training included how the second line replaced the first line, the second with the third, along with a number of other maneuvers. The most important formation of all, however, according to the veterans of all ranks, was the Century formation of the *testudo*, famous throughout their world. The word "tortoise" was appropriate, because what was a group of men aligned so that there was an arm's width between them would suddenly contract into a compact formation of men standing shoulder to shoulder, with men of the inner eight files and from the second rank backward, lofting their shields above their heads to protect themselves and their comrades from missile weapons, whether it be arrows, javelins, or from a sling, the latter of which they had been told was favored by the rebelling tribes, thereby creating an armored shell. In forming the *testudo*, there was a small blessing for Artorius; because of his spot on the left side of the formation and in the last rank, all he had to do was turn his shield outward a bit more than normal, while the upper half of the shield held by his comrade in the Ninth Section protected him from above. Men on the opposite, or right, side, like Pullus, were forced into choosing between shifting the shield to their weapon hand, or holding the shield across their body, which was not only awkward but required a fair amount of strength and endurance. None of his comrades were surprised when Pullus chose the latter method, and it was one time that Artorius was thankful for his diminutive size; a couple inches taller and he would have been forced to hold his shield above his head.

"The quicker you get into *testudo*, the better your chances of living to see another day!"

This, and variations of this rang in their ears, and the *Tiros* of not just the Tenth but every Section quit counting both the number of times they heard this admonition, and the number of times when, sometimes without warning, Crastinus would give three short blasts on his bone whistle. As the *Tiros* learned, marching in *testudo* was a tricky proposition, and if Artorius had been asked to describe it, he would have said it was more a shuffle than a walk, making their progress agonizingly slow.

"Form *testudo*!"

Gradually, the First Century learned to move quickly, aided by both Crastinus and Vinicius, through their *viti* and the encouragement it provided until, finally, after performing the maneuver what most agreed had to have been at least twenty times, the Pilus Prior grunted, "Well, you're not the worst I've ever seen."

It was a day each of them would remember, the first time their Pilus Prior had given them any praise at all, however qualified.

Similarly to the milestone of learning to force march, there was another that *Tiros* were evenly divided about, and that was when they were finally allowed to start sparring with each other after having been forced to face their weapons instructor; in the case of the Second Cohort, this meant Vinicius, who had emerged from every bout without so much as a bruise, even against Pullus. *Tiros* like Pullus, Domitius, and if he was to be believed, Didius had been looking forward to this day, while men like the Mallius brothers and Vellusius seemed resigned to it, but for Optio Vinicius, it also gave him the opportunity to at least partially solve a problem with his Century that had been building for a few weeks. The issue was that Spurius Didius was a cheat; of this Vinicius was certain, while the problem was that he was very good at it and hadn't aroused anything more than suspicion, which was especially galling to Vinicius. It had started innocently enough; Didius was clever enough not to win every throw, and as any sharp operator knew, it behooved one to lose more than they won in the beginning. Then, over time, he had become "luckier"; once his tentmates learned their lesson, Didius had begun moving from one tent to another until, of the ten sections, eight of their Sergeants had come to Vinicius to voice their suspicions about Didius' actions, and they had all urged him to go to Crastinus, but he had demurred, assuring them he knew of a way to at least temporarily suspend the *Tiro*'s predations on his comrades. His cause was aided, unwittingly, by Didius himself, his hatred and envy of Pullus having reached the point where, every time Vinicius selected Pullus as the *Tiro* he would demonstrate a new skill, Didius could be counted on to make some sort of comment about it, always under his breath but loud enough for Pullus and the others to hear. The fact that what this meant for Pullus in practical terms was that he received far more than his share of bumps, bruises, and the occasional cut was lost on Didius, although from what Vinicius could see, he was the only one in the section and the Century who felt this way, the other men perfectly content for someone else taking a beating.

This was why, on the day sparring among *Tiros* began, and Vinicius pitted Didius and Pullus for the very first bout, as he dragged his toe to create the line for the two contestants to toe, without looking up, he whispered to Pullus, "I'm not deaf or blind. The only thing I'll tell you is that you're forbidden to kill him. Understand?"

Pullus gave a sober nod, and Vinicius was pleased to see that he didn't appear pleased, or overconfident...but his jaw was set in a tight line that the Optio had never seen before. If anything, Didius looked as if he wanted to be elsewhere, but the entire Century was there, forming a four-sided square, and as always, the wagering was brisk. Vinicius made a last-moment check, tugging on each of the padded sleeves that were worn during sparring sessions, followed by the wicker faceguard that had been a development created by Pompeius Magnus, then doing the same with Didius before moving out of the way to the spot from where he would judge the bout.

In seeming repudiation of Vinicius' assessment that he was taking this seriously, Pullus called out, "*Ave,* Didius. How long will it take me to make you my whore?"

This excited the onlookers, most of them chuckling, although there was a smattering of curses and gasps that indicated some support for Didius.

"Why don't you come and find out, you *cunnus*?" Didius shot back, clearly more angry than worried now.

"Be careful what you wish for, Didius," Pullus replied, but he was also moving as he said it, and to Vinicius' eyes, it confirmed his suspicion that, when properly motivated, *Tirone* Pullus could move with blinding speed.

Pullus had drawn the training shield up hard against his shoulder, and he used it to slam into Didius' own protection with an impact that Vinicius was certain he could feel up from the ground and through his legs, and despite his own feelings about Didius, the Optio was impressed that, while it did send Didius reeling backward, he managed to keep his feet, something that Vinicius was certain none of the other men in the Century could do, even the veterans. However, Didius was also spared by Pullus, because rather than launching a thrust that, even with the padded undershirts used for training, would have at least driven the wind from Didius' lungs, Pullus used his *gladius* as a slashing weapon. Instantly, Vinicius understood what the *Tiro* was up to, striking Didius on his upper right arm with a backhanded slash, then when Didius desperately shifted his shield over, repeating it against his left, but doing it several times in a row, while Didius was totally on the defensive, his padded sleeves only partially softening the blows. He's punishing him, Vinicius thought, by weakening his arms so that Pullus can finish him over the top of the shield. Even as this thought flashed through his mind, Didius began to respond, but instead of well-aimed thrusts, he was essentially flailing away, all of which Pullus blocked with an ease that certainly wasn't

lost on the spectators, who were now baying for blood. By
Didius' fourth thrust, Pullus had disdained even using his
shield, parrying his opponent's attacks with the *rudis*, making a
sharp cracking sound that was similar to the sound of striking a
stake, but even louder, as he knocked Didius' *rudis* to the side.

His face expressionless, Vinicius called out, "Careful about
showing off, Pullus. It's sloppy and can become a habit."

Since his back was to Vinicius, Pullus bobbed his head
once, but then took a step backward, relieving the pressure on
Didius and allowing him to reset himself.

Pointing around at the grinning faces with his *rudis*, most of
whom were now openly cheering him, Pullus challenged, "Hear
that, Didius? It sounds like your comrades don't care for you
very much."

Didius, now as enraged as he'd ever been, spat on the
ground and sneered, "What do I care about those *cunni* for?"

Instantly, the good-humored cheering turned into curses and
shouts of derision by the men of the First Century, and Vinicius
could barely hear Pullus counter, "Oh, I don't know. Maybe
because one day you'll have to rely on them to save your life."

This was Pullus' first mistake, one Vinicius immediately
noticed, reminding himself to mention to Pullus that it wasn't
wise to use the same trick or tactic twice, because as before, he
had launched himself at Didius while he was still speaking,
except this time, Didius was ready for it. If anything, this second
impact was even more brutal, arousing a chorus of "oohs" from
their comrades, and Vinicius heard what he was certain was the
cracking of at least one of the shields, something he'd only seen
happen two or three times. Nevertheless, boss to boss, the two
combatants stood, exerting all their strength against each other,
neither of them able to budge the other. This was when
Vinicius' suspicion about Pullus' innate superior strength was
confirmed, seeing Pullus drop his hips by going into a tighter
crouch, then an eyeblink later, with a huge bellow, uncoiling his
body in much the same manner as a *ballista* suddenly releases
its energy when the pin is pulled. Didius' feet left the ground by
several inches, his face registering his shock as his mouth
formed an "O" of surprise and causing an explosion of roiling
dust when he hit the ground, flat on his back, both arms

outspread in an unconscious reaction to falling backward. Before he could react by drawing his shield back over himself to protect his body and head, Pullus was astride him, and had the point of his *rudis* pointed directly at his throat. Wooden *gladius* or not, Pullus possessed more than enough strength to shove the point down and end Didius' life right then, but instead and in obedience to Vinicius' warning, he backed away from Didius.

"You make this too easy," Pullus said contemptuously, whereupon he made his second mistake, this one having real consequences.

Turning to face the side of the square his section was on, Pullus, with a broad grin, lifted both arms, still holding the weapon and shield out from his body, mimicking the gladiators they had all seen during festival games celebrating their victory, and, Vinicius allowed, he felt somewhat responsible, because he took his eyes off Didius as well, meaning that he didn't see the *Tiro* climb to his feet to go at a sprint towards Pullus' back. The Optio was just opening his mouth, while Pullus, seeing the expressions on his comrades' faces as they registered the threat posed by Didius' charge, was just beginning to turn when, with a vicious force, Didius struck Pullus with a low, slashing blow aimed right at Pullus' kidneys with the flat of his *rudis*. The sound was audible over the cheering, and Pullus dropped to his knees as if his legs had suddenly decided to stop working, while Didius compounded his own first error with a second, allowing Pullus to climb to his feet and spin about to face him.

"Who's the whore now?" Didius taunted, but instead of answering Didius, or even acknowledging he had said anything, the large *Tiro* turned and looked directly at Vinicius.

Should I let him? he wondered, so that for a span of heartbeats, everything seemed suspended before, finally, the Optio gave him a slight nod, thinking, You're in the gods' hands now, Didius, as Pullus resumed the bout, and this time, Pullus didn't talk. Instead, what he did was unleash a fury that neither Vinicius nor any of the veterans of the 10th had ever seen before. Truly, if Vinicius had been grading Pullus on his form and technique, he would have informed the *Tiro* that he had failed, miserably, but he knew this wasn't about anything other than the raw, savage fury of an immensely strong man with lethal skill. Pullus' *gladius* arm was a blur of motion, raining down blow after blow after blow as Didius, with growing desperation, and what looked like a growing panic to Vinicius, could barely keep his shield up in a position to block them, his shield arm being driven back towards him with every thrust, or downward with every slash. The square had fallen silent, another thing that Vinicius hadn't witnessed before, with every man standing, mouth agape, so that the loudest sound was the harsh panting of the two combatants. Pullus was certainly tired, Vinicius saw, but Didius actually reminded the Optio of the weakling Artorius the way his mouth was hanging open as he tried to draw enough breath into his lungs. Then, without warning, Pullus suddenly relented, stopping his onslaught and, even more unusually, stepping back to allow Didius to gather himself. What are you up to, Pullus? He didn't have to wait long for his answer, and it happened because of a habit that Vinicius had tried to correct, not just with Didius but with several new men, something that Pullus had clearly spotted. When some men became fatigued, they tended to forget the importance of technique, specifically in keeping their shield in a perfectly vertical orientation. Most commonly, tired men let the top of the shield tip forward a bit, which created more of an opening for a thrust, but what Vinicius didn't see coming was Pullus suddenly lunging, except that his first offensive move was with his shield, bringing down the bottom edge of his shield hard against the bottom of Didius' own, which when combined with Didius tipping his shield already, gave Pullus the gap he needed to execute a backhanded slash above his opponent's shield, but with his wrist twisted so that, as Didius had done to him, it was with the flat of his *rudis* that he struck Didius right in his nose, crushing the wicker faceguard as if it weren't even there and creating a shower of blood as Didius, screaming in agony, dropped both weapon and shield to drop to his knees to cover this face, his hands instantly covered with blood. For his part, Pullus simply turned and, ignoring Vinicius, walked past him to where his comrades were waiting, while the shocked silence was only beginning to end as men comprehended what they had just seen.

It was still quiet enough for Vinicius to hear Domitius say,

"As much as I hate him, I do sympathize. I know what it's like to be hit like that by you."

Vinicius was walking over to Didius, who was still on his knees, moaning in pain, but he heard Pullus answer simply, "I hit him harder."

Reminding himself to find out about that exchange, Vinicius reached Didius, who still clutched his nose, but when he extended a hand to help the *Tiro* up, Didius angrily slapped it away, an offense which could have gotten him flogged, but fortunately for Didius, Vinicius' thought was, You've been punished enough.

Climbing to his feet, Didius' voice was muffled by his hands, but he was understandable, and loud enough for everyone to hear him demand, "Well, are you going to do something? Isn't there some sort of charge you can write against him?"

There were gasps of shock from the others, none of them having left, including Pullus, and even Vinicius was slightly bewildered.

"And what would I write him up for?"

Instead of ending this, Didius glared at him as he shot back incredulously, "What for? You saw what he did to me. There are rules against striking the head and face in training!"

"Just as there are also rules against striking a fellow Legionary when he's not prepared. You had been knocked down, *Tiro* Pullus bested you, and the bout was over."

"I didn't capitulate!" Didius insisted, and Vinicius lost his patience, doing something that he rarely did, and in fact hated to do, raising his voice to snap, "More fool you, because Pullus had finished you. The fact that you're too stupid know it isn't his or my fault. Now," he ordered, "follow me to the *medici*."

Unfortunately, there was no way Vinicius could avoid leading Didius past Pullus, so he wasn't surprised when the injured man hissed, "This isn't over!"

"Any time you want another beating, I'm happy to oblige." Pullus said this so cheerfully that Vinicius had to hide his smile as they walked past.

As he expected, Vinicius was summoned to the Pilus Prior's

tent at the end of the day, nor was he surprised to see Calienus standing outside, clearly waiting for him.

"Let's get this over with," was all Vinicius said, then rapped on the block of wood that hung outside the tent that was larger than the tents of the other Centurions, save that of the Primus Pilus.

The size of the tent wasn't a reward as much as it was a recognition of the fact that a Pilus Prior was responsible for all six Centuries, and as years had passed and the Roman army became more organized, more records were created, which had to be stored and carried with the Legion wherever it went.

Crastinus' chief clerk thrust the flap open, then stepped aside to allow Vinicius and Calienus in, telling them, "The Pilus Prior is expecting you in his quarters."

The other difference between rankers' tents and that of all Centurions was the leather partition that bisected the tent, creating essentially two rooms, and the Optio shoved aside the flap that served as the doorway, where Crastinus was seated behind the small folding desk.

Pointing to two of the stools in front of the desk, Crastinus wasted no time. "What do I need to know about what happened today?"

"It's been building for some time," Vinicius spoke for the both of them, which suited Calienus perfectly. "*Tirone* Didius hates *Tirone* Pullus, although I don't know why with any certainty."

Before he could continue, Crastinus asked, "What's your guess?"

"Jealousy," Vinicius answered instantly, which was supported by a nod from Crastinus in a sign the Optio took meant that he had just confirmed the Centurion's suspicions. "And," Vinicius allowed, "Didius *is* strong, there's no doubt of that, and technically, he's competent with his *gladius* and shield work. But Pullus..." he paused as he searched for words, settling, somewhat unsatisfyingly, on, "...is on another level."

Crastinus nodded again, but then he surprised both men when he asked, "Did I tell you what I learned back when they first started working the stakes? About who trained him?" Both of them shook their heads, and Crastinus went on, "The instant

I saw him working the stakes, I saw he knew what he was about." His features split into a grin. "Except for your grip. I wish I'd been there to see that."

This caused Calienus to laugh, but while Vinicius didn't, he did smile as Calienus told Crastinus, "You should have seen the bruise. He had me look at it that night because he was worried that the Optio had ruptured his guts. You can still see it now, but it's fading."

Now Crastinus laughed, then continued, "So when I asked him who trained him, he told me that it was Quintus Ausonius!"

"Cyclops?" For one of the few times, Vinicius' face expressed his feeling of surprise to a degree anyone who didn't know him would be able to recognize and identify it as such. "How's that? He said that he'd never pick up a *gladius* again!"

"I've heard about him," Calienus said. "Didn't he fight for Sertorius?"

"A lot of us did," Crastinus interjected. "But he saw the worst of it. He lost his eye at Saguntum, then after Sertorius was murdered by that *cunnus* Perperna, he went back home."

"How does he know Pullus?" Vinicius asked, and Crastinus laughed again.

"Cyclops is his brother-in-law!" he exclaimed, slapping one hand on the desk. "Can you believe that? He married one of Pullus' sisters. That's who trained both Pullus and his short friend Domitius."

"Domitius is almost as good as Pullus," Vinicius said. "He's faster, certainly. He's short, but he's strong."

There was a brief silence, then suddenly Crastinus' voice hardened, and he looked directly at Vinicius. "And when were you going to tell me about the other problem with Didius?"

To his credit, Vinicius didn't attempt to dissemble or stall for time, something that Crastinus noticed and appreciated.

"Because nobody's caught him, Pilus Prior," Vinicius replied evenly. "Nobody has come to me with any kind of proof. So," he shrugged, "I decided that I might be able to solve two problems at once."

Instead of replying to his Optio, Crastinus turned to Calienus, asking bluntly, "Do you know how Didius is cheating, Sergeant? Is he cutting you in?"

"No, Pilus Prior," Calienus replied calmly, but Vinicius, being closer to Calienus, heard the anger there, and he felt it wise to speak up.

"He's not gambling for money, Pilus Prior," Vinicius pointed out. "He's gambling with and for...other things."

Fortunately, Crastinus understood immediately, since this had been a problem plaguing the men wearing a transverse crest for centuries at this point. As far as the army and most Legates were concerned, who stood watch wasn't important, just that someone was standing it. Similarly, if a man wanted to risk being indebted to a comrade for all manner of favors, as long as it didn't impact the efficiency of the Legion, it wasn't a problem worth the effort it would take to solve. The one thing where there were actually regulations in place was in the gambling of the wine ration, although this was largely ignored, unless a ranker ended up getting drunk, then usually a good flogging, or as it was universally referred to as a striping, cleared the problem up, at least for a time.

This explanation was sufficient for Crastinus, signaling his tacit acceptance of Calienus' innocence by asking him, "What do you think we should do, Calienus?"

Calienus considered a moment, then answered, "Considering the beating he just took from Pullus, I think Didius isn't going to be eager to leave our tent anytime soon because he'd have to hear about it from the rest of the Century."

Crastinus snorted at this, informing the pair, "Oh, it's all over the entire Cohort now. Everywhere I go, it's all the men are talking about. So," he nodded, "I think you're right that he's not likely to show his face." Returning to the original matter, Crastinus asked both of them, "Was it as bad as I've heard?"

"It was for Didius," Calienus answered, and this time, Vinicius joined Crastinus in laughing, although the Centurion's lasted long enough that he had to wipe a tear away.

Vinicius was still smiling, but his tone was serious as he assured Crastinus, "I've never seen anything like it, Pilus Prior." He considered for a moment, then explained, "It's not just how strong he is, and it's not just his speed. He has this...fury in him that I've never seen before, in anyone."

"Do you think he can ever beat you?" Crastinus asked, but

while it might have been in a teasing manner, the Optio saw that Crastinus was serious.

And, at his core, Aulus Vinicius, while taking pride in his skill, was also honest, particularly with himself, which was what prompted him to answer soberly, "Once he's seen battle, yes, I think he could."

Titus Pullus was destined to never know that he had just been praised by Aulus Vinicius to a degree that the Optio had never offered about anyone before, but it was a moment that both Calienus and Crastinus would remember.

Calienus' prediction about Didius proved to be accurate, at least as far as his wandering from their tent, but he also chose to spend most of his time inside the tent during their free time. One of the camp physicians had done what they could to straighten his nose out, but both eyes were blackened, while the nose was swollen to twice its normal size. While he said as little as possible, when he did speak, his voice had a nasal quality to it that was completely unlike his normal speaking voice to the point that Calienus wondered if it would be a permanent change. It wasn't, but while the bruising faded and the swelling went down, Spurius Didius' nose would never look the same again. What concerned Calienus the most was what Didius had planned for Pullus, but after a few tense days, it became clear that Didius had been at least temporarily cowed by his ordeal at Pullus' hands. However, what impressed Calienus the most was how Pullus behaved towards the other *Tiro*, essentially ignoring him completely, and whenever one of the others began veering the conversation towards the topic of their bout, even when Didius wasn't within earshot, Pullus stopped them, usually with just a glare.

Meanwhile, the training continued, and intensified, but the *Tiros* of the Tenth Section had adapted to the increasingly strenuous activity, although with one exception. After barely managing to stay with the Century on two more forced marches, Artorius had once again fallen out of the formation, and was informed that one more failure would result in his dismissal from the Legion. From Calienus' perspective, the only reason Artorius hadn't already failed was due to the efforts of the man who stood next to him in formation, Domitius. Without hesitation, Domitius worked with Artorius, helping any way that he could; in fact, Calienus knew that on the two marches Artorius had managed to complete, it was because Domitius had offered to carry some of Artorius' equipment in his own pack. Although he was willing to turn a blind eye, it was only to a point, which was why Calienus took Domitius aside just before the next march and warned him that Vinicius would be checking the packs of every man in the Century; when Domitius asked why, Calienus explained that Vinicius had been tipped off about a man in the Fourth Section who was doing the same thing for his close comrade, and it had aroused Vinicius' suspicion. This was a lie; it had been Calienus who had alerted Vinicius about Domitius' actions. It wasn't that he wasn't sympathetic, but Calienus' sympathies actually lay more with Domitius because the young *Tiro* refused to see what the rest of the section, and most of the Century saw, that Quintus Artorius didn't possess the inner iron that it took for a life under the standard. His ultimate responsibility as Sergeant, however, was that his section become as strong as he could make it, and in the case of Artorius, he was certain that it would be a case of addition by subtraction, and as Calienus suspected, the first time that Artorius was required to carry his full load, he dropped out, although this time it was after the second rest stop on the return march. That didn't matter to anyone, save perhaps Artorius and Domitius, who seemed far more upset when Artorius finally returned to the camp, prompting an argument between Pullus and Domitius that Calienus, who had gone into the tent, ended up overhearing since the others were gone and the pair thought they were alone.

"Vibius, do you really think Artorius is trying his hardest?" Pullus asked, then voiced Calienus' own thoughts as he added, "To me, it looks like he's doing this more for you than for himself."

"I believe he's putting everything he has into his extra work," Domitius shot back, and Calienus heard the anger there, perhaps more than the comment deserved, which told Calienus that this had occurred to Domitius as well. "He can't help it if he's not as strong as you, Titus. Not everyone is; in fact, few people are, yet you seem to think everything should come as easily to them as it does to you."

"*Edepol!*" Calienus heard the surprise and indignation in Pullus' voice. "Who says that things come easily to me? I have to work as hard as anyone else."

Even through the leather walls, Calienus heard Domitius' sigh.

"I know you think you do, Titus, but I don't think you have the slightest idea just how much stronger and better you are than the rest of us. Haven't you seen not just us, but the other men in the Century stop to watch you when you're going through the drills?"

This, Calienus knew, was the case, but Pullus' tone expressed his doubt. "What of it? I'm sure that they're just watching me because I stick out, being so large." There was a silence, then Pullus added in what was clearly a plaintive voice, "I can't help it that I was born this large, Vibius. Do you think I wanted to kill my mother because of my size?"

"No," Domitius sighed again, "I know you can't, and you didn't. But," his voice hardened, "that's not what it is at all, Titus. You make these drills look easy. I know; I hear the other men talking. There are even men betting on how many barbarians you'll kill in your first battle."

That was true, Calienus knew, but what he would never reveal was that he was one of the men wagering. Whatever they were going to say after that was interrupted when Atilius and Vellusius came trotting up, breathlessly informing the other two *Tiros* that there was a wrestling match taking place over in the Third Century. The four of them hurried away, and Calienus waited for a moment before emerging from the tent. He was in a thoughtful mood; he had learned a great deal from that short conversation, but what would stick with him was the knowledge that Titus Pullus didn't just take his size for granted, and was actually conflicted about it. If, Calienus warned himself as he ambled down the street, following the sounds of men cheering a wrestling match, he's telling the truth; somehow, Calienus was certain that he was.

At last, after two weeks and two months of waiting, the *Tirones* of the 10th Legion were finally issued their real weapons and allowed to take the leather covers off their real shields that they had begun carrying on marches while still using the training shields for sparring. For the veterans, it was a day for them to remember as well, but almost unanimously, their thoughts went back to when they had been the eager and excited *Tirones* who, at last, had been rewarded for their efforts by at least appearing to be real Legionaries.

On that day, however, Crastinus put it differently, telling them, "It's just that the Legate can't afford to waste any more time on trying to make sure you don't stab yourselves instead of the enemy." His face was set in its normal expression, which *Tiro* Pullus had memorably commented in the first days of training that made him look like a *numen* was holding an invisible but extremely malodorous turd right under his nose as he added, "Most of the Centurions are wagering that we'll lose half of you in our first battle anyway. I know that I am."

As Crastinus intended, the grins and cheerfulness as the men held their newly assigned *gladius* in their hands and commented to each other on how light the real weapon was vanished instantly, their expressions now universally a scowl at Crastinus' jibe. Good, he thought, that made them angry, and now they're determined to prove me wrong. By this time in training, the relationship between the *Tiros* of the First Century and their Centurion was composed of almost equal portions of hatred and devotion, depending on the moment and what Crastinus was doing with them, or to them...which was exactly how it was supposed to be; it wouldn't be until after their first battle where, if he did his job, the balance would shift away from the antagonistic feelings they held for him to one of respect that came from the recognition that everything Crastinus had put them through was for a higher purpose, keeping them alive.

Three days after receiving their weapons, in late May, which was already well into the campaign season, Quintus Artorius rose along with his comrades, going through what had become an ingrained habit where there was little wasted motion, and once more, he had to force himself to break his fast, while at Domitius' urging, he consumed three more cups of water than normal, but he did so as listlessly as he had consumed the evening meal. Somehow, he had managed to survive and stay with the others on the march from the camp the day before, and the Second Cohort had been blessed by Fortuna to be responsible for placing the picket stakes that lined the dirt wall of their marching camp, which was considered the easiest duty next to being the guard Cohort standing watch during the construction. Because the tasks that were required of a ranker when preparing to march were now so ingrained, Artorius packed up and brought his *furca* outside the tent, then strapped on his shield without having any memory of doing so. When the call to assemble sounded, he simply followed the others as they fell into formation in the Cohort street along with the rest of the Second, but there was a somnambulistic quality to his movement that alerted Crastinus, who stood watching Artorius as he stumbled more than walked to his spot. In a few quick strides, Crastinus stood in front of Artorius, and with his open hand, slapped Artorius across the face.

"You still asleep, Artorius? Eh? Well," he poked Artorius in the chest with his *vitus*, "you're going to need to stay awake on the way back, because you know what happens if you fall out again, *neh*?"

Artorius surprised Crastinus, and himself, by managing to focus on the Pilus Prior long enough to respond, "I understand, Pilus Prior. And I will obey."

That's the most words he's spoken in the last two days; this was the thought that flashed through Domitius' mind as he stood next to Artorius, making no attempt to hide his concern as he studied his comrade's face as Crastinus stalked away. The command to begin the march sounded, and Artorius stepped off with his Century, thankful that today, while they were nearer to the rear of the marching column than the front, they were ahead of the baggage train, but it still meant the dust was thick and choking, since this march was with the other three Legions. Even men like Pullus had difficulty drawing a clean breath, coughing and gagging as he spat out globs of dust that turned to mud, while Artorius withdrew within himself with every passing mile. He managed to keep up until the first rest stop, but within a couple miles after the march resumed, once more, Artorius found himself stepping aside as he slowed, watching his comrades leaving him. Somehow, Domitius didn't notice immediately, absorbed in his own misery as he struggled with the dust and the pace, once again set by Caesar, but when he did, he didn't hesitate. Moving aside himself, the Tenth Section was now only eight men, but when Calienus, who saw what Domitius was doing, called out to him to remain with them, Domitius pretended not to hear; at least this was what he claimed later. From Artorius' perspective, Domitius seemed to just materialize out of the dust, coming to a stop as he waited for Artorius to reach him.

When he did, Domitius asked, "Can you carry my javelins?"

This seemed a nonsensical question to Artorius; had Domitius run out of patience and was actually trying to weigh him down more? Despite this thought, he felt his head nod up and down, and he learned what Domitius had in mind.

"Here, take mine," he said quickly. "Then hand me your *furca*."

It took a span of heartbeats for Artorius' mind to comprehend what was required of him, but without a word, he reached out and grasped Domitius' javelins, while the other *Tiro* grabbed Artorius' *furca*, demonstrating his own considerable strength despite his size by lifting it from Artorius' left shoulder to place it on his right, now burdened with more than eighty pounds.

"Let's go," Domitius said. "We need to catch up."

Numbly, Artorius followed Domitius, or tried to, but he was already lagging behind again when, once more from out of the dust, another figure appeared.

"All right, Artorius," Vinicius said encouragingly, "come with us. We're going back to the Century. You don't want to be left behind again, do you?"

It wasn't that Artorius wasn't grateful, nor that he didn't want to answer, but he knew that he couldn't afford the extra effort it would take to speak, so he simply nodded as Vinicius grabbed his arm and broke into a trot. For the rest of his days, Artorius would have no memory of how or when he was returned to his Century; it was just as if one moment he was left behind, then he found himself back with his section. Domitius made no attempt to hand Artorius his *furca*; in fact, he would carry it by himself the rest of the march, creating a small sensation among his comrades. As far as Artorius was concerned, he didn't have the strength to lift his head, so instead, he just watched the back of the feet of his Ninth Section comrade to make sure that he didn't step on them. Consequently, he was unaware of the almost constant examination of him, not just by Domitius, but by the other members of the section who would either lean a bit forward to peer down the rank or shorten their stride a half-step so that they could see Artorius from behind. When they spoke of it later, the consensus was unanimous; Quintus Artorius was unconscious, yet, somehow, he still managed to march with them, for a time at least. By the second rest stop, Artorius was gone again, but this time, he wasn't even in sight when the horn sounded the end of the respite, and it would be the last any of his comrades would see Artorius in uniform. The only other excitement came when the Mallius brother they called Romulus offered to take Artorius' *furca* from Domitius for the last part of the march, but not only did Domitius refuse, it angered him to the point that harsh words were exchanged between him and both Mallius brothers since, unsurprisingly, Remus leapt to his brother's defense. It finally required a sharp word from Calienus for them to subside, so Domitius was still carrying both when they marched into camp.

The Cohort marching drag found Artorius, collapsed on the side of the road and barely conscious, his condition serious enough that the Centurion ordered one of the wagons to stop long enough for the *Tiro* to be thrown into the back. The wagon driver was concerned enough to empty a flask of water over Artorius' head, which revived him to the point that he understood where he was...and that his time in the Legion was over. If, that was, Crastinus hadn't been lying to him. As he learned very quickly once they were back at camp, the Pilus

Prior had been serious, and in fact delegated the task of dismissing Artorius to Optio Vinicius.

"If I see his face, I know myself well enough to know that I'd thrash him," Crastinus had growled to Vinicius, which wouldn't have surprised the *Tiros* at all if they had heard him say this. They would have been staggered if they had heard him say soberly to his Optio, "I failed with that boy, Vinicius. I should have spent more time with him."

While Vinicius had only known Crastinus for about five months, he had seen enough to know that Crastinus wasn't just speaking to hear his own voice, and that he took every loss of a *Tirone* from the harsh training personally, seeing it as a failure of his leadership.

Therefore, he wasn't speaking falsely when he assured Crastinus, "Pilus Prior, you could have spent every moment with Artorius and it wouldn't have mattered." With a shrug, he said simply, "Some men just aren't made for the Legions."

The worst part for Artorius was when he was escorted to his tent to retrieve all of the equipment that Domitius had carried back to camp with him. He had already been issued a civilian tunic and had surrendered his *hamata*, helmet, and everything else that had been on his person, which was how he appeared to the section as they sat in their accustomed spots around the fire, as just another citizen, with one exception; he was still wearing his *caligae*.

"Go get your gear, Artorius," Vinicius spoke softly, but he stood slightly apart from the others, just out of the circle of firelight as he watched Artorius walk to the tent.

The normal chattering and rattling of dice in a cup, although it was now Atilius running the game, abruptly came to a stop when Artorius materialized out of the darkness and entered the circle of light from the fire. None of them, save one, looked up from the ground, but in the case of Domitius, it was Artorius who felt too ashamed to meet his eyes as he entered the tent. He was dragging out his gear from where Domitius had stowed it in the exact manner that they had been taught by Calienus all those weeks before when he heard some murmuring, then a shadow fell across the wall of the tent.

He didn't want to, but Artorius straightened up and turned

to face Domitius, who broke the silence by saying quietly, "I'm sorry, Artorius. I wish I could have done more."

This was too much for Artorius, and he hated himself for the sudden rush of emotion that made Domitius start to shimmer in his vision, but he gave a violent shake of his head.

"I'm the one who should apologize, Domitius. You did more for me than you know. I...I just don't have the strength to be in the Legion."

There, he had said it; he had finally acknowledged a truth that he had sensed almost from the first day, that his enlistment had been a mistake.

Domitius said nothing for a moment, then asked, "What are you going to do now?"

Artorius surprised himself by laughing, one of the only times he had ever done so, and admitting with what was almost a cheerful tone, "I have no idea."

Before Domitius could respond, he was joined by Scribonius, who voiced his own regret at not helping more, but then he stepped closer to Artorius and extended his hand, palm up. Artorius caught the glint of silver, and once again, his composure was threatened.

"I know that the army doesn't give you anything but that tunic," Scribonius said quietly. "Here, there's twenty *sesterces* to help you when you go back to Italica."

"I'm not going back to Italica," Artorius answered instantly, because this was the only thing that he was certain about. "I'm not going back to tell my father I failed."

"What are you going to do?" Scribonius echoed Domitius, which elicited a shared chuckle between Artorius and Domitius.

This time, Artorius said, "Maybe I'll stay here in Scallabis. It's bigger than Italica. I'll look for work."

"You might want to buy new shoes," Scribonius suggested, which surprised Artorius, but when he asked why, Scribonius explained, "Because someone might see you wearing those *caligae* and think you're a deserter. You're too young to have done a full enlistment, and you're not maimed."

It was, Artorius recognized, good advice, and he promised to do so. By this time, he had gathered up everything, and for one last time, he hoisted his *furca* to take back to the *Quaestorium*. Stepping outside, the others were in essentially the same posture, staring down at the ground, although Vellusius looked up and gave him a solemn nod, which seemed to shame the Mallius brothers, Romulus murmuring something that Artorius couldn't make out while Remus copied Vellusius. Didius was pointedly ignoring him, but this didn't surprise him. What did was when, just as he was reaching the edge of the firelight where Vinicius was waiting, someone called his name. He turned to see that it was Pullus, who had stood up to face him.

"May the gods favor and protect you, Artorius," Pullus said. "I wish you well."

Then, without waiting for a response, he turned about and dropped back down onto his seat. To a man, they were all certain that this would be the last time the men of the Tenth Section would ever see Quintus Artorius again.

A week after Artorius' dismissal, Caesar deemed that the 10th Legion was sufficiently trained, which the men learned by the announcement that, at last, the 10th would hold its first lustration ceremony. Normally performed in Januarius, the one exception was in the case of an army where there was a new Legion like the 10th that was recently formed, and while it was an important ceremony in its own right, it was doubly significant for the *Tirones* of the 10th because, after the sacred rites were performed, the Legion was ordered to remain in place.

By this point in time, all of them had at least seen Caesar, some of them close enough to touch him, but today, he was standing on the rostrum attired in his muscled cuirass and wearing the red general's cloak called the *paludamentum*, and once the other Legions were gone, he began speaking, starting with one simple word, "Soldiers!" He stopped then, knowing that it would take a moment for the meaning to register, because this was the first time he had addressed these men as such, and while he hid it well, he was pleased to see the sudden ripple of movement and the rustling sound as the men realized that they had done it, they had become Legionaries. "Today is a great day for you, and for Rome!" When he spoke to large groups, Caesar had been trained to pitch his voice higher because it carried farther, and he continued, "You are about to be entered into the rolls of the brave men who have served Rome so well in the past, covering both our eternal city and themselves in glory!" Raising one hand, he swept it across the formation in the direction of the Centurions. "Perhaps some of you will elevate yourself to the glory and rank of the men you see standing before you." Pausing a beat, he said soberly, "Perhaps not." Another beat passed. "What *is* certain is that some of you will die, if that is the will of the gods. But," his voice strengthened, "if it *is* the will of the gods that you die, it will be up to each of you to choose *how* you die. And, in dying well, you add even more glory and fame to Rome, to your tribe, to your family, and to yourselves." There wasn't a whisper now, to the point that Caesar could hear the rippling sound made when a breeze lifted his *paludamentum*, and he made sure to move his head across the Legion in an unmistakable signal that his words were meant for every single man. Returning his gaze to the First Cohort and the eagle standard held by the *Aquilifer* standing next to Favonius, Caesar finished, "I hereby declare that the training of the 10th Legion is completed, and they will be marching with me as we crush this rebellion by the barbarian tribes of Hispania!"

Even if he had wanted to say anything else, he would have been drowned out by the sudden roar of almost six thousand male voices that were raised in both celebration and in a promise they would fulfill their duty to him as their Legate, and to Rome. Satisfied, he gave Favonius a nod, turned and hopped down from the rostrum, then strode into the *Praetorium*.

When the new Gregarii of the First Century were dismissed by Crastinus, they were informed by their Pilus Prior that, for the first time since their training began, they would be allowed to leave the camp.

"I'm standing for the first round of drinks," Crastinus announced, amused at the looks of astonishment on the faces of the men, "but after that, you bastards are on your own!"

Dismissing them, he was content to watch as for the first time since they had arrived, they behaved like what they really were: a bunch of teenagers or in their early twenties, boisterous and excited, congratulating each other and themselves for achieving what all but a select few often doubted they would, becoming a Gregarius. No longer a *Probatio,* or a *Tirone*, but a full-fledged man of the Legions. Following along behind, he saw Vinicius stop to wait for him, and they exchanged a smile.

"So, who do you think are contenders for who gets the drunkest the fastest of the new meat?" Crastinus asked Vinicius, who considered for a moment.

"Fronto," he said, naming a man of the First Section who they had caught more than once trying to persuade one of his comrades to surrender their wine ration, since there was no regulation against this. "Then I think Manius," who was in the Third Section. Finally, he said, "And Atilius."

Crastinus grunted, then elbowed Vinicius. "Five *sesterces* says that it's Fronto."

Vinicius countered, "And I say Atilius."

They spat and shook hands, then Crastinus turned serious. "We're also going to need to watch for a few scores being settled."

Vinicius nodded, certain that he knew who would be at the top of the list, but he was curious to know. "Aside from Didius and Pullus, who else are you worried about?"

"Dolabella and Varus," Crastinus replied, naming two close comrades of the Fifth Section. "They had some sort of falling out, but Rufio either doesn't know or won't say what it was about."

"Knowing Rufio," Vinicius said confidently of the Sergeant of the Fifth Section, "he doesn't know, because if he did, he'd tell you."

"I agree," Crastinus nodded.

By this time, their conversation had led them past the Cohort area on their way out of camp, heading towards one of the ramshackle huts that were a feature of a semi-permanent military camp, always constructed close to the camp and outside the walls of whatever town or city so that they fell outside the jurisdiction of the *duumviri* who ran the administration of the municipality in the name of Rome. As time passed and the shantytown grew in size, an informal system that had been around for as long as anyone could remember had developed, whereby those *tavernae* and brothels were claimed by men of different Cohorts and Legions. Because the three other Legions present, the 7th, 8th, and 9th, were veteran Legions, they had been given access to Scallabis, while the officers of the 10th, and now the new Gregarii had the shantytown. Where Crastinus and Vinicius were headed was a *taverna* that was for the First and Second Centuries of the Second Cohort.

By the time they entered the *taverna,* dubiously titled The Happy Legionary, one of only a handful of titles used to by proprietors to advertise that they catered to men of the Legions, they had agreed on who needed to be watched, while Crastinus pulled out his coin purse, slapped it on the counter, and told the pockmarked man behind the bar who was missing three fingers on his right hand, the sign that he had once been under the standard, "Crack open a half-dozen amphorae, Glabius, and get ready!"

By the time the men arrived, Crastinus had already consumed three cups of wine, so when the new men entered, they were greeted by a very different Gaius Crastinus, who bellowed, "Welcome home, boys!"

Once everyone had arrived, Crastinus waited for their cups to be charged, then began circulating the room to offer each man his arm, offering up some anecdote that involved them, and even when it was something that had angered Crastinus in the moment, or seemed to, Crastinus related it in a humorous tone.

Naturally, Pullus was easy to spot, and Crastinus wasn't surprised to see that he was standing with Domitius and Scribonius, and he saved the trio for last, waiting for Domitius and Scribonius to return to the counter for another cup so that he could get Pullus alone, bellowing, "Well! Here's the hero! Hasn't seen a battle yet, but he already has those Lusitani *cunni* shaking in their tracks!"

He had made sure to raise his voice, and as he intended, it evoked a rousing chorus that was composed of both approbation and jeering, although to Crastinus' ears, it was mostly good-natured. Nevertheless, not everyone was happy, and Crastinus saw Didius out of the corner of his eye, glaring at the back of the big Roman, who looked both mortified and pleased and blushing furiously.

The young Roman actually kicked at the packed dirt floor, looking down at it as he said, "I certainly hope I can live up to your belief in me, Pilus Prior."

"You will, boy," Crastinus assured him with a laugh. "You will, I have no doubt of that. Once I saw you working the *rudis*, I knew that you'd be one to watch." Crastinus slapped Pullus on the shoulder. "Just save some for the rest of the boys, eh?"

Then he was moving on; as Pilus Prior, he had to go visit each of his Centuries in their spots in the shantytown, and after a brief conversation with Vinicius, he slipped out the door. By the time he got back, he thought with amusement, the bet Vinicius made would be settled one way or another.

Didius wasn't the only one who watched the exchange with Crastinus, but Calienus' attention was evenly divided between Pullus and Didius, and despite being across the crowded room, he was certain he could feel the hatred radiating from the latter man. For an instant, it appeared as if Didius was seriously considering attacking Pullus, from behind again, Calienus thought contemptuously, and he tensed, ready to leap across the space. If Didius intended to, the arrival of Domitius back from the counter coincided with Crastinus walking off, prompting Didius to turn away, stalking off towards the counter and another cup. Calienus crossed the room, just in time to catch Domitius give Pullus a playful punch.

"Aaaaah, quit moping about, you big ox!" He heard Domitius tell Pullus, who had a thoughtful and troubled expression on his face as Domitius continued, "You'll be fine and you know it. He's right; you'll probably kill so many of those barbarians that there won't be enough for the rest of us."

Pullus didn't see Calienus approaching, and he was clearly unconvinced. "I hope it works out like that. But the truth is, none of us really know." Suddenly, he lowered his voice, but Calienus had gotten close enough to hear him continue, "I mean, nobody truly knows how they'll react until it happens, *neh*? So for all I know, I may find that my knees turn to water, and I piss myself like a girl."

Once again, Calienus was impressed, and he agreed, "That much is true." Pullus whirled about to look down at him with a startled expression, but Calienus continued, "Nobody really knows what they'll do the first time they face the enemy, unless they're," he used his head to jerk it in Didius' direction, "a liar or a fool like him." Pullus glanced over to where Didius had begun talking to the handful of men who were at least friendly to him. "All you can do is this," Calienus said, "rely on your training, and put your trust in the man next to you." Reaching up, Calienus grabbed Pullus by the shoulder, his voice becoming intense as he assured Pullus, "The rest will come much easier than you think. When the moment comes, trust me, you'll know what to do." Done with Pullus, Calienus turned to Domitius, and said seriously, "And both of you need to watch each other's back at all times."

This made Domitius laugh.

"All right, Sergeant, but we haven't started the fighting yet!"

Calienus shook his head, and for the second time, used his head to indicate Didius, saying seriously, "I wasn't talking about the Lusitani. I'm talking about him."

When the pair looked beyond Calienus, they saw that, despite being surrounded by laughing comrades, Didius had his cup to his lips, but was looking straight at them with a malevolent stare. Calienus moved away, and quickly enough, thanks to a couple cups more wine, both Pullus and Domitius quickly forgot Didius and his enmity. And, as he had been certain, Vinicius won his bet on who got the drunkest, the evidence being finding Atilius sprawled in the middle of the muddy road back to the camp, snoring soundly.

The next morning, there was no vestige of the affable, comradely Pilus Prior Crastinus who entered all ten tents of his Century bellowing at the top of his lungs, and it was the misfortune of the Tenth Section that he started with them first. Pullus found himself dumped out of his cot by a booted foot, but he was fortunate that, at the same time, Crastinus was using his *vitus* on Domitius, still lying on his cot next to Pullus, then as quickly as he arrived, he was gone, his progress marked by his bellowing voice and the alarmed shouts of the other sections, leaving the Tenth Section behind in an uproar.

"What was that about?" Pullus demanded of Calienus indignantly. "We were sworn in yesterday!"

Calienus had been forewarned about what to expect, and he explained to his tentmates, "What happened yesterday was unusual. Normally, you'd have completed all four months of training before swearing in, but Caesar's anxious to move because it's already late. So he had you sworn in earlier than usual. It didn't sit well with some of the Centurions, I'll tell you that." Anticipating the response, he hurried to add, "The Pilus Prior wasn't one of them, though. I heard him telling Optio Vinicius he thinks the Century is ready to go right now." He paused, then gave them a grin as he finished, "The Second Century is another story."

Their feelings assuaged, the men made preparations for what would be the final part of their training with the entire army of four Legions, the first, and last, time they would do so in training. After another march, two marching camps were created, with the even-numbered Legions in one camp, and the other two in the second. The next day, a mock battle was performed, while Caesar had ordered the building of a tower so that he could stand above the dust and confusion to watch. No other Legate that Crastinus had ever served under had done as much, but his immediate thought was to wonder why it hadn't been done before. Along with the crashing of the wicker shields and *rudii* that had been hauled to the site in wagons, the Centurions worked on the variety of maneuvers that they anticipated they would be facing in the field, the shrill blasts of bone whistles, blown notes by the *Corniceni,* the men who carried the large curved horn called the *Cornu* in every Century, and bellowed commands creating a cacophony of noise that, as time passed and the men gained experience, they would be able to use to determine the course of a battle and how they were faring. Wisely, at least in the opinion of Favonius and the other Primi Pili, Caesar had made it clear that he wouldn't be judging which of the two groups was the winner or loser, not wanting any animosity between the Legions that should be focused on the rebelling Lusitani, the first tribe that Caesar planned on subjugating, nor did he order one side to emulate the battle tactics of the enemy they would be facing, which was the one aspect of Roman training that Caesar found wanting, but there was only so much flaunting he could do of the ancient customs. Much emphasis was made on moving from a marching column into a battle line, whereupon the order was immediately given to collapse back into a column in order to simulate a march that culminated in contact with the enemy, a battle, then a pursuit of this enemy. How to conduct a fighting withdrawal was the last maneuver to be practiced, but the opinion among the Centurions of all four Legions was unanimous, that they would never be forced to use this in battle. As Caesar expected, on their return to Scallabis, he was leading a fit and well-trained army, ready and indeed eager to face the enemy.

Two nights before the army was departing on campaign, the men of the 10th were given permission for the first time to go into the city of Scallabis, albeit with strict warnings about what parts of the city they were to avoid because they were now where the three senior Legions congregated, none of the two hundred forty Centurions wanting their men to be responsible for a brawl. In the Tenth Section, opinion was almost evenly divided about whether to go into the shantytown or the city, with Pullus, Domitius, and Scribonius preferring to stay in familiar surroundings, while Vellusius announced that he was fine with his new close comrade Scribonius making the decision. The loss of Artorius had proven to be a blessing for Vellusius, who had been miserable with Didius, and he had approached Calienus for advice.

"Your close comrade is the man you trust the most," Calienus had counseled, then reminded Vellusius, "He holds the second copy of your will, he's the man who, if your life depended on it, you'd look to him before anyone else." Vellusius said nothing, but he looked so miserable that Calienus patted him on the shoulder and assured him, "I'll take care of it." That night, he had called Didius, and surprisingly, Atilius aside, and told Didius bluntly, "I don't think you're the right match for Vellusius, so I've decided that you and Atilius are now close comrades."

"You can't do that!" Didius protested, although he had no idea if this was true, which Calienus was counting on, and the Sergeant shot back, "Can you point out the regulation that forbids a section Sergeant from making that change?"

"You know I can't," Didius snapped; his illiteracy, while he was far from the only unlettered man, was still a tender subject with him, and while he was angry, he also knew he was defeated.

Not once did he glance over at Atilius, who had been standing there as a mute witness, and it wasn't until after Didius stalked away that Calienus turned to Atilius and said quietly, "As we agreed. You get an extra wine ration once a week, and for the next month, your name is at the bottom of the list for *cac* details."

Atilius only nodded, and Calienus knew that the new Gregarius was far more concerned with the wine than the prospect of missing out on some unpleasant task, but he was also the only other member of the section who had anywhere near Didius' passion for gambling. For his part, Calienus was surprised that when the men left the camp, Didius and Atilius were together, along with the Mallius brothers, who were chattering about the spot they had stayed at the night before they enlisted. The Sergeant had also been wavering back and forth about going into the city, but Vinicius, *Tesserarius* Cordus, the third in command, and two of the other Sergeants had persuaded him that there was a brothel that he would regret not visiting for the rest of his days. Following the stream of men heading for the *Porta Praetoria*, the gate that led directly to Scallabis, he quickly forgot Didius and Atilius and the other sundry items that were part of his duties.

Didius was secretly happy that Atilius didn't appear upset that they were now close comrades, but he was still angry at Calienus. However, he was also nervous, because he had made a decision to do something that he had expressly been told not to do, and that was to visit Marcus Surenas, or as he now knew him, his uncle Gaius Didius. He considered actually telling Atilius in the hope that his new close comrade would come along, but he decided against it.

Instead, for one of the few times in his life, Didius actually made an attempt at amiability, telling Atilius, "If you know of a good place for some wine and a whore, we can go there."

Atilius didn't look over at Didius as he answered, "I don't know much about Scallabis, and what little I know, I can barely remember."

"Ah, that's right." Didius nodded, recalling hearing Atilius recounting his story of why he had shown up a day late. "You were robbed and knocked out, I remember now."

For a brief instant, Atilius considered telling Didius the truth as a sign of trust in his new comrade, but it was a fleeting thought, so he only nodded. And, he thought, it's pretty much the truth; I'm not lying about not remembering much, just why I don't.

Aloud, he said, "Once we get through the gate, maybe I'll see something I remember."

The gates were open, the *duumviri* warned by Caesar to expect even more Legionaries than they had gotten accustomed to over the previous five months, but while neither official was happy about it, they also knew better than to argue the point with the *Praetor*. Didius and Atilius were about midway down what was a line of groups, some with just two men like themselves, and others, like those containing Calienus numbering a half-dozen and more. The street torches were being lit by the slaves, but while some of the men didn't pause inside the gateway, knowing exactly where they were heading, most of the men of the 10th, particularly the *Tiros,* came to a stop as they discussed their options for exploring.

"They told us we're not supposed to go south of the Forum," Didius commented, then he gave Atilius a nudge, giving him his version of a grin as he added, "That must mean the pickings are so good that those bastards in the other Legions don't want to share. Maybe that's where we should go."

Atilius shook his head, but his objection wasn't based on

the idea of disobeying orders, but for a more practical reason, which he indicated by pointing to his tunic. "They'll know we're from the 10th because our tunics aren't as faded as theirs."

Didius was chagrined, realizing this was true, but he wasn't about to admit that; instead, he said, "It's going to be full dark. The only way we get caught is if we're spotted around one of the torches. And," he added, "once we're inside some place, you know how dark they are."

That, Atilius realized, was true. Besides, he reasoned, this would be one way he could show Didius he could be trusted.

"Let's go," he said. "You're right, as long as we're careful, we should be fine."

Didius' smile was genuine, for him, and he slapped Atilius on the back.

"Here's a man who thinks the way I do! So let's go see why those greedy bastards don't want us men of the 10th snooping around, eh?"

What befell the two new close comrades wasn't at the hands of the men from another Legion, but it was caused by Atilius' faulty memory. Initially, once they crossed the Forum and entered the southern half of the city, they behaved with caution, attempting to appear as if they were just a pair of Legionaries from the authorized Legions but moving to the far side of the street at every corner where there was a torch in a wall sconce. Fairly quickly, they saw that none of the other men were even giving them a glance; they were just another couple of Legionaries out on the town for a last night of debauchery. It was when the distinctive stench unique to pigs assaulted their nostrils that Atilius felt a stirring of something, but he said nothing, telling himself that there was probably at least a dozen of these around the city. Then, when they rounded a corner, Atilius came to a dead stop, looking across the street at the small crowd standing outside a two-story building with an oil lamp hanging above the door to illuminate a faded sign that was barely legible. Since neither Atilius nor Didius were literate, what the sign said didn't matter, but the appearance of the *taverna* triggered in Atilius a memory.

"I remember this place," he told Didius. "The wine tastes like piss, but it's cheap. And," he pointed up to the second floor, whose shuttered windows still leaked out light, although it was the sounds of passion, real on the part of the customer, and counterfeit on the part of the woman providing the service that confirmed Atilius' words, "there's a brothel right upstairs."

"Looks like a good place to start," Didius agreed, then crossed the street, but the pair experienced a moment of anxiety when, just as they reached the door, four men emerged, all of them wearing the same soldier's tunic.

Because of the lamplight, Atilius was certain that the comparison between his and Didius' bright red tunic that was only slightly more faded than when they were issued three months earlier and theirs that could only charitably be called red would be instantly obvious. To the relief of both of them, only the last man out even gave them a glance, but he only nodded and resumed his conversation with one of the others. Didius looked over his shoulder and shot Atilius a grin, then stepped inside as Atilius followed. Pausing just long enough to scan the interior, Didius spotted an empty table in the corner, leading Atilius to it and, in what would turn out to be a fateful decision, took the seat facing the counter at the back of the *taverna*, leaving Atilius to sit facing the door.

"A couple of cups to start the night," Didius said, beginning to think that Marcus Atilius wasn't a bad sort after all and Fortuna might have had a hand in Calienus' decision, while Atilius sat down, nodding enthusiastically and smacking his lips, replying, "Why stop at a couple?"

Didius' laugh sounded more like a bark, but it was genuine, and he slapped the table to exclaim, "Now, I like the way you think!"

This was the moment when a female wearing an apron and carrying a round wooden tray approached, catching Didius' eye, but while he noticed how she came to an abrupt halt, then spun back around to scurry around the tables back to the counter, he assumed she had forgotten something.

"Do you remember enough about this place to recommend one of the girls upstairs?" Didius asked, then before Atilius

221

could respond, he added, "Normally, I like them young, but by the gods, right now, I'd fuck a goat!"

Atilius laughed, agreeing, "Same here. But," he shook his head, "the only girl I remember is..."

If the owner hadn't bellowed something unintelligible first, he probably would have succeeded in bashing Atilius' brains out with the cudgel he was lifting above his head, but while the other customers who saw what was about to happen only gaped in surprise, Didius actually leapt to his feet, and just as the man, heavyset and with a black beard that hung down to mid-chest, began to swing the club down, Didius took a step forward as he launched a straight punch that struck the owner on the point of his chin. As Atilius and the other men of his section had learned, Didius was the second strongest man in their tent, and between this and the fact that the owner essentially ran right into the blow, there was a meaty sound punctuated by a noise that sounded a bit like gravel being crunched underfoot as the bone of his lower jaw was shattered. It was the way he landed, already unconscious, the back of his head smacking the wooden floor that caused another sound that was similar to the first one that arrested everyone for a couple of heartbeats, including Didius, who stared dumbly down at the man, the slowly spreading stain around the man's head glistening in the lamplight. The silence was broken then by the shrill scream of the woman that Didius had barely noticed, and he looked up from the man he was close to certain was dead to see her, one hand on her mouth, pointing at Didius. This, at least, was his initial thought, but then he noticed this wasn't the case; she wasn't pointing at him, she was pointing at Atilius, who had gotten to his feet and turned around, his mouth hanging open in surprise.

"*That's him!*" she shrieked, the shock on her face transforming into something else, and again she screamed, "*That's him! The one who...*"

Whatever she was saying was drowned out by the shouts of the other customers, which included a fair number of Legionaries, and they were also on their feet now, every one of them looking directly at Didius and Atilius.

"Follow me!" Didius snapped, but he was already moving

for the door.

To his credit, Atilius didn't hesitate, while one man, not a Legionary but some sort of tradesman by the look of him, stepped in between Didius and Atilius, meaning that it was Atilius' turn to inflict punishment, although he was content to lower his shoulder as if he had his shield hard up against it, slamming into the man's midriff and sending him flying backwards. The man still almost foiled Atilius' attempt to escape because of his body serving as an obstacle that caused Atilius to stumble, and he would have fallen if an immensely strong hand hadn't snatched a handful of tunic as Didius kept him on his feet. Then, they were out the door, leaving the *taverna* in an uproar, dashing for the nearest corner, both of them having been taught the same skill by their fathers, although neither of them was aware of this. It was actually Atilius who violated one of the rules by risking a glance over his shoulder, but while several men had spilled out into the street, and a couple even began running in their direction, his experience told him that their hearts weren't in it and they wouldn't be pursuing the pair far. Nevertheless, while they slowed down once they made the corner, they still moved at a trot until they reached the forum and crossed it back into the area that was safe for the men of the 10th before they stopped.

Both of them bent over at the waist with their hands on their knees, and Didius panted, "Pluto's *cock*! What was that about? Why did that *mentula* want to bash your fucking head in?"

Atilius didn't answer immediately, catching more of his breath before he answered, "I don't know, Didius! I swear it!" Straightening back up, he eyed Didius with a newfound respect, and gratitude. "But whatever the reason, you saved my bacon, Didius. And," he offered his arm, "I owe you for that."

For his part, Didius was assailed by a number of emotions, some of them in direct conflict with each other. To begin with, this was the first time in his life he could recall being praised for what could be considered a heroic act that was on behalf of someone else, and while his face remained impassive, he was moved. The fact that he had assumed that the man who was clearly the owner of the *taverna* was, for some reason, about to attack him and not Atilius was something that Didius would never divulge.

"That's what we're supposed to do for each other, *neh*?" he said gruffly, accepting Atilius' grasp. Then, with a laugh, Didius added, "I just didn't think it was going to be in a *cac*hole in Scallabis. I thought it would be against one of those barbarian bastards." There was an awkward silence then, which Didius broke, clearing his throat, then admitting to Atilius, "Actually, I wasn't entirely honest with you about something, Atilius, when I said I didn't know anything about Scallabis. I *do* know of a place on the north side of the Forum we can go." Suddenly uncomfortable, Didius fumbled, "It's just that it's somewhat...complicated. The situation, I mean." Deciding to throw the dice, Didius confessed, "My father didn't come with me to Scallabis to stand for my enlistment. He sent me to see a man he said would be able to take care of it. And," he shrugged, "it turned out that he's my uncle."

"That's good, though, isn't it?" Atilius replied. "I mean, I know that they allow an uncle or grandfather to stand for you."

"He's not the one who stood for me," Didius confessed. "He found someone to do it."

"Why?" Atilius was confused now.

"Because I'd always thought he was dead," Didius answered honestly. Initially, this was as forthcoming as he was prepared to be, then he realized that he wanted Atilius to be with him when he talked to Gaius Didius, so he went on, "And my brother and I thought that our father killed him in a...dispute," he finished, knowing how lame this description sounded.

But, just as Atilius didn't know that Didius had assumed the man was coming for him, Didius didn't know that Atilius' background was, in many ways, remarkably similar, so he wasn't surprised at all; again, his question was more practical in nature.

"Will your uncle be glad that you came to see him before we leave?"

"I doubt it," Didius admitted, but Atilius simply shrugged.

"There's only one way to find out. So," he turned to face the northern wall, "how do we get there?"

Primus Pilus Favonius summoned his Pili Priores first thing the next morning to get a report on how the men of the new Legion had comported themselves the night before, and after listening, he was quite pleased.

"So it sounds like the boys behaved for the most part," he summarized once he listened to the other nine Centurions. "We only had one brawl in the Third Century of my Cohort, but it was broken up quickly and nobody's on the sick and injured list." His battered features split into a grin then, and there was no mistaking the pleasure he took in saying with a chuckle, "But the same thing can't be said for the 9th."

"I heard something about that," the Tertius Pilus Prior, Tiberius Carfulenus, spoke up. "Some trouble with a citizen?"

"Oh, you could say that," Favonius answered, still smiling. "Apparently, some bastard was stupid enough to come back to the *taverna* where he raped a barmaid. A barmaid," he added, not smiling as broadly now, "who was actually the owner's daughter. The owner attacked the ranker, and if what they're saying is true, the Legionary killed him with one punch."

This elicited a chorus of murmurs and a couple of low whistles, and Crastinus said, "Good thing it wasn't someone from the 10th, because the only ranker I know who could do that is Pullus in my Century."

Instantly, the competitive nature that was a feature of the makeup of Centurions of Rome surfaced, just as Crastinus knew it would when the Quintus Pilus Prior, Gnaeus Arvina, scoffed, "*Gerrae!* I've seen Pullus, Crastinus, and no doubt he's big and strong, but he's a boy! My man Tullius would throw him around like a sack of grain!"

"Neither of them match Bassus," the Nones Pilus Prior, Lucius Silanus, interjected. "He was the wrestling champion of the 2nd Legion for the last three years!"

"See what you started?" Favonius said dryly to Crastinus, who gave him a grin.

"We don't have time to do it now, but when we come back, I'm willing to put up some money that says Pullus can whip both of them," Crastinus challenged, and very quickly, the subject of the killing of a *taverna* owner was forgotten.

Chapter Five

His name was Marcus Creticus Appius Piso, and he was one of the six Tribunes assigned to the newly formed 10th Legion by the Legate and *Praetor* Gaius Julius Caesar. The fact that he was never once referred to by any of his names by the men he, in theory, commanded was something of which he was, and would be unaware of for his time with the Legion. Piso, although he preferred to use the Appius name because it was more prestigious and, through his mother, he was of a minor branch of the Appius Claudius family, was one of the fine young men of Rome who, once they decided on a public career, took their first step on the *cursus honorum*, the list of offices that culminated with Consul and of which Tribune was the first. There were civil Tribunes and military Tribunes, but Roman society being what it was, the posting to a Legion was considered the more prestigious of the two, which was why Piso had asked his father, who was a Senator, to use his influence to secure the post. The fact that Piso was completely unsuited for the military, and in truth was something of an idiot, was something that Piso was unaware of nor would he have believed it if he had been told, even by his father, who did know his son was a dullard. In this, however, Piso wasn't unique, and it was another feature of Roman society that has been shared by other cultures before and since, the idea that somehow the men of a family who in previous generations were capable of and performed noteworthy deeds somehow passed the qualities that made them great down to their descendants, when the truth was that Piso was just the opposite. This wasn't why he earned his unfortunate nickname, however; it was his fondness for sweet pastries that he couldn't seem to control that made him almost too corpulent for service, combined with the kind of pale complexion of a man who preferred to recline on a couch inside his father's large villa on the Palatine, or their country estate outside Alba Longa, that was reminiscent of the finally milled wheat that made the bread that graced the finest tables. More than anything, however, it was his habit of puffing up his chest and thrusting it out when he felt the need to remind someone who had offended him of his lofty ancestry that earned him the nickname Doughboy. Indeed, his time with the 10th would be so undistinguished for any positive reason that the new *Tiros* who would go on to survive and serve at least one full enlistment would only remember him as Doughboy and never by his name. It wasn't just the men of the ranks who viewed him as largely incompetent; it was a view shared by the Centurions, and most importantly, it was shared by Caesar. However, while Caesar wasn't normally overly concerned with traditions, especially those that were observed simply because things had always been done a certain way, there were political issues that meant that Caesar was resigned to the young Tribune remaining as part of his staff. Where Caesar drew the line was in the tradition that dated back to the earliest days of the Republic, where the command of the entire Legion was rotated on a daily basis among the six Tribunes.

While it was true that few Legates adhered to this, most of them, including Pompeius Magnus, were content to perpetuate the fiction by going through the part of the morning routine where one Tribune turned over command to the next, with the understanding that this was nothing but ceremonial. Caesar wasn't willing to do even that, precisely because he was certain that Doughboy, along with one or two other Tribunes of the twenty-four spread between the four Legions would actually try to exert some sort of authority because he was so dense. That he had done so once had earned Caesar a visit from Primus Pilus Favonius, who told him flatly that putting Doughboy in a position of any authority over this newly formed Legion before it saw battle would be a serious mistake. In a move for which Caesar would become famous throughout the Legions he commanded, the Legate deferred to Favonius' judgment, and informed all of the Tribunes that they wouldn't even be going through the pretense of rotating command, and that they were to issue no orders to any Centurion on their own authority. He had also assured Favonius that, in the event he or one of his Centurions was approached by a Tribune with orders, they could be certain that it was at Caesar's direction.

Consequently, all of the Tribunes, Doughboy included, became little more than glorified messengers, but while all of them were aware that this was the case, only five of those attached to the 10th accepted it. Fortunately, for all involved, the Tribunes had virtually nothing to do during the three months and one week that the 10th was being trained, but now that the orders had been issued to prepare to march against the Lusitani, Doughboy was determined to make his mark on these men. He might have been unaware of his nickname, but he knew that they didn't respect him, and he attributed this to Caesar's unfortunate and, frankly, wrongheaded decision to keep the Tribunes from exerting any authority, a tradition that dated back centuries, about which Caesar seemed to care about not a whit. To correct this, he had decided to supervise the Second Cohort in particular, for the simple reason that their Pilus Prior, a vulgar, scarred man named Crastinus, was second only to the Primus Pilus in not hiding his disdain for a superior officer. By rights, he should have chosen Favonius, but while he told himself it was because he was aware that Favonius had responsibility for not only his own Cohort but the entire Legion, the truth was that while he was scared of Crastinus, he was terrified of Favonius. Consequently, on this day, he was making what was essentially a large circuit of the Second Cohort, determined that by the end of the day, these men would know his name.

For the new *Gregarii*, as hectic as training had seemed, it was nothing compared to what it took to get ready to march in earnest this time, with the prospect of facing a real enemy. And, while they all professed to be eager to set out to one degree or another, Calienus knew how much of this was just the bluster and bravado of young men about to face the unknown. As he knew it would, there was one event that brought the reality of what faced them home, and that was the order by Pilus Prior Crastinus that every single man make a will. Each Gregarius was required to do so, which meant that it was an opportunity for the clerks and literate men in the ranks to make extra money, or perhaps a favor or two in exchange for writing it out. Any man in the ranks who aspired to climb the promotion ladder had to be literate, because the Centurions and Optios were required to be able to read and to do figures as part of their job making requisitions and writing reports that had become more prevalent after the Marian Reforms. In the Tenth Section, Didius, Atilius, and Vellusius were completely unlettered, while the Mallius brothers could write their names and a few simple words. He wasn't at all surprised that Scribonius was by far the best educated, and he had actually slipped up once and admitted that he also spoke and wrote Greek, but Calienus was somewhat startled to learn that the final two members of the section, Domitius and Pullus, were also literate.

One evening as they were sitting around the fire, he asked curiously, "Domitius, where did you learn to read and write?"

"My mother," Domitius replied with a shrug. "Since I wasn't going to be part of my father's tanning business, she thought I should learn how to read and write so that I could find work more easily."

"How did your mother learn?" Calienus asked; it was unusual for women in their society, particularly in the Head Count, to be educated to any degree.

Domitius actually looked startled, and he didn't answer while he chewed his bread thoughtfully, trying to remember. Finally, he shrugged and replied, "Actually, I have no idea. It never occurred to me to ask."

Satisfied, Calienus turned to Pullus; by this point about a week before the march, Calienus had learned enough about Pullus to know that his father loathed his son, a sentiment which the son returned in full measure, and that Pullus' father was a farmer, and a drunk. The combination of these facts didn't seem to lend itself to the father teaching his son to read and write, but when he asked Pullus who had taught him, the large youth shifted uncomfortably, glancing over at Domitius, silently communicating to his friend, who spoke up on behalf of his friend.

"Actually, I did," Domitius admitted, then shrugged. "He helped me with our training with Cyclops, so I returned the favor."

Despite being literate, this didn't mean that Pullus and Domitius were up to the task of writing a will, and this was where Scribonius stepped in, and in fact, volunteered to write out the wills for every new man in the section, two copies apiece, one of which was given to the Century *Tesserarius*, Aulus Cordus, while the close comrade kept the other. The wills were written on sheets of vellum, for which the army would deduct the cost from their pay, of course, and at Calienus' suggestion, the copy carried by the men in their pack was wrapped up in a waterproofed cloth. Watching his charges carefully place their comrade's will in the bottom of their pack, Calienus felt a twinge of nostalgia, and a bit of sadness, remembering both the feeling he was certain the others were experiencing when he had done this for the first time, but this inevitably led to remembering the death of his first close comrade, Publius Capito. It had been Calienus' responsibility to fulfill Capito's wish that his ashes be sent to his parents, along with the sum of money that Capito had had in his Legion account, which was also held by the *Tesserarius*, and since Calienus had learned his letters by then, he had written a message for them as well. As a veteran, Calienus knew the high likelihood that at least one of his new comrades would be performing essentially the same function in the near future, but that, unfortunately, came with life under the standard, and while Calienus was cautiously optimistic that the section would acquit itself well, he also knew that there was only one way to find out.

On the day before the march, Doughboy had managed to insert himself into the middle of the work being performed by the men of the Second Cohort, chastising those men who didn't snap to *intente* when he made his first pass, then criticizing their slow progress on the next, completely oblivious to the fact that he was a large part of the delay. He had decided to start with the Sixth Century, telling himself that he would save the First Century for last, not because he was afraid of Crastinus, but in his opinion, that Century was the least disciplined of the Cohort, defining discipline in terms of how deferential they were towards him; that this was due to the men feeding off of their

Centurion's contempt for him was just one more thing that escaped Doughboy's attention. By the time he had reached the Third Century, he had varied his routine a bit, choosing to perform a snap inspection on a man who had eyed him with an expression that indicated his lack of respect, or just because he didn't like the look of the fellow. Not surprisingly, Doughboy was completely dissatisfied with what he found; a smudge on a man's helmet, or a scratch on the coat of varnish applied to the Legionary *baltea* brought with it the command to correct this deficiency immediately. Equally unsurprising was the fact that some of the men of the Third fell behind their comrades in their assigned tasks to the point that it drew the attention of their Centurion, the Princeps Prior Marcus Gabinius. Compounding their misfortune, Doughboy had already waddled out of eyesight when Gabinius happened upon four of his men occupied with tasks that weren't what he had ordered. Within a span of a couple heartbeats, Gabinius was using his *vitus* liberally on the unfortunates until, between yelps of pain as they covered their heads, one of them managed to gasp out the reason they seemed to be disobeying their Centurion, that they were obeying the orders of the fat Tribune who had just been there.

"Pluto's cock," Gabinius snarled, and while he felt a bit sheepish about lashing out, he certainly wasn't going to apologize, although he assured them, "I'm going to talk to the Pilus Prior so that he can put a stop to that idi..." He bit the word off, knowing the rule that Centurions were to never utter anything that could be construed as disrespectful about superior officers in front of the men, and he managed to correct himself, "...Tribune from meddling."

He strode off, his one sop to the men he had punished unjustly was pretending not to hear them cursing him under their breath. Unfortunately for the men of the Second Cohort, Crastinus was in a meeting with the Primus Pilus, and by the time Gabinius learned this, Doughboy had already managed to visit the final two Centuries, leaving confusion and consternation in his wake.

Doughboy had certainly noticed the huge Gregarius before; there was simply no way to miss the man who stood a head or more above most of his comrades, and who was so broad across the shoulders that Doughboy felt sure that he took up two spots in his rank. He had never been this close to him, however, and the youth was even more impressive, and daunting to a man like Doughboy, who had never been athletically inclined in his life and hadn't seen his own muscles since early childhood. Even before he reached the First Century to inspect them, he had chosen to make an example of this Gregarius, but that resolve seemed to evaporate the instant he got within a couple paces, so instead, he chose the man's diminutive comrade, whose head didn't quite come up to the giant's shoulder. The pair were working together, their assigned task gathering up the stakes and carefully coiling the guide ropes of their section tent, which was now collapsed, with their backs to him as he approached.

"Gregarii!" Doughboy snapped in what he considered a commanding tone; how the men described it would have infuriated him, but what was important was that both of them instantly straightened up, turned and came to *intente*. Pointing down to the smaller man's *baltea*, which was perfectly varnished, he said severely, "There's a scratch on your leathers, Gregarius. I spotted it a dozen paces away!" He took care to keep his gaze pinned on the short man in an unconscious attempt to send the message to his comrade that his ire was directed at only one of them. "What do you have to say for yourself, eh?"

By the time Doughboy had reached the First Century, the most common response to his chastisement had been an initial protest by the chosen Gregarius, which meant he was completely unprepared for the short Gregarius to respond immediately, "Absolutely correct, sir. Won't happen again, sir."

Doughboy's reaction was one of bemusement; he had already opened his mouth in anticipation of what he assumed the Gregarius would say based on his prior interactions with the rest of the Cohort, and it remained hanging open as he tried to think of an appropriate response. Making matters worse, he could see at the edge of his vision the large Gregarius who, while he maintained a straight face, he could see was fighting to keep from laughing.

"Very well then," he finally managed. "Just make sure it doesn't happen again." Doughboy knew that he should be moving along, but his feet seemed to be stuck to the dirt, and he stood motionless for several heartbeats before, clearing his throat, he said, "Right. Well, I must go. There are many duties to attend to."

Spinning about, he tried his best to march off, but the truth was that his thighs rubbed together when he moved in this manner, so within a few paces, he was back to his normal gait, which he knew was undignified but couldn't seem to help. Compounding his problems, he clearly heard two voices roaring with laughter, and for an instant, he was tempted to turn back around and make an issue of it, but he decided he had made his point. The Second Cohort knew who Marcus Creticus Appius Piso was, and that he was not a man with whom to trifle! They would remember his name now; he was sure of it.

"How many times did Doughboy come by?" Crastinus asked his Centurions and Vinicius, once he had returned from meeting with the Primus Pilus and had been approached not only by Gabinius, but by Gnaeus Calpurnius, the Centurion in command of the Fourth Century.

"At least three times with me." Gabinius spoke first, but this earned a snort from the Hastatus Posterior, Tiberius Fronto.

"Only three?" Fronto scoffed. "He walked back and forth through my Century *five* times, and he stopped one or two of my boys every fucking time. That," he became apologetic, "is why we were the last to finish, Pilus Prior, I swear it!"

Normally, this wouldn't have been enough to assuage Crastinus, but Fronto had the good fortune that, even with the delays, the Second Cohort had reported its readiness to march before any other Cohort, even the First, putting Crastinus in a magnanimous mood. Vinicius had remained silent, although this wasn't all that unusual because he was taciturn by nature, but when Crastinus glanced over at him, he shrugged.

"He only made one pass through the First."

"*Gerrae!*" Calpurnius exclaimed. "How did you get that fortunate?"

"I'm not sure," Vinicius admitted, then after a slight

hesitation, he allowed, "although I saw him bracing Domitius and Pullus. Then," he offered another shrug, "he just walked away and I didn't see him again."

"Pullus probably terrified him just standing there." Crastinus chuckled, although the other Centurions' reaction was more muted, most of them only smiling.

There was one exception, and it was Fronto, who for reasons nobody could guess, had taken an intense dislike of a *Tirone* that wasn't even in his Century.

"I'll still put up twenty *sesterces* that he *cacs* himself and rolls up into a ball in his first battle." This engendered some mutters of disagreement, but Fronto completely missed the glance exchanged between Crastinus and Vinicius, addressing Gabinius instead, who was clearly the most skeptical one. "You know how those big men are, Gabinius! They're so used to being stronger than everyone else, but when they meet a man who isn't afraid of them, they fall apart!"

"Some do," Gabinius agreed, "but that's not always true."

"Bah!" Fronto spat on the ground. "Maybe one out of a hundred!"

"I'm not sure there are a hundred men Pullus' size in the entire army," Calpurnius pointed out, laughing as he did so because he didn't want to get dragged into another quarrel with Fronto, who was by far the most disagreeable of the Centurions of the Second Cohort.

And, in his private opinion, much of Fronto's enmity came from the fact that he was the shortest of the Centurions, and he suspected that there had been a large boy in Fronto's past that created this visceral hatred, although he would never say as much. What he did say aloud was to nod in the direction of the Pilus Prior and his Optio.

"Maybe you should ask them what they think, since they trained the boy."

Somewhat surprisingly, Crastinus didn't respond, deferring to Vinicius to speak for the both of them with a nod.

"I don't think you need to worry about that with Pullus," he said blandly, but then didn't elaborate.

Fronto, however, was unimpressed, and he repeated, "I have twenty...no, make it *fifty sesterces* saying that I'm right about him!"

Crastinus rubbed his chin, looking thoughtful, then gave a curt nod, saying, "I'll take that wager."

With that, their business of the moment was done, and the Centurions returned to where their men were now sprawled on the bare ground where their tents had been now that everything had been packed.

Watching them walk away, Vinicius waited for them to be out of earshot, then said, "Rubbing your chin was a nice touch."

Crastinus gave a short laugh, admitting, "I thought that might do the trick." Nudging Vinicius, he grinned. "This will be the easiest money we make."

"Even split?" Vinicius asked.

"Of course!" Crastinus replied indignantly. "You trained him!"

Vinicius didn't reply directly, asking instead, "Does he know yet?"

"What?" Crastinus glanced at him, then understood. "No, not yet. It all depends on what kind of action we see first."

They both turned to look where Pullus was lounging against his pack, watching and laughing as one of the Mallius brothers was telling some sort of story that even had Didius giving the grimace that was his version of a smile.

"Which one is that?" Crastinus asked, and Vinicius had to think for a moment before he said, "That's the one they call Remus."

"He's a storyteller, I see," Crastinus commented. Then, turning back around, he said, "Let's see what kind of stories he has to tell in a month."

The four Legions, marching in numerical order, departed Scallabis at dawn the next day, heading north for the Durius (Douro) River, the river that marked the southern boundary of Lusitani territory. And, because of their new status, it meant the 10th was consigned to marching behind the baggage train, which was now at its full complement, each wagon and cart fully loaded with their cargo, along with more than three thousand mules, one per section for all two thousand, four hundred sections in the four Legions, one each for the Centurions with the exception of the Primus Pilus, who had a wagon of his own, and Pili Priores, who shared a wagon. Then there were the wagons for the officers, the Tribunes traditionally allotted a wagon apiece, but in another departure from custom, Caesar had ordered that cut in half, so the baggage of two Tribunes was in one wagon. Not surprisingly, this had been extremely unpopular with all twenty-four Tribunes, but only five of them had been foolish enough to insist on an audience with Caesar, while only one of them was assigned to the 10th; the fact that each of the unhappy men had been the five Caesar had identified as potential problems early on was no coincidence.

Despite the prospect of eating the dust of the other three Legions and wading in the filth produced by so many animals, the spirit of the men of the 10th couldn't have been higher, with the new Gregarii choosing to stand lining the *Via Praetoria* on both sides as Caesar and his staff led the army through the wooden gates. Unlike a marching camp, the permanent camp outside Scallabis had wooden walls, and it would be waiting for the return of the army in a few weeks, or months. Rank by rank, the Legions of Rome marched to war, to a combination of cheers and good-natured taunts between the veteran Legions who paraded past.

"There's the 10th, boys!" a veteran of the 7th called out. "In the rear with the gear, where there is no fear!"

This was met with roars of laughter by the veterans, while the 10th jeered and someone from the First Cohort of the 10th shot back, "They're saving the best for last!"

This was the tenor of the moment, while the new men like Pullus and Domitius, who had been dreaming of this since Titus was ten and Vibius eleven, stood there grinning from ear to ear at the sight of the Legion eagles, carried by their *Aquilifer*, parading past, the sun glinting off the gilt silver wings, while the red Cohort standards carried by the *Signiferi* were all new, a deep rich red with gold stitching.

Pullus and Domitius were far from alone in their exultation, and even Didius felt his heart filling with pride at this sight of Rome's power at its most potent. That it was competing with the knot in his stomach that had sprung up the day the departure on campaign had been announced was something that he didn't divulge to anyone, even to Atilius, despite the fact that, as far as Didius was concerned, his close comrade had proven himself to be a loyal, if not friend, then at least comrade.

On their night in Scallabis, Didius had almost talked himself out of going to see Marcus Surenas, but it had actually been Atilius who had convinced him to do it, albeit in an unconventional way.

"For all you know, you may be dead in a month," Atilius had put it bluntly. "Do you want to die not knowing exactly what happened between him and your father?"

While Didius didn't care for the callous manner that Atilius displayed when talking about his possible demise, neither could he argue with the logic, so he led Atilius in the direction of the Temple of Apollo. This was in the authorized area for them to be in, but both of them kept glancing over their shoulder, more out of habit than any real concern that their pursuers were still searching for them. As it had been outside the place where they had run into trouble, there was a small knot of men standing just outside the brothel, but Didius led Atilius to the plain door two buildings down. He stood there long enough that Atilius was about to open his mouth to urge him to make up his mind, and it was seeing this out of the corner of his eye that got Didius moving, and he reached out and rapped on the door. There was a window next to the door, but it was shuttered, although they could see there was at least one lamp lit. He was about to knock again, but heard the scrape of a footstep, then the door was opened, just a crack and part of a barely visible face appeared.

The only way Didius identified the person was by the voice, recognizing it as Surenas' as the man snarled, "I thought I told you to never come back here!"

"You did," Didius agreed, but when it was time to say something else, he realized he had no idea what he really wanted. Consequently, he just blurted out, "We're leaving on campaign in a couple of days. And," he tried to sound as if it was no moment, "if the gods aren't kind, I may not come back."

Surenas said nothing for a long moment, then while only fractionally, spoke in a softer tone, "Yes, I heard that the army is marching. But," he persisted, "that doesn't explain why you're here, boy."

"Did my father kill someone and make you take the blame for it?"

While this was what he wanted to know, he hadn't intended to ask this while standing outside, but it did catch Surenas off balance, and he demanded, "Who told you that?"

"Nobody," Didius assured him. "I just worked it out for myself that that's why you disappeared."

"Well," Surenas sighed, "you're wrong." Without warning, he opened the door and took a step backward as he said, "You might as well come inside. I don't want to be talking about this where others can hear." This was when he saw Atilius for the first time, and while he did not shut the door completely, he closed it slightly as he demanded of Didius, "Who's this?"

"This is my close comrade," Didius explained, then swallowing, he added awkwardly, "He's my friend."

"Do you trust him?" Surenas asked, and Didius nodded without much hesitation, but he saw this wouldn't suffice, so he said, "Yes, I do."

Surenas grunted, but he allowed Atilius in, who introduced himself, receiving only a curt nod, then Surenas lifted the lamp from its holder next to the door as he commanded, "Follow me."

They did so, following Surenas into the room where Didius had met the man who turned out to be his uncle, but it was the shadowy figure on the opposite side of the room that caught Didius' eye.

"Get us some cups, Vara," Surenas commanded, then pointed to the opposite side of the table for Didius and Atilius. The man addressed Atilius for the first time, pointing at Didius and repeating, "And, do you trust him?" Like Didius, Atilius nodded, but this was obviously acceptable to Surenas, although he warned, "If he's anything like his father, you're likely to regret it."

Naturally, this angered Didius, although the fact that he would have essentially agreed with his uncle's assessment of his father as a fundamentally dishonest man created a confusing mix of feelings. However, he also sensed that Surenas was baiting him, and he reminded himself of why he was there, so instead, he didn't say what was on his tongue.

As Didius had suspected, it was the young girl who came and wordlessly set three cups on the table, then without being told, picked up the pitcher that was already on the table, and poured each of them a cup full.

"You can go back to sleep," Surenas told her, barely giving her a glance, and like a *numen*, she vanished into the darker part of the room. Lifting his cup, Surenas said, a bit grudgingly, "May Fortuna, Mars, and Bellona watch over you and your lot as you put those barbarians in their place." He didn't wait for them to acknowledge the toast, putting the cup to his lips, taking a drink, then putting it on the table. "Now, what do you want to know?" he demanded.

"Just what happened," Didius answered. "We always thought that you were dead, but you're here, under another name. So," he shrugged, "I tried to think of the reasons why you had to leave Gades, and that seemed the most obvious one."

"Well," Surenas allowed, "you're on the right track. Yes, there was a killing, but it wasn't your father who was the killer." He picked up his cup to take another sip, and Didius was certain he saw a slight tremor in his hand. Lowering the cup, Surenas said, "It was me."

"Who did you kill?" Didius asked.

"One of the *duumviri*," Surenas replied flatly, while Didius gasped, and even Atilius, who was determined not to say a word, gave a little cough. Ignoring them, Surenas was staring down into his cup as he explained, "His name was Numerius Placidius Cossus, and," his mouth twisted into a sneer, "he was a greedy, grasping little *cunnus*. He bribed the *Praetor*, whoever he was every year, to remain as one of the *duumviri* going back at least ten years." Suddenly, Surenas looked up sharply at Didius, frowning. "Do you remember your grandfather? Our father?"

"Only vaguely," Didius replied, which was true; what he remembered of the Didius *paterfamilias* was the smell he associated with the man, of sour wine, rotting teeth, and body odor over and above what was normal for the people of their class. Sitting there, Didius also remembered something else, that he had been terrified of his grandfather, not so much because of the man himself, but because of the fear his own father had towards him.

"Old Spurius was a cunning bastard." Surenas gave a short chuckle. "He set this thing up with Cossus when your father and I were still pups. But then, Old Spurius died, and Cossus thought he would take advantage of us. He demanded an extra ten percent over what Old Spurius had been paying him to look the other way on the docks." For the first time, Surenas showed signs of real anger. "It was true that our business had grown down there, but he thought he was entitled to wet his beak over and above the agreed amount." Surenas, growing agitated now, slammed one hand down on the table with a sharp crack, and with enough force that some of the wine sloshed out of his cup. "That's not how business is done! An agreement is an agreement!" Pointing directly in Didius' face, Surenas thundered, "You remember that, boy! We may be thieves, but we never reneged on an agreement!"

Didius didn't like having anyone shove a finger in his face, but while it irritated him, he was actually more amused, and he actually laughed.

"What's so funny about that?" Surenas snarled.

"Because you've been gone a long time, Uncle," Didius replied evenly. "My father breaks agreements all the time if a better opportunity comes along."

Surenas stared at him, still angry, then suddenly exhaled and slumped over, saying tiredly, "Which was why Old Spurius wanted me to run the business. He knew your father, and he knew that Aulus wasn't made of the right stuff."

The effect Surenas' words had on Spurius Didius was complicated; on one hand, he felt vindicated in his judgment that his father wasn't the right man to run what was in essence a family much like the Atilius family, devoted to criminal activity, just on a much larger scale than the late Gaius Atilius. Still, he couldn't say he liked his uncle speaking of his father in this manner, yet again, he remained silent.

"But, what Cossus did was wrong, and your brother and I agreed on what needed to be done." The laugh he gave was laced with bitterness and regret. "We rolled the dice for it, and I should have known better." Surenas' eyes lifted from the table to pierce Didius. "Did Aulus teach you all of his tricks? Say what you want to about him, but I've never seen a better cheat at dice."

This made Didius acutely uncomfortable, which Surenas immediately noticed, and while he didn't say anything, he did look embarrassed and offered his nephew an apologetic glance as Atilius had to hide a smile because he had known this for some time. Not because Didius had told him, but because, frankly, he had admired Didius' skill and had thought, If my Tata, or I for that matter, was that good, I wouldn't be in the Legions now.

Seeing that Didius didn't intend to comment, Surenas continued, "My other mistake was that I trusted your father to set things up so that I could do the deed in a way that it wouldn't be traced back to us. Cossus already had plenty of enemies, thank the gods." He laughed, but with a bitter edge to it.

He fell silent, and Didius waited for him to continue after his uncle took another sip, but he set the cup down and seemed as if he believed he had said enough.

Finally, Didius couldn't wait any longer, and his impatience showed as he demanded, "Well? What happened?"

"What happened," Surenas replied immediately, sounding more tired than angry at being prodded, "is that your father arranged things so that I didn't get caught outright, but it turned out there was a witness who knew me."

"Who?" Didius asked.

"You never met him," Surenas assured him, then explained why. "Because your father had him...taken care of."

"Then that should have solved the problem, shouldn't it?"

"It did," Surenas answered, then offered Didius a twisted smile, "for your father. You see, he somehow found out that Old Spurius intended on handing me the control of the business, which meant that Aulus would be working for me. I'm two years older than your father, but things like that never mattered to him. So," he heaved a sigh, "his price for taking care of the witness was my agreement to leave Gades and allow him to run things."

While this made sense as far as it went, Didius saw something that didn't fit into this explanation.

"Why didn't you let him take care of the problem, then go

ahead and run things like Old Spurius wanted?"

This earned Didius a glare from Surenas, who asked scornfully, "Weren't you listening a moment ago, boy? What I said about agreements?"

"But he did that to cheat you!" Didius protested, only vaguely aware that for the first time in his life, the concept of fairness became more than something the weaklings that he and his family gulled used as an excuse for the flaw of these fools thinking things should be fair. "The gods wouldn't punish you for that!"

Surenas' response was a snort that might have been a laugh.

"I'm not worried about the gods, boy. And," he admitted with a shrug, "all in all, your father did me a favor." He leaned forward, and for the first time, Marcus Surenas reached across the table and placed his hand on Didius' arm, squeezing it as he assured his nephew, "I have no regrets about how things turned out, Spurius. If I'd stayed, I would have been forced to kill your father before he killed me. And no matter how I felt about him, he's still my brother. No man should be forced to kill a brother."

Didius was embarrassed, feeling his face grow hot, but he was also touched; this was the strongest sign of affection he had ever received from a male member of his family, and he felt his eyes begin to sting.

To change the subject, he asked suddenly, "Was what my father told me about his time in the Legions true?"

Surenas' initial reaction was one of confusion, then his expression cleared quickly, and he asked, "What did he tell you?"

Didius went on to relate what his father had told him about marching with Sura against Mithridates, and by the time he was finished, Surenas was smiling and shaking his head.

"That wasn't your father, boy," he said quietly. "That was me. Oh," he added, "your father was going to join with me, but then at the last moment, his nerve failed. He said that one of us needed to stay behind to keep an eye on Old Spurius."

By this point, when Surenas said this, Didius was not only not surprised, he was certain that his uncle was speaking the truth, but he did feel a twinge when he asked, "What about my grandfather? Did he even serve?"

"That," Surenas nodded, "is true. Old Spurius was one of Marius' Mules."

Then, there was nothing else to say, and Didius cleared his throat before saying awkwardly, "Yes, well, we have to get back to camp. I just wanted to...thank you," he fumbled.

Surenas stood, then offered his arm across the table, and said, "If you come back to Scallabis...come to see me so that I know you're safe."

When they left his uncle's and Atilius didn't say anything, Didius came to a stop, trying to decide how to broach the subject.

"About my father," he began, but he got no further.

"I won't say a word about any of it," Atilius assured him. "Especially about his lying about being in the Legions."

"T...Thank you," Didius said, but Atilius just shrugged.

"You're not the only one with a father who's nothing more than a big sack of *cac*," he said simply.

And throughout their time in the Legion together, Atilius never spoke a word about it. That night, before heading back to camp, they decided to sample the brothel two doors down from Surenas' home, then joined their other comrades who were going to be marching the next day streaming out of Scallabis. In what would become a pattern, of the two, Atilius got much drunker than Didius, to the point that he needed Didius' help to stagger back to camp, just making the curfew set by their general for the beginning of the midnight watch. At the time, Didius didn't think much of it, putting it down to nerves about what lay ahead, something that Didius resolutely refused to think about, which he thought was the wiser policy.

For Calienus, the night before departing on campaign wasn't a new event, and like many men under the standard, what he had done the night before embarking on his first campaign was what he did on the night before this one, which meant that, while his lust was sated, his head was pounding in much the same way it had when he embarked on his first, and subsequent campaigns. While he would never admit it, Calienus had a strong streak of superstition, and he reasoned that Mars and Bellona must have favorably viewed his choice to debauch for, not just this but every campaign starting with his first, what he knew might be the last time. To that end, he and Vinicius went into Scallabis, but only after coming to a mutual agreement that they wouldn't discuss anything related to the Legion, a promise that lasted through their second cup of wine.

"I think," Vinicius said suddenly, without any emotion in his voice, "that this is going to be my last campaign, Lucius."

During his years under the standard, Calienus had heard men solemnly declare that the upcoming campaign would prove to be one too many, and in his experience, they were wrong at least as often as they were right...but they weren't always wrong. And, he knew, as did others, that a handful of those men, for whatever reason, welcomed death and essentially enabled a foe to take their lives, thus fulfilling their self-proclaimed prophecy. It was something that men never spoke of, except in the immediate aftermath when, as usually happened, warriors talked of what they had just undergone in an attempt to try and make some sense of what was, when all was said and done, a nonsensical event, but once that day passed and their fallen comrade had been purified by the flames and his ashes interred in the jar that a Legion always carried with it, it was never a subject for discussion. Now, as Calienus heard Vinicius' somber prediction, he tried to think if there had been any signs that this was his Optio's frame of mind.

Nothing came to him, which prompted him to blurt out, "*Gerrae!* What kind of nonsense are you talking, eh?" He forced himself to laugh. "I've never known you to be one of those doomsayers who declares that they're a dead man walking!" Only a bit more seriously, he prodded, "So, what's this about, Aulus?"

Vinicius shrugged, but Calienus saw that his friend wouldn't take his eyes off his cup as he frowned down at it, finally admitting, "I don't really know, Lucius. It's just a...feeling that I have. And," he shrugged again, and there was a note of resignation in his tone, "I can't explain it because I've never had it before."

Not knowing what else to say, Calienus adopted a cheerful manner and lifted a hand to signal one of the serving women. "Well, if this is destined to be your last night getting drunk and fucked, we might as well make it a night for you to remember, eh?"

This did make Vinicius chuckle, and he certainly held up his end of the unstated challenge the Sergeant had laid down, matching Calienus cup for cup, and when it was time to satisfy his other urges, afterward, he was back to his normal self as far as Calienus could tell, and the next day, Calienus could have been excused for thinking that the conversation was a figment of his imagination. Once they were assembled in their marching formation, after having been forewarned by Crastinus of their spot in the column and knowing that it would be at least two parts of a watch before the 10th actually moved, Calienus dropped to the ground on his spot in the formation, and using his pack for a pillow, did what veterans did, knowing that sleep was a precious thing. Before he dropped off, he watched the men of his section, although he still thought of them as boys, with a slight smile on his face. Unlike some of the other veterans, Calienus didn't jeer the new men for eschewing the chance at rest to instead go and stand by the *Porta Praetoria* to gawk at the rest of the army march past them. In fact, he was one of the few veterans who would openly admit to his new comrades that he had done the same thing when they had embarked on his first campaign against Mithridates, under Lucullus. It was, he reflected just before he dropped off, an impressive sight after all, seeing the might of Rome on such potent display.

Romulus and Remus had followed the example of Calienus, going into Scallabis one last time, and like their Sergeant, they were feeling the effects of their last night. Unlike Optio Vinicius, however, neither of them even considered the possibility that it would be either one of them, or both, who would return in an urn; that introspection would only come later, when going into battle took on a more concrete form than it was at this moment. Instead, they joined the others to watch, and they were as spirited in their exchanges with the men of the three veteran Legions as they marched past as their comrades. It quickly became apparent that there was a contest developing about who could offer the wittiest jibe, or retort to a jibe, and

Remus got into the spirit of this almost immediately. As the 7th marched past, the bantering was rather basic, with taunts by the men in the more veteran Legion aimed at the youth and inexperience of the 10th, while the men of the 10th countered about the need for their Legion to be formed because the 7th was clearly not up to the job. It was all in good fun, and there were broad smiles and laughter by the men who were targeted by a taunt that they considered witty, and this extended to the men of the 8th who were next. Romulus, while enjoying the back and forth, was also noticing that, in the spirit of competition, the insults were becoming more pointed, and he did wonder if there was an invisible line that his brother or the other wits standing along the *Via Praetoria* would cross with these older, more experienced men that would trigger a confrontation. This didn't stop him from urging his brother on, or any of the others for that matter, but it was with the men of the Eighth Cohort of the 8th Legion when Remus uttered a retort that would serve as fodder for laughter around the fires for the next couple of days.

It began with one of the rankers on the outermost file, a man with a long, pink scar that followed his jawline, who called out mockingly, "Did any of you precious young lads at least get a chance to get your cocks wet before you march with us? I'd hate for you to die only knowing what your hand feels like!"

Perhaps if Remus had immediately replied when the comrades of the 8th's man were still roaring with laughter, it might not have created the excitement, but Romulus could tell by the grinning glance his brother gave him that Remus thought he had come up with a reply that would prove superior, which made him wait until the noise died down, and he was right.

"Why, yes," Remus shouted, just as the laughter was dying out, "and your mother told me to tell you to be sure and write!"

The noise created by the men of the 10th, and as Romulus saw, some of the men of the 8th, dwarfed the previous uproar, while it prompted the 8th man, who Romulus could see was actually angry, to bellow, "My mother's dead, you *cunnus*!"

And, before Romulus, or anyone, could counsel caution, Remus shot right back, "Well, that explains why she smelled so bad and just lay there!"

It was impossible to hear Remus' opponent bellow because

of the hooting and even more uproarious mirth, but it was also impossible to misinterpret his action, which was to drop his *furca* and come rushing, straight for Remus, fists clenched and face contorted with rage. It was also a foolish thing to do, not only because Remus was surrounded by his brother and other comrades of the 10th, all of whom were ready to defend him, but because the ranker's Optio had been paying attention. Before the ranker made it three steps out of the formation, his discarded *furca* causing the man immediately behind him to stumble over it and creating a bobble in the otherwise uniform motion of men on the march, the Optio was on him.

Slashing down with his *vitus*, and since on this first day they were in full uniform, aiming for the ranker's torso, which was protected by his *hamata*, instead of the man's legs, which might have hobbled him, the Optio roared, "Get back in your spot, you *cunnus*!"

The ranker's rage suddenly dissolved as he instinctively covered his head with his arms, despite wearing his helmet, but it was his yelps of pain that Remus and the other men of the 10th found the most humorous.

For his part, the ranker, who had stopped his headlong charge to head back towards his *furca*, protested, "But he insulted my mother, Optio! You know that she..."

"I don't care if he *did* fuck your mother, Lupus!" the Optio snarled, which only added to the hilarity, and Romulus actually thought that the Optio might have heard the exchange. "You know you don't break ranks, for any reason! But *especially* when we're on the first fucking day of the march and we're still in the fucking camp! You're not a *Tiro* like these *cunni*! You know better!"

The now-identified Lupus scurried back, dodging his Optio's last swipe to snatch up his *furca*, then had to scramble to catch up since the column hadn't stopped to accommodate a ranker with a grievance, and their last sight of Lupus was of him looking over his shoulder glaring at them.

"This isn't over!" he shouted, which earned him another smack from the Optio, who was essentially herding him back into the formation.

Unsurprisingly, this was met with shouts of derision and

taunts that any time Lupus wanted to tangle with the 10th, he knew where to find them.

Romulus, however, tugged on Remus' sleeve, and not wanting to shame his brother, spoke so that only he could hear, "That's enough, Quintus. You don't always have to get the last word or prove you're cleverer than someone you're arguing with."

Remus, rather than being chastened, laughed and shoved his brother, exclaiming, "Says who? Besides, just because Tata isn't here, that doesn't mean you're in charge of me."

This, Romulus thought with a sigh, was true, but besides Remus' defiant tone, his brother noticed that, for the rest of the time they had as the first of the 9th marched past, he fell back on more banal taunts. By the time they were summoned back to their respective Centuries, the Mallius brothers, along with their fellow rankers who had watched the procession, were not only awed by the sight of Roman might, they also felt more secure in the likelihood that they would emerge from whatever came next unscathed; after all, they reasoned, what barbarian tribe, no matter how formidable, could hope to withstand what they had just seen? To one degree or another, every man who stood there on the *Via Praetoria* watching their comrades in the other Legions marching past would think back to this moment, some with amusement, some with regret, and some with sadness at what they would learn was their naivety.

As had become their habit, the close comrades Scribonius and Vellusius naturally gravitated towards Pullus and Domitius, which on the surface was understandable, since in their ranks, Vellusius stood next to Domitius, who was now officially the smallest man in the section, and Scribonius stood next to Pullus. This was only part of the reason, however, because as opposite as they were in appearance and demeanor, each of them felt an affinity for the man marching next to them. While Domitius could be loud and boisterous; not as loud as Remus, certainly, while Vellusius was more taciturn by nature, the two *Tiros* had discovered they shared more than just their diminutive stature when compared to their own close comrades, they enjoyed and appreciated each other's outlook. The same was true, albeit for different reasons, with Scribonius and Pullus, with their largest and most powerful comrade admiring Scribonius for his cool, calm, and measured demeanor, but more importantly, for Scribonius' intellect and willingness to share what, to Pullus and the others was a vast amount of knowledge. Conversely, Scribonius esteemed Pullus, and while it was certainly based in his respect and recognition of Pullus' physical prowess and skill, to Scribonius' own surprise, he was impressed by the giant Roman's raw intelligence, learning that, while he was literate in only a rudimentary sense, he had a consuming curiosity and desire to learn. Despite the fact that Pullus had never divulged his ultimate purpose for enlisting, Scribonius had intuited that his tentmate possessed a burning ambition that, as time progressed, Scribonius would compare to that of their general. At this moment, however, it was more of an unformed thought, and the four of them were completely absorbed in the spectacle marching past, although this was only partially true with Scribonius. For him, watching the army of which he was a part departing to go to war evoked a number of emotions, some of them quite painful, because Calienus' instinct that there was more to Scribonius' story than he had divulged was a good one; this was not Scribonius' first time standing in a rank, marching off to do battle with an enemy. The result of this was that, while he pretended to be as impressed as his younger comrades at this sight of Roman power, the thoughts that always lurked there on the edges of his mind were now pushing themselves into his consciousness, the image of neat ranks of men marching in step evoked as much sadness as any positive feelings.

Therefore, it was with a variety of emotions that the newly formed 10th Legion watched their more experienced comrades marching past before falling into the spots that they had spent the previous months learning, picking up their *furcae*, and making themselves ready for their turn to begin the march. If there was any unanimity with the almost six thousand men of Rome's newest Legion, it was in their collective desire to return to Scallabis, alive and whole; that this was close to an impossibility did not make it any less of a desire on the part of any man. Above that, there were men who desired to do more than just survive, who wanted distinction, to prove that they were worthy of acclaim and reward, and while a few, a very few of them would achieve that end, there was only one among them who would become a legend to all of those who marched for Rome...his name was Titus Pullus.